CW01506856

Lomond's Awal

A Novel

by Alison Demarco

Editor and Technical Advisor, Lianne Pipskyj -

lpipskyj@gmail.com

David Mackenzie Assistant with research and composition

Book Cover by www.kontemptcreations.com

First edition 2019

First published in Great Britain in 2019 by

Alison Demarco

1B Robbs Loan Grove

Edinburgh EH14 1 SJ

Lomond's Awakening 978-0-9932165-2-7

ACKNOWLEDGEMENTS

Many thanks to all my amazing friends and family: son Daryl, Daughter Tara, their Father Ramon, and grandchildren, Demmie, Shinade, Romeo, Ashton and Sienna. To my close friends Tracy Avella, Maria Rutherford, Andrena Greenan, Lianne Pipskyj, Dave Mackenzie, Neil Ward, Lorraine Allen, Jane Nottage, Ruth Williamson, Kyle Young and everyone else in my inner and outer circle.

Special thanks to the energies in the Universal Consciousness that have guided and led me on my incredible inspiring and joyous journey.

For those who would like to know more, you can visit Alison's website on:

www.AlisonDemarco.com

Email: alisondemarco646@gmail.com

Other books by Alison Demarco

The Signature From Tibet 978-0-9932165-1-0

Dark Storm Golden Journey 978-0-9932165-3-4

Lomond's Awakening 978-0-9932165-2-7

Own Your Power Cards 978-0-9932165-0-3

COMING SOON 2020.   LOMOND'S JOURNEY

FORWARD

By Phamie Gow

Everyone has a 'blind-spot', and it is in that space, where there are undiscovered realities and combinations of sights, sounds and senses that go beyond the expected normal conduct of living as a human being. Once we realise this, it is only then, if we are brave enough, and conscious enough to enter and embrace the unknown, and unveil the Truths of our own existence and True purpose. It is there, in that 'blind-spot', or perhaps we could call this a 'coma-spot'; an enlightening realm where we see all the colours of life and much more and expand the visions of our hearts and minds beyond the imaginable.

Phamie Gow is an International musician and composer with purpose.
www.phamiegow.com

ALISON DEMARCO

Alison Demarco, International Speaker, Author, Visionary, Self-empowerment Guide, reads people's lives to their benefit.

Alison is one of the world's fastest and most accurate personality, and temperament assessors. Having been deemed by some experts as the world's #1 Spiritual Guide and Visionary due to her ability to reads people and their lives as if they are an open book. Alison has been seen and heard on BBC TV, ITV Lorraine Kelly Morning Show, Channel 5, House Busters with Russell Grant, Radio, and featured in the National & International Media.

Alison is a Colour Therapist, Kirlian & Energy Practitioner, NLP Practitioner and Self-development expert & Life Coach.

As a specialist in the language of colour, Alison uses colour to tune into and uncover the root cause and issues that are holding her clients back from being 'in their element 'and offers them the 'how to' lead a happy, successful life. During a reading it is not unusual for Alison to relay messages from people's loved ones who have passed over. Alison has touched the hearts and souls of countless individuals worldwide for over three decades.

Alison offers Guidance and Support in the workplace, and uses a colourful Team Building System to understand personality & temperament thus creating balance and harmony for the team members.

Author of *Dark Storm Golden Journey. The Signature From Tibet* and *Lomond's Awakening*, she is an experienced and entertaining speaker and lecturer, runs workshops worldwide, offers numerous self-development webinars, & Private Readings, as well as facilitating her accredited Colour Therapy/Colour Language and Personal Assessment
Face Reading/Temperament Courses.

Demarco makes her home in Edinburgh, in the United Kingdom.

Email: alisondemarco646@gmail.com

Website: www.alisondemarco.com

LOMOND'S AWAKENING

PART 1
CHAPTER ONE

Lomond couldn't figure life out at all. Adults! What do they know? On and on they droned about the most boring things: the washing, the ironing, cleaning the brass and silver. Then there's the issues with money—the scrimping and scraping. Her mother insisted on showing her how to darn her own tights, and her father's socks, just to save a few pennies. Is she ridiculous or what? They were constantly chastising her for daydreaming, forever demanding she study-study- study. *You must to go to university and earn the proper qualifications needed for a good, well-paid job Lomond, one with a secure pension at the end of it to see you through old age!'* Old age? She hadn't had much of any age yet! Surely you don't just get born to be caught up in everybody else's plans for *your* life? Surely *your* life is here and now and meant to be enjoyed? Not run purely for some unknown event way into the future. School was okay; she had fun there at least. Well, fun bending and breaking the rules and diktats; she could after all. It was her father (and six other parents) who'd saved it from closing. *They'd* raised the money to buy a new property for the all girls school; an old three-storey, Georgian house. They even pitched in extra to help convert the old run-down building, all just to keep it going. Didn't that buy her some clout or at least a say in things? *You have to learn while you still have the opportunity. Soon you'll have to work for a living and you'll need a profession, a well-paid job to help you build that "nest egg."* Their constant, depressing reminders tormented her as she made her way between classes: *"Life is a race against time!* Then there was all the information. Plastered on school notice boards and crammed into text books. Teachers pontificating in their strangled voices:

    'Girls, remember! You are here to learn and education is a serious business.' 'Mark my words, this will all come home to roost one day' 'One more word out of you, young lady, and it's detention!'

    'Just you dare,' Lomond would muffle in retort, 'I'll punch your lights out, you stupid twat.' So, they forced it into your brain for *what*? For some fancy piece of paper and to have some boss promise you *anything* like a decent wage. Then, get married, get a house and have kids, get to cooking and cleaning.

All so your kids can get stuck in the same shitty, boring routine? And at the end of it all...you all just die. What is the bloody point?

Sunday lunch had just finished and Lomond was in the kitchen washing the dishes in exchange for an hour listening to Radio One's Pick of The Pops with Alan Freeman. That morning, her parents had dragged her to the obligatory 11 o'clock weekly church service. Her mother believed this would somehow give them absolution from any and all of their past and present sins. The words to *Pleasant Valley Sunday* drifted into the room and she turned off the hot water tap so she could hear it properly. *The Monkees* were the best; they even had their own T.V. Series. Lomond was in love with the drummer, Micky Dolenz. She believed wholeheartedly he would fall in love with her; if and when they ever met. *The Monkees* and *Top of The Pops* were the only two programmes they let her watch. She turned the dial on the old black radio, praying her mother wouldn't burst in and switch it off completely; s*he* hated noise, especially the kind made by pop music. Forgetting the dishes, Lomond started twisting and twirling around the room, singing along. The words made so much, as if they were written for her. It made her happy to think someone else got her view of life, she wasn't the only one to think as she did.

No! She definitely wanted more from life; *much* more. Although still unsure what it was exactly and where she would find it; at fifteen, she was fired up and determined to find out.

The week flew by and Friday came; the night her parents allowed her to go to the ice-rink. The only place they allowed her to go on a week night. Little did they know, Lomond didn't always go to there as agreed though. She loved excitement; she *craved* it in fact. Her friend George, a local motorcycle mechanic, supplied this perfectly in the form of a gigantic state-of-the-art motorbike he named "Power." Lomond's parents forbade her from going near *any* bike, much less George's "monster", as her dad called it. That was another thing they did that irked Lomond no end; their nagging *on* and *on* about the dangers of riding on a bike. How bike riders were famously irresponsible; prone to speeding, dangerous driving and accidents. How a bike offered no protection whatsoever and a crash usually left the victim paralyzed, or worse. Her mother repeated endlessly, the list of horrors she'd heard happen to those *foolish* enough to get on a bike as a litany or a Hail Mary to the High-Priestess of Conformity.

'Just look at poor Jimmy Law, he'll never use his legs again. Surely he'd be better off dead than a cripple!' Lomond would roll her dark green eyes at the thought, her slim and well-developed legs wriggling in frantic boredom. What the hell did they know anyway? They just want to control her. Why couldn't they just trust George? He was a great mechanic, there wasn't anything he didn't know about bikes and he'd ridden them for years. What is it about parents? Were they all like that, or was it just hers? Maybe it was because she was an only child; or was it something else? She couldn't remember a time when her mother (it was always *her*) didn't put her down. It had gone on since the year *dot!* In fact, both her parents had brainwashed her. Thinking any differently to them was not allowed. Thinking for herself was out of the question. They couldn't bear it when she started challenging them and their ideas.

'*How* exactly will God punish me?' '*Why* does he punish people, anyway?' They never liked that at all. As a child, she'd been curious about the mysterious colours she saw radiating from things.

'Why do colours dance and weave in and out of everything?' she'd asked. Then, when they threatened to take her to a child psychiatrist to have her head examined, she never mentioned it again. As far as Lomond was concerned now, disobeying parents was routine. The normal way of doing things, it's what teenagers had to do! Lately, disobeying had become synonymous with *freedom*. Someday, she thought, *I'll ride off on that bike and never come back!* She had dreams of travelling the world, and George was part of that plan. In her spirited imagination, she ventured along straight running roads, mile upon mile, riding pillion with George. With a song in her heart and freedom at her fingertips, the wind would be sweeping through her golden streaked, light brown hair. Her mother, Beth, would be standing forlorn at the kitchen sink, looking out of the window for her only daughter who'd gone and would never return. No household chores. No more school for this brazen, free lass. She felt a sense of silent satisfaction. Not long now, only four weeks and she'd be sixteen. Legally free to leave home at last. *I'll finally be an adult, a free agent*, she thought. *I'll show them*! Tonight, she was going to meet George come hell or high water! So, what if a neighbour, or someone from the local pub saw her and told her father. Nope, the thrill of being on the back of "Power," holding on tightly to George, that was *all* that mattered. Living every moment with excitement, that was the master plan and she knew best how to do that. So, this Friday afternoon, with the chores done and tea wrapped up, Lomond rushed around madly from the bathroom to the bedroom. The clothes were thrown off, skin tight jeans and bright turquoise

T-shirt pulled on, then the final touch, her powder-blue jacket. Her hair was curled and coiled strategically, not too much make-up; *Mother will make me wash it off.* Then, ready at last, she crept downstairs and across the hall, tiptoeing towards the front door with her ankle length black leather boots held in one hand. She glanced at the big clock in the hall with its grandfatherly tick, it was nearly seven. With her hand on the brass knob of the front door, she took a deep breath and kept her voice casual,

'Bye! Back later.' The chimes began their chant as her mother appeared in the kitchen doorway.

'Going skating?' she inquired in her Speaker-of-the-House manner. Lomond avoided eye contact and called over her shoulder a steady,

'Yes.'

'Remember, Lomond, you are *not* to go on that motorbike. Be home by ten and not a minute after!' Lomond bent down, pulling on her boots and quickly zipping them up before hurrying down the road without looking back.

Beth was wound tighter than a watch spring. She didn't want Lomond going out at all, even though she knew that was unreasonable. She was just so easily riled these days; found fault with everything. Even the sight of Mac's tall lanky frame sucked into the big armchair, set her off in a frazzle; especially the way his watery-blue eyes traced the contours of weather woman's hour-glass figure on the TV.

'Touch of frost tonight,' he commented needlessly, in his hollow monotone voice. 'Hope Lomond's not going out on that damn bike.'

'Certainly not!' assured Beth, her eyes widened to assert her authority. 'I can't imagine *what* she sees in that dirty boy, *anyway*. He never even wipes his feet when he comes in. You'd think he'd appreciate being allowed to come into such a fine home as this.' she said turning to leave the room. 'Oh, Mac, look what you've done!' When her husband glanced over the side of the armchair, he saw his cup had inadvertently dribbled chocolate onto the plush new beige carpet. 'Pitiful! The bloody dog can do better!' said Beth demeaningly. Mac hung his head and mumbled under his breath.

'Think I'll take the dog for a walk, maybe he'll teach me how to behave like a human then.' Mac had long felt totally untrained.

'You say something?' He got up silently, sweeping his thinning grey hair back from his forehead and shuffling his tired lean body out of the room; hoping to avoid his wife for the rest of the evening.

Beth strode into the lounge and walked over to the large gilt-edged mirror above the fireplace. She peered at herself, checking her favorite bright red lipstick was still intact. She pouted her thin lips provocatively- in a way her husband had never witnessed - and tilted her head sideways; checking the face powder she'd applied that morning was still visible. Lomond had criticized her colour choice; said it was too white, made her look starved and ghost-like. Beth knew better. Lomond seemed to live in her own little world and her refusal to live and behave in Beth's was a constant irritant.

Shuffling over to the walnut desk, she sat down and positioned her long legs at an angle; just as she'd seen proper ladies do from the movies. She opened a drawer and looked down at the list of invitations to be sent on behalf the Women's Guild, for which she was chairperson and proud of it. She enjoyed addressing the envelopes, making things formal. Then she began: *Mrs. Belinda Blaine*, wildly looping the capital "B's", her favourite letter of the alphabet she decided, she smiled as she imagined Belinda marveling enviously at her fine script.

CHAPTER TWO

Lomond gathered the folds of her powder-blue jacket and clutched them tight to her bosom. The cold evening air had made everything in sight take on a haze of frost. She shuddered about the lie she'd just told her mother, but then she thought about George waiting for her at the bottom of the road and her pace quickened. *That's worth any lie! I won't let those bampots ruin it for me!* She envisaged George pulling off his helmet, his light brown hair falling away from his smooth brow. They'd cruise around the city whilst the Edinburgh night life was in full swing, through the Grassmarket and down Lothian Road. Like a queen on her gleaming chrome steed, they would pass girls her own age standing shivering outside nightclubs, whilst she would be snug, feeling the warmth of George's body as she pressed against him; they would do anything to be like her.

Why should she feel bad about lying? Before her mother was any the wiser, this adventure would be over anyway. She'd be tucked safely up in bed. She'd never know Lomond would have been having the time of her life. When she thought about it, her stomach began to flutter in a way that nothing else made it do;

warm and alive with a vibrant energy. Now she was almost
dancing down the road to where George and Power would be.
Power, the most beautiful name for a bike ever, they'd decided.
At the bottom of the hill there was no sign of George or the sound
of his beast of a machine. She sat on the stone wall above a bench
and waited. There was rarely any traffic around this part of the city.
The wall was overhung by huge trees, like stark and brave
sentinels looming over her, their reaching limbs cast strange
shadows on the pavement below. Lomond felt the chill of the night
air penetrate her jacket. Her eyes searched the curves of the road in
both directions, straining to detect her hero's approach. No sound
but the wind, it was making her ears tingle. She tilted her head
back and looked up, the waking stars were beckoning her. She
reached out her delicate fingers as if to touch the bright blue star
nestled in the cleft between branches. *Up there is my true home,*
she thought. She felt certain she could live happily ever after on
one of those glittering stars; certain that once upon a time she had
been a star among stars.

The roar of the bike dragged her back to earth and her heart leapt;
George with his handsome rugged face and deep-set brown eyes.
She thought about the last time they met, the fleeting touch

of his lips on hers and a warm glow radiated inside her. The bike appeared around the corner, a moving gleam of chrome and striking red. He pulled back the throttle as he approached and Lomond scrambled off the wall; was ready to skip over to him with excitement. *This is not how grown-up ladies behave,* a voice inside her resounded. Instead she kept her feet rooted to the ground and gave him a quiet salute. She was Lomond, young, free and in control. The bike came to a quivering halt and George kicked out the side-stand, planting both feet on the ground. He pulled off his black helmet and she noticed the sweat on his brow; he'd been somewhere, she didn't know where.

'Sorry I'm late.' He was smiling. 'Bit of business to do first. Fella wanted me to check out a G-Reg Honda,' Lomond pouted and George wiped his brow, 'and… I was halfway down the road when I remembered I didn't pick up your helmet! I got you a new one, see. I went all the way back, but can you beat it, I couldn't find it. So, I grabbed the old one instead, here. You okay?' Lomond was no longer listening, all she wanted to do was get on that glorious bike and get out of there. The thought of her father out-and-about walking the dog, made her anxious.

'Hurry, George! Let's hit it before I'm seen.' He paused for a moment, watching her put the helmet on. He loved the crooked little smile she always seemed to have on her pretty heart-shaped face. He bent in close to her and saw the twinkle in her dark green eyes through the visor.

'Where d'you wanna go babe?'

'I don't mind, let's just get going!' she breathed. George swung his leg over the bike and reset his helmet. Then, with his left foot, he kicked up the side-stand and edged forward invitingly. Lomond placed one hand on his broad shoulder and swung her slim frame into position behind him.

Instantly she felt his body press against hers and vibration of the grumbling engine coursed through her. Without warning, George clunked into first, revved the engine and sped off down the road. Lomond screamed out in pleasant surprise as she hung on for dear life. Her heart always set off racing when George set Power free. He'd taught her how to be at one with the bike, she knew to lean into the bends with him. She felt the bike shudder as George released the throttle and they began to speed off heading west out of Edinburgh. On her left she saw the signpost for the Ice Rink, one of her favourite places. Just up ahead, the traffic lights turned to green as their bike approached and imagining for a second she was royalty, Lomond gave a regal hand wave. Now on their right,

Edinburgh Zoo came into sight and she felt a tinge of sadness for the poor caged animals, she empathised with them so much; too often felt as if she *herself* was caged. The village of Corstorphine came into sight and George began to slow down, just in case there were any Police traps ahead. He hated the Police. Cruising through Corstorphine, Lomond glanced at the shop windows; the butchers, bakers and florist, the hairdressers and Woolworths; a cheap shoddy shop according to her mother. Past the shops, houses came into view and George released the throttle again. Lomond's excitement grew as she realised he was heading for the airport, a quiet country road at this time of night; she was in for a thrilling ride.

Lomond pulled on the strap under her chin to make her helmet feel snugger. George was shouting back something about wild foxes, she couldn't quite hear him but she nodded anyway. She wrapped her arms tighter around his waist and giggled. Her jacket was billowing out so much she felt it might lift her from her seat. She imagined her body moulding into the huge framework and noticed the moon rising over the horizon. Its pale-yellow light softly touched the crowns of fluffy clouds as they swirled and danced in the twilight. *The adventure was beginning!* Lomond imagined the bike taking flight and skimming across the sky; up into the heavens. Bearing right onto Turnhouse Road, George tilted Power artfully into each bend, the engine roaring as he picked up speed in between. The bike was his pride and joy and he knew her intimately. Then, glaring white lights illuminated the road up ahead and Lomond found herself looking up to avoid the glare. She caught sight of the indigo sky and her heart expanded into the wonder of infinity. Stars of every colour began cascading all around her in a volcanic shower; flooding her consciousness. *Are we flying?* Up ahead she saw a long dark indigo tunnel and her body felt weightless as it began travelling towards it. Faster and faster, she was catapulted through, a blaze of white lights brighter than the sun blinding her vision. Then, everything stopped and all she could see was a tiny blue-black coloured dot in the distance; an iridescent pinpoint. She tried to focus on it, waiting for her eyes to adjust to the darkness.

Next, without warning she was being propelled towards it at shocking speed, a burst of silver light exploded all around her and now she's looking down at herself lying on the road in her powder blue jacket and cracked helmet. It looked as if she were asleep. *What part of me is seeing this? How can this be? This kind of seeing, it's...different. I just need to expand and I can see everything. Or contract and I can see just one wee bit. I'm looking now at the bike; the beautiful bike.* She saw the pillar box-red of its fine paintwork and the red of another vehicle; the silver chrome of car and bike embracing, prismatic shards of light-shattering glass and for a fleeting moment a memory of something terrible and overpowering. *The bang... Yes!* There was an unyielding impact, searing pain and from her viewpoint, she noticed now a scarlet red stain appearing on her jacket, oozing out from under the cracked helmet.

What happened? George, where is George? She felt she wanted to go back and look for him but she didn't know how. Now there are ambulance attendants bending over her motionless body. *Why aren't they tending to George, too?* How could she get them to look; get their attention? She had no mouth to make a sound. No fingers to reach out and tug their stiff yellow jackets. She watched as one of them lifted up the lids of her eyes. The other held her wrist and was looking down at his watch. Their voices sounded muffled and distant.

'Looks like a head injury.' Then there's a stretcher, a neck brace and another man appears. He's saying something, his words are full of anguish.

'I think I killed her! She came out of nowhere, she did, I swear, I never saw her!' The ambulance men are trying to calm him down.

'That's such a big bike for a wee lass,' he shakes his head, 'Are you sure *she* was riding it?'

'She's the only one here.' answers the other. They lift the stretcher carrying Lomond's limp body and slide it through the open doors of the ambulance.

'Careful now, careful! Keep the neck stabilized.' The doors slam shut and in an instant, she is overcome by an excruciating pain. At the same time, she feels herself being sucked back up the dark indigo tunnel before being spat back into the blinding white light of the here and now.

CHAPTER THREE

Her eyes hurt; *God, how they hurt!* The searing white light flooded her whole being, leaving her unable to connect to anything. She felt herself floating upwards, losing all sense of herself or where she was. It was as if she was *becoming* the light, her form fading and diluting, on the brink of dissipating into the air. Then, she felt a violent jolt and she was sent spinning upwards, the force like the sudden opening of a parachute. This feeling of velocity was followed by a sensation of freefalling. The same whirlwind of energy that had propelled her through the tunnel began tossing and turning her on the whims of erratic thermal currents, like a feather. In a breathless silence she wondered how it was possible to be here, yet not. It was in this unseen form that she began to *experience* the light, realising there are different ways of seeing, feeling and thinking. Somewhere in her mind's eye there was the image of being above the clouds, looking at the world upside down. However, no matter how hard she tried, she couldn't get a fix on the land below, or the sky above, for that matter. It was as if she were lost in some kind of mystical *Limbo,* yet still aware of the sensation of movement and the light. A sense of calm washed over her.

Just then, the light began manifesting as a living feeling thing in itself, not just a tool to illuminate perception. Individual beams coursed through her, with each one possessing a unique vibration and creating different sensations within. She desperately yearned to reach out and touch one; her mind telling her this would connect her to her former earthly reality. She needed sight and touch to bring her back down. Yet, in this nether-realm, she was discovering quickly that her former sensibilities were of no value. There were no references or signposts here, nothing to focus on. There was no need for any of it. Lomond gave up searching for answers, surrendering herself entirely to the energies that tingled through her. It was at this point that for the first time in her fifteen years of existence she felt a sense of freedom; *total freedom.* She allowed herself to be carried along. Like a swallow surrendering to the air currents, she coasted along with the flow of energy; perceiving every change in its speed and direction. She realised she was no longer bound by her limited physical form. Instead she had become something else. Something that was simultaneously expansive yet absorbent, pliable and resilient. Cocooned in a kind of warm and protective energy, as if electrically shielded as the glaring light reflected and reverberated all around her. Abruptly she came to a stop and for a time she hovered, suspended in nothingness. Then from somewhere, a high-pitched buzzing filled the emptiness, barely audible, but there. She strained to identify the source. *Is it inside my head?* Unable to decide, she could do nothing but embrace it and as she did so, it was as if every living cell within her was being soothed and sedated. In an instant, just as soon as it began, the buzzing stopped and she was enveloped in silence. Then they came, colours of every hue pouring into this void with her, connecting with every inch of her being. First a beam of yellow penetrated her solar plexus, swelling her with a feeling of happiness. With it, images of brightly-coloured insects, bees, birds and flowers being nurtured by the sun's rays flooded her consciousness. She marveled at how the intake of colour could make her feel such joy. A desire awoke inside her and suddenly she was overcome by the need to learn more about life, about nature and the cosmos. The lively yellow morphed into violet, instantly relaxing her. She saw the church her mother had taken her to every Sunday as a child. She'd been captivated by the way the light shone through the stained-glass windows, casting prisms of colour on the floor. A realisation occurred to her. It was the atmosphere within the church that had drawn her to it. She'd felt at home there, at one with the silent energy of the place. Yet somehow, over the years, she had found a way to block out this energy, shunning the comforting silence. Now, as the violet rays beamed around and though her; she felt she'd finally allowed it back in and she felt strangely complete.

As the beams continued, Lomond was thrilled by this vast arena of colour; vivid and luminous colours she had never experienced in everyday life. It was as if her happiness and sense of self was alive within them, each one a faithful friend, there to help her become free at last. In this place she felt there was some kind of purpose and in some way, she was part of it. She just didn't know how or why. She felt totally unified with this energy, in this realm.

Was this what they meant when they talked about being moved by the spirit?

Lomond began to focus on the colours that attracted her most, and as she did it was as if she became that colour. She thought of the rocket shaped Lava Lamps in the window of Iconic Design in the Edinburgh Grassmarket. She would often visit the little shop, pulled inside by the wonderful colours emanating from all the different lamps. The owner called them his 'Astro Lamps'. She liked that. She'd been particularly drawn to the pink one.

Captivated by the way the ball of wax divided and multiplied as was heated by the bulb in base below. Marvelling at the way the tiny pink bubbles floated up and down in the clear liquid. *Softness, love, and nurturing* had radiated from them. Now as she conjured pink rays and absorbed them into her, she experienced those very same feelings. It was extraordinary. It smoothed the hard edges of hurt and pain she had become used to and she luxuriated in it. Then the pink rays did something quite unexpected. Before her eyes, a diminutive and rather tubby, dumpling of a woman materialised from the pinkness. Lomond seemed to recognise her.

'Mrs R!' she gasped and in an instant memory came back to her. Her parents constantly banishing her to her bedroom for misbehaving, the room was painted pink. She remembered the first time Mrs. R. had appeared at the bottom of her bed. Lomond had been worried this peculiar lady dressed head to toe in pink was part of her punishment. But then her calming gentleness quickly won Lomond over and they became fast friends. They had wonderful tea-parties together where Mrs. R would pour imaginary tea from a large china tea-pot into small delicate china cups. They would add imaginary sugar and milk and stir each cup with an imaginary silver teaspoon. Both Lomond and Mrs. R would raise their cup to their lips and pretend to drink them; with the obligatory pinky finger extended outwards of course; so many years ago. *Maybe she can tell me where this place is?*

'Mrs. R, it's so nice to see you again!'

'It's lovely to see you again too again lass.' She answered in the same sweet tone that had always soothed her as a girl, 'Can you tell me where we are?'

'It's a wonderful realm of vibrating energies, accessible to some through the mind with special practice. Although you've been projected here without your free will,' her tone held a note of intrigue. Before Lomond could consider what she'd said, Mrs. R added, 'It was our destiny to meet again my dear. You closed down our colour connection so long ago; although unintentionally I'm sure.'

'I *did*?' answered Lomond, wondering what she meant and how she'd managed that without even trying.

'Not to worry, these things happen,' Mrs. R answered smiling, 'You're here now. But, it's up to you to decide if and when you return to your earthly life.' The words alarmed Lomond. Until now she'd assumed this was some kind of dream and she just needed to wake up. Mrs. R was telling her she had a decision to make. That she had some kind of power to decide between life and death. *How was that even possible...how would she even do that?*

She knew she wanted to be alive...didn't she? Suddenly Mrs R was gone and she felt herself become unfettered and falling; tumbling into the unknown...

CHAPTER FOUR

Mac and Beth stood helpless before the large and forbidding metal doors; somewhere in there was their daughter. Beth's hand shook as she slid on her red-rimmed reading glasses to look at the notice. *ACCESS WARD 15…ICU…WAIT FOR ADMITTANCE.*

'This must be Intensive Care' she said pointing at the sign. Silhouetted figures glided to and fro behind the frosted glass…ghostlike. Fear about what might lay beyond rooted them both to the spot. A green-uniformed auxiliary worker passed by them in the corridor and they both looked at him hopefully.

'Press the buzzer,' he said. 'Someone will come.' Mac sucked in his breath as he reached out and pressed the shiny chrome button. After a few seconds the doors swung open, seemingly of their own volition and facing them, was a young nurse.

'Are you the parents of the girl just admitted?' Her tone hid the fact she'd seen the look of terror and uncertainty on countless faces before theirs.

'*Yes…*' Mac's voice sounded far away, distracted. He just wanted to see his daughter.

'We're Mr. and Mrs. Mitchieson.' clarified Beth.

'Please, if you'll follow me.' The nurse led them along a corridor to a door plastered with a larger than needed *No Smoking* sign. Inside was a bland and poky waiting room. The nurse left and they sat in silence with their hands resting nervously on their laps. A few minutes later, a young woman wearing a bright, chalk-white coat arrived. The sight of her made Mac's throat tighten and his head began thumping. As she spoke, her words sounded muffled.

'Hi, I'm Dr. Robb,' she said. 'I'll be the primary contact for your daughter, Lomond.' She paused a moment as Mac and Beth stared at her eagerly. 'I'm afraid Lomond has been involved in a motorcycle accident.' A small sound escaped from Beth's lips and her hand flew to cover her mouth. 'She's sustained an injury to her head and we think this has caused some internal bleeding inside her skull. Mac was shaking his head and the colour had drained from his face. 'That's all I can tell you at this point. We're still in the process of carrying out tests to rule out any other injuries. As soon as we have Lomond stabilised, a nurse will come for you and you can go see her.' She added, attempting to soothe the troubled couple.

'I want to see her *now*!' Mac burst out. 'She's my...she's our daughter!'

'This is all his fault!' screamed Beth, 'Where is he?'

'I'm sorry, Mr. Mitchieson, but I'm not sure what you mean? As far as we've been told, there were no other casualties, she was admitted alone.'

'She was with him! She was on that bike with him! We warned her about this!' Beth's face was twisted in rage.

'Where is he?' demanded Mac, 'I'll kill him!' Dr Robb looked confused,

'I'm sure you'll understand we have to follow hospital policy and right now our primary concern is to stabilise your daughter. I understand your concern entirely, but at this point we need you to remain calm and patient.' Dr. Robb was firm but kind. She knew it was hard for a parent to stand by and wait idly. She was sure she would feel the same in their position. 'Would you like me to ask an auxiliary to bring you some tea or coffee? I'm afraid our vending machine is out-of-order, as usual.' Mac and Beth looked at each other in desperate resignation.

Ten minutes later, they were still sitting in silence sipping lukewarm, milky tea and nibbling on stale biscuits. The mechanical ticking of the wall clock seemed to be slowing time down; it was a real discomfort zone. After what seemed like an eternity, a nurse with kind eyes and a slim build came for them.

'Don't be alarmed when you see Lomond,' she explained as she ushered them towards the ward. 'Since she is still unconscious, we've had to connect her to a ventilator, to help her breathe. This is just routine procedure, something we do with all patients who are in this way.' The ward had nothing of the hush and soft glow he and his wife had expected. It seemed to be thriving on some kind of controlled chaos, a constant ebb and flow of medical staff darting back and forth between bays, looking expressionless and exhausted all at once. There were as many overhead lights as you might find illuminating a fairground. Their bright strips glared and blinked as they walked under them, Mac had to shield his eyes. A strong clinical smell wafted around his nostrils and the *swish* and *thrum* of mechanical devices filling his ears, reminding him this was somewhere people met their end. The décor was sterile and bare, with each bed cordoned off by stiff green curtains. Some of these were open, exposing bodies inside attached to a varying array of disconcerting machinery. Clipboards hung at the end of the metal beds and it was clear some of the people were hanging on to their lives. It all felt so undignified. They came to stop at one of the cubicles and the nurse pulled back the curtain.

'Here we are' she said, beckoning them inside. 'She is still unconscious, but we've managed to stabilise her'. Mac and Beth were unsure about going anywhere near Lomond. The first thing they noticed was the clear flexible hose coming out of her mouth and running up to the ventilator. Her chest expanded and contracted rhythmically together with the machine. The sound was disturbing and the whole scene highly upsetting. Through tears, Beth looked at the monitor on the other side of the bed, it displayed Lomond's vitals, her blood pressure, temperature, heart rate and other things she thought must be important to monitor. Her eyes took in the array of equipment before coming to rest on her daughter again. Her head bandaged and held in position by a wide neck brace. It was so surreal. Anguished thoughts were buzzing like hornets at the windowpanes of Macs mind. *How could this be happening? Is this really my daughter? This lifeless thing drained of all colour, being kept alive by a plastic tube? How could I let this happen?* He thought he'd done everything he could for his daughter; *everything*. Now he questioned whether it had been enough at all.

Nurses and doctors came and went all evening, taking blood, fiddling with machines and writing up notes. Yet still, the only information they could provide was that Lomond was in a stable condition for now. The longer she sat staring at her daughter, the worse the dull throb in Beth's head was getting. How many times had she told Lomond about the dangers of motorbikes? So many times she had disobeyed her and now, here they were paying for the consequences of Lomond's outright stupidity. She hated hospitals. She wished she'd brought her pain pills along, the ones kept hidden at the back of the medicine chest behind the aspirin. She never felt so helpless or out of control. Mac sat with his head cradled in his hands. Every time he looked at Lomond, he felt sick, he really couldn't stomach this serious injury stuff. Trying to distract himself, he thought of their dog Shuna all alone in the house. No doubt, she would be whining, not knowing where they were. The curtain swished open again and they both looked up hopefully. It was just the ward sister coming to do checks. As she was leaving, she told them they could get some rest in the visitor's lounge if they wanted. Up until that point, neither of them had even thought about getting any sleep.

'When do you think we'll know what's wrong with our daughter?' Beth asked with a little more sharpness than necessary.

'We should know more by morning I should think,' the sister answered 'but probably best at least one of you stay nearby for now, just in case any snap decisions need to be made.' After she left, Mac rose from his seat, scraping the legs of the metal chair against the newly polished, tile floor. He needed a cigarette.

'I'm going to stretch my legs,' he stated, 'I won't be long.' Beth neither flinched nor looked at him.

It was around 3:00 a.m. when Mac finally joined Beth in the visitor's lounge; he'd been sitting with Lomond while his wife went to get some rest. Leaving a chair-space between them, he sat down and began rustling through the pages of an early edition of *The Mail*. After a while of staring at meaningless words and pictures, he gave up and put the paper down. Maybe it was time for a wee snooze. He folded his arms and let his chin drop towards his chest. Now he was still, he realised his heart was racing and he tried to slow it in unison with the tick of the clock.

They were both startled awake by another doctor. Mac looked up at noticed it was six o'clock. He introduced himself as Dr. Guthrie, a neurologist. *Dr Gavin Guthrie* Mac read from his ID badge; he didn't look much like a Gavin. As he spoke, Beth wore a smile that never quite reached her eyes; her face was void of any emotion at really, a look those who knew her were well used to seeing. Mac noted the peculiar way the doctor was stressing certain words. It sounded like an Indian twang, although he never looked Indian at all, maybe he grew up there. Dr Guthrie explained Lomond was in a state of profound unconsciousness or what is more commonly called, a coma.

'A coma?' repeated Mac, 'But, how? For how long?'

'Well, that's difficult to predict,' he answered, 'although she is stable and her organs seem to be working fine, we are still helping her breathe with the respirator. Your daughter sustained a significant impact to her head; it is quite usual for people to remain in this state after a head injury. Although the scan seemed to show no bleeding in the brain, I'm afraid we won't know until if there is any lasting damage or not until she wakes up. Also, if she doesn't start breathing on her own soon, we may opt to perform a *tracheotomy.*'

'A trachi what?' Beth questioned.

'It's a procedure to help her breathe more easily once we take her off the respirator.' Dr. Guthrie explained. 'At the moment, the tube carrying oxygen to Lomond's lungs passes through her mouth and down through the Trachea, putting pressure on her vocal cords. Since we don't want to cause lasting damage to her voice, we will feed the tube in lower down, through her neck.'

'Through her neck?' Beth exclaimed as Mac recoiled in horror. 'Will she be able to speak normally again…when she wakes up?' asked Beth. The doctor did his best to reassure them.

'Unfortunately, there are no certainties with comatose patients. The length of time a person can be in a coma can range from a few hours or days to weeks, months, or even years. This is what will determine Lomond's degree of recovery.'

'You mean she might not be able to talk or walk again? Mac sounded overwhelmed.

'From every indication,' Dr Guthrie's tone was kind and steady. 'Lomond appears to have been quite lucky. No cracked or broken bones, just a nasty laceration to the head and a lot of bruising to her face, arms and legs. This will become more pronounced over the next week or so but it will fade. We will be keeping a close eye on her brain activity and neurological state, along with all her vitals. If there is the slightest worsening of her condition, we will act immediately.'

'Act, how?' asked Beth, bracing herself for a worst-case scenario.

'Well any drop-in blood pressure could indicate an internal bleed below the skull plate, which means we would have to operate. If she remains stable once we take her off the respirator, we will move her down to the High Dependency Unit, but please don't worry. Lomond will get the same round-the-clock care there.'

Mac and Beth were unsure whether this was all good news or not. Dr. Guthrie suggested that for the moment, they might want to go home and get some rest. Someone would contact them immediately if there were any changes or cause for alarm. Then he was another shadowy silhouette fading into the background behind the vault-like doors.

The morning traffic was at its peak as they both stumbled wearily out of the hospital and to their car. On the drive home, neither of them spoke for fear it might set-off a verbal blame game. As they sat struggling through rush hour, Mac thought about all these people going about their normal daily routine, none of them had any idea about the night they'd just had, what they'd been through. Shuna greeted them like a dog possessed. She had never been left alone all night before and it was clear she'd made the most of it. As if by way of commentary, a large hole had been chewed out the doormat, it now read "ELCOME." The plastic telephone receiver was gnawed to a pulp and she had chewed right through the cable too. A box of stick matches were reduced to wet splinters and the entire house was littered with the remains of three shredded silk-covered pillows and a weeks' worth of newspapers. The debris and destruction lay strewn across floor like poignant dog offerings. By

9:00 a.m. the three of them were in their separate beds. Beth and Shuna both sound asleep, exhausted by their efforts. Mac on the other hand, lay staring at the ceiling torn between regret and anger; where the hell was George? He couldn't understand how Lomond had ended up in hospital and he was no-where to be seen, they must have him in the police station.

CHAPTER FIVE

Feelings of relief swept over Lomond as she found herself back in a world of colour. Moving, swirling, expanding and contracting; these were the colours she had known as a small girl. Suspended in this *nowhere and nothingness*, she was filled with a sense of freedom; freedom and peace she had only ever had glimpses of. Momentarily, she indulged herself in a game of colour-floating; slipping effortlessly between the vibrant energy waves. Immersing herself in a meandering sea of purple one moment, before rolling onto beams of yellow the next. After a while, Mrs. R came back into her mind. Since their first meeting, more memories of the relationship they had shared when Lomond was a little girl had come back to her. The fun and laughter, the mischief and sense of security Mrs. R had given her had all but gone and all she had were these memories. Lomond knew the colour pink connected her to Mrs. R, and she felt she really needed her right now. She focused all her thoughts on the colour and after a few moments, a mass of vivid pink energy, moving in a frenzied, fragmented manner appeared before her. As it began to settle, the plump and smiling figure of Mrs. R materialized from within it.

'Wow! That was amazing. I just concentrated all my energy and focused all my thoughts towards you and the colour and now like magic; you appear right in front of me!' Lomond lowered her voice to a whisper. 'Since I can see you and we can speak to each other, what does this mean, does it mean we are both dead?'

'No, lass, you are still among the living on earth but I, well, I suppose I am dead on a physical level, but my light, my consciousness is very much here and alive.' Sensing Lomond's confusion, Mrs. R continued. 'Unlike you, my physical life ended long ago – long before I came and visited when you were a wee girl; when your light and its power attracted me to you. Lomond was eager to know more about this apparent light within her. *How did Mrs. R know about it when she was unaware of it herself? Where was it and why had she never come across it before?* There were so many questions she wanted to ask, but she kept quiet, anxious she might miss some vital point if she interrupted.

'It seems easy to explain but I can see it's hard for you to understand. Although my body died, a part of me, maybe the real me, didn't. Some might call it consciousness, an essence or soul; but to me it's *light*. Well, this didn't die, it just returned to its elemental state.' Lomond could not contain herself any longer.

'But if you're dead and I'm alive, how are we

communicating?' There was a hint of suspicion in her voice. 'I mean, am I light like you now?' Mrs. R smiled.

'You have a gift Lomond. You can move out of the physical world and return to it at will, you can travel to other times and places. Very few can do this, especially in this modern and materialistic world. But it's something you need to understand, I mean *really* understand and control. There is great power there, but you must learn to master it.'

'So, you're saying, I've moved out of the physical world, or my light, my essence has, and that is how we are communicating? And at some point, I can go back to my physical world?' Lomond was musing to herself as well as seeking confirmation from Mrs. R.

'Yes. Your light, your energy, can move between these states. Everything both here and in the physical world is connected. Where we are now, where we have been and where we will go, they are all the same. It only changes form and substance from one life or realm to the other.' She explained, 'Light and energy, in all their forms and colours, vibrate and resonate across all space and time.' Lomond was trying her best to understand, sifting through the images and thoughts going through her mind. 'You know about Déjà vu and premonitions?

The times when you think you've been somewhere or done something before; or when you think of a person or something, and then you meet them or that something happens? Well, these things act as a bridge; a connection between worlds and states of being.'

Lomond marveled at the myriad of colours dancing and weaving around them, around everything, and she felt connected to something greater than herself. Feeling both intrigued and uplifted, she felt a sense of wholeness and peace. A wave of pink energy surged towards her and Mrs. R evaporated inside it. It washed over her and Lomond felt an instant sense of determination. Her adventurous spirit swelled and burst out through her in rays of red energy. When she focused on this feeling, the intensity and vibration grew more intense. This must be the power Mrs. R was talking about. Exhilaration and excitement caused the red to become more vivid than she had ever seen and with this, her head began to throb; she needed to bring some calm. Next a ball of orange was rushing towards her, as if someone or something was pushing it her way. Then, she became the orange and with it she was awash with joy and elation. Traumatic memories and emotions seem to lose all their significance. Visions of the accident re-played in her mind, but she felt no fear, nothing. Not at the sight of the bike lying in the road with its back wheel spinning pointlessly, nor the vision of her body lying motionless as blood pooled around her skull, nothing. Then, at breath-taking speed, the scene was gone, and she was somewhere else.

The orange morphed into yellow and she was moving, travelling across huge expanses of time and space. She felt and she saw the sun beaming down upon the Great Pyramids and suddenly it was as if she possessed the knowledge of the ancients. It all played out in her mind, right in front of her. She felt the truths behind ancient mysteries, the essential connections with the natural world the sages had maintained for a millennia; truths and wisdom that have been lost to science and modernity.

'I've come back to help you.' Lomond hadn't noticed Mrs. R had returned until she heard her calming voice.

'Help me how, and to do what?'

'You are still in the space between physical life and death. It's like a void from which you must seek a way out. Yes, you can feel colour and light here, but I believe with your power, you can give them substance in the physical world.' With this, Lomond stared to understand more clearly. It was more than a choice between life and death; it was about adding something to her life for the better, living the alternative.

'You have already begun your journey,' Mrs. R said, interrupting her thoughts, 'it's time to use your power now, time to think for yourself; search for the colours you feel. You will know which one to follow.' A rainbow of colours swirled around the words of Mrs. R, pushing and jostling with each other as if trying to seek Lomond's attention. Then slowly, a dense indigo light began to push its way into her mind. It seemed to pull her into its influence as it stretched out like a tunnel in front of her.

'How and where Mrs. R? What am I to do? *Please don't leave me.'* wailed Lomond.

'You can do this, I'll come with you, but you have to concentrate on the tunnel, clear your thoughts and picture it in your mind, just the indigo tunnel'.

CHAPTER SIX

That evening when Mac and Beth got to the hospital, they discovered Lomond had been moved to the High Dependency Unit on the ground floor. A nurse met them there and spoke encouragingly. Although Lomond was still on a ventilator and being fed by a drip, the team were hopeful she would be breathing on her own soon. Mac and Beth passed by rows of patients occupying the ward. Some had masks over their mouths, others, nasal canellas feeding oxygen into their lungs. Unlike Lomond though, many of them were sitting up in various states of recovery.

'Think I'll go for a smoke,' said Mac as they neared the bed. Like many fathers, husbands, sons and brothers, hospitals made him queasy. Beth never responded. Her eyes were fixed on the young doctor checking Lomond's vitals. After a few moments, she sat on the metal-framed chair next to the bed, the last words she spoke to Lomond echoing through her head,

'Lomond, you are *not* to go on that motorbike.' How she wished her suspicions had been unjustified. That damn blue jacket, why hadn't she noticed? Lomond never wore that to the bloody ice-rink. Feeling bitter and angry she looked around for Mac, where was that fool when she needed him.

A young nurse with shoulder length curly hair and a wispy fringe passed by Mac in the corridor.

'Anywhere I can get change for the vending machines?' he asked searching his pockets.

'Not at this time of night, I'm afraid,' she answered in a velvet tone, 'You're Lomond's father, aren't you?' she added hesitantly.

'Yes' replied Mac, noticing a softness in her brown eyes.

'Do you mind if I speak with you for a moment?'

'Yes, of course,' he answered, looking over his shoulder for any sign of his wife, grateful she wasn't within earshot if it was bad news.

'I'm Lorraine,' the young woman said, reaching out her hand, 'Lomond's primary-care nurse.' Mac's brow creased with worry as he took her small hand in his. 'There's nothing to be concerned about,' she assured. 'I just wanted to introduce myself. I'll be in the ward later and…'

Suddenly her attention broke as someone shot by them. Mac shrugged politely but continued.

'Yes, you'll meet my wife then, Beth. She's with our daughter just now. It's a difficult time…' He noticed she wasn't quite listening. Her eyes were on the figure of a young man in a leather jacket galloping along the corridor. *The leather jacket.* Macs mouth fell open and flames of rage shot through his body. It was George, *that spineless idiot, how is he even here?* Without another word, he was hurtling, stiff-legged down the glossy tiled corridor leaving Lorraine startled and wondering. When Mac burst through the swinging doors at the end of the corridor, he was disappointed to find himself at the bottom of an empty stairwell. Panting, he looked up but there was no sign of anyone. If it was that bampot, he was long gone. Out-of-breath, Mac made his way back to the HDU. As he passed the nurses' station, he noticed the same doctor they'd met earlier, Dr. Robb. She was bent over a file, whispering intently to the ward nurse.

   'The police want to interview her as soon as she comes round. They think there was another rider on the bike, a driver. They're coming to speak to the parents' Mac froze, he couldn't believe his ears. How could they possibly think Lomond was alone in the first place? He hurried back to Lomond's cubicle to tell Beth; she was going to hit the roof. He was still breathing heavily as he sat next to Beth.

   'Where've you been?' she hissed, almost accusingly. He realised he would need to choose his words carefully. Turning to speak to her, the look of disdain on her face silenced him; he'd need to build up some courage first. Just then, Lorraine appeared to check on Lomond. She stood at the foot of Lomond's bed with a reserved smile.

'Hi, I'm Lorraine, Lomond's nurse,' she directed towards Beth.

'Oh,' responded Beth, 'pleased, I'm sure.' Lorraine began her checks on Lomond, seemingly un-phased by the tight-lipped response. They both watched her as she decoded the digital read-out from the monitor and added notation to Lomond's chart.

'She's doing fine,' Lorraine said, almost absently. 'pulse is even, heart rate steady, respiration clear.' She checked the drips and started changing over one of the bags containing a saline solution. 'Did you find him then?' she asked, glancing at Mac.

'Uh…no, he must have taken a lift or slipped out the side door,' Mac realised his tone sounded shifty and he threw the nurse an imploring look, it was too late.

'Find who? Who were you looking for?' Lorraine glanced apologetically from husband to wife, sorry to have set something off. If looks could kill, Mac would have dropped down dead on the spot with the way Beth was staring at him. The moment she left the room, Beth was on Mac.

'Well? Who did you see?

'Beth, I don't know for certain. I only saw him from behind for a moment, but it might have been that George.'

'What?'

'It may have been him. I can't say for certain…'

'What's that bloody half-wit doing here? Why is he not been arrested?' Beth was absolutely seething.

'There is something else,' he added, knowing better than to withhold anything his wife might find out herself alter. Beth cocked her head and crossed her arms expectantly, 'I overheard Dr. Robb talking with one of the nurses. Seems the police have only just realised there was another rider, but they must not know who it was, they're waiting to speak to Lomond and us, it must have been that George.' Beth's thoughts began to surge. *Where is George? Here in the hospital? Surely they would trace the bike back to him. Oh my god, they must not be able to. So it was all his doing and now he was on the run? He wasn't even man enough to stay at the scene. He'd seen their daughter lying there for dead in the road and he'd done a runner, and now he was prowling about the hospital like some rabid dog. How dare he?*

'That despicable *coward*!' she blurted out, 'You let him get away!' Mac shuddered off his chair.

'For God's sake, woman, what did you want me to do? Chase him around the whole building?'

'For once, just be a man and protect your daughter" she spat back.

Just then, Lorraine reappeared clutching an envelope for Lomond, walking in on them with Mac backed up against the wall like some cornered animal. Beth rose quickly from her chair and declared almost honourably,

'Mac, I insist. You take my chair, it's much more comfortable.' Then, turning to Lorraine, she added, 'His poor back. It's always giving him trouble.' When Beth did her *royalty* act, she did it most convincingly. It was easy for Mac to imagine a glittering tiara perched high on the tight-knit perm of her coarse brown hair. The nurse waited as the couple awkwardly exchanged chairs.

'Special delivery,' she declared, handing Beth the envelope. 'This was left at the front desk.' Beth opened the get-well card and read it to herself: *Lomond—Be Strong, Girl! We Love You!* It was signed, Maria, & Tracy, her two best mates from school.

Suddenly Beth was overcome by feelings of guilt. She wanted so much to reach out to Mac, to hold on to him, but she couldn't; showing weakness was just not her style. Mac must have noticed the tears rolling down her cheek because he reached out and rested his hand on her thigh. In response, she slipped her hand into his, for the first time in years. Her face was full of anguish as she spoke.

'Surely we don't deserve this. What did we do to be punished this way?' She could already hear the voices of their friends and neighbours, gossiping about what awful parents they must be. Mac looked at his wife of many years with the tears smearing her thick mascara. Although his heart was touched, he knew Beth was only considering her own pain; not Lomond's or his. As always, everything was about her. She seemed incapable of seeing things from outside herself. What could he say? In all their years together, she'd never really heard him. Despite this, as they sat holding hands, the years rolled back to the first time he'd timidly reached for her hand. Sitting in the stalls at the Regal Cinema, they had watched Rhett Butler eying Scarlet O'Hara as she descended the grand staircase in *Gone with the Wind*. Mac gave her hand a gentle squeeze, reminiscent of that day; knowing well those innocent moments were now just faded snapshots. Beth glanced coyly at Mac—in the same way she had back then- before casting her eyes back to their daughter. As they sat watching dark red blood coursing through the tube and into Lomond's lifeless body, a shock realisation hit Beth. It mattered, it mattered terribly that Lomond should live.

CHAPTER SEVEN

'Now, watch carefully,' Mrs. R told Lomond as she slowly enveloped herself in a blanket of deep indigo. 'To leave this spirit realm and travel to another, we must prepare ourselves. See how I draw the colour towards me and do as I do.'

'Where do you get it from? How can you be all pink one moment and indigo the next?' Mrs. R smiled.

'You create it in your mind, lass. Just focus on the indigo around me and surround yourself with that same energy. Draw it right in through the top of your head and fill your body with its vibration.' Then, just like that, Mrs. R disappeared into a cloud of deep purple-blue, right before Lomond's eyes.

'Go on now, you can do it.' Mrs. R was urging her from somewhere beyond. Let yourself bathe in the colour.' Lomond willed herself to relax and something began to happen. Steady waves of indigo were washing over and through her, bringing with them a deep sense of calm. A distant memory awakened; visions of a dark starry sky, feelings of a profound spiritual connection to a wondrous blanket of twinkling lights. Suddenly she felt Mrs. R beside her and they were floating together through this tunnel of colour, weaving in and out different tones and hues of indigo.

'Now we can travel between the different realms,' announced Mrs. R. 'we can come and go wherever we choose.' Lomond had never felt more alive. The idea of being free to slip between different realms of energy filled her with ecstasy. From somewhere inside her came a deep realisation, she had known all along. Alternate spiritual dimensions did exist and now she was experiencing the wonderful sensations of weightlessness and freedom she imagined would be possible there. They began picking up speed. The vibrant colour whipped up a cool wind as they hurtled through the deep tunnel, plunging them somewhere into the unknown. Then, they stopped. So abrupt that the tunnel vanished, sucked into a void behind them. In its place, the pure light of a morning sun dazzled Lomond. They had arrived in the physical realm.

It took a few moments for Lomond to adapt to her surroundings, for things were not quite as she remembered them. Matter was no longer defined by edges or contrasts between light and dark. Instead, everything appeared through a luminous mist. As if the mist itself was a manifestation of the things beneath it. Looking more closely, Lomond saw a myriad of colour energies weaving intricate patterns, each tone and hue seemed to be vibrating in its own unique way. She was nearly overcome by emotion. Then, there were erratic shards of light and she in a hospital ward. Tubes and bags and wires connected to noisy machines. Two people sitting at the foot of a bed with their heads bowed.

'My parents!' she cried.

'Yes,' Mrs. R said, 'who do you think is lying there?'

'I can't make out . . . .' said Lomond. The fact virtually no colour energy was radiating from the body on the bed made it difficult to discern an identity.

'Look harder,' Mrs. R said ominously. Lomond attuned her mortal senses and focused in on the figure lying there.

'My God, is that me? That is me!' The dire condition of her physical body reflected by the way she lay there; like an empty colourless husk left blanched white by the sun. Lomond looked at her parents. Her mother was dominated by fiery red and spikes of purple colour energy. Like red-hot flames from a coal fire, they danced and wove around her, standing out like a beacon compared to the uneven flashes of blue and green emanating from her solemn father. Mrs. R. seemed to be able to read Lomond's thoughts and emotions.

'As you can see dear, your mother is engulfed in red. There is a lot of anger there; frustration, regret.' Lomond nodded her consensus. 'Interestingly, part of her true nature, her real *inner* self, gives off purple vibrations. This means she is fundamentally spiritual; despite how she may appear or act. I know she has suffered deeply in her life and is haunted by a lost love. She's also very intuitive; though at the moment, this energy is so subdued it's barely visible.' Lomond's curiosity was piqued.

'Mrs. R, what do you mean, "haunted by a lost love" and what about an 'inner' self?' Purposely avoiding the first question, Mrs R explained that every human has an *inner* and *outer* self.

'The *outer* self is public,' she said 'it is the part of us we share with others. Our *inner* self is that which no one can access, unless we choose to share it. The *inner* self consists of the layers of experiences we've encountered in this and past lives. The *outer* self our façade, the way we want the world to see us. It reflects our patterns and conditions, our learnt behaviours.'

'But where does it all begin, Mrs. R.?' Lomond asked. 'I mean, what's at the beginning?' Mrs. R smiled at her eagerness.

'In the beginning there were five elements: *earth, air, fire, water* and *ether*. These were the first aspects of nature humankind became aware of and they were key in defining the beliefs in their earliest gods as well' Lomond couldn't fathom what she meant by this. 'As well as being fundamental to our individual experiences and worldviews, these elements are also universal and intuitive.

You've heard the expressions, "a down-to-earth" or "fiery person?" or someone being "wishy-washy" or "airy-fairy?"' Lomond nodded. 'We intuitively understand the meaning of the elements as they are used to describe human characters. More interestingly, and I think this will especially interest to you, they can also be seen in an individual's face and overall size and shape of their body'

'The elements do? Really?'

'Yes, indeed they do lass. We'll learn more about that another time.'

'What about her then?' Lomond asked. Her mother was the one person on earth who posed the greatest mystery to her, and Mrs. R. had long known of the tension between them.

'As you can see Lomond, aside from the red and purple, all her other colour vibrations are weak; this is what happens to people who suffer emotionally. Their colours weaken. Their vibrations weaken and this is when physical and mental illness can take a foothold. Clearly, over the years, Beth, or your mother, has suffered a great deal; mainly because she harbours secrets. She carries a deep emotional burden that has festered in time. It spills over into her relationships, with you and your father.' Lomond nodded, a knowing truth in her eyes. For as long as she could remember, her mother had never seemed happy, never. As bad as her relationship had always been with Beth, the way she treated her father was almost unbearable. Lomond had often wondered why he bothered to marry such a mean woman in the first place.

'Will she ever change?' Lomond asked, already predicting the answer.

'No one can say for certain, but change can come about. Look there, you see the violet? It's there, just waiting for her to acknowledge. She has to wake up to her spirituality first. Only then will she find peace and harmony within herself. The she will heal her wounds and be able to move forward in life. Without spiritual understanding, this may never happen.' Forgetting for the moment all the frigid indifference she and her father had long suffered at her mother's insensitive hands, Lomond asked,

'What old wounds?' Mrs. R. spoke carefully.

'Lomond, your accident has been a catalyst—a trigger, for your mother to acknowledge her suffering and that which she imposes on others. An opportunity for her to re-examine the decisions made throughout life. She carries many regrets and like all of us who are in conflict, the colour vibrations she emits reflect the deep struggle between her inner and outer selves.'

'Regrets, decisions, conflicts, she hides them all so well. Anyway, I'm just amazed at how differently each colour vibration makes me *feel*.' Lomond said, losing interest in her mother's issues.

'Lass, the energy emitted by each colour tells you something very important. It's a special intuitive language and you are just beginning to learn its codes, its *secrets*.' Mrs. R. gave Lomond a second to let all this sink in before prompting her, 'Tell me what you *feel* about the colour *green*.' Taking in a deep breath, Lomond searched her mind for the right words to express a colour by feelings.

'I see myself lying on freshly-cut green grass. I can actually smell it. My heart is at peace and I feel as though I want to stay in the greenness of the countryside forever.' Lomond was smiling at the sensation she was experiencing. 'In fact,' she added with a tone of exhilaration, 'I would love to live off the land, maybe on a farm. With green I feel at one with myself, as if I touched something that made my heart soar.' Mrs R was nodding.

'And *blue*?' she asked. Lomond began to draw in the colour blue, revelling in the fact this was becoming effortless now. Again, she was surprised at the effect.

'If sounds could fall like water this would be it' she said. 'I can hear and see in my mind the crashing of crystal-clear water, cascading over the face of a rocky hillside and into a pool at the bottom. I feel blue flooding into my throat, as if I should be speaking, or singing or reading aloud or telling a story. Yet, at the same time I feel tired,' she said, a yawn overtaking her. Then, Lomond spoke no more as her mind became quiet and a deep stillness washed over her.

'Beth is someone who'd certainly benefit from blue vibration' muttered Mrs. R. Then, as if to avoid having to explain her deeper meaning she vanished into the ether.

Alone, Lomond set out in her energetic form to explore the hospital. Being able to expand and contract at will, she found she was able to scan the colour energies of other people. Observing patients, nurses and visitors, she soon discovering others were void of colour; their energy barely perceptible. She floated along with a nurse who wheeled a trolley into a ward. Inside, the energies of nearly all the patients were dim and fading. The nurse stopped at the foot of each bed and counted out tablets or filled medicine vials. Lomond noticed that when the nurse approached and spoke to each patient, her colour vibrations became dominated by blue.

'Hello, Mrs. Jones. Having a wee nap, are we?' 'Did that handsome son of yours visit today, Jenny?' 'Oh, that is a pretty plant, Mrs. Dobson, seems you have an admirer!' In response to the nurse's soothing blue aura, some patients were inspired enough to sit up and chat; others gave her a wave or nod. The nurse with the medicine cart then cut down a corridor until she came to a side-door that was standing ajar. She paused before looking in. Just inside was a man in a well-starched white lab coat, standing with his back to the door. He was mumbling and writing intently,

'What's that, nurse?' he asked.

'Just thought I should mention I saw a boy, a young man really, he was trying to open the door to the pharmacy. When he saw me, he turned away, as if he'd got the wrong door. I'm not really sure, I don't know. He had a funny look on his face. It struck me as suspicious.'

Thank you, nurse,' he said dismissively, 'but, I am solely responsible for the security of the pharmacy and it is not your job to remind me about locked and unlocked doors!' Taken aback, the nurse nodded apologetically and said nothing. Lomond watched on as she resumed her round; the soothing blue energy- so dominant moments before started to fade away. Her luminosity dimmed as she continued her duties with faltering footsteps and her eyes fixed to the floor. Lomond followed her down the hallway and into the room where her body lay. She watched smiling as she handed her mother an envelope; it looked like a greeting card. When Beth finished reading the message inside, she looked from the nurse to her husband, her face became pale and she started to tremble. The colour energy around her shifted drastically, as if she were having an emotional crisis. Then she saw her parents hold each other, just for a few moments, but in a way Lomond had never seen before.

CHAPTER EIGHT

Finishing her shift at 7.00am, Lorraine slipped out of her uniform and caught the 7:20am bus home. She could have walked - and often did- but she had stops to make and didn't want to be out long. After buying milk and fresh rolls from the local co-op and a copy of *The Scotsman* from the newsstand, she walked the short distance towards her second-floor flat. She glanced up at the drawn curtains resisting the morning light and envied the occupants their sleep. She climbed the stairs and quietly let herself in. She would wait until her flat-mate Helen left for work, only then would she run a nice hot bath and soak the stresses of the hospital away.

Recently, Lorraine had begun to resent Helen and she felt bad about it. She resented her boisterous, over-the-top behaviour and loud habits. They exhausted Lorraine and opposed her more conservative upbringing. Most mornings, it seemed the moment Helen heard her come in, she would get up and streak around the flat ahead of her. Into the bathroom, rushing around the kitchen, the tell-tale signs of her rushing left strewn behind her. You needn't be a detective to track her movements, that's for sure.

Lorraine knew Helen would get around to cleaning up after herself, eventually, but it annoyed her; she lived by the old adage,

"Cleanliness is next to Godliness." Her nurse's sensibilities taught her that mess meant germs, germs meant unclean and unclean was an outbreak waiting to happen.

In truth, their relationship hadn't always been so strained. When the two of them had first met, Lorraine had been drawn to her sunny, carefree disposition. Aware she herself was on the *too-serious* side; she hoped some of Helen's verve and audacity might rub off; just a little. However, it didn't work out like that; Lorraine had misjudged. Helen's *sunshine,* as she came to discover, was in fact, a limelight that only shone when she was basking in the centre of it. Now things had reached the uncomfortable stage they had; Lorraine resented herself for feeling this way. It was unfair, especially as she had encouraged the relationship in the first place. The more unfair it felt, the more Lorraine withdrew into her shell like a delicate mollusc. It made her feel like a 'safe' but not-so-very-nice person.

The pictures on the wall shook as her rambunctious flat-mate jerked the front door closed. In no time, Lorraine had run the tub and eased herself into a reverie of bubbles. With a deep, musing sigh, she tried to empty her mind of the day's events. It drifted to the young man she'd seen with his hand on the pharmacy door. She thought about Lomond, the patient in bed eleven. What an unusual and beautiful name. *Would she be one of the lucky ones who'd come out of their coma unchanged?* She wondered about Lomond's parents; their relationship seemed so strange. They certainly didn't act like the best of partners. Having witnessed more parents struggling with sick children than she could begin to count, she'd seen this all before. It seemed another case of the child being the only glue holding them together, a constant blame-game bubbling below the surface. She'd decided long ago that she didn't want it to be like that for her, but she wondered whether anyone who matched her hopes and expectations would ever come along.

Men often asked her out; even a few of the doctors. Yet, Lorraine always managed to come up with an excuse to say no. Her disinterest seemed to annoy her flat mate Helen. In fact, she had for a time, wondered about Lorraine's sexual preferences. Meanwhile, Helen harped on about keeping her eyes open for her own 'Mr. Right'. Lorraine wondered just how many 'Mr. Rights' needed to come and go before Helen's would actually appear. So far, it seemed every man she met became *the one, the answer to her dreams* overnight. It all seemed so pointless and shallow the way she flitted from man to man; letting each one into her bed; it was no wonder she was known as easy around Edinburgh.

However, Helen professed to know better of course. To her, men were attracted to her exceptionally sexy looks *and* her bubbly personality; that was what they fell in love with. So, it was with this belief that she flaunted her *assets* at any handsome, well-heeled man who gave her a second look.

'A girl's a fool not to use what Mother Nature gives 'er!' she'd boast, heaving up her sizable bosom.

After pulling herself out of the bath, Lorraine dried off and pampered herself with soft, sweet-smelling baby powder.

Slipping into her pyjamas, it was 9.30am when she finally fell into bed and almost immediately, she was in a deep sleep. When she woke, the last rays of winter sunshine were cutting low into her room and across the far walls. For a while, she lay there peacefully watching the way the angled slats of the window frame reflected violet on to the pale blue wall. She was fond of her room; it suited her. Sufficiently feminine yet understated. She liked the way the rose-flowered border created a clean edge against the ceiling she'd painted a bright white. It provided a pure backdrop for the varying-sized luminous stars she adhered to the ceiling. She loved the way they gathered the light and emitted a warm glow, long after the darkness of night delivered silence.

She let her eyes roam upwards and imagined an inner journey she had yet to take. Lorraine had enrolled in an evening massage-therapy class, but since they conflicted with her night-shift at the hospital, she had only attended two before she had to drop out. Just last week on her way to the hospital, she ran into one of the other students. Innes was a tall and somewhat dull-natured young girl with long, limp brown hair and old-fashioned horn-rimmed spectacles. Recognising each other, they had stopped to chat. Finding Innes surprisingly easy to talk to, Lorraine realised you should never judge a book by its cover. She told her she was a nurse and explained how the evening class wasn't quite what she was looking for and in the spirit of sharing; Innes told her how she was studying at Edinburgh College of Art and earned money as a cleaner at the house of her Spiritual Guru, Tyrone. With great enthusiasm, she talked about his meditation group. He was very experienced and worldly; he'd travelled throughout India and Tibet for over a decade and had he had run a little spiritual enlightenment group in Edinburgh for years now. Noticing a spark of interest, Innes wrote down the address,

'Why don't you drop by and check it out next Saturday? I'm sure you'll find Tyrone fascinating!'

'I need to check my shifts and see if I am off.'

'What hospital are you at?' asked Innes.

'The Royal Infirmary.'

'Oh, my friend is in the Royal at the moment. I really want to visit her but I'm a bit scared.' she stated

'Maybe I could meet with you and take you in, who is it you want to see?'

'My friend Lomond, we were neighbours for years, we had great fun. She was really wild, you know. I was older than her but we got on so well, she seemed older than her years.'

'What a small world, I look after her, so that is even easier. Let me call you and we can sort something out' said Lorraine.

Lorraine woke from her sleep after the Friday night shift and lay in bed contemplating. She wasn't so sure about the meditation group after all and Helen had invited her out to the pub too.

'Come on Lorraine, it won't kill you to go out once in a while! We can go out for a pizza afterwards as well' she'd coaxed. Now Lorraine was torn. She'd put her off so many times in recent weeks. Perhaps she *should* go—in the name of good will, if nothing else. On the other hand, she really wanted to check out this new meditation group conducted by the mystical Tyrone. Throwing off the covers and swinging her legs over the edge of the bed, her feet sank into the softness of the lush blue, shag-pile carpet. She caught sight of her reflection in the wardrobe mirror. Studying herself for a moment, she smoothed her shoulder length Auburn hair and took in her slim frame and perky breasts. She looked so different without her nurse's uniform on, she hardly recognised herself. It struck her now, just how long it had been since she'd thought about her figure and her femininity. Wrapping a blanket around her shoulders and plunking herself down on a thick cushion by the fireplace, she reached for a box of long stick matches. Gazing at a half-burnt candle, she struck one and lit a candle, the first flicker and swell of the flame sparking her fascination. Drawn in, she watched it steady and pucker before blossoming into a vibrant, and colourful beacon. The glowing nimbus made her feel warm and secure. She studied closely all the varying hues. The yellows, oranges and reds dancing within, the way the violet surrounded, contained and shielded it. She pondered- as many have in this twilight of mind-*What is life really about*? *Where am I going? Will I know when I get there*? And most importantly, *who am I*?

The front door slammed, jolting her back to the present. It was Helen returning from work. Remaining silent in the candlelight, she hoped her flatmate would assume she was still asleep. A moment later the music came on in the living-room; some new band from America she'd been raving about. She could hear groceries being unwrapped in the kitchen, the tap opening full bore in the bathroom. A moment later the bedroom door flung open.

'Hey, why are you sittin' in the dark?' Helen exclaimed, snapping on the bright overhead light. 'Come on, no layin' about, Lorraine. Get dressed. We're goin' out remember? You can have a bath after me. Mind and wear that turquoise-blue dress you have, your diddies look *outrageous* in it' Helen said, indicating Lorraine's proportions with her hands. 'Oh and wear your hair down for a change!'

'Look, Helen, I'm not sure I'm really in the mood to go out. Besides, I've been asked to go round to someone else's place tonight as well.' Although dying to ask, Helen knew better than probe into Lorraine's private life. Instead, she said,

'Okay, tell you what, you can come down to the pub and have a few drinks and meet some people I know, a right bloody lot of knob-heads, but they're a good lot, and after that, you can go on to your friend's place. What d'ya say? You in?' Lorraine had to agree that Helen's plan seemed reasonable enough but she couldn't ignore the fact she didn't have much in common with her friends at all. She wasn't interested in getting drunk or high and she didn't find their conversations interesting at all. She'd often wondered why she couldn't fit into their carefree lifestyle; but she just couldn't; it just wasn't who she was.

Lorraine tried on the turquoise-blue dress Helen suggested and Lorraine wasn't wrong; it clung tightly to her slim body; enunciating her small waist and modest perky breast. However, the plunging neckline, nearly to her navel was far too revealing for Lorraine. She'd loved the dress on the rack, but now she realised she'd bought it out of impulse, rather than planning to actually wear it out. She had to admit though, she did look downright hot in it. Almost too embarrassed to look at herself in the mirror, she quickly slipped it off. It certainly wouldn't suit a meditation group anyway. In the end, she resigned herself to an ankle-length, blue cotton, Gypsy-style skirt and a simple white, embroidered peasant blouse. Helen poked her nose around the door and saw the turquoise-blue dress lying crumpled on the bed. Her face was a mixture of jealousy and admiration as she realised her friend would attract men no matter what she wore.

'You look *fabulous*.' she encouraged. 'How 'bout me?' she asked, spinning around playfully; almost daring Lorraine to proffer criticism. Lorraine quickly took in her appearance and the obvious intention of it. The fullness of Helen's bosom pushed the low-cut yellow top to the limits. The tight-fitting black skirt stretched across her voluptuous hips, stopping well above her knees and displaying her full and shapely tanned thighs, for all to see. Lorraine smiled; she knew the evening would probably end with Helen wondering off with someone she'd just met to spend the night in their bed. She'd stumble home after sunrise with her clothes wrinkled and her hair like a birds nest. No doubt he'd be 'the one' and a week or so later, she'd be back on the prowl again.

They shared a taxi to The Bandwagon in Frederick Street. Helen insisted on paying the fare, but she also took the opportunity to express her views on cigarette smoking to the taxi driver.

'My clothes are stinking now because of you smoking that

bloody cigarette while we're in your taxi, we should get a discount.' she complained.

'Listen here hen, either you pay me the right fare or see that red box over there, that what's called a phone box So, I'll just take myself and ma cigarette over there and call the police. Oh, and guess what, see when yer pie eyed later this evening and it's me you flag down to take you home, you'll no be grumbling then aboot the smell of my cigarette then. No, you'll be thanking me for stopping and taking you home. So, what'll be hen, pay or jail?'

Lorraine had been to this pub before, but she was hardly a 'regular' unlike Helen and her gang. The Bandwagon had a lounge area upstairs and, in the basement, a stage where lots of different bands played live. Lorraine followed Helen down the stairs and towards the entrance. She stopped to smile at Jock, the bouncer who instantly recognised Helen and opened the door. She headed straight for the bar, which was heaving. Helen pushed her way through, smiling at the men as she did so. Once the men saw her, they would then of course gravitate towards her; a strategy that worked well for her in the past. At the bar, Helen ordered their drinks. The barman smiled.

'Your usual Helen, a Blue Lagoon? Twelve and six please darling.'

After paying for her drink, she turned and caught sight of a group of her mates.

'Be right over, guys!' She waved enthusiastically, her voice carrying above the perpetual din of shouts and laughter. Lorraine took in the little crew at a glance; mostly young men, well boys really. Amongst them she spotted a short and attractive girl with a halo of bubbly blond hair. This young woman seemed at ease with the guys. Not shy or simpering, neither bold nor brassy. There was an air of confidence about her. Lorraine decided that if she were to talk to anyone, it would be her. However, no sooner had they pushed their way through the writhing bodies, the bubbly blond had disappeared and Helen effectively took over the room. The men seemed to be enjoying her bold, off-colour sense of humour. Before long, all eyes were riveted on her flatmate and Lorraine found herself standing uneasily to one side, wondering why on earth she'd agreed to come in the first place.

The band Shorty Rogers and the Wranglers burst into life and 'You Ain't Nothing But A Hound Dog' blasted from the stage. The body heat and chatter grew intense and Lorraine began to feel a bit lightheaded. She downed most of her drink, but that only seemed to make things worse. Then out of nowhere, a snapshot of her encounter with the ill-tempered pharmacist came to mind. Why had she even bothered? He was well-known for being abrupt, bad-tempered even. What had she set herself up to be belittled, to be dismissed so disrespectfully? She tried to push the image out of her mind, but it wouldn't go. She breathed in and out slowly; even trying to tune-in to Helen's inane conversation for a moment. But his haughty face and dismissive tone kept echoing in her ears. Feeling the blood rushing to her brain, she felt as though she were at the centre of a volcano about to erupt. Her head started spinning and she felt her legs begin to buckle beneath her.

'Hey, grab her, Fred!' Helen's voice rang out above the others.

'Hey, you alright, lassie?' said another voice.

'She's my flat-mate. Sit her down over there.' Suddenly, Lorraine found herself in a chair in a dark corner of the room.

'Sit here whilst I go and get you some water.' a young man said. She dropped her head and tried breathing in and out, slowly and deeply; just as she'd been taught. Breathless and with her mouth so dry she couldn't speak, she longed for a cool drink of water. Her eyes searched through the crowd for her rescuer.

Warily she looked to her left and discovered an odd-looking couple sitting beside her. Gaunt and wiry and with a hungry look about their eyes, they seemed to be peering at her with poised lips. 'Room for me to perch beside you?' It was her knight in shining armour, returning with the cool water as promised. Lorraine sipped the glass until it was empty and her head began to clear. 'Have you eaten?' the young man inquired.

'No, I'm okay, really.' Lorraine answered, feeling embarrassed now and realising in truth, she hadn't eaten since early morning.

'We could go round the corner for a bite. This place is way too noisy for me any way.'

Noticing Helen worming her way towards them through the crowd, Lorraine got up quickly, thanked her rescuer and gave her flat-mate a short wave. Then she made for the door. As she glanced back, she noticed Helen was already taken in by this tall, handsome, glassy-eyed specimen who'd obviously had several too many. Lorraine wouldn't expect to see her home until the next morning. Outside, she breathed in the cool fresh air and regretted agreeing to come to the pub. She considered going back to the flat to watch some TV, but she realised she couldn't face another Saturday night alone.

Feeling the perspiration under her arms, she thought maybe she should go home and change. *Just do what's best for you, Lorraine,* came an almost inaudible whisper from somewhere.

CHAPTER NINE

It's funny, Lomond thought from her place in the vast expanses of the energy realms, *how easily I've been able to ignore my colourless, lifeless body lying there in the hospital bed.* Now it was time though, time to reunite with her body and resume her life; as screwed-up as it may be. Oh, yes, she loved the freedom and power of these energy realms, but there was still so much more she wanted to see and do in the real world. Besides, she told herself, if things got too painful or fagged-out, she knew what to do to return.

'Mrs. R., do you think the doctors and nurses will be able to fix me?' she asked. It was the first time she had shown any desire to return.

'Lomond, there is a nurse who can and will try to help you, as will the doctors. But in the end, it all comes down to you. Only you alone know your true desire and is able to build the pathway to your future. You must choose when to return to the physical world, you have to will your way back.'

'The question is *how though*?' Lomond mused as Mrs. R. gave her a reproachful, impatient look. 'So, is my recovery all to do with energy and colour? Is that it? Am I supposed to form a cloud of colour around my body to replace what I lost? Like, if I replace all my colours, I'll get better, and If I don't, I'll die? Is that the trick?'

'Lomond child, think of it this way. Every thought, every action and every aspect of your surroundings is made of *energy*. This energy is *colour,* felt in the form of *vibrations*. Recovery for you is all about your state of mind. Clear thoughts create a pure state of mind, and a pure state of mind is one that is detached from all its negative patterns. A silenced mind, in a relaxed and peaceful state will provide healing to the body. This is the *fire* that fuels life. By keeping your mind in its purest state, through purposeful intention, your colours will naturally intensify and your energy will be restored.' Lomond tried to grasp the crux of what she must have to do. So much of what Mrs. R. said seemed like a riddle to her. Why couldn't she be more direct and just spell things out?

'The fact is Lomond, so many people have very little understanding of themselves and those around them, or even of life itself for that matter. For example, most humans desire close friendships, people to share their life with, it is in our very nature. Yet so often, this is not something realised or considered important by society. Our development into fully evolved human beings, who know how to interact and improve our personal relationships, is not something we seem to learn through interaction. In reality, we're left pretty much to our own devices to discover our needs. Our well-being, success and happiness is our own responsibility. The only means we have to discovering our true selves, and learning about others, is through observation. This must be objective to be of value. We must be detached from prejudices and preconceptions and be in control of our attentions.'

'Mrs. R., do I not need to return to my body first and find a way to fix it, before I can do all these fabulous things?'

'Lass, our time together is limited, so listen carefully.' Lomond nodded. 'To perceive properly, we need our mind to be still and silent, open to the sights and sounds around us. We must be receptive to colour, energy, shape, form, vibrations, and movement; not just those *around* us, but *inside* us too, the workings of our minds and bodies. We cannot allow ourselves to be conditioned by outward pressures. In the end, this will only prevent us from being inwardly *free*. When is the last time you gave thanks for *anything* Lomond? For the food you eat, the house you live in, your parents, your friends or even the universe for supplying all of the wonderment of nature?' Lomond searched her memory for such a time, but to no avail. Instead, she tried to absorb all that Mrs. R. was sharing.

A troubling scene took control of her senses. In her mind's eye, she saw ambulance attendants carrying her lifeless body on a stretcher away from the scene of the accident. *Was that my fate?* She thought. *Was the purpose of my life to end up some casualty on a road all along?*

Suddenly, she was engulfed by orange colour. It was pulling her. Vibrating a spirited frequency that excited and reminded her of what it felt like to be alive; *truly* alive. She knew with certainty; she needed this colour. It was the medicine that would heal her physical body. Mrs. R. chimed in on cue:

'Spot on, lass. Your body has shut down from the shock of the accident and this has caused a chemical imbalance. The orange will stimulate your adrenal glands and help bring your energy levels back to normal.' Lomond hovered above the hospital bed, looking anxiously down at her motionless body; it was if it belonged to someone else. She could feel her anxiety and will grappling with each other as she filled her essence with orange energy. Then, she projected it towards her form and in silent wonder; she watched it wash over and engulfed her body like a golden ocean wave, sending an electrifying charge to everything in its course.

'Slow down, slow down!' Mrs. R. warned. 'You must *never* go too quickly into the orange, or you may not come out. Healing with colour energy is about balance and harmony, the correct timing.' Lomond was almost certain she had seen a flicker, a slight flutter of the eyelids. Before she could say anything, she felt herself being pulled away; sucked back into the indigo tunnel. Her physical self became a pinprick in the distance as she was projected upwards into another realm of colour. Then, the tunnel was gone and they were both hovering above Edinburgh Castle.

Beneath its dark, foreboding walls, lamp-lit routes fanned out, giving the city a wheel-like interconnectedness. Lomond began roving the city *via* her energy: to the north, she flitted towards the gleam of the Forth Estuary, with its two bridges spanning the Firth to Fife. To the south, beyond the city outskirts, she coasted by the rolling Pentland Hills. Circling back to the east, she soared over Arthur's Seat; the great city landmark crouching like a resting lion, the hump of its back sitting over the sharp edges of Salisbury Crags. Below the crags, the old and new stood side-by-side; the poky council flats contrasting the stone eminence of Holyrood Palace. From there, she skimmed the cobbles of the Royal Mile, heading directly to the castle esplanade and ducking under the ramparts, she swooped dizzily through the shoots of tomorrow's daffodils studding the slopes of Princes Street Gardens. Then, as the two-colour energies, Mrs. R. and Lomond re-joined and passed back down from the castle, directly into the vibrations of a Saturday night in the city. They passed over popular pubs, *The Barbeque Grill and Restaurant, Deacon Brodie's, The White Hart* and the *Forrest Hill Bar.* Lomond revelled in the boundless sensation, elated as she drifted unnoticed in and out of spaces below. They passed through Greyfriars' Churchyard, where the small terrier dog seemed to be transfixed on the words and actions of its master. Then, they floated back towards the hospital to where Lomond's body lay in the HDU. They scanned the wards and corridors for the nurse.

'She isn't here,' observed Lomond.

'Come.' said Mrs. R. and the pair departed the hospital. Lomond glided behind Mrs R. as she led her to another area in the south of the city. They entered a stone tenement building and found their way into a dimly lit room. Inside was the unmistakable and vibrant blue-violet energy of nurse Lorraine sitting with a blanket around her shoulders. For a while they both hovered, colour energies in waiting, observing.

'She's meditating,' said Mrs. R. 'Do you see the violet? Why don't you join her? Go investigate my dear.' She added with gentle encouragement. Without hesitation, Lomond dived head-first into Lorraine's colour. At first, the vibrations felt peaceful and inviting, but then came a harsh intrusion; a blast of blood-red entered the violet. Then Lorraine was shocked back into the present as loud noises ensued, shouting, banging doors and raucous singing.

'Bloody *amazing*!' said Lomond. 'But what was the red? So much noise and confusion coming from one person, I feel rattled,'

'Oh, that was Helen,' Mrs. R. stated matter-of-factly. 'She's a real pill, always trying to run away from her sense of hopelessness. She fills her life with parties and noise and commotion to block it out.' Lomond decided to stay close to Lorraine. They floated behind as the two girls left the flat and headed to *The Bandwagon*. There was a mad rush at the pub; it felt like a volatile volcano waiting to blow. Lomond was nearly overwhelmed by the chaos and harsh odours filling the small space.

Minutes later, she was pleased to see Lorraine also made a bid for freedom. She followed closely behind her as she left the pub and hurried down the hill towards India Street. At the top of some stone steps, Lorraine stood in front of a foreboding door with two stone lions sitting regally on either side. She hesitated before taking a few deep breaths and ringing the bell. To her surprise, it was her old neighbour and friend Innes who opened the door. In a whisper, she invited Lorraine to take off her coat and shoes before instructing her to select a pair of Asian slippers from a row laid out beneath an ornately carved, wooden bench set along the entrance wall. Lomond and Mrs R. were listening close by.

'Am I too late? asked Lorraine nervously.

'No, there's still one or two others due yet. There are usually eight or nine of us. Come on through, I'll introduce you to Tyrone.' As Lorraine bent down to pick up the slippers, she became rooted to the spot. Her eyes were drawn to the carvings on the bench. She recognised the symbols. The all-seeing eye, a downward pointing pentacle and the Sabbatical Goat who's name she could not remember. A cold shiver ran down the length of her spine. She flinched as Innes touched her arm before leading her gleefully down the hallway and into a room on the right. It was dimly lit and was adorned with splendid Oriental rugs and floor-to-ceiling tapestries. Lorraine felt an uninviting vibration and there was a powerful cloying aroma of incense; she thought it was sandalwood or dragons' blood maybe. At the far end, she noticed a table with two tall white candles burning on it. Between them sat a beautifully carved Buddha made of jade. Lorraine's eyes were drawn to the statue, with its serene, almost hypnotic gaze. Suddenly, she forgot the fear she had felt from the symbols on the bench. This is what she'd hoped to find coming here, tranquillity, simplicity and serenity.

She hadn't noticed the others in the room nor the tall, imposing figure who emerged from a shadowy recess and moved towards them. It was their host, Tyrone. Immediately, she felt alarmed and on guard in his presence. His high cheekbones and the grey pallor of his face spoke of untold, dark secrets. His thinning, silver-streaked light-brown hair was swept to the right and he seemed detached, cold, and haughtily aloof. His demeanour struck Lorraine as the antithesis of the gentle and serene Buddha. Suddenly, he was standing before her, his near black eyes locked on to hers.

'Welcome to our little circle,' he said, reaching for her hand. 'My name is Tyrone, and you are . . .?' His tone was both demanding and condescending. His eyes reminded fixed as if trying to mesmerize her.

'Innes suggested I join your group, I'm Lorraine' she muttered nervously.

'Ah . . . Lorraine!' Tyrone said knowingly. He flashed a

beguiling smile that made her feel he was trying to peer deep into her soul. A wave of dread washed over her. Unable to hide it, she grimaced and took a step backwards. She had hoped to meet a kind, caring and insightful person who could help awaken her spiritual side. Not this intimidating man who made her feel utterly vulnerable. As he shuffled away to greet other arrivals, Lorraine told herself that perhaps she'd misread him. After all, she'd never been in the presence of a *truly evolved being* before; as Innes described him. Perhaps she was mistaken, she was still a little off from her experience at The Bandwagon earlier after all.

'Trust me, Lorraine, he's really not so bad,' whispered Innes. 'Just wait till you hear him speak. He's quite *amazing*, really he is.' Lorraine sensed some kind of school girl crush vibe coming from her friend. Forcing herself to smile, she turned to Innes and said, 'I'm Sorry, was it that obvious?' Innes nodded and flashed a smile back. Lorraine looked again at the jade Buddha. With one hand held high, the palm out, index and middle finger raised; he held a posture that captured attention, in a way that was neither beckoning nor commanding. The other hand lay resting on his lap, the palm turned upwards. There was healing in his gesture and Lorraine began to relax. Two more people shuffled into the room; young Bohemian types. Lorraine was glad she wasn't the last. She watched as Tyrone worked the room, always greeting the newcomers with the same cagey smile playing at the corners of his eyes. When all those expected had arrived, he proceeded to his hand-carved, high-backed ebony armchair and eased himself regally onto it. Everyone else chose a brightly-coloured cushion and sat reverently, cross-legged on the floor in front of him.

Lorraine and Innes were side-by-side and anxious buzz filled the room. Raising his hands to bring quietude, Tyrone rose from his chair and bowed to the 'alter' by his side. He made a sign in the air above it with his right hand before ringing a little brass bell three times. The room grew so silent Lorraine could hear her own blood rushing around her body. Tyrone was poised ready to address his silent *worshippers*. Another rush of uneasiness crept through Lorraine and her eyes were drawn to symbols carved into the front of the alter. She noticed they were the same as those on the bench in the hall: *Is this some kind of cult?* She wondered.

 'Friends, old and new, you are all here tonight to learn the art of meditation, to learn new philosophies, new doctrines and new ways of perceiving life; to become *enlightened* if you will. As most of you know, my name is Tyrone and I can guide you along your spiritual path to *enlightenment*. I have studied many different belief systems over my lifetime, and I have visited many temples and places of worship throughout the world. I've studied with the world's greatest spiritual masters.' He paused long enough to receive adulation and acknowledging nods from his followers. 'As many of you are aware, my visits to India were perhaps the most life-changing of all...' His worshipers continued nodding at each other. Lorraine was growing increasingly uncomfortable; she couldn't shake off this uneasy feeling. Something just didn't ring true about Tyrone's shameless self-promotion. He struck Lorraine as a common hustler, a con artist, a slick, snake-like oil salesman bent on convincing his customer to buy a new car or house, or Fountain of Youth miracle cure. The negative thoughts would not go, not even with the collective breath work and relaxation session he led them through next. She only found herself with more doubt. *Is he putting these people into some kind of mind-controlling trance? This was a mistake!* She almost shouted aloud. *What was I thinking?* She noticed Innes was looking at her as she fidgeted nervously. All the while, Lomond and Mrs. R. were hovering above, silent energies in waiting. Mrs. R. pointed out the frenzied way Lorraine's colours were moving.

'She's quite uncomfortable, and rightfully so. Look at the red dominating her. She's transcoding Tyrone's colour vibrations and it's making her leery. Her sixth sense is activated. She's sensing the *true* nature behind his façade, but its alarming and confusing her, poor thing.' Lomond adjusted her sensors so that she could feel what Lorraine was feeling. 'You see lass, there will always be some who take advantage of those who aren't able to recognise them for what they truly are. We can learn from this though, by not giving these types of individuals the attention they feed on. If everyone in this group could recognise their own and others' *true* selves and use their energy and attention to support and sustain it, then harmonious relationships would follow. Charlatans like this 'Tyrone' would cease to be a threat.'

'Is Lorraine in danger?'

'Let's just wait and see.' Mrs. R. Instructed.
Lorraine could feel her senses over-loading. She was seeing nothing but red as she suppressed her outrage. She had to force herself not to stand up and shout: *'You crazy bampot*! *Con artist…cheating fraud*!' She could feel those around her being sucked into a spiralling black hole, Tyrone's dark satanic vortex. His drone became wholly hypnotic.

'Now, focus on relaxing each part of your body . . . *focus* on your muscles . . . *focus* on your extremities . . . *focus* on letting all the tension leave your body.' His voice was now a vague echo in the back of her mind. She felt her resistance dropping, could feel herself being drawn in against her will; his pull was so powerful. Intentionally, she shifted her attention to the flickering flames of the candles; there was a place of peace there. She saw the orange of the flame as if it were right before her eyes. It was comforting, empowering. Then as she gazed, she suddenly saw a face within the flame. It was the face of Lomond; the girl under her care. It seemed like she was trying to communicate with her. She strained to hear what she was saying. Then her words became crystal-clear.

'Help me, Lorraine. Help me to heal. You can do it; you know you can.'

'I'm doing my best,' she whispered under her breath. It was loud enough to draw Innes' attention. 'I'm using all that I know. I will keep trying, I promise.'

'Use the *orange,*' Lomond was saying. 'Use the *orange* colour' Just then, Lorraine felt the colour of the flame enter into her body, finding its way to the very core of her being. The expansion of this energy felt so soothing; it was like nothing she had ever felt before. She promised herself that she would sit with Lomond as soon as she reported in for her next shift. She needed to discover what this connection was between Lomond and the colour orange. For now though, she realised it was time to separate herself from Tyrone's darkness and so, aided by the vibrant orange energy, her escape suddenly felt effortless. Taking Innes' hand in hers, she whispered into the young girl's ear,

'Sorry, but this isn't for me.'

CHAPTER TEN

Another two days passed and Lomond was finally taken off the ventilator. Since she was able to breathe with the aid of an oxygen mask alone, it was decided inserting a tracheal tube was unwarranted. Still, the clock was ticking. Lomond hadn't gained consciousness and statistically, the longer she remained 'under' the lesser were her chances of a full recovery. Lorraine had covered aspects of coma during her nurses training. Yet, since experiencing the 'vision' of Lomond in Tyrone's meditation room, she was convinced that deep inside, her *inner* self had awareness; maintained a conscious connection with the waking world. She'd read numerous accounts from both insider and outsider perspectives about people being in comas for months, even years sometimes. Ultimately, it was usually their friends and family members who drew many of them out of their altered state of consciousness. They worked with them using touch, sound, or smell to awaken their sleeping senses. She was also fascinated to learn of the many coma patients who had given accounts later about being aware of those trying to draw them out.

She knew instinctively that touch was so important to almost all areas of patient recovery. She had even experimented with synchronising her touch with the breathing of a comatose patient in the past. Whenever she was on duty and the opportunity arose, she would monitor and strengthen Lomond's respiration through touch. Taking a hold of her hand, she would apply gentle pressure as she exhaled; relaxing her hold as she breathed out; gentle and steady. On one particular day as she administered this method, she noticed a flickering behind Lomond's eye lids. The monitor registered increased brain activity at the same time. It was only a small reaction, but it provided promise. Lomond's friends, Maria and Tracy were her most loyal and regular visitors and Lorraine encouraged them to come, the familiarity of their voices might help bring her around, she'd tell them, *whisper gently in her ear.* Lorraine would ask them to let her know immediately, if they noticed the slightest change; any change to her breathing, a flutter of the eyelids, a twitch in the finger.

Today, she was due to finish at 2:00pm, but she decided to stay longer. She was desperate to try envisioning the orange flame she'd experienced at the meditation group, to connect with Lomond, and now there was an opportunity. Lorraine had no idea if it would work, but she'd made a promise to them both that she was going to try. Sitting quietly at Lomond's bedside, she held both of her hands and concentrated on the orange in her mind. Again, she could hear Lomond's voice saying, *Use the orange . . . Use the orange colour!* With her eyes closed and in just a few seconds, she found her way back to the orange she'd felt that day. It filled her very being and she felt the energy travel through her own body and into Lomond's; like an 'energy transfusion'. As they were locked in this embrace, the head nurse appeared looking to speak to her. She'd started to notice Lorraine staying beyond her shift.

'Go on, get *off* with you!' the old crone scowled. 'Haven't you been *warned* about this? We *can't* have you getting emotionally involved with the patients. Be off this minute, or you'll find yourself on Geri-ward duty!' Although Lorraine considered all patients' needs equal, working the Geriatric ward was considered something of a punishment; it was quite unpopular with the other nurses. Reluctantly, she got up and left Lomond's room, the nurse following her all the way to the exit door.

Lomond was bursting.

'Mrs. R. It was bloody unbelievable.' she cried. 'The way the orange moved from Lorraine into me. I could feel it rush through me, from my head, to my throat, to my heart and right into my stomach. I could feel what it was like from inside my body. I could *feel* each part of me tingling, like electricity running through me.' Now on a pure high, Lomond wanted to know how many times Lorraine would have to send the orange energy into her body to make her wake up. Surely there must be someone else who could help? Or maybe there was another, even better colour that could be used? So many questions swirling and she couldn't wait for answers. Even in this alternate reality, patience was clearly not one of Lomond's virtues.

'Please, just *let . . .nature . . .take . . .its . . .course!*' Mrs. R. warned. 'Can you not just be still for now and realise these things take time Lomond.' Clearly irked by Lomond's impatience, Mrs. R. departed without another word, leaving her to her own devices. Barely noticing, Lomond was torn between realms. Though tempted to sit and wait for her physical body to awaken, she really wanted to explore the indigo energy that had swathed her in the meditation room. She was curious to discover if it was the room itself, or the presence of the meditators, with their combined and concentrated energies, that was the source of the energy. Lomond made her decision and headed back to the shadowy room where Tyrone held court. Even with no-one physically present, the room was filled with an inky transparency. Through it, centered on the

Buddha, she saw a strange golden light. Moving through the flat, Lomond found the self-proclaimed 'meditation master' in a spacious sitting room. Tyrone sat with his arms spread wide over the back of an oversized, luxurious, dark-green velvet settee. The floor-to-ceiling bay windows looked out onto a small enclosed garden, hidden behind tall black wrought-iron railings. The room was cluttered with piles of newspapers and magazines competing for space and a selection of cuttings, torn articles, and letters were spilled out on the surface of an antique mahogany writing desk.

Lomond tuned in to Tyrone's thoughts. He was contemplating the last meditation class. There had been a new girl there, this *Lorraine*. He knew she'd be trouble. He knew the type. She wasn't the first like her to find their way into his little group. She was no mindless follower. At some point, he realised she would start to question his authority, his sincerity, probably even his methods. Time was money and money was essential to his present worrisome circumstances. It angered him that she seemed so able to resist his charm. That *anyone*, without his vast experience, someone who had never travelled to India, not met a genuine guru, could be so intuitive. How could she be so untouched by his charisma when others seemed to fall under his spell so willingly?

He couldn't control her and he felt she could see through him. Despite his lifelong quest for enlightenment, Tyrone had never *really* understood the spiritual world, no matter how hard he'd tried, and God how he had tried. He'd never connected. He'd never seen a ghost, never felt any hint of phantasmic energy nor had he experienced a *vision*. It was his little secret. He was completely devoid of the spiritual rapport he professed to have attained. Tyrone thought now of the other girl, Innes. *Sweet Innes.* Unlike Lorraine, she'd fell for his charms so quickly, it was like taking candy from a baby. Now she *adored* him and was more than obliging to prove it. He was her *savior*. He had no mind to dissuade her; it suited him to be worshiped. It suited him to have enough money and power to influence those around him. It enabled him to perpetuate the lie about who and what he really was. He'd discovered long ago that ignorant people respected two things more than anything, money and class. To him, people believed position meant credibility and for most of his life Tyrone had used this naiveté to gain power and status; the smoke and mirrors that kept his sycophantic followers from seeing into his dark past.

Lomond's energy moved towards Tyrone's desk. Intrigued, she

stared at a group of six small black statues sitting in a semi-circle beside a small gleaming paperknife. As she looked closer, she realised they were actually grotesque, gargoyle-like figurines. One statue in particular stood out, with its whole head formed in the shape of an eye. Suddenly the energy in the room shifted, as if there was a build-up of electrical power. She turned to stare at Tyrone, but he was oblivious. She watched as waves of black energy vibrated and swirled around his desk before the mist-like black mass, gathered momentum and began heading towards her. She could hear a deep booming sound coming from its core and she knew that soon, she would be engulfed in its folds. For a while she was frozen with fear, but then, from somewhere in the depths of her being, she focused on pulling up her own energy. It manifested as a mass of white light and she projected it towards the advancing blackness. For a moment, it felt as if all her energy was being sucked out of her, like balloon being thrown upwards without its knot being tied. Then, a sudden noise jarred her senses. A harrowing scream and the sound of smashing glass as crystal teardrops rained down from the enormous chandelier in the center of the room. Lomond watched as it swung precariously from side to side from its ornate rose centerpiece.

Then, there was a crack, an explosion of electrical static and a blinding flash. Lomond was stunned by the unseen force. As she recovered, she noticed the black swirling mass being sucked into the carved statues. Then silence. There they sat as if nothing had taken place. Her attention was now directed towards Tyrone. She noted an array of colours surrounding him. Most dominantly was a dull and drab green with a tinge of washed out indigo. There was no sign of otherworldliness here. What was it about Tyrone that did not stack up? Was there some kind of evil in this house, was it him? One thing was certain, something had been long neglected in Tyrone; something left to fester, decay and corrupt in a most pernicious way. Without any doubt, he was most defiantly *not* who he claimed to be. Lomond watched him shuffle over to the antique corner cabinet. He parted the hand-etched glass-paned doors and took out a bottle of *Glenfiddich* malt whisky. There was a look of displeasure on his face as he poured himself a stiff measure in a tall crystal glass. He skulked over to the couch and dropped heavily onto it, bottle and glass still in hand. Closing his eyes, he lifted the glass to his lips and bottomed it before tilting it a second time. No, there was no sign of otherworldliness here.

CHAPTER ELEVEN

A week had passed since Lorraine attended the meditation group. Despite the gut-level distrust she felt towards Tyrone, she decided she'd go one more time. Stronger and more positive feelings now motivated her. During the past week, she'd luxuriated in the orange energy, drawn to it as a moth to a flame and she knew why. It was healing; to Lomond, and to herself. If there was something positive to be derived from Tyrone's group, she was now able to take it in without fear; she felt she would be able to resist him. Catching the bus to Queensferry Street, Lorraine alighted and strolled over to Rankin's Fruit Shop. For a few minutes, she stared in through the large windows, allowing her senses to be tempted and teased by the colourful and highly polished fruits and vegetables. She noticed the person serving a customer behind the cigarette and sweet counter. It was Johnny, a school friend of hers. He looked up and waved when he saw her. The last time she'd spoken to him, he'd told her proudly that he was the new Saturday 'tattie-laddie' in Rankin's. She guessed he must have been promoted to counter sales now. Dragging herself away from the dazzling array of fruits and vegetables, she headed for Law & Forest. The amazing aroma wafting out from the up-market grocers stopped her in her tracks.

Squinting in through the window, she spied a little girl sitting on a high stool eating a chocolate biscuit while her mother talked with the man serving. Behind the counter, were dozens of magnificent spice drawers with brass handles, lined up against the back wall. She swithered about buying a quarter of their delicious meat paste, it was only 2 shillings after all. The brother of one of her friends worked in this shop. A while back he'd gloated to her about taking the weekly cooked meat off cuts from under the counter, across the street to the butcher. She'd been amused at his description of how the butcher would run a slice of bread through the mincer; to remove all raw meat before slicing his cooked meat. Changing her mind against buying the meat paste, she decided to get a bend on. Walking past the Milk Bar, she saw no-one she knew through the window, so she cut back across Shandwick Place and reached Binns Department Store where she paused to look at the outfits the mannequins were wearing.

Quickly, before she was tempted to buy, she headed for Charlotte Square and walked down the hill into Queen Street. As dusk descended, she watched her shadow contracting and expanding under the old-style streetlamps that fanned the broad pavement with their arcs of soft-orange light. She felt warmed and protected by their glow. As she crossed the street, Lorraine began to think of times long past. Days like she'd seen in old films of a humming lamp-lit city. She heard the *clippity-clop* of shod horses' hooves as they pulled people in fancy carriages and carts full of wares along cobbled streets, delivering coal for firesides, milk and butter for waiting housewives and gallant gentlemen for fashionable ladies of the New Town. Funny, she thought, how the area is known as "New Town" when it's over two hundred years old now. She arrived at No 6 India Street, calm, grounded, and feeling in charge.

A group member with long black hair and donning a floor-length white robe greeted her at the door; he introduced himself as Acolyte Fingal. Lorraine quickly switched her shoes for slippers and proceeded down the hall to the dimly-lit, tapestry filled room. She slipped in beside Innes who welcomed her with a warm hug. Sensing her presence, Tyrone turned and flashed a troubled glower. The two altar candles splashed a violet-rimmed gold into the indigo light and in that moment, Lorraine was glad she'd come. Then it happened again. A glowing ball of orange colour appeared. It was Lomond. She was trying to tell Lorraine something, but she couldn't make it out. Lomond faded before flickering brightly and then she heard her.

'Lorraine!' She was calling her name. The warming breath of orange penetrated through the crown of Lorraine's head. She offered no resistance as it tingled down her spine…into her solar plexus . . . and into her belly. It was warm and vibrant and she felt herself glow within it, as if enveloped in a great orange halo. Suddenly, all the members of the group seemed to notice the radiance around the new girl; including Tyrone. A series of *Oohs* and *aahs* filled the room as everyone saw and sensed she was somehow special. Lorraine rose to her feet and they all cleared a way for her to pass by. Her heart surged as she realised, she had begun a journey of the spirit. What Tyrone offered was now insignificant. All that mattered was the pathway she had discovered to the spiritual realm and the endless possibilities this offered.

As Lorraine left Tyrone's toxic flat, her main hope was that her journey would continue, that it wouldn't end there where it started. Once outside, she decided to walk home. She felt radiant and lightheaded as she made her way across the New Town, up the Mound and over towards the Meadows to Marchmont. Helen came into her mind and she realised she wouldn't be in the flat. She was *gaga* for Bobby, her new squeeze; a seemingly loving young man who rejected any form of work, or conventional lifestyle; a real free spirit.

'This time it's for real!' Helen had cooed. She was going to travel the world with him. Never mind that she was clueless and would do anything for Bobby without question. Lorraine could think of several reasons why this relationship was doomed from the start. As Lorraine passed the Royal Infirmary and headed down the walk into the Meadows, she was glad to leave the tall, cloistering buildings behind her. She snuggled her coat collar around her neck and gazed longingly up at the night sky. With the harsh city glare and the lamps in the park blinding the view, she was disappointed she could hardly see any stars. A thought crossed her mind and she mumbled to herself.

'This park really isn't really safe at night, so I guess it's a good thing all the lights are here!' Then she spotted something. A zig zag of darting red amidst an inky-black silhouette. She realised that, whoever it was would intersect her path in a matter of moments.

'Mrs. R' breathed Lomond. 'Look at that guy. There's something very dodgy about him'

'Good observation, dear. The huge swirling masses of red and black surrounding him most certainly spell trouble' confirmed Mrs. R., her tone matter-of-fact.

'Can't we…shouldn't we…do something?' Lomond pleaded anxiously.

'Like what, Lomond? As yet, he's done nothing wrong. We can only watch and wait.'

'Shouldn't we send her some kind of message?'

'No, Lomond, it's up to Lorraine, now. She has the orange energy inside her and she can use it to conquer her fear, and cope with this situation. That's what it's for, and besides, it's not our place to interfere.'

Lorraine had her eyes fixed on the dark-hooded, slightly-hunched figure as it approached, weaving erratically back-and-forth across the path. At first, she thought the individual was drunk; but no, there was something not quite right about the gait. It was forceful, as if intent on deception. As the figure neared, her fears were confirmed, it was a male and his hand was resting on something inside his leather jacket. She felt a stab of fear and her heart drummed inside her rib cage as the adrenalin pumped fiercely around her body. She glanced around with urgency, praying to see someone else near, anyone she could run to for help. She wanted to shout out to him that she had nothing worth taking, that she'd donated all her change to a collection bowl, she didn't even have bus-fare, but she realised he probably wouldn't believe her anyway. If it was even money he was after. Terror filled her, what a fool she'd been, feeling so powerful and self-assured. Where was all that strength now when she needed it the most? She felt the blood drain from her legs as she came to a standstill. *Hell,* she was drawing attention to herself. Surely, she could do something more than just stand and allow herself to be attacked. Then, it was as if everything played in slow-motion as he ran up to her with something clutched in his hand. There was a soft *fffttt* sound as whatever it was, flicked open. A blade reflected the lamplight like a shard of polished mirror. He grabbed at her long silk scarf and pressed the knife to her throat.

'Give it me, ya eejit, just, giz it!' His voice growled between clenched teeth. 'Get on with it, if you've nae cash, geez that watch. Now bitch…I ain't got all bloody night' He hissed.

Then, as Lorraine stood eye-to-eye with this guy; a strange thing happened. Instead of being consumed by fear, she felt pity and curiosity. Her attacker noticed this too.

'What about your sister?' she asked him. 'How'd you feel if someone treated your sister or your mother like this?'

'I ain't got no bloody sister. You think I'm havin' a laugh do ya? Just gimme the damn watch or I swear I'll cut your bloody heed off!'

'Your mum then, fancy a world where she has a knife put to her throat in the middle of the park by someone like you?' Lorraine pressed, sensing that she'd hit a nerve.

'You radge *bitch*. Who gives a shit! You *wanna* die, is that it?' he said, pressing the blade harder. The sweat was beginning to trickle down his face.

'Your mum gives a shit…and your *sister*. I'll bet you do have one, *don't you*?' The guy was now sweating profusely and the hand clutching the knife began to tremble.

'You'll figure it out, you will, I promise' said Lorraine. 'First, you gotta let me go. Just walk away, before you do something you can't undo.' His face fell and then slowly he released his grip and lowered the blade.

'Bloody messed up this is.' he mumbled as he backed away. Then, Lorraine watched as he turned and with his shoulders hunched, he disappeared into a line of bare cherry trees under the cover of darkness.

She wondered where on earth the words she'd spoken had come from. Did he have a sister? Somehow, she felt he did. As she headed home, she walked with a renewed sense of confidence. In the face of danger, she'd stared it down. She'd dug deep and found an inner strength she never knew she had.

CHAPTER TWELVE

Despite the harsh reality check, Lorraine continued to pass through the Meadows on her way to and from work. For one thing, it was convenient. For another, she felt driven to face her fears. Chances were, she wouldn't be accosted again, but there was always the possibility. Knowing this she consciously walked tall and with confidence, testing herself. Her flat in Marchmont lay on the south side of the Meadows. During the daytime, many people walked along the tree-lined avenues, students mostly, but professionals too; people who lived and worked in the city and enjoyed the scenic atmosphere. Now it was spring, the crocuses were in full bloom, the "clowns of the flower kingdom," as she thought of them with their little tops billowing and ballooning in the gentle March breeze. Lorraine relished the sight of their orange centres, clasped by petals of yellow, white, or purple. She relished at the sight of the orange as a cat relishes its comfy bed.

Although still unconscious, Lomond was on the mend. Maria and Tracy continued to drop by the hospital regularly. Tracy had brought in a tape player so she could play Lomond her favourite songs. She was convinced Lomond was telling her which songs she wanted to hear. Whenever she or Maria would suggest a particular song she might want to listen to; they were certain she would gently squeeze Tracy's hand. For her part, Lorraine continued to send the healing, orange energy out to Lomond whenever she had the opportunity - when taking her readings, giving her a sponge-bath, or when straightening up her bed clothes. It had been two weeks since the night of the accident and the situation was reaching the critical mark. Despite being stable, patients who remained in a coma for longer than this often sustained physical and mental issues to overcome later. There was just no way of knowing until she woke up. The doctors were watching and waiting and a few of the nurses had their fingers crossed. Lorraine was sure she would wake up soon, she had to.

The connection she felt with her was so strong it was becoming intrusive. Lomond had even started visiting Lorraine in her dreams.

One morning after a particularly strange and haunting dream about Lomond, Lorraine woke full of energy. It was as if someone had injected her with happy serum during the night. She skipped out of bed and drew back the curtains to let in the light. Deciding it wasn't enough, she climbed on a chair and removed them from their runners; she wanted to let in as much as possible. More importantly, she decided she needed to feel free. With an overwhelming urge to sing aloud, she switched on the radio. The song, 'These boots are made for walking' boomed out and she sang along wholeheartedly. Feeling empowered, she decided when she got to work, she would finally tell that crabby ward nurse about things that escaped her. *In case you are unaware, touch is excellent therapy for a comatose patient. They need to feel the warmth and energy of another human being. Monitoring them isn't enough. We need to be pro-active and interactive. You'll see. You'll see the results!* Yes, today she felt more alive than she had ever remembered feeling. She felt ready for an adventure and she sensed that one was coming. She decided she needed someone to love and share her life with, and she was ready. As she strode to work, people seemed to look at her, young and old, all attracted to the positive energy radiating from her. In the Meadows, a little girl threw her a ball and a man on a bench looked up from a book he was reading, losing his place. A grim-faced, middle-aged woman who worked at the local Co-op cracked an acknowledging smile, for a change, although secretly envious of the young nurse's positive aura. Lorraine proceeded, up the broad avenue where the homeless camped out with their sleeping bags and grubby blankets on the wide grassy verges. She stopped and sighed as she neared the bus stop, looking at the hospital driveway by the entrance leading to A & E. All along the tree-lined avenue, people liked to hang out, she knew many of them by sight now and most of them acknowledged her.

Once a week, a pavement artist claimed a pitch here. A tall, barrel-chested guy with a clean-shaved head and rings ornamenting everywhere; through his nose, eyebrows, ears, lips and chin, and as most suspected, in places best left unseen. There was practically no more room to pierce flesh and Lorraine liked him for his cheery grin. She was also fond of the white-whiskered old man who wore a grey tweed coat in all weathers.

He always tipped his tweed cap at her come rain or shine. She thought the tall, red-haired young busker with the old and battered acoustic guitar was so good. She often saw him with his instrument strapped across his back, waiting to be prompted to perform. He was one of the few street musicians who didn't make you feel compelled to drop money into his old and battered guitar case. You did, if you were in the mood and he was singing a song that caught your fancy. As she passed this morning, she listened to the words he sang.

'Good mornin' star shine, the earth says hello. You twinkle above us. We twinkle below'

How sweet, she thought tossing a shilling into his case. He glanced up at her and smiled and she smiled back, noticing his large turquoise looking eyes. She'd often thought of making a request but hadn't so far. Then, she noticed someone at his side, a young man with straight light brown hair dressed in black leather biker's gear; he didn't seem to belong there. Lorraine gave him a coy smile and to her surprise, he smiled back. Her heart skipped a beat and she felt a little giddy. She was still humming the tune of the busker's song as she walked on. Meanwhile, there amongst the colour vibrations, Lomond was aghast.

'George. Bloody hell! I've been so focused on myself; I'd forgotten all about him.'

'They come and they go.' replied Mrs. R. impassioned.

'You don't get it, you probably never even had a boyfriend.' Lomond bemoaned. Mrs. R. was half-tempted to fill her in on the details of her life, or rather, her *many lives* on the earthly plane. Instead she resisted; there was still time for that yet.

'Take a long, hard look at your so-called *love.*' She instructed. 'What are his colours?'

Lomond gazed at George, but no matter how hard she tried, she could see no colours whatsoever around him. He seemed ghostlike, more of a vapourific apparition than a living, breathing human being.

'His colours are so faint.' She cried, the shock and fear apparent in her voice. 'They're so…dull. Is he ill or something?'

Mrs. R. thought a moment before answering.

'We need to know a little more about this lad before we come to any conclusions.' She said and Lomond was momentarily taken aback. Until now she thought she knew a great deal about George, but now she realised, she actually knew next to nothing. Their time together had always focused on riding on his bike, *Power.* It was the flashiness of his bike that first attracted her to him, she remembered now. For that matter, she hadn't really known him all that long at all.

'Well, what about his mate with the guitar, then?' Lomond diverted. 'He's got loads of blue and turquoise and other colour energies weaving in and out and around him. *That,* I can see.'

'Let's just wait.' said Mrs. R. and Lomond sensed she was deliberately withholding something. True enough, there was much more Lomond would later find out.

Unknown to anyone, including himself, when he left the scene of the accident that fateful night; he was scarcely aware of what had occurred. The impact had thrown him clear off the bike, over a hedge and onto a haystack; as if picked up and tossed onto the pile by a farmer's pitchfork. Though the soft landing had saved his life, he was knocked unconscious. He knew nothing of the caravan of commotion taking place; the ambulance and police sirens wailing, the grumbles and stares of passers-by and gawkers. When he finally came to, he had no idea how much time had passed only that he felt sick to his stomach. Oh, so sick.

After a while his mind cleared and he was convinced Lomond was dead, that he'd killed her. As he lay there in the darkness, looking up at the starry sky above, he wished it were him instead. All that really mattered was *gone*. She was everything to him. When he was with her, for the first time, the mistakes of his past didn't matter. Even though he knew it was *Power* that had first attracted Lomond, he'd been hopeful it might become more. But now... all kinds of thoughts raced through his mind. *What have I done? What the bloody hell have I done? The police! Do they have Power? Was it wrecked? Have they traced it to me? Whatever I do, I have to avoid them. It looks like I just better disappear.* When his senses finally slowed, he set off across the countryside, staggering through fields and hedgerows as disconnected thoughts flashed through his mind. He remembered not being able to find his helmet. Nothing added up. Shivering, he hugged himself and rubbed his arms briskly to try and keep warm. The wind threw hoarfrost into his face as he pushed on in the darkness. At last, he spotted the clock at the Haymarket Station; it read seven o'clock, He realised it must be morning because the streets were desolate. Stumbling along Morrison Street, he finally reached his attic bedroom in the flat he shared on Grove Street, forgetting entirely how he got there.

Inside, panic began to set in and he wondered how long he had before there would be a knock on his door. One thing was for certain, he couldn't go back to the garage. Soon, *everything* would come out. Even now the police were probably looking for him. The only good thing, he thought, was that no one at work knew exactly where he lived or worked; he hadn't even told Lomond, even when she'd asked. He'd told her the last thing he needed was an angry father banging down his door. His credo had long been, 'Don't

Trust Anyone'. He kept his lips sealed and his personal life safe. Of course, he knew nothing would stay that way forever. Staying clear of the authorities had been his priority for years and he'd become an expert in side-stepping what he didn't want to confront. Some had chased hard on his heels, like when he skipped out on the rent or borrowed money he couldn't repay. For most of his life, he'd lived day-to-day. He knew the way of the streets, cadging from bakeries, the back doors of food chains and soup kitchens; surviving on hand-outs and easy marks. It was a desolate life, competing with boggin' nutters, but he was better at it than most. Truth be told, he'd often longed for a companion; a 'partner-in-crime,' so to speak. He thought Lomond may have one day fulfilled this dream…but now *this*.

As George fell onto the dirty sheets of his single bed that morning, he somehow found a happy thought. He remembered the first time he ran into his pal Mint in the Meadows. That was a great day. As well as being amazing on guitar; he was smart and wise; he seemed to know everything about everything. George could sit and listen to him singing his little ballads all day long. Nearly nodding off, George jumped up.

'Yeah! I need to go see Mint.' He said aloud. Then,

throwing on his leather jacket, he raised the wide collar up tight around his neck and pulled the door shut. As he did, it crossed his mind that he might never be able to return.

On his way to the Meadows, glimpses of the night before kept flashing into his conscious mind. He could remember clearly picking Lomond up at the bottom of the hill; how he'd been late, he hadn't been able to find the new helmet he'd bought for her; how she'd climbed on excitedly and nuzzled up against his back. They'd instantly become *one* with *Power*, riding headlong into the stinging wind with no thought of their destination.

Everything beyond that was a blur of fragmented, disconnected images. *Bloody hell! Did I kill Lomond? Did I lose control of the bike and kill her? Is that what I did...?* Then the realisation hit him. *The hospital! Why didn't I think of that before? They would've taken her to the hospital.* Getting his bearings, George doubled his pace and headed straight for the Infirmary. It was only as he was about to push his way through the Accident and Emergency entrance, he realised he'd better find another way in.

The police could be in there waiting for him for all he knew.

Quickly proceeding to the rear of the building, he slipped in through a service door and made his way to the nearest information desk, making certain to avoid eye contact with anyone he passed. After seeing the coast was clear, he found the courage to enquire at the main reception. When he was told a young woman by that name had been admitted the night before, and was in the High Dependency Unit, George could barely contain his sense of relief. Though desperate to find out more, he knew he'd better not draw any more attention to himself. So, with just a "thanks," he headed back the way he had come. Noticing several of the kitchen staff milling around the service door, he took the exit to the stairwell. Climbing a flight of stairs, he hurried down the hall, passing several nurses as he did so. Moments later he burst through a side-door leading to the parking lot, the sense of freedom like none he'd ever experienced.

'Bloody hell. She's alive.' He cried. 'Lomond's alive!'

CHAPTER THIRTEEN

'Hey, man. Where ya bin?' asked Mint as George came sauntering up later that morning.

'I took a run up north,' George lied, spinning things out. 'Weather's god awful, nothin' much doin' up there anyway.'

'How's your job at the garage going?'

'*Ahh*…same old shite; they take you on then they don't wanna pay ya. Ask for a fair wage and it's like "been nice knowin' ya."'

'Ah, that's harsh, man. Ever thought about setting up on your own? You could do cheap repairs on bikes—you know, on the side, like, word of mouth.'

'Shit, if you tell me how to get started with nowhere to even hang my jacket and I'll have a go!' George said. He wanted to steer the conversation away from work, half-jokingly he said;

'Hey Mint man, how about teachin' me some guitar? Then you and me, we can maybe hit the road, see the world and all that.' Always fanciful, Mint struck a deal with George, they even shook on it. Mint would teach him a few chords, then, they would head down to the scrap yard and see if they could salvage a bike for Mint. George would fix it up for him. Although he wasn't really into bikes, the idea of touring the continent for a summer seemed to excite him.

'That would be a real real gas, eh?' Mint said. Deep down George knew he was only fanaticising, but he played along anyway.

'What about passports?' asked George.

'Ah, nothing to it, mate. You just get kitted up with a photo, fill in the forms and pay the government some money and you're away. Although I hear you sometimes have to go Glasgow to pick it up.' He expected George to crack a coltish smile but was surprised to see a grim expression come over his friend's face.

'Hey, man, what's the flack? You got troubles?' George quickly pasted on a false grin.

'Hey, man, you know that song… that *"Get Around"* one, I cannae mind the words, but I really like it. You ken, the one by the Beach Boys?' Mint nodded and began to strum the tune as George tapped along with his foot. Just as he was finishing, a young woman in a nurse's uniform wandered by. She stopped and listened for a minute before tossing a shilling into his open guitar case. Mint smiled and she grinned back. Then, noticing George; she flashed him a coy smile too. Hiding his secret pain, he forced himself to smile back; realising it did his heart the world of good.

As she walked on, Mint turned to George and started chuckling. He'd bore witness to it all; the shy glances between them and the way her warm smile cheered up his buddy.

'I think she's into you, man. She was definitely checkin' you out!'

'Shit man, I don't know what you're on about…seems she liked you well enough to spare you her change though. ' he said, attempting to divert attention from himself.

'She seems a real sweetheart, George. Very cute!' Sure, George could see the young woman was attractive, but he wanted to know more about her and he didn't want to give Mint the wrong idea. Next, he'd be making him the subject of his new ballad or something.

'So, you've seen her before?' he asked casually.

'Hah! I knew it, old buddy.' Mint grinned in smug satisfaction. Then to George's embarrassment, he started playing another song;

Loving you could be so easy, loving you could be so good! Yes, Mint was right, he was interested in getting to know the nurse, but not for the reason his friend thought. In fact, George recognised her from the hospital and he figured she might help him find out more about Lomond. After pausing to consider his next move, he decided to change tactics; he'd play along.

'Okay, man, you got me. Yeah, she's super cute and I think I might like to know her better.' Mint smiled knowingly.

'Tell you what, mate. Be here tomorrow morning at eight o'clock and you might see her, if she's on the morning shift. Otherwise, you'll have to come back around two o'clock in the afternoon and you'll catch her then okay? Oh, and one more thing, mind and name your first-born after me when the time comes ok? Jokes aside, George knew he would need to be smart about this. Chatting-up the nurse would be a great way of finding out more info on Lomond, but first he'd need to smarten himself up a bit.

Taking the back roads to his attic flat, he approached stealthily from the adjoining property; watching and listening for a while before creeping up the stairs and slipping inside. Straight away he rummaged through his dirty clothes, hoping to find anything that looked (and smelled) half clean. Managing to dig out an old pair of jeans that had somehow escaped being splashed with grease and oil; he laid them out on the wooden floor and smoothed them out with his hands; giving them a "piker's iron," as he called it. Then, he remembered he had a black T-shirt that wasn't too bogging. It had a hole in the back, but he'd look presentable at least if he wore his black leather jacket over the top. If he wanted to convince the nurse to help him, he had to look harmless. He lay down on the bed to plan his next move and within moments exhaustion took over him.

The sound of loud banging woke him up with a start. Holding his breath, he went to the window and peeked out through a crack in the curtains. *Please don't let it be the law.* A man dressed in a dark suit was standing at the front door with a clipboard in his hand. *Bloody petitioners, probably want me to help save the whales or some bloody thing like that!* He knocked again and looked up at the windows causing George to let go and pull his head back quickly. A few moments later, he peered out again. The man had given up and was moving on to the next block.

'Who's gonna bloody save *me*?' He said sighing deeply.

Then, looking at the clock, he was shocked to see it was 7.30am. How the hell did he manage to sleep right through the afternoon, and all night? Then he remembered, dammit…that nurse! George threw on his clothes and slipped out the door, locking it behind him. Deciding it best to retrace the covert path he'd taken the day before; he made his way through the alleys and back passageways.

As he did so, Lomond came into his mind.

Snippets of the accident flashed in his head like surreal memories not completely his own. If he ever got the chance to talk to her again, what would he say? How much should he tell her about what happened? He didn't want to ruin his chances with her, but some things are best left unsaid. Forgotten. One thing was for certain; he'd have to find the courage to apologise. Of course, then there were her parents. He knew they'd never accept him and why the hell should they? They wanted something better for their daughter and why wouldn't they? *Shite*! What if the truth—the *whole* truth came out, which it probably would eventually? What would they think of him, what would *everyone* think of him? Especially if they found out he'd been in trouble with the police in the past? *Shite*, maybe it was better not talk to Lomond after all. How about a card or a letter, he thought? He could make up some bullshit about not wanting to run into her parents at the hospital, or some *pish* like that. Yeah, that made more sense. Just throw in an apology, too. Yeah, a letter, that was a better plan.

Even though his handwriting was like a child's scribbling, he'd write the note and get that nurse to deliver it; she should have no problem just delivering a letter for him at least.

It was 7.45am when he made it to Mint's little patch of green. The sun had yet to climb over the rooftops and trees to fend off the night frost. Mint was rubbing his hands together briskly as George approached.

'Hey, man, you look dapper today. Here, take the guitar. Your hands gotta be warmer than mine. See if you can strum those chords, I showed you.' George was glad to have something to temporarily distract him from the nurse and worrying about Lomond. Awkwardly, he tried to wrap his hand around the neck of the guitar and force his stubby fingers to stay put the way Mint had shown him; his pal did it so effortlessly. Learning to play was turning out to be way more difficult than he imagined. Noticing, Mint went behind George and held his thumb in place so that it wouldn't slip, helping him contort his fingers into the new configurations. Neither of them believed George actually had the patience to learn guitar, but neither of them would say it out loud. A few minutes later they were interrupted by the sound of female voice.

'Oh, so you play the guitar too?' said Lorraine softly. George looked up in surprise to see her gentle doe-eyes fixed directly on him.

'Uh, just a bit.' he stammered, not wanting to disappoint her.

'Well, I'll be back later to hear you play then.' she said smiling before heading off, she seemed in a bit of a rush. George handed the guitar to Mint and hurried to catch up to her.

'Uh . . . you work at the hospital, don't you?' George said as innocently as he could manage.

'Yes. That's right.' She nodded. 'Yes, I do.'

'Well I…I'd like to ask you about a patient, if that's okay? You see, hospitals kinda freak me out, and…'

'I understand,' Lorraine said, stopping to flash a smile. 'Do you know which ward they're in?'

'Well, no . . . but her name is Lomond.'

'Lomond? Oh, sure, I know her!' Lorraine said with a note of surprise. Then her gaze dropped to the ground, her look tentative. George noticed and found himself on the verge of panic.

'She's alright, isn't she? I mean…' His voice so filled with anguish Lorraine felt obliged to speak frankly.

'Well actually, I'm sorry to say, your friend is in a coma. No broken bones or internal injuries as far as we know, but she's still unconscious and we're monitoring her closely.'

'Oh no!' George let out a soft, agonising groan before

turning away. Lorraine wanted to say more but withheld; she was already late for her shift and patient information was supposed to be confidential after all.

'Are you a family member?' she asked.

'No, I…you see, we…I…' He looked into her eyes imploringly and Lorraine felt a sense of what he was trying to say; her heart softened; this was a troubled young man.

'Listen, can you meet me here after my shift?' she asked, 'just after two? I'll see what else I can find out about your friend.' A look of relief was evident on George's face as he nodded in agreement.

'Listen, if it's any solace, I don't think she's in any immediate danger.' Lorraine added and with that, she turned and walked towards the employees' entrance of the hospital. Just before she passed through the gate, she turned back and gave George a friendly wave.

'Hey, did I call it or did I call it, man!' grinned Mint as George returned. 'She fancies you…got yourself a date just like that eh? *Casanova!*' George felt confused. It was true, he liked her. He liked her shiny auburn hair and her smile too; she seemed to do that a lot. At the same time, thoughts of Lomond tormented him. He couldn't let her down. Not now. The truth was though, he'd *already* let her down; with his bike, the accident and now she was in a coma. What the bloody hell was he thinking? Then he thought of Lorraine and hoped she'd show up at 2pm.

CHAPTER FOURTEEN

George would need to ask Mint to front him some cash. He hated the thought, especially since his friends only source of income was from playing, but he could see no other way. His pockets were empty and he needed to be able to take Lorraine somewhere, to offer her a bite to eat, or at least a coffee. When they met after her shift, he suggested they go to The Canny Man's Pub in Morningside; he knew the owner who also had a small garage beside the pub. The Canny's was a well-known watering hole with secluded and quiet corners. They dawdled their way from the Meadows up to Morningside and got there just as it opened for the evening. On the way Lorraine filled him in on situation with Lomond. Although she was doing okay, they wouldn't know for certain about any damage until she came out of the coma; *if* she came out of it. As concerned about Lomond as George was, he found himself eager to know more about Lorraine. Over a couple of lagers, which was about as much as he could afford, Lorraine told George all about herself. She found him surprisingly easy to talk to. She was an only child. Her parents had worked in the building trade; her mother was the company secretary and bookkeeper; her father and his four-man crew took care of the construction. After some years, her mother had grown tired of the business and tired of her workaholic husband. When a young builder joined the company, they struck up a friendship that grew into a secret love affair. Then, after several months, the guilt became too much for her mother. She came clean about the affair and asked her husband to leave.

Lorraine's father had been furious about the revelation and in response he'd thrown them both out of the family home; Lorraine was only five years old at the time and she never saw her father again. Her mother had remarried; but her step-father was another disappointment. When her mother got sick, he abandoned them too. At just thirteen, Lorraine become the sole provider and carer for her mother. She died in her arms two years later and she'd been on her own since. It was this loss that had inspired her to go into nursing.

Lorraine studied George while she was talking. She was mesmerised by his dark eyes; his gaze seemed to reach deep into her soul. Sometimes his expression became quizzical, particularly when she spoke about her profession, working in a hospital with the constant smell of death and sickness and the personal care they had to provide; it was all so foreign to him.

The thought of such responsibility both horrified and grossed him out. What if a nurse made a serious mistake, like giving a patient the wrong medicine which killed them? He admired Lorraine for her intelligence and obvious love of her job. He'd never imagined he could hold a conversation with someone so… sophisticated and proper.

He told her all about his past. The pain of not knowing who his father was, of never knowing his mother either. The foster homes, which he had no recollection of where they were until he was moved to Edinburgh when he was nine years old, each one no better than the last. He lived each day with bullying, the abuse and constant fear. He confided with her that he used to cut himself, that it felt better to inflict pain on himself than having to suffer it at the hands of others. At least then he was in control of his destiny, even if it was dark and self-destructive. He could see no way out, no reason to go on. He'd never felt able to share so much of himself with anyone before. He was scared he'd told her too much, but he couldn't help it, she had a special way of listening; she seemed to really hear him. It was so different with Lomond; they never talked. He was simply her escort, her chauffeur. She wasn't interested in him; just his bike. Then he found himself confiding about her. He explained how he'd been the one with her on the night of the accident. They'd been out on his bike. It was a cold night and the roads had been icy. He stopped abruptly. Realising he'd said more than he ever meant to, but god only knows it was too late.

For a moment, it seemed as if Lorraine were appalled. How was she going to deal with his heartfelt confession? He eyed the door nervously, expecting her to get up and leave at any moment; but she never. Instead, she took his hand and squeezed it affectionately.

'Go on,' she encouraged 'it's okay. You need to talk it out.' He took a deep breath and went on. He explained how he felt so trapped, caught up in it all, not knowing what to do for everybody's sake. He was miserable with guilt; if only he'd paid better attention to the road that night. He couldn't get the images out of his mind; the accident, the aftermath, Lomond lying helpless in the hospital. It was all because of *him*. The thoughts were constantly careering around his head, like rats crazy to escape from a rusty cage. He wasn't even sure now what was real and what was his imagination. It was such a relief to tell someone.

'George, I can't even imagine how you must feel, but you can't place all the blame on yourself. Remember, Lomond could have refused to get on the bike, knowing the conditions of the road. That was her decision. What about the other vehicle? Surely some of the responsibility lies there too?'

'Yeah, I guess so' said George solemnly, 'but truthfully, I don't even know what really happened. I still can't remember. I don't know if I lost control of the bike or....'

'Listen,' Lorraine interrupted, 'call it fate, or bad luck or whatever. The accident was a combination of circumstances that happened to fall together. You, the bike, Lomond, the weather, the car, they're all separate pieces of the puzzle, and you never had control of them all. I think it's important you keep in mind that the *reality* of the accident, of *any* 'accident, for that matter, involves things beyond our control. Beyond anything we can foresee.' Lorraine could see from his expression that he still couldn't accept he wasn't to blame. 'Think about this. If your nature was fixed, and your world contained you alone; how would you learn and mature to adulthood? Life is in a state of constant change George. It's not fixed or stable. If you look at the all the different elements of the accident, you can see they are separate but interdependent. It happened because they converged at that very moment. You've become focused on only one aspect of the accident: *your* part and now your own guilt. I can't say that you did everything *right* that night, but accidents are just that; it was an accident.' Then Lorraine remembered what had brought the two of them to this place. 'Can I ask, do you feel you've ruined your relationship with Lomond now? That you've lost her friendship?' George was quiet for a while before answering.

'Yes, I do. Even if she wakes up, how could she ever forgive me? I just wish things could go back to how they were before.' Lorraine could feel the pain in his eyes, she wanted to take it away.

'You know, I've been meditating for a bit now and it's really helped me; it's amazing how breathing can help clear the mind. Just by meditating on the anger I feel, I've learned to replace it with compassion. Positive thoughts can be a real source of happiness and joy.' She gave a half-smile before continuing. 'I didn't think it would do anything for me at first. I was holding so much from my childhood. I felt so much hate for my father and my step-father; what they'd done to my family. I thought that was the only way I could ever feel. But then I began to see him in a different light. I remembered the stories my step-father told me when he was drunk, about how his father used to beat him and then somehow, I found compassion for him.' George was nodding.

'When I think back about the time, about how much of it I've wasted wishing for this or that, for things to be different, well, now I can see things from a different perspective. It's all just stuff; none of it has any *real* value, it never has. In reality, *everything* is just an impermanent thing.'

'How can I change the way I think?' George asked, sounding perplexed. Lorraine smiled.

'It starts with waking up I think, realizing your negative thoughts and creating new, more *positive* ones. I know it all sounds corny, but when you can see the negativity in your thinking and change it, you'll be able to let go of the past and start sharing more joy with others.' George was momentarily silent. Then he smiled and said,

'Wow, I couldn't follow all of that; but a lot of it does make sense. Maybe I do think of everything in a negative way. It's just that…'

'I understand,' Lorraine said. 'I really do.' George looked conscience-smitten.

'What is it?' she asked, squeezing his hand.
'You know I invited you to eat with me…well the truth is, I had to borrow money from Mint, just to pay for these drinks. I could bullshit you with some mince about hard times, but…'

Lorraine smiled and stood up.

'Come on.' She said. 'This is a problem easily fixed.'

Back at her flat, Lorraine prepared them a simple but tasty meal, chicken curry with rice. She lit a candle and they ate together in her room. Afterwards they held hands and she was open to his advances. She offered no resistance as he softly touched the nape of her neck. Timidly, she looked at him and then they kissed. The magic of discovery was in the air as things that had never happened to Lorraine before were happening. Slowly they undressed each other and allowed their attraction take its course.

He surprised her with his gentle touch. In the morning light, Lorraine couldn't believe what she'd done. She'd allowed a man to stay the night, in her bed; something she'd never done before. She knew if Helen found out she'd never hear the end of it. She'd never slept with a man after just one date before, but she felt no regret. Even with Lomond looming in the back of both their minds, it was as if they had found something special. As she lay in his arms watching the first rays of morning sun fill the room, the thought back to her classmates in school. Many of them had sex as young as fifteen. By sixteen they were drinking, smoking and taking pills.

She could see that most of them had issues, they were hurting inside for some reason or other; angry at a parents' breakup, suffering physical and mental abuse, annoyed that a new stepmother or stepfather was on the scene. She understood how these life-changing events took their toll on young people, they were only acting out. Their troubling, rebellious behaviour shielded them from the pain; as dangerous as it was. Some of them became addicted to drugs, others couldn't start the school day without a swig of liquor. A few of her classmates got pregnant and were whipped off to the doctor or forced along to an abortion clinic. A few even had their babies, babies that were later passed off as a sibling or cousin. Some girls were quick to leave the nest, desperate to shack up with their clueless, immature boyfriends, sadness and tragedy almost always befell them. Lorraine was the safe one. Despite her own experiences and the trauma, she had gone through. She always felt sorry for her friends with their upside-down lives; on their dangerous paths. Many of them saw her as boring and stuck up; someone who thought she was better than everyone else.

'You just need a good flangin', you do. That'll set you straight you clueless twat.' They'd laughed. One older girl had even taken such a dislike to Lorraine, she held her arms behind her back while three others punched her in the chest and stomach. Despite this, through it all, Lorraine felt nothing but sympathy for them. Somehow, after her mother's death, she realised that smoking, drinking, doing drugs and having promiscuous sex would never take the pain away. Instead, she was drawn to the idea of helping others deal with their pain and suffering, so she enrolled in nursing school. Now she thrived on the comfort she brought to patients like Lomond.

Lorraine slipped quietly out of bed and into the bathroom to freshen up. She stood naked before the mirror and laughed to herself when she thought of Helen's face. She would be more than amused; she'd be *amazed* to see her now. No doubt they'd have a good laugh about it, they'd see each other in a whole new light now. She boiled the kettle; soon it would time to leave for work.

George awoke to the smell of fresh coffee warming his senses. Last night felt like a dream, but one look around the room removed any doubt. This wasn't his bedroom. He noticed Lorraine's clothes, slung haphazardly over the back of a chair; his lay in a dingy heap on the floor beside him. He jumped out of bed and threw on his jeans and T-shirt; the hole he'd sought to disguise

was much larger now. *Christ, will she still like me this morning.*
Will she regret what we did? Did she enjoy it? I think I
told her too much? The door opened and George startled. Lorraine
peeked in and smiled.

'I bet you take sugar.' she said, holding a cup of black coffee.

'Two please.' He said. She took two cubes from the porcelain
sugar bowl on the tray, dropping them in with a *plunk plunk*. They
stood looking at each other, he in his torn T-shirt and Lorraine
wearing a lavender silk robe, her breasts and pink panties just
visible beneath. George opened his mouth to speak, but Lorraine
went to say something. She realised.

'No, you go on, please' she gestured.

'No, you first.' He replied and they stared at each other
bashfully before both laughing. Then they moved towards each
other, leaning in for a kiss. George tasted sweet coffee and cream
from her lips. He struggled to imagine anything finer than waking
up each morning to this. Was this even a possibility for him, this
sort of happiness? Or was it a myth? He felt a little awkward that
she was going to work. The thought of bumping into Mint at the
other end of the Meadows; he'd see them together and draw his
own conclusions. He realised he didn't care. He didn't want to be
without her just now and if it didn't matter to Lorraine, why should
it bother him?

On the way to the Meadows, Lorraine told George about the young man who'd accosted her with a knife.

'Just let me get my hands on that wee fud' he said, without thinking first how immature it sounded. 'You know, you shouldn't be walkin' back on your own, 'specially at night.' He added, putting his arm protectively around her shoulder. Even though there were many *what-ifs* and *buts* to be sorted out between them, it felt right. 'Listen, how about you tell me when you finish work and I'll come meet you, walk you home?' She smiled and pressed her face to his chest.

'You know, the funny thing is, I think I saw him in the hospital; that same kid.'

'What d'you mean? Like a patient, or just someone wandering around the corridors?'

'Well, I saw someone that looked just like him. He was young, no more than sixteen, and it was after visiting hours. I have this strange feeling that it was the same guy who tried to rob me that night.'

'Hmmm, think I'll ask Mint if it sounds like anyone he knows.' George said.

As they crossed Melville Drive and got onto one of the paths that crisscrossed the Meadows, George spotted Mint in the distance.

'There he is now, getting out his guitar.' said George, and arm-in-arm they sauntered over towards him. He greeted them with raised eyebrows but his face was a look of no surprise. A few moments later, Lorraine was bidding them both goodbye, kissing George softly on the lips before heading off towards the infirmary for her shift. George decided to hang with Mint for the day; he wanted to share his good fortune with someone and he had things to ask him. He and Lorraine had agreed to meet and go swimming together later, to the Warrender Baths on Thirlestane Road. In all his zeal to spend more time with her; it never occurred to him he'd need swimming trunks.

CHAPTER FIFTEEN

Lomond was fuming, *Livid*, teetering on the very edge. Feverishly, she was weaved through purple, red, and orange, with no intention of stopping. It was only when Mrs. R. threatened she would leave that Lomond slowed down.

'Don't go, Mrs. R. Please don't do a runner on me now.'

'What has got you in such a state?' Mrs. R. asked, somewhat feigning her ignorance.

'Don't you know?' she cried. 'The whole of Edinburgh must know. I've never seen two people so sickeningly happy in my whole feckin' life!'

'My goodness, but that's a good thing no?' she teased.

'Good? Are you taking the bloody piss? C'mon Mrs. R. she's supposed to be looking after *me* and he's supposed to be *mine*!' Lomond was making such a fuss; she was in danger of upsetting the inter-dimensional balance. There was a chance she might even skid out of the colour realm and lose the ability to return to the physical dimension. Realising she must assume control of the situation quickly, Mrs. R. moved towards Lomond and with lightning speed, she sent masses of pink energy to the distraught young girl. It engulfed Lomond; sending calm and love her way, but it wasn't enough.

'I mean, he's supposed to be with *me.*' Lomond cried. 'What's happened? This wasn't part of the deal.' She was losing the grip on what she was saying.

'He's *supposed* to be with you? There is no deal, Lomond,' replied Mrs. R. 'Don't you get it yet?'

'No *deal*?' Lomond was incredulous. 'She's my nurse. She's supposed to have *my* bloody best interests in mind, not her own pleasure.' Mrs. R. had no intention of letting Lomond off lightly. In fact, she had secretly hoped for this eventuality, it was time to teach her a lesson or two.

'What did you expect? At the moment, you're here. You've made no conscious decision to return to your body. Life goes on without us Lomond. Everyone has a right to happiness; including your nurse Lorraine. Let me ask you this lass, did you even care for George, like really care about him?' Lomond was silent as she thought.

'Well…of course I did.' She fired back but Mrs. R. gave a doubtful look.

'Is that so? Come on child, be honest with yourself. Was it actually George who attracted you? Or was it his bike, his lifestyle and the fact that other young girls envied your relationship?'

Lomond hesitated, confused about what to say. She wanted to defend her feelings; but a part of her realised her jealously was both immature and selfish.

'Of course, sharing common interests in life is an important aspect in the quest for love and happiness.' Mrs. R. offered. 'But being at ease with that person is another. You're still young Lomond. To try and control someone, to convince yourself they *belong* to you will only create huge emotional problems further down the road. One day you'll discover that real *love* is having the freedom to love whomever you choose. The heart wants what the heart wants and all that. None of us have the right to *demand* someone love us if they don't, or to control who they feel attracted to,

'But he promised to stand by me no matter what…forever and ever.' Lomond protested, half ashamed of her own justification.

'*Forever and ever?* Come on, lass, take off your rose-tinted glasses. How many times have you exaggerated or said things you didn't really mean in the heat of the moment? Things you never expected someone to take seriously?' Lomond grimaced; she hated being reminded of her weaknesses. Mrs. R. was administering a harsh dose of reality. 'Child, it's easy for loneliness to pull us down the wrong path in our relationships. Our ego, fear, the desire for power and money; all these things can give us a distorted view of others, the need to seize control. Inner peace and a solid sense of self are critical to our overall well-being. While feeling a part of someone can be emotionally rewarding, it can be a hurtful experience too if taken too literally.

If we become consumed by jealousy, envy and greed, it can create a life full of regrets. This can lead us to depression and ultimately, deep unhappiness. I know reality can be a bitter pill for many to swallow, but if you're expecting everyone to put their life on hold, until you're ready to come back to the land of the living, then you're in for a rude awakening. Life does not revolve around you. It is going on now, even as we speak.'

Lomond could feel her self-control slipping away. She couldn't understand the pain she was feeling at Mrs. R's words; it hurt as nothing ever had. It was as if the walls she had created around her own little world were finally crumbling and she could do nothing to stop it. She felt helpless and furious all at once. She resented having to witness the way Lorraine and George were connecting, simply because she listened and showed concern. It was never this way with them. Now she could see how it affected him, having someone show interest, really caring about what was on his mind. Then she felt guilt. She had never given George the kind of attention he needed; the kind Lorraine had. This made their connection all the more unbearable as it was so different from the relationship they had; it all seemed, so personal. 'Ranting and raving to yourself won't change anything.' Mrs. R. declared. This was the harshest medicine of all, because she realised the woman was right.

'Don't you see, lass? Now's your chance to change the direction of your life; to create your future and develop your inner self,' Lomond sighed in resignation. 'Here, let me explain a few things that'll make it easier for you.' Said Mrs. R., and although still pouting, Lomond listened; accepting it was for her own good. Yet all the while, the thought of Lorraine with George was eating away at her.

'Lass, it helps to understand the differences between the *conscious* and *subconscious* parts of the mind; to help you realise what you can and cannot control. Our subconscious mind is internal and subjective. Think of it as the night-time, like when you are asleep and unaware of what is real and what is happening. The conscious mind is like the daytime, when you are aware to all that is around you. The subconscious takes over when the conscious mind relaxes or goes to sleep and vice versa. Think of the things you do habitually, all the time. The things you do without thinking. Remember when you learned to ride your bike? Once you mastered the skill, you paid little attention to the how, you just got on the bike rode it, like flicking an autopilot switch. It's only when some outside distraction, like a loud sound, a strong odour or a powerful image draws our attention away that our subconscious alerts us to come back to the task at hand.'

Lomond thought she was following this explanation quite well, she even seemed to remember something about this from school. 'Do you know Lomond, when we listen to someone speaking, we only hear only a limited number of words at one time; what psychologists call a 'chunk.' All the while, the subconscious is busy filling in the blanks, functioning *symbolically* and considering the appropriate reply; or sometimes the *inappropriate* reply. How do you think our bodily functions work, like how does our heart beat, our lungs breathe and how do we digest our food? Well, they all function without us actually having to do anything, they're involuntary actions led by the subconscious; and thankfully so. The subconscious mind has some bad habits too, it can register our negative thoughts as fact, because it has no sense of reason. But it can also do something very special that the conscious cannot; it is capable of sensing other people's moods and feelings and it can alert us to danger. These are all skills you can and will develop Lomond.'

'So, the subconscious, I guess it just happens, I never really thought about how.' Lomond said.

'Have you ever thought of someone and the next minute they phone you or you see them? Well, that is what we call telepathy, and believe it or not; you can actually develop this ability.' Lomond was deep in thought, what Mrs. R. was saying resonated with her; she found herself being carried away trying to recall times she had these experiences.

'Lomond wake up, you're dreaming again. I need to tell you about the *conscious* mind. So, the conscious mind is objective, it's literal and it functions externally. Think about all the times you focus on outside stimuli, sounds, sights, tastes, smells and physical realities that trigger your senses. Imagine your conscious mind as the sun.' Lomond nodded, the visual concept working in her mind's eye. She was becoming increasingly impressed by Mrs. R's vast array of knowledge.

'Wow, does everyone in the spirit world have as much

knowledge as you?'

'Yes. In this realm, we never stop learning, there is so much to understand.'

'So, when I was last in Tyrone's house and I stared at the statues on his desk, the one with an eye for its head. It seemed to draw me into it; almost as if I was being hypnotized by it. Then something really strange happened. I felt as if I was being attacked by some kind of evil. Do you know what that was all that about then?'

'Oh dear, yes I do and it's not good at all. To begin with, the symbol of the eye as signifying dark forces is as old as time, it's a supernatural omen reputed to be able to lay some kind of specific spiritual curse.' Lomond shuddered at the thought. 'It is believed to cause harm, illness and even death. You know, the eyes are the gateway into a person's soul and maybe you've heard, or even used the phrase, "Stop giving me the evil eye?"

So, I think what happened to you there was, your energy homed in on the eye symbol and you made a connection to it, to its spiritual force.' Lomond was frowning as Mrs. R. continued. 'I can see you are wondering how energy can be contained in a statue? Well, what do you think happens when someone repeats a verse, prayer, a mantra over and over again towards a specific thing?'

'To, be honest Mrs. R, I've really no idea, does it become it, maybe?'

'Correct. In a way it does Lomond. The intention of the words becomes embedded within the object. So you see, if Tyrone has been repeating evil mantras with a focus on that statue, then it will contain the vibratory energy of those intentions. Think of all the statues, carvings, paintings and artifacts seen all around the world. Religious relics, statues, royal objects the list is endless. Well, they all give off a vibration; an energy. They need no written explanation as they generate their messages to the world by their very existence. They transmit subliminal vortices of information to be picked up by our subconscious mind and played out by us in our conscious mind in everyday life; without ever knowing or understanding the link. These frequencies broadcast their messages all the time and you, Lomond, you are intuitively able to decode what they represent.'

'But *how* do I use all this information, in the *real* world, when I go back?' Lomond asked.

'Hmmm…well that's a little more difficult to explain, lass,' Mrs. R. said. 'First of all, it's quite valuable to understand that our living body is not totally who we are, it is the vehicle that allows the five senses to send messages to the brain which then decodes them as our reality. Our reality is based on our beliefs and values; the things we have learned from our peers and teachers. A short moment ago, you were day dreaming and I asked you to wake up. It is important to be awake and living in the moment as much as we can Lomond. This helps us consider and process what we are *actually* saying when we speak; the meaning behind the sounds. But to do this requires us to separate the real from the unreal in our conscious minds. Also, we must recognise we all have the ability to make choices in life, and as long as we do, we can directly affect our lives. We must resist judging others and allowing the judgment from others to affect us, this will help us become centred, grounding and balance. If we accept everything that we experience *as* just that "an experience", nothing more or less, then we can begin to affect any situation. Science shows that people who exert control over a situation, who make an effort to surmount obstacles in their way, become less stressed by negative events. Also, people with a greater sense of self-love, get sick less often and recover quicker when they do.' Lomond was silent as she contemplated all that Mrs. R. had imparted. There was so much to take in. She felt she understood, but the more she considered it, the more doubt and frustration crept in.

'Well, that all sounds perfectly *wonderful*, Mrs. R., but I can't just *change*. I've been this way forever. It's who I am!'

'Well, no, you certainly won't change with *that* attitude.' Mrs. R. admonished; her patience was beginning to wear thin. 'You know, even as a baby you…' She caught herself before she said anymore, but was too late, Lomond's ears had pricked.

'What do you mean, even as a baby?' Lomond quizzed, 'Tell me, what did you mean by that? Is there something you're not telling me?' Mrs. R. was cornered.

'Uh, I just meant that if you don't learn to exert self-control, the picture you have in your mind of George and Lorraine will get locked in as the very symbol of emotional pain, and once it's locked in.'

'Oh, so, you're saying I should just forget all about George? Go off like I don't give a shit? That's your bloody solution?'

'No. I only meant that putting things in perspective will help you.'

'You know, I've a good mind to go visit the earthly realm without you, Mrs. R. and I've a good mind to give that backstabber Lorraine a dose of her own medicine.' Lomond threatened, although she couldn't think what the dose of medicine was. Mrs. R. recognised the dire seriousness of the situation. Entering the indigo tunnel in such an agitated state could keep Lomond from ever being able to return to her body. Planning violence, or carrying out any violent act, could well bring about her death. She quickly fumbled, looking for a way to dissuade Lomond from hurting anyone else, and herself.

'Oh, lass…just this once try to see a different perspective. Think about how you would feel if you observed your own thoughts about George and Lorraine. Imagine you are looking in on this relationship from afar?'

'What does that mean?' Lomond snorted.

'Try to become an observer of your own thoughts'.

'Oh, and just how do I do that?' Lomond fired back sarcastically, hostility now oozing from her.

'Okay. Just think of your mind as an organ, a part of the body you can manipulate and change; you have the power to tell it what to do. Use all your senses. What do you see? What do you hear? Be still and breathe deeply. If you can calm your body, your mind will follow. Remember, suffering is a condition of your own mind. A state created and sustained by you alone. It is not a physical reality; unless you make it so. Now, Lomond, what are your thoughts? What are your feelings? What do you see and hear?' Lomond decided to take on Mrs. R's proposition as a personal challenge.

'Okay, I'll play along,' she said, opening her inner eye. 'Well, I see George and Lorraine. It's like watching a movie. They're together, walking through the Meadows, holding hands.' Mrs. R. could see the images playing in Lomond's mind.

'What are they doing now?' she asked.

'Well, nothing really. They're just talking. Looking at each other and smiling.'

'And?'

'Well, they look pretty happy. I can *feel* their happiness.'

'How does that make *you* feel Lomond?'

'Well, George was always good to me, so…I, I know Lorraine's been trying to…aw *shit*!' Lomond moaned.'

'What is it? What's the matter?'

'All of the sudden I don't feel angry at them anymore.'

'Can you think of any reason that might be?' coaxed Mrs. R and despite having a strong desire to shield her own feelings,

Lomond found herself opening the door to her inner thoughts.

'Well, seeing George without his bike, I realise it's not actually *him* I'm attracted to. In fact, I can't even see myself spending my whole bloody life with him.' She paused, allowing her mind to absorb this new insight about herself. Mrs. R. smiled. Then Lomond said,

'You know, I have no expectations of him anymore. I can accept that they're together, I mean, why not? The funny thing is, I think I actually feel happy about it. I feel free. I mean, I still care about what happens to him; but I realise he's not the one for me.' Lomond was somewhat stunned by her own feelings and now she felt an urge to re-enter the indigo tunnel, to visit Lorraine and George one more time, just to confirm her feelings.

So, drawing in the colour, she was suddenly projected back down the tunnel, with Mrs. R. following close behind. She was experiencing a new sense of awe as it dawned on her, she could take control of her own mind and her thoughts. S*hit*, it was crazy to think that she'd never tried it before. Why had she accepted inner pain as her only possible reality, like it was an inescapable given? The idea now seemed absolutely absurd. In this new frame of mind, she perceived an energy that was infinitely compassionate, empathetic even. Mrs. R. hovered nearby as Lomond continued to wrap her mind around this new realisation; then she followed her as she made her way to look in on George and Lorraine.

When they found the happy couple, they were locked in an embrace; caressing each other as they talked and laughed together. Lomond observed a new mist around George; dominated by pink and blue. She thought back to her time with him. Their hurried conversations: usually centred around how much she despised her parents and the obstacles they put in the way of her freedom. Or how he would go on about bikes, how much he adored them. Once he confided in her, there was nothing he liked better than a bike that wouldn't run; something to work on bringing back to life.

'Funny how a lot of men with earthy temperaments seem to become mechanics,' interjected Mrs. R. somehow aware of her thoughts. 'They lose themselves in the tinkering and tampering, not unlike a surgeon, I suspect.'

'What was that… did you say *earthy*?'

'Sorry dear, for a moment I forgot myself. Yes, he has an *earthy* temperament; of the element *earth* and the colour green. The element relates to his personality, but it can be seen in his physicality too. See his long, slim neck? How he tilts his head? His clumpy boots and the way he walks—slow and slightly hunched over. The fact he always finds a wall or tree to lean against; as if he needs support to hold himself up?'

'Wow, I did notice that,' said Lomond.' But I never thought

of it like that before.'

'With his earthy temperament, having someone he can share his thoughts and emotions with is critical to his well-being. That's the only way he can put his pain and suffering into perspective'

'He's suffered a lot of pain?'

'Indeed, he has dear. And the more he expresses himself, the freer his mind will become. Once he learns to trust, he'll be able to create more positive thoughts and find inner happiness, just like we were talking about. As he becomes *one* with his own true nature, the colour turquoise will become more prevalent in his aura. When you become more observant of those around you; you'll begin to recognise the different elemental qualities in people of course.'

'That's really interesting.' said Lomond to her own surprise. 'I can see how that would be very handy!' She thought for a moment before asking. 'So, what about that Tyrone then? What's he all about?'

'Oh, Tyrone,' said Mrs. R. making little effort to disguise her contempt. 'He has a *water* temperament, dear, blue in colour. As you saw, he's short and dumpy, with small shoulders and a stubby neck. Like most water temperaments, he pretends to tire easily and tends to lounge around a lot. Of course, he's also very stubborn and set in his ways; he clings to the past. He does, however, have an exceptional memory, but it's a pity he uses it to take advantage of others. And all because of the regrets he carries. He's tormented by memories of an unpleasant childhood and his own sense of inferiority. He convinced himself he's unworthy, something his father taught him and his mother reinforced. Now his self-loathing controls him; his insecurities are at the forefront of his mind every moment of every day.

Despite his self-proclamation of being able to connect with the world of spirit; he has unwittingly blocked any natural intuition that would have gained him access to other realms.'

'Wow, that explains a few things then.' Lomond commented before adding more excitedly, 'Okay, me now, do me please.'

'Oh, you're an easy one, lass. You've a *fire* temperament. Red is your colour. Quick movements, fast thinking and sometimes, irrational behavior; it's all part of the fire energy. You crave excitement and with your rapid metabolism, you can burn off calories with ease; something people of the other elements may come to envy about you as you grow older.' Mrs. R. said rolling her eyes. 'You need movement, travel. Constant new projects on the go in order to be content; and more than any other element, you need to be in *control*.' Lomond smiled smugly, although she felt uncertain if that were a compliment or a criticism. 'Though you feel you should be the one leading, your quick temper and even quicker tongue can sometimes rile people. Oh, and your colour. You've no doubt heard the expression 'red with rage'? Well, I'm *sure* you can think of times when you've been so angry that you actually felt *red*?' Though somewhat uncomfortable hearing her own short-comings listed, the accuracy fascinated Lomond.

'What about you, Mrs. R.? Tell me about you.'

'Me? Well, I'm an *air* temperament and yellow is my colour.' Then, instead of elaborating as she had with the other descriptions, she stopped abruptly and lowered her head, as though she had drifted off somewhere else. After a few moments she continued, her voice full of melancholy. 'You wouldn't guess it now, but when I was of the physical realm, I wore stylish clothes and lots of make-up. I loved to look just so. ' A sly grin appeared on her face but Lomond sensed an awkwardness in her, as if she were hesitant to reveal herself. There was more to her than it seemed.

CHAPTER SIXTEEN

It was beautiful Saturday. Lorraine had the weekend off and George was coming over; they'd been seeing each other for a week now. She hoped he might like to go to the meditation group with her, but she wasn't counting on it. She was sure George would not get on with Tyrone; they were from entirely different worlds. Tyrone was phony. Hell, she didn't even trust him herself. He was too *insincere* for anyone as *real* as George.

According to Innes though, Tyrone had promised there would be a visit from an especially important and wise man this evening. This man was supposedly a bit of an enigmatic character, and all that was known about him was that he came from the Black Isle. Tyrone had apparently persuaded him his group was worthy of his presence. Lorraine was intrigued. Was he a charlatan like Tyrone, or was he the real deal? She wondered what a modern Celtic "hermit" would look like. Would he be dressed in a sack-cloth and ashes; as she'd heard ascetics did? Maybe he'd be wearing a long white tunic, or sheepskins strategically draping his otherwise naked body. Regardless, she was intrigued and knew she wanted to go. She hoped she could persuade George to join her.

There was also her flat mate to contend with. Helen was desperate for George to meet her boyfriend, Bobby. *We can all go out together on Saturday*! She'd shrieked in excitement. *That'd be so fabby*! After talking it over, it was decided. Lorraine and George would stop by the meditation group for a bit before meeting up with Helen and Bobby at The Bandwagon later.

As soon as they arrived, they were ushered inside by one of Tyrone's loyal acolytes; a grinning doe-eyed girl in her mid-twenties named Amie. Immediately, George felt totally out of place. The stench of incense and the snooty surroundings made him feel a bit antsy; he was much more at home with bike parts strewn around and the smell of motor oil hanging in the air.

Being here stirred up insecurities about his background, reminded him about being poor. He grappled with feelings of inferiority and contempt. *What must they think of me? Well, who do they think they are, anyway*? Tyrone made things infinitely worse by extending a long-fingered, languid hand towards George before wrapping him in a full-body embrace. George found this so uncomfortable, he had to hold back from throwing him off and telling him he was not into guys.

He was also disturbed by the way Tyrone leered at the bodies of the female members in the group.

'You can't trust this loon.' he whispered to Lorraine. She felt just as uneasy and was regretting bring them both along. Just as she was about to motion for them to leave; the visitor made his grand entrance. They had no choice but to stay put and squeeze in next to Innes.

The so called 'holy man' turned out to be visually unremarkable. A slim, stooping figure who looked in desperate need of soap and a haircut. His straggly silver hair and beard looked matted and dirty. He shuffled to the front of the room and turned to face them all, his bushy white eyebrows hiding deep-set eyes. Maybe this was how all hermits looked Lorraine consolidated.

He started to speak, telling them a little of his past. He was born in the Black Isle, into a crofting community. His father was a shepherd, as was his father and his father before him. The Hermit impressed them with his storytelling skills. He told them fantastic tales of recent times, and the ancient ways. Finally, he introduced them to the purpose of his visit.

'Tonight, my friends, I am here to speak to you about a small part of the ethos I base and live my life by – *breathing*. Not just your everyday shallow breathing but breathing techniques which enable me to connect to a weightless sense of being and the natural rhythm of the universe. It is in this weightless state where infinite possibilities exist and where my mind is set free to roam at will.' Puzzled faces glanced at one another around the room, the hermit carried on. 'When we take time out of our normal routine to sit quietly in silence, allowing ourselves to breathe deeply and rhythmical, we can begin to set our mind free, we can develop our awareness and understanding of what our life purpose is. I can see that you are all sitting here shallow breathing, this does little for your mind, body or soul, you are simply just existing. Deep breathing techniques ignite our *willpower* leading us, and motivating us forward into a greater consciousness, where peace, and happiness reside.' The room was deathly silent as he continued. 'Many people find themselves initiated into the spiritual life through the misfortunes they suffer. We need not allow life's challenges to drive us to dark desperation. True, they do this to many, but, if we look at them for what they really are, they can lead to our ultimate truth and re-connect us to the 'I', where no limitations exist, no sadness resides, simply only peace, joy and happiness. By becoming an observer of our thoughts, we can free ourselves from any unfavourable thinking and emotional entanglement. We are then able to choose our attitudes, our perceptions and the outcome of our experiences.' Out of the corner of her eye, Lorraine was surprised to see George appeared to be hanging on every word. The hermit stole a sideways glance towards Tyrone, then faced the audience. 'As individuals, we should be able to recognise when our motives are driven chiefly by self-gratification, the desire for acquisition of mental, emotional and material gain. Consider all conditions, patterns and ideals you have set for yourself, or were set for you by others. Ask yourselves, if they serve you well, or not? People formulate ideas and beliefs about what we experience; we rarely *truly experience* anything. We must learn to see through our own and other's verbiage. Can you always distinguish between what was *thought* to have occurred and what has *actually* happened? We use words to describe an incident, a feeling. A feeling however can only arise from a thought. Fear is merely an illusion, created from a thought, which is lodged in your memory bank as an experience, these *feeling*s are then experienced by the body.' A majority of those in the room were nodding in affirmation. The Hermit was beginning to win them over. 'Breathing is the breath of life, *the way*, so, develop and connect to the power of the breath and go deeper into *your* mind for this is the way to harness the willpower of the energetic blueprint of spiritual wholeness, health and happiness. Love dispels fear. Love is *truth;* on this you can depend. Forgiveness is not necessary if love for every living thing exists within you.' Lorraine and George exchanged a knowing look. 'Discover who you really are, your purpose and importantly love yourself.' The Hermit brought his hands together next to his heart and bowed his head.

Much to his surprise, something in the Hermit's words hit a nerve. It felt like a *revelation*. Lorraine had also become so engrossed in the Hermit's narrative; she never noticed its effect on George. As everyone was getting up and quietly slipping out of the room, George remained seated, lost in his own thoughts. Then she noticed the Hermit's eyes were fixed directly on George. As he raised his head, he appeared to be drawn into his gaze. Was he using hypnosis…or telepathy? Then, as if unspoken words had passed between them, she watched as George stood and approached the old man. With everyone else gone, she suddenly felt like an intruder. She crept out of the room and waited for George outside; uncertain if she was doing the right thing. Standing face-to-face, the Hermit spoke directly into George's heart.

'Tell all you know young man; you will be protected. Deal now with your problems or life will deal with you.'

CHAPTER SEVENTEEN

Racing through the indigo tunnel with Mrs. R., Lomond continued to put into practice all that she had learned. Mrs. R. had encouraged her to seek out and study a special kind of person; someone pure of soul who understood their own mind; a mature individual who had shed their worldly possessions and most importantly; who radiated pure compassion. Realistically, how could Lomond possibly find such a person in the city? It would be more difficult than finding a needle in a haystack.

'Trust, lass, *just* trust.' she said with an encouraging nudge. 'Come on now, out through the tunnel you go.' Moments later, Lomond burst out and into the pulsating atmosphere of a Saturday night in the city. Despite the hustle and bustle, she was immediately drawn to a beacon of golden light. Without hesitation she headed straight for it. It led her straight into Tyrone's meditation room where a wise looking old man was leading a session. She was beyond surprised to find George and Lorraine there too. This 'guru's' golden light was intense; so intense she knew it must be rare. She had seen it once before, surrounding the ornately carved jade Buddha. She observed the way it filled the whole room, how everyone was affected by it; even those with experience and knowledge. They were all absorbing the gold colour; as if basking in the sun's enriching rays. Even in her spirit-form, Lomond too was affected. She could feel its richness and the soothing tranquility beneath; a warming -intense joy. The session ended and everyone began filing out the room quietly, including Lorraine. Only George remained. Lomond watched on as they stood facing one another, the old man gazing deeply into his eyes, into his very soul. A thick cord golden light projected from his "third eye" and George flinched as it pierced his forehead. However, he remained surprisingly calm and still. Although she could not hear the words the old man was saying, she saw George lower his head and nod in accordance, before turning and leaving the room. *Where was Lorraine?* She wondered.

Tyrone and Innes re-entered the room a few moments later. Tyrone and the Hermit came to rest on large armchairs at the head of the room. The rest of the group returned, resuming their places on the floor, but George and Lorraine were nowhere to be seen. Innes sat at the feet of the two men, glancing from one to the other in awe and adulation. Lomond felt troubled as she watched the innocent delight radiating from her youthful face.

Tyrone raised his hand to bring silence before commencing, his voice steady and authoritative.

'We humans are a curious lot. We doubt, we theorise, we question and we seek proof but, unlike myself, the majority of people never stand still long enough, or quietly enough, to hear or witness and therefore miss out on the reality of spiritual communion. I, for one have worked for decades using my spiritual, creative and intuitive knowledge, and I have instructed others in how to develop theirs. Now is the time for us to work together, even harder than before. To redouble our efforts in spreading this knowledge, I will lead the way to a balanced future for all of planet Earth.' Heads nodded around the room in agreement. 'For the good of humanity, we must all take responsibility. We have reached the point in evolution where there is a distinct need to move into a new dimension of healing. A dimension which I know only too well, that brings the: spiritual, intuitive, creative, scientific and academic aspects of society together, to create balance. From the beginning of recorded time, the greatest prophets, philosophers, poets and even scientists have been 'inspired' by divine knowledge. I too have experienced such knowledge. I know only too well that divine communion is a crucial factor in my work. Please make a promise to yourself to return here to continue your learning before

you leave this sanctuary and go back out into the mundane world.'
The Hermit was not smiling as he rose to leave.

'Goodnight and blessings to all.' He said before bowing out
of the room slowly. Tyrone followed him; ignoring Innes who was
left sitting on the floor before the two empty chairs.

'Hmmmmm . . . well, I'm not really convinced about
Tyrone's little speech.' Remarked Mrs. R. somewhat mockingly. 'I
suppose we can admit there is *some* truth in it, but he's so trapped
in his own ignorance and impurity of thought he just can't see
beyond.' Lomond was taken aback by the harsh evaluation; it was
snarky, even for out-spoken Mrs. R. 'That poor girl!' Mrs. R
spurted, shaking her head derisively. 'She believes every word that
self-absorbed cretin says.' Again, her unapologetic callousness
surprised Lomond. She considered Tyrone, in all his ignorance. He
was so *egotistical*; he hadn't taken on board anything the Hermit
had shared; except the parts that supported his own message. It was
obvious he was driven by a delusional sense of self-importance. To
Lomond, the fact he was oblivious to the Hermit's golden energy
as it rained down on him was most telling; even the majority of his
lowly followers were attuned to that. Instead, he strutted on, intent
on upstaging everyone in the room; blind to the wisdom
surrounding him.

'Both Tyrone and Innes are caught up in their own little worlds of deception' Mrs. R. hissed; not to hold back any longer. 'Him with his own importance and her, she's delusional about a future with that charlatan. It's all so pitiful. They're in for a serious fall…' She was stopped short by the look of reproach on Lomond's face. 'Oh, don't fret, wee one.' She chuckled. 'It'll be of his own doing, he's always his own worst enemy.' From somewhere in the corner of her mind, Lomond became aware of a tittering between Mrs. R. and another; like a private joke that didn't involve her. At first, she found it difficult to accept another presence, she had gotten used to being alone with Mrs. R. in the spirit realm. But then, as the tittering broke out into full-on laughter, it was so infectious she found herself caught up in the hilarity, despite having no clue what it was about. Then she realised who had joined them in the colour realm, it was none-other than the Hermit. He and Mrs. R. were basking in his golden presence and beckoning her to join them.

'So, this is the one who is to discover me?' said the Hermit in a most unpretentious tone. Lomond pondered his meaning.

'Lomond, *breathe* in his essence while you can.' Mrs. R. adjured. 'He will not be easy to find once you have returned to your physical body.' Lomond realised there was much more to this teacher than was revealed in the company of Tyrone.

The clamour at The Bandwagon was at its max. The music was deafening and everyone was competing to be heard; screaming at the tops of their lungs. George was in no mood to mingle with people who were so flighty and superficial. He was angry with himself for betraying his social standards, to be mixing with these privileged posers. The world never seemed to tire of pissing on him.

'Wanna drink?' someone screamed in his ear. Reactively, he swung his fist and nearly connected with Helen's face; the look in his eyes was *murderous*. Mortified and realising he'd probably ruined it with Lorraine; he grabbed his khaki fishtail parka from the chair beside him, quickly put it on and did a runner out of the club; leaving Helen in a state of shock and fear. Noticing her friends' despair, Lorraine went into panic. She ran out into the street, not knowing if she would find him, and unsure if she wanted to. Violence was a hard thing to accept from anybody. Like many women, she'd had her share of angry and violent young men in her life. She ran to the corner and spotted him. She could see his agony as he sagged against a lamppost, the fur trimmed hood pulled up over his head and his head buried inside the crook of his arm. He seemed to sense her cautious approach. Unable to face her he begged:

'Please, Lorraine, go away. Just go away. I'm telling you, I'm no good. I've never been any good. A woman like you, you deserve better than a total fucking twat like me!' Lorraine placed her hand gently on his shoulder.

'George, let's go to my place. We can talk there.' Without looking up, he stretched out his arm and brought it around her and drew her forcefully against him. 'Did it have something to do with *me*?' she asked the breath almost squeezed out of her body. 'Was it something I did?'

'Hell, no!' he said vehemently, holding her at arms'-length by the shoulders now. He looked at her and his eyes widened helplessly, searching for the right words.

'Was it Helen?' Lorraine asked, looking for a way to help him. 'I know she can be quite…did she say something to offend you?'

'For Christ's sake, no.' he answered hotly whilst backing away. 'You don't get it, do you? It wasn't *you*; it wasn't *her;* it wasn't *anybody*. It's *me*. No one could *ever* understand unless they've been through it.' Lorraine felt like weeping. She realised she understood nothing of what troubled him; she was unable to find the words to comfort him. George seemed so alone and she wondered if he might ever let anyone else in. She took him by the hand and they made their way back to her flat. Walking in silence, the rhythm of their footsteps seemed to calm him. As they crossed the Meadows, an owl hooted into the night. They looked up and saw it sitting on the branch of a Chestnut tree, its wide, wise eyes staring down at them. Lorraine noticed a wave of calm come across George's face.

Later, as they held each other on her bed, fully clothed, they heard it again.

'I think that's the same owl.' She whispered, her gaze searching into the darkness. 'What do you make of that?' Beside her, George's body gave way to small tremors as the emotions he'd kept buried for so long rose to the surface and began to spill over. She held his head close to her bosom and ran her fingers gently along the creases of his eyes, not saying a word. After a while, his quiet whimpering subsided and he began to talk. The words uttered more measured and thoughtful than she had ever heard from him.

'It was an owl. It was an owl that kept me sane.'

'An owl?' she answered, intrigued.

'Aye. It lived in the tree outside my bedroom window. If it

wasn't for that bird, I swear, I would have . . .' he grew silent and she waited, sensing he was about to share something of great importance. Eventually he began again. 'I hated him so much, but I didn't have the courage to stop it. He'd sit on my bed every night just staring at me. Sometimes his hand would move towards me and he'd stroke my face. I'd try to slap it away, but he just kept on going. It would move down my neck, to my chest, to my stomach. I'd jump up and try to run but he'd slap me hard across the face. Then he'd reach between my legs and…' She felt his body go tense and she held his hand tighter, willing him the strength to continue. 'After he…well, he'd get up and leave the room, crying. Can you believe it? He was the one *crying* and I'd lay there trembling in the darkness. I'd stay that way until the sun came up. But then there was the owl…it was there outside my window. It seemed to understand my pain. It was the only one who did.'

Over the coming days, George opened up to her. Bit by bit, he shared things he thought he would never share with anyone. He talked about the *faggot warden*. About his seemingly innocent words, how he used them to try and disguise his real intentions.

He spoke out of the relentless pain that dwelt in his heart, weighing it down. Lorraine listened patiently and quietly but inside she felt total anguish for this young boy who'd never had anyone to love and protect him. A boy who had learned to harden his heart and hit back, to strike out first before anyone could hurt him again. He told her how he had gone into every new foster home with the fire of new hope ignited inside him. *Maybe this would be the home he'd always dreamed of. Maybe here he would find the love he never had.* George described one occasion where he'd been forced to wash and polish the cars of all the staff at the home; one after another without a break, and for what? Just for standing up for himself, for refusing to accept their bullying. He'd nearly passed-out from the exhaustion. His arms ached so badly he could barely lift them for days. Worse still was *the routine as it was called.* He was made to stand flat against a wall from morning to night, no water or food; not even allowed to use the toilet. He'd been deprived of sleep; caned on his bare buttocks until they bled. He was slapped, punched and beaten; separated from the other kids his age. He didn't know what he did to deserve it, but despite everything, he refused to give in. There was something inside him that kept him going. For so many years he'd held on to the hope that someone would come to his rescue. But no-one did. Eventually the constant abuse began to change him. It became his undoing, even in the nicer foster homes he'd stayed in. He began to lash out, sabotage any chance of happiness. He was misunderstood and feared and this led to constant rejection. He began to realise it was too late for him, he would never learn to control his anger. He would always be that troubled kid, the undesirable who would never adjust. The outsider. The delinquent. Lorraine's heart bled for him. Now he had reached an all-time low. He couldn't believe he had lashed out at a woman. It shocked him to know that he was capable of such vile behavior. Lorraine listened to his confessions with non-judgmental warmth and gentle encouragement. She knew that now he had opened the door to his troubled past, it was important to set it all free. He talked about how eventually, as a teen, he had come to accept the abuse, accept the mental and physical anguish as a part of his life. Then there was the day his anger became unleashed. He'd come to the defense of a younger child, he finally snapped. He smashed his fist into *that faggot's* face, again and again; breaking his nose and bloodying his mouth. He felt no regret. He was removed from the home immediately. Taken into juvenile custody and kept there for weeks; to await his punishment for injuring that disgusting predator. Later in court, he felt nothing but contempt as the warden stood in the witness box and painted the worst possible picture of him. His expression had been almost smug as he testified against George.

Now he felt a new fear, a fresh anxiety. Instead of seeing his persecutor's face, he saw the face of Lorraine's father testifying against him and he felt crippled by guilt. *What had he done to Lomond? Would she suffer all her life because of him?* He believed he should be punished. Lorraine realised nothing she could say would change his past, but she believed that with time and by having someone by his side, the pain would subside and his heart would soften. She had love to give him.

　　'He said I should come clean about everything.' George told her eventually 'That I would be protected, but how? Surely no one will ever believe me!' His torment was distinct. Lorraine knew he was referring to the Hermit. She had been curious about their encounter and now she knew advice the wise old man had imparted.

　　'George, don't you see? You've told *me*, you've told me everything. I believe you *will* be protected. I just know it.' Although he wanted to argue against what Lorraine was saying, inside he felt she was right. Telling her had brought him a huge sense of release and now, suddenly, the Hermit's words seemed to ring with an element of truth. There was only one thing left to do, he told Lorraine. He needed to go to the police and confess.

CHAPTER EIGHTEEN

Innes checked the family '*in-out*' board in the hallway. As
expected, her parents were '*in.*' Her brother, Ian, had marked
himself '*in*' too, but she knew better. She was used to covering his
back on a Saturday night. When the pebbles bounced off her
window, she'd slip quietly downstairs to let him in. It was their
little secret. They'd always stuck together. Even when their
interests had begun to diverge as teenagers, the bond between them
was a strong as ever. It was them against the world. While she
waited, she took out her pastels and began recreating an image of
the Hermit. She managed a fair likeness of his features: the hawk
nose, the ruddy veined cheeks and piercing blue eyes; but there
something was missing. A quality she couldn't pinpoint. Was it his
silvery, salt and pepper hair? Was it curlier, or thinner? Maybe it
was the chin, more square or pointed? Innes studied her drawing
with a critical eye and was about to make the hair thicker when she
heard a subtle rustling, together with a strong sensation there was
someone else in the room. She glanced around to see the curtains
were wafting gently. *Oh, it's just the wind* she told herself. She
noticed the goose-bumps prickle up all over arms. A part of her
didn't quite believe her explanation. She went over to the window

and stood a while, looking down at the street below. It was her favorite daydreaming spot. A moment later she noticed her brother, Ian, crossing the street.

Boldly, and somewhat miraculously, weaving his way through oncoming traffic. At one point he even signaled a car to a halt.

Eventually, he meandered his way onto the pavement. *High again.* She thought. *Loaded out of his little mind.*

Just then, two burly men appeared out-of-nowhere. They walked directly up to Ian in a way she knew meant trouble. She watched helplessly as one moved in and pinned him against a railing, the other thrust his face in close to Ian's, talking at him before punching him hard in the gut. She saw her brother double over in pain before toppling over onto the pavement. She couldn't hear what was said, but the hostility was clear. Ian gestured helplessly, turning his palms up in submission. Whatever they wanted, he didn't have it, or he didn't want to give it up. Was it Money? Drugs? Knowing her brother, it could be either. She resisted the urge to run down and intervene. The man punched her brother again, this time in the ribs. As they turned to leave, she caught their faces in the street light. One had heavy-set angular features, a wide brow, flattened nose and chin. His short, greasy black hair was swept back. The other man's face was round, with large wide-open eyes and a mop of unruly blond hair that looked perpetually uncombed. His face was vicious looking. A moment later they jumped into waiting silver Ford Escort and drove off. Their registration number was too obscured in shadow to catch it. Innes ran down to help her brother as he struggled up the porch steps; when she opens the door, he collapsed in her arms.

'Ah, sis, I was…'

'Ssshh…Mum and Dad' ll hear us.' But he was oblivious, in another world; he started ranting and raving. There was no calming him down. Innes had no option but to call an ambulance. When it arrived a few minutes later, Ian thought they'd come to arrest him. He resisted with insane strength, staggering and flailing his arms around wildly. Innes and her parents stood by helplessly as the paramedics restrained him onto a stretcher before injecting him with something to sedate him. She wanted to ride along in the ambulance with him, but her father refused to allow her, shaking his head in disgust. Instead they followed the flashing blue lights in the family Mercedes. Innes felt like a child as she sat in the middle of the back seat while her parents took turns grilling her. She had no choice but to tell them the truth; she regretted it instantly.

'You knew he was lying about his whereabouts! How *dare*

you keep this from us, young lady?' Her mother screeched.

'What the hell did you think would come of lying for him? You should have told us about it all whenever it all started.' Ranted her father.

'How can we help our own son when we've been kept in the dark?' Her mother's eyes were full of fire. 'How could you?' Innes' mind raced and her heart felt heavy as lead. Her parents made her feel like the outsider, as usual. They were always been too busy with their own lives to be involved in their children's; with their dinner parties, important meetings and other *obligations*. They'd never talked to them, they never listened. *What kind of people are they*? She often questioned. *Some people just shouldn't have children*. She'd come to that conclusion long ago.

At the bottom of Liberton Brae, the ambulance sped through the red lights; her father slammed on his breaks and swore under his breath.

'Don't just sit there missy,' he spat 'explain yourself!'
Innes had no words.

'This is all your fault you know,' her mother said with contempt, 'you've been covering up for him, and now look at him. It would never have come to this if you'd used your brain.'

The tension in the car had reached record levels.

'If we'd known what was going on, we'd have been able to sort it out long before now.' Her father's stare was fierce. 'Such a bloody disappointment, the pair of you. Such bloody disappointments!' Innes erupted; she couldn't take any more.

'You would never have believed me anyway, even if I did try to tell you. You never listen to me, ever!' The tears had started streaming down her cheeks. 'According to you, I'm always overreacting, or exaggerating. All you ever do is doubt me!' she screamed. 'That's s all you *ever* do!' The outburst seemed to momentarily stun her parents. It was her father who spoke first.

'What's the use of crying like a wee baby?' he mocked. 'You want treated like an adult, you'd better start behaving like one then.' The response from her mother surprised her.

'Donald, that's not really fair.' She intervened. 'Naturally she's upset. Ian is a grown man now.' He turned on his wife, chastising her for interfering.

'*Interfering*?' Her tone was incredulous. 'At least I bloody try. Not like you sitting up there in your little ivory-tower all day, avoiding coming home.' Now she was crying. It didn't faze him.

'Oh, so now it's *my* fault for the way these brats have turned out? My fault for working my fingers to the bone, just to make sure you all have a nice home and all the things you want; bloody spoilt they are, and you too. You've never wanted for anything and look at how things are now. Innes is just like *you*. Never bloody satisfied, constantly finding fault and shifting the blame!' he was shouting now. 'And him, he's just a big girl's blouse that one, your delicate little Ian!'

No wonder she hadn't told them about any of her brother's problems, no wonder. What would they have done about it anyway? They would have just screamed at her and pointed the finger.

She thought about her brother. She knew for some time he'd been using drugs and she hated it. But she also understood why he did it; to block out his home life; to find a replacement. A "high" to replace the sadness he felt. But he'd become an addict. Not just hooked on the drugs but addicted to the belief they were the solution. Now things had gone too far. Innes knew his loneliness well. They had come to accept the disconnection from their parents. Essentially, they were four individuals related by blood and occupying the same space, that's it. There was no bond. Clearly to them, *parenting* was a job title and that's it. There was no interpersonal responsibility involved. Children were subjects to be owned, not nurtured.

She hung her head. She was so very tired of it all. They were both victims of a much larger disease; dysfunction.

'What right do you have to tell me I interfere?' her mother hissed, 'how would you know, you're never home!' Now they had become more focused on themselves than their son in the ambulance racing ahead. Being a clerk at a prestigious law firm, her mother took everything too seriously. Sure, she still saw to it they got to school, had a freezer full of easy meals and nice clothes on their backs. What more should she be expected to provide? What more could they possibly need? Now they had grown, she took pride in the fact they were self-sufficient, more than other young people their age. But she overlooked a fundamental aspect of being a parent. Just like her workaholic husband, she chose to ignore their need for love and affection; convinced herself that material things were a fair substitute. She was blind to the fact they had grown up to be lonely, needy, and insecure. Totally unaware they were searching for a way out, any way out.

Her parents continued to pass the blame back and forth as they raced towards the hospital and Innes felt physically sick. *Stop this merry-go-round and let me the fuck off.* She wanted to scream. Would they ever show care or the slightest bit of compassion for anyone other than themselves? She wanted to tell them she'd met someone wonderful. Someone who had taught her the importance of mercy and kindness; that we're all connected as beings. The words came out before she realised.

'Do you know, I was telling my spiritual mentor Tyrone all about you both, about how you are and do you know the conclusion we came to? If you put your own bloody self-importance aside for once, you might actually understand why your son behaves the way he does. You might even see how much we've both suffered at your egoism.' Her mother looked as if she'd been slapped.

'Innes, what are you talking about? I've never heard such stupidity. Whoever this fool is, it's time you stopped seeing him. It's clear he's corrupted your mind!'

'For Christ sake, *enough* with this hocus-pocus nonsense.'

Her father countered barely listening. 'It's a firm hand Ian needs…that's all, a firm *hand*! And you, young lady, you're part of all this mess as well remember. The sooner you both get over this

ludicrous, juvenile behaviour; the better life will be for all of us!'
Innes shook her head in disbelief and defeat as the continued the
drive in silence.

CHAPTER NINETEEN

Lomond luxuriated in the realm of lightness she now resided in; she could easily imagine staying there forever. Her vision was clearer, her hearing more acute and her senses keener than they ever were in the physical realm. It was as if she were fully awake in every moment. This state of mind made her spirit soar. Before she'd encountered the Hermit in this blissful domain, she had never considered the possibility of conscious humans being able to enter another realm, even temporarily. She wondered how many others might there be dipping in an out of other realms? *Could there be dozens, hundreds, even thousands more like the Hermit, moving in and out of other dimensions at will?* Witnessing him spiral back into his physical body had been a true revelation, an awakening of the highest order. According to Mrs. R. he was able to propel the energy out of his body whenever he wished; he'd attained a superior level of enlightenment. Lomond wondered if she would have this ability too; once she was back in the physical realm. The thought she might intrigued and encouraged her. She'd been told finding the Hermit might not be so easy; he was the *special soul* Mrs. R. had bid her to look for. Regardless, Lomond decided transferring the learning experiences from one realm to another would be easy; a piece of cake.

'Lass, you'll be lucky to remember anything at *all* of this realm once you return to the physical world. You should prepare yourself for this; the adjustment is difficult for most.' Lomond was unprepared.

'What? I won't remember what I've learned here…about colour…and energy…personalities, none of it?' Her tone was full of panic and disappointment.

'I'm afraid not.'

'Well, what's the bloody point in me being here then?' she demanded. 'I mean, what's the point of learning all this if I can't use it in real life?' To Lomond, it made no sense; it was a serious flaw in the inter-dimensional system.

'If you desire a crossover, a memory, you must sow the seeds of recollection. You need to leave clues for yourself to find later, drop some proverbial bread crumbs if you like. These will activate your learning from the colour realm and allow you to retrieve and apply it in the physical world.' Lomond's face reflected her confusion and sense of betrayal. '*Remembering* comes automatically.' Mrs R. added. 'It occurs through association triggers and requires little, if any effort. *Recollection*, however, requires more. It's a different kind of association; far more subtle.

It may manifest as *Déjà vu*, the feeling you've met a particular individual or visited some place before; but you can't remember when or where. It's up to you to work it out, to recognise the clues. You must assemble the fragments of images and sensations that will help you make sense of these clues. It's like building a puzzle from seemingly random pieces, without knowing the picture in advance.' Lomond tried to imagine what Mrs. R. was describing. 'These moments will come at unexpected times. They will appear as random flashes, images and incomplete thoughts. You will sense they are coming from the back of your mind, from somewhere logical. Their true origin will be hidden, but you must act on them to recollect. Lomond found it difficult to imagine the processes being described. Back in the physical world, she'd never conceived being able to pass through walls, or see rainbows of colours and their energies. *That's sci-fi, right? People can't randomly watch events unfold and others go about their lives from afar, from other realms. What would be the point of having a physical body if you could fly here and there at will? The realities of the physical realm wouldn't really make sense then. The very existence of humankind would be without any purpose.*

'Mrs. R., why is it so hard to travel between the realms?' Lomond asked. 'I mean, when we're in our physical bodies, why can't we remember how?'

'Because the physical body doesn't do the travelling,' Mrs. R. stated. 'It's only when our minds are free of the body that we can achieve the necessary state. Sometimes we do this unconsciously, in our dreams. I'm sure you can recall times when you felt as though you were flying in your sleep? When you felt your body were so light you were floating? You may have even found yourself able to look down at your sleeping self as you are able to now.'

'Yes, yes I've done that!' Lomond responded.

'Do you remember the feeling of falling when you were in that state? Of waking suddenly just before you hit the ground?'

'Yes, I know that feeling,' Lomond answered with a shudder. 'It's terrifying!'

'Well, that occurs when you are just about to wake. Something has most likely disturbed you in your sleep. The sensation you experience when you *jump* from your unconscious to conscious state is your energy jumping back into its physical home, your body. Because of the shock of returning so quickly to your body, for a few moments you're left with this unsettling, out-of-body sensation. Ironically,' said Mrs. R. with a smile, 'children can move between the realms quite effortlessly, at least until they're told they can't. It's a natural ability we're all born with, but it doesn't stay with us unless it's encouraged. We lose it as we grow up and learn the need to fit into the world of adult sensibilities. The thing is, most adults have limited spiritual insight. They become *rational*' Lomond couldn't help think of her own parents with their all too sensible ways. 'As children mature into adults, most of them close up. They suppress and eventually forget their metaphysical inclinations, their natural connection with the spirit world. Very few manage to maintain this this into adulthood,' Mrs R. spoke sadly and Lomond was beginning to feel, to recall how her own spiritual curiosity had been stifled in this way.

'But what's the point of it all being forgotten. It ain't like the 'Normans' are gonna believe you've been there!' Lomond sought to reason and prepare herself.

'Darlin'; it's all part of a much bigger picture. Throughout time, spiritual seekers from all over the world have used methods to empty their minds and gain access to the spirit-realm; to transcend the limitations of their physical bodies and reach higher levels of consciousness. Some have discovered the secrets of energy travel. Through years in isolation they have become more than earth-bound flesh- and-blood; they have mastered how to evolve into other states of being.

In the modern world, the concept of advancing the human spirit has hardly been a priority for world leaders, people in power. They go to great lengths to keep the masses ignorant. For the advancement of social conditioning, we are told what is normal. Dictated about how we ought to live, learn and behave, everyone is expected to follow the grain. Connecting to the spirit-realms is a long way off. This is one of the main reasons why so many young people end up taking drugs and alcohol. They are yearning to reach an altered state of consciousness.'

'Really?' Lomond said, surprised.

'They want to discover their true nature, to feel at one with their inner and outer self. Instinctively they know this lies beyond earthly confines. When we feel we are in our element, we are actually in our purest state. In this pure state, there are endless possibilities to train the mind to leave the physical body and explore other realms, other dimensions. There are many beings that have discovered this process; souls like me try to spread the word.'

As Lomond contemplated Mrs R.'s words, she realised she'd always want to connect with colours and their energies, to feel the prisms of light running through her being. This led her to consider that returning to her lifeless body might be too much of a sacrifice. Who would really miss her anyway? Her parents? They didn't care about her happiness. And what about George? He'd left her on the roadside to die. Her friends all had lives of their own. Why go back to that shallow existence when this realm had so much more to offer? She thought of Tyrone's meditation group; trying desperately to see a connection between the people there and other realms. She decided only a few members had any true potential. The Hermit for sure, perhaps Lorraine, maybe even George. She thought about Innes, who was overburdened with problems of her own, her brother's, her parents' and Tyrone's. Yet it seemed she was still so devoted to finding a spiritual path. She seemed permanently anxious, depressed and emotionally exhausted. Lomond wondered if she had the stability needed to make such a leap into the spirit-colour realm. She realised they all had stifling burdens; layer-upon-layer of perpetuating problems that needed to be separated out from the realms of spirit.

CHAPTER TWENTY

There was something about Mrs. R.'s, unannounced departure that triggered a thought in Lomond; was this her way of indicating she was on her own now? That whatever remaining time she had left in the spirit realm, was hers to use as she chose? What if she decided to remain in this realm forever? It was her decision to make after all…wasn't it? She planned to use her time wisely. Lomond drew in the dark and soothing indigo colour and wrapped it around herself like a cocoon of light. Then she set out to find Innes. Knowing she had to empty her mind of all thoughts and tune into her friends' energy; she visualised Innes. Holding a picture of her firm in her mind, she slowly inhaled and exhaled several times until she felt herself gravitating in her direction.

Upstairs in her room, Innes had been drawing but now she stopped. Her troubled expression indicated she was uncertain about something. Lomond noticed her already pale energy had faded to a mere whisper. Seeing she was feeling unwell, Lomond did something she'd never done before: she swirled the energy she cast, transforming it into a gentle breeze. Though the night air was still, the curtains fluttered playfully and Innes' long brown hair flew up in wisps.

She looked up, getting to her feet and walking to the window; a curious look on her face. There she spotted her brother, Ian; on the street below. Lomond also saw him. She could see his disturbing colours; near black, with flashes and streaks of violet and white. *Addiction* was the first thought that came into her mind; yet something about him was familiar. Then she realised. He was the one who'd confronted Lorraine as she walked through the Meadows that night. Lomond hung close to Innes as troubling events unfolded. Seeing the brother and sister together, Lomond could feel the loneliness they shared; she sensed there were deep-seated problems. Being with her in the back of the car, it was clear how her parents had substituted love and nurturing for discipline and ambitions. They treated their children as objects, part of a misguided process expected to play out like a fairy tale. Lomond stayed with her as the ambulance came to a screeching halt at the Emergency Department. She was there in the waiting room as the doctor approached to ask questions. She watched on as Innes cowered into a small ball in the chair after she left. Her parents were nowhere in sight.

'Hello Innes, my name Detective Sergeant Jordan. I've been called in by the hospital staff, due to the nature of your brother's injuries.' Innes nodded. 'I've spoken with your parents. I understand you witnessed the events that occurred, your brother's attack? Would it be alright if I asked you a few questions?' Despite her despair, Innes sensed something keeping her upright, as if she was being held. It was a comfort. Suddenly she no longer felt alone, or helpless. *Yes, I would like to help.* As she drew courage, her bag fell from the arm of the chair, seemingly of its own accord. Pencils and markers tumbled out and fooled around the floor.

'Perhaps you'd prefer to go out somewhere more private?' the detective asked. Innes looked at her and nodded. She gathered her drawing tools and the two of them stepped out into the corridor. She was led into a small side room with a table and chairs.

'You let Ian into the house tonight, is that correct?' D. S. Jordan asked, pen and pad in hand. Innes cleared her throat before answering.

'Yes, I let him in.'

'Was anyone with him?' Innes looked at the detective. Beyond her starched grey trouser suit, her eyes were kind and considerate.

'Not when I helped him into the house, but I did see two men before that, when I was upstairs looking out the window.' She responded.

'What did you see exactly?' asked the DS, scribbling into her notebook.

'I saw them shoving and threatening him. They had him pinned against the railing outside our house. One of them held him while the other punched him in the stomach.'

'Can you describe the men for me?' An expression of doubt came across Innes' face. 'It would be a great help if we could get some idea of who we're dealing with.' Detective Jordan added, her tone hopeful.

Confusion contorted Innes' memory as she tried to picture the faces of the men. After some time she was able to manage a rough description.

'Are you interested in art?' The detective asked as she led her back along the corridor. Then before she had a chance to answer, 'You know, when I was a wee lass, all I ever wanted to do was draw horses.' she said fondly. 'Any free minute, you would find me with my pencils and pad, sketching away.' Innes began to open up. She told her she loved art, she hoped to continue her studies at

Edinburgh Art College. It was the way in the D.S was looking for.

'I'd *love* to see some of your work.' Jordan said, prompting Innes to stop and pull her pad from her bag. Standing in the middle of the corridor, the detective flipped through the pages. She noticed several well-drawn, rough portraits.

'Wow, you have a knack for capturing the real likeness' she complimented. You know Innes, anything else you can remember about the men you saw, anything at *all*, would be so helpful. We'd like to track them down. Based on similar reports, we suspect they are prolific drug dealers. If we you can give us a solid description; it could help us break up one of Edinburgh's most notorious drug gangs. Do you think you could draw them for us?' Although fear made her reluctant, Innes wanted to help; if for no other reason than to help her brother. She agreed to try and draw the faces of the men she'd seen under the street light. DS Jordan handed her card over; telling her to contact her as soon as she had something, day or night.

'It's not just Ian you'll be helping, Innes. You'll be helping a lot of other young people who've been targeted by these thugs.'

That night Innes spent hours sketching and re-sketching, until she was satisfied. The next morning, she contacted the D.S. She had two likenesses of the men she'd seen.

'This is what I can remember of them,' she told the detective when she arrived at Innes' home. The Detective smiled as she held the images at arms'-length.

'These are fantastic, thank you so much!' she stated with a distinct tone of satisfaction. 'these could be just what we need to help us find the men responsible.' Innes felt good to have been able to help, but a part of her was afraid. She knew that if they did find them, the police would her to identify them in person and then she might be called as a witness. She'd have to go to court and testify against them. The thought of this terrified her so as much as it would if she were waiting for her own trial.

CHAPTER TWENTY-ONE

George awoke to the sun streaming in through the sheer bedroom curtains. He opened his eyes a slit before closing them again. For a while he basked in the warmth of the sun and the sound of Lorraine's soft, rhythmic breathing beside him; enjoying the contentment. But then the illusion burst. Reality flooded in like a dark cloud and his mind churned with worry and anxiety. *You must tell all.* The Hermit's words of advice replayed. *Like it was that simple.* Sure, Lorraine thought it was, but he needed a plan. He needed to think things through. He could just turn up at the station and own up for leaving the scene, for being the one driving. But then what? How was he going to keep himself out of prison? How could he afford a lawyer to represent him? What if Lomond's father insisted he pay compensation on top of whatever punishment they gave him? Lorraine stirred beside him, snuggling in closer. Suddenly, his faith in the Hermit's advice had waned.

Over coffee and toasted hot-cross buns, tension was growing. Lorraine promised she would stand by him no matter what, she loved him. She said the words, but to him they were just that. The right words people say because they think that's what you want to hear. *Would she really stay in a poky little attic room waiting for me to come out of prison? Or would she go on with her life as if I never existed?*

'George, we'll take things one step at a time.' she tried to reassure him. But nothing could soothe his mounting fear. Fact was fact: he'd be a dead-weight around her neck and it wasn't fair to her. She should find someone else and move on 'What about this?' Lorraine suggested. 'Let's speak to someone who knows more about this than us. We can find out the worst that can happen; for leaving the scene of an accident? Surely it will still go in your favour if you come forward now, better *now* than not at all eh? We can ask around, just to be certain.' Even with this new possibility, George's heart was racing and his breaths getting shorter. The desire for everything to be back to how it was before the accident overwhelmed him, he felt so hopeless. It was affecting his reasoning. He searched his mind frantically for a place to run and hide from the truth. Seeing the rising panic, Lorraine took his hand in hers. 'I know it'll be rough,' she said soothingly, 'but you've got to make the first move. It'll be far worse if you sit back and do nothing. Please, let me ask around and see what I can find out.' George could see the logic, but he needed to confide in someone other than Lorraine. She was too close. More and more he found he couldn't think clearly in her presence; she was starting to stifle him. Mint's face flashed into his mind. He trusted Mint, trusted his judgment.

'I'll go talk to Mint about it,' he said. 'He knows a lot of people.' Lorraine agreed he was a good place to start.

'Okay, just let me throw something on and I'll come with…'

'No, I need to do this myself.' He interrupted. 'I'll let you know how it goes.'

'Well, okay,' Lorraine answered; her expression somewhat crestfallen. 'If that's what you think you should do.' George pulled on his boots, slipped on his jacket.

'Yeah, that's what I'll do, he'll be able to help.' Then without another word, he stepped out and pulled the door shut behind him.

His gaze was fixed straight ahead as he made his way to the Meadows, heading straight for Mint's usual pitch. His friend saw him coming and waved from a distance.

'Well, if it's not lover-boy!' he teased as George came striding up. His expression changed when he saw the look of concern on George's face.

'Trouble in Paradise mate?' he asked, half trying to lighten the mood.

'Have you got a few minutes?' George asked.

'Anything for you buddy.' With the sun climbing into the near-by grove of alders, they sat on the grass under a shady Elm and Mint listened intently as George told him his story; nodding in understanding and encouragement.

'Do you know anyone we could ask about the likelihood of prison, of how much time?'

'Sure,' Mint said, looking thoughtful, 'I know a DS we can ask on the sly, he's *cool*. He'll know I'm askin' for a mate but he won't ask questions. I'll just have to owe him one.' George relaxed a bit. 'For my money's worth, it'll all hinge on Lomond pulling through though.' Mint added and George's face fell. 'Hey, don't sweat it man. It'll work out.' Mint struck a chord on his guitar before adding philosophically, 'It ain't like you meant to do it, and there were lots of other factors involved.' Now he sounded like Lorraine. 'I'll let you know as soon as I hear something.' George nodded and thanked him before heading off.

Back at Lorraine's flat, he told her about Mint's D.S. friend and his opinion it would depend on Lomond's recovery. Lorraine agreed Lomond's case looked positive; she didn't mention there were cases of coma victims who never recovered consciousness.

'I've got another idea,' she said. 'I think it would be good for me to talk to Lomond's parents, to persuade them you might be the one person who can bring Lomond back to consciousness, that we need to find you…for her sake.' George was quiet some time while he mulled this over, he knew they hated him, but he was running out of options.

'Aye, why not.' He agreed reluctantly. 'Maybe if they ain't so fixed on havin' my head on a spike, they might not make things worse for me at least.'

'Oh, one more thing,' Lorraine said, 'before you talk to police, it might help you to go back to the scene of the accident, to try piece things together. Maybe it'll jog your memory, give you something to use as defence.' Since the accident had occurred at night and George hadn't got back to his room until the next morning, it was clear he'd lost some time. He remembered seeing the clock at Haymarket Station, but before that, everything was more or less a blank. He agreed he had nothing to lose.

Back on night shift, Lorraine made her rounds. She entered Lomond's room where the girl lay still. Her eyes were closed and wore nasal specs with tubes inserted in each nostril, one for oxygen, one for the drip-feed. Lorraine checked her vitals and reflexes for any significant changes. Sliding a chair up to the side of her bed, she sat down, took her hand and closed her eyes. She took a few breaths and focused her mind. She began reciting names she knew would be familiar to Lomond, the names of friends and family who'd visited. Maria, Tracy, Innes… her mum and dad and the dog, Shuna. Seeing no reaction, she leaned in close and whispered in Lomond's ear, '*George.*' Instantly, Lomond's eyes flickered behind her eyelids and one eye seemed to want to open. Lorraine's heart skipped a beat. *I'm onto something.* Then, as if in slow motion, Lorraine felt herself become light. Her ears strained to a sound, like the buzz of electricity. She watched as a soft and airy mist descended from somewhere above. Slowly it engulfed her and everything in the room seemed to vanish, everything except Lomond. She felt somehow connected to this girl lying on the bed and a feeling of peace washed over her. Lorraine smiled as she noticed Lomond's lips part. A hand on her shoulder startled her back into the room. Confused and shaking, she turned to see another nurse standing beside her. Looking back at Lomond, she thought she saw the quiver of a smile play on her lips. She squeezed her hand, and something in her seemed to respond. It was clear they were somehow linked. She wasn't sure how and where but she suspected it was beyond the physical realm.

In the spirit realm, Lomond felt connected to Lorraine; physically and through the senses and for a moment, she felt the mass of her own body as she lay on the bed. The appearance of the other nurse and the sensation of Lorraine's energy jumping back into her body caused Lomond to jump out of hers again. The last thing she heard was his name, George.

Now she found herself with him. He was alone. He was headed for The Grassmarket Mission. He was hungry, couldn't remember the last time he had eaten. The usual woman was there ladling out bowls of broth from an old-fashioned stainless-steel jug; a selfless old lady who always had a kind word. Magenta shone richly from around her and Lomond could sense her warm, open heart. Magenta energy signified composure and genuine nurturing love. Helping others was clearly second-nature to her and she radiated compassion.

'What's up today luvvy?' she asked with a toothy smile.

'Oh, same old shite.' George replied, frowning, accustomed to dishing out a bit of free advice with her delectable broth, she spoke wisely.

'You know George, I used to be full of negative thoughts once.' He looked up guardedly. 'See, my husband was a boozer, he beat me, gambled and one day just up and left me for a younger model. He was a real *bawbag*, if you excuse my crudeness. Caused me so much sufferin' in our marriage, a dark cloud always seemed to be followin' me round. Then after he was gone, it was as if I finally started to wake up. All my depressin' and negative started to fade. Replaced by positive happy ones of how it used to be before he came into my life. I realised I'd allowed bitterness to take over. I created my own prison I was livin' in, not my husband. I realised that until I unlocked the door to the outside, I'd never be free or find peace. I could never be the real me. I had to *choose* to view my life differently, see it for what it really was. Once I walked out of that prison, I was free to do whatever I *chose*. Since then, I've never let my thoughts control me. Feel myself again. It didn't happen overnight of course; it took a bit work. But I did it. And George, you can too. We all have the ability. You can choose to leave your troubles in the past and get on with your life, find happiness.' She smiled as she handed George his bowl of soup.

Pondering the old woman's advice to George, Lomond's thoughts turned to her father, Mac. It suddenly occurred to her that he'd all but slipped from her mind. Now she realised she really missed him. Pangs of love and compassion for what he must be going through rose suddenly to the surface. It struck her how selfish she'd been. Despite their differences, he was her dad. She knew he'd be distraught at seeing her lying in a hospital bed hour after hour, day after day. She knew he'd be chain-smoking and pacing the floor in despair. She felt a sudden rush of love for him and wondered why this hadn't occurred to her before. No thought of her mother came to mind.

CHAPTER TWENTY-TWO

When Lorraine arrived on the ward on Monday evening, Lomond's parents were already there. *She* was seated with a stern and impatient look on her face whilst her father paced the floor; looking lost and frustrated.

'We want to thank you for the care and attention you've shown our daughter.' Mac said sincerely as she entered the room. Her first thought was to minimalise her part. Perhaps tell them she was only doing her job. However, she knew that was far from the truth and far from what Lomond's parents needed to hear right now. Her involvement had gone against hospital policy, moved way beyond the professional, to a deep and profound personal interest. In order for her to bring up the subject of George, she'd need to show she had a special interest in their daughter.; but she'd have to be tactful. She considered telling them she had been speaking the names of people in Lomond's life, that she had reacted to the utterance of George. She decided this might seem a bit too suspicious, they would wonder how she knew him. She was still working out a way to broach the subject when Lomond's mother spoke.

'You know, nurse...uh...Lorraine, Lomond's birthday is

coming up soon, she'll be sixteen on Friday. We were thinking of having a little party for her. What do you think? Maybe invite a few of her friends over, just close ones of course. We could even have a bit of cake and ice-cream...,'

Beth sounded hopeful.

'I think that's a wonderful idea, Mrs. Mitchieson. It could be very helpful for her recovery. Hearing her friend's voices could have a very positive effect.' Inside, Lorraine was secretly delighted. It was also the perfect opportunity for George to make his entrance. Excited at the prospect of a party, Beth went off to discuss details with the floor nurse, leaving Lorraine and Mac on their own.

'What do you think her chances really are, Lorraine?' Mac asked wearily, as if bracing for the worst prognosis.

'Personally, I think they're pretty good, Mr Mitchieson,' she replied. 'You just wait and see.'

'Oh please call me Mac.' Lorraine nodded.

'Of course, well *Mac*. You see yesterday, I sat with her for a while and I'm quite sure I saw her smile, just for a fleeting second but a smile nonetheless. I'd been reciting the names of her friends, you know, *Maria* and *Tracy* and *Innes,* the one who sent the lovely hand-drawn cards. I mentioned a name I overheard one of the girls say, it seemed like this person was quite important to her. When I said the name I'm certain her eyes flickered. I can't be a hundred percent sure she wasn't just dreaming, but…'

'What name was that?' Mac interrupted. Lorraine took her chance.

'Emm…it was *George*. Is he a classmate…a relative…a boyfriend maybe?' Mac winced.

'Well, yes, I suppose that's how Lomond might think of him; as a boyfriend. But he's nothing but trouble. It was his bike they were riding when the accident happened. And instead of coming forward to take responsibility, or see how Lomond is, he just disappears. We don't want to hear how or where he is, unless it's behind bars!' Lorraine thought carefully. How was she going to persuade the grieving and rightfully angry father?

'Mac, I think I may be able help,' she said. 'I really want to help Lomond.' She had his undivided attention now. It was now or never. I might know how to find this George.' Mac looked at her suspiciously.

'So, it was him I saw.' He said under his breath. 'I bet the torag has been visiting Lomond on the sly. Mac was lost for words; he couldn't bring himself to show his frustration to the woman dedicating so much of her time to care for his daughter.

Lorraine continued.

'I know this may be the last idea you'd normally consider, but if I could get word to him, do you think he should be invited to the party?' Mac's eyes narrowed with contempt. Why should they invite him to a gathering of people honouring his daughter?

'I wouldn't normally suggest it Mac, but I think it could make all the difference for Lomond,' she encouraged. 'Whatever your differences, his presence, perhaps his voice, they could be just what Lomond needs to help her regain consciousness.' *Lomond smiled from somewhere above. She realised just how much she was missing her old life and she felt a deep longing to reclaim it.* Lorraine could see Mac was partly convinced on the idea.

'As far as we know, he's wanted by the authorities though.' He said.

'Well, why don't we cross that bridge when we come to it? If he can help Lomond, and he's willing to do it…' Mac followed her logic; he just wanted his daughter back.

'Okay, if you can manage it, go ahead and ask him.' Lorraine broke into a radiating and encouraging smile and taking his hand, she said,

'Everything's going to work out, I'm sure of it.' Mac looked into her hopeful eyes. He was relieved to hear words of encouragement. However, he never imagined his daughter's saviour would come in the form of her offender. Just then, Beth returned with her birthday approval.

'There can be no candles due to the oxygen, but the party is allowed, as long as there are no more than eight people in the room at once; cake and ice-cream is fine too.' She took a pad and pencil from her handbag and began making a check-list of things to buy, things to do. It took a few minutes for her to register Mac was bursting to tell her something.

'What is it?' she snipped and Mac cleared his throat before speaking.

'Dear, Lorraine thinks she knows how to locate George.' Beth's eyes widened in surprise and deep suspicion, 'We've had a chat about it and I agree. We think it would be a good idea to invite George to Lomond's birthday. His presence might be exactly what she needs to bring her back to us.' Beth glared blankly from her husband to Lorraine as she tried to fathom their plan. The hostility bubbling under the surface was tangible. This was the *last* thing she'd expected to hear.

'*What?* Did I just hear you right? You're suggesting we invite George? The very same irresponsible lout who's near killed our daughter and ran off to avoid jail? You want *him* to attend

Lomond's birthday party?' Beth was incredulous. Mac never responded. Instead he turned calmly to Lorraine.

'Alright,' he said kindly, 'we won't ask how you know his whereabouts or why you think you can convince him to risk being arrested. But, if you can persuade him to come Friday night, I think it's worth a shot, for Lomond's sake.' Lorraine was relieved, but she kept her composure; finally, an opportunity to set things right. Beth grabbed her handbag and stormed from the room.

CHAPTER TWENTY-THREE

It was dusk when George got off the bus opposite the Maybury Hotel. He started out along the airport road, passing the row of houses set back from the road and before long he was heading out into the open countryside. As he neared the destination, he suddenly felt sick inside. But he knew he had to do it. He needed to visit the scene of the accident and try and relive the night, the best he could. He needed to recall what had actually occurred; if he was to make any kind of case for himself to the authorities. Lorraine had said something about his *inner sun* and something about his *ego* deceiving and misleading him. His head was beginning to hurt with all her mumbo-jumbo. He appreciated her help, but her rose-tinted views were getting tiresome. All she seemed to do was *think, think, think*; but she still didn't seem to understand how he really felt. However, he realised he might not be here, revisiting the crime scene, if she hadn't pushed him. As walked along, dark thoughts took hold of his mind, pulling him into the present drama and self-doubt. *Why am I making this journey now and not before? Was I waiting for all the pieces of the puzzle to fit into a safe, reassuring picture? Was I waiting for my fears to be proved right?* He pulled the collar of his jacket up tight against his neck. A chilly breeze was coming from the north-west; from the direction he was heading. From the Maybury Hotel, there was a mile of roadside for him to walk along before he reached the bend. As he made his way along the road, he remembered the way the bend had come upon him; much quicker than he'd expected. He saw remembered the blinding lights, the bike skidding and the sensation of it sliding out from under him. Then nothing. He didn't even recall the wailing of sirens he was sure that followed. He continued, where was it? He beat his hands together to generate heat, and out of nervousness. What about his helmet? He wondered if he would find it.

Walking steadily, it took him nearly twenty minutes to reach the bend. It was a junction where another road joined from the east. Just beyond, he noticed a small row of houses and a farm. This was where it happened. He was sure of it. Here he crossed the road. It appeared much less ominous than he remembered it. He noticed a hedge running along the road side. He peered over it and back to the road. In the dimming light, he could just about make out a heap of tussled straw. Then a memory came. That was the spot where he'd landed; it had probably saved his life. It looked like a field that grew vegetables and the straw was down to protect them from the frost He must have been thrown clean over the hedge. A few yards further along he noticed a gate. He pushed it open, ignoring the NO TRESSPASSING signs, wandered into the field. He sat down on the bed of straw and glanced up at the late afternoon sky; just as an airplane was passing low with its landing-lights blinking. The sound it made seconds later told him it had landed nearby. He heard the lonely whistle of a distant train. The noise jogged his memory again. It was the same sound that had led him to the railway line that morning. With renewed enthusiasm, he stood up and began searching for his lost helmet. No luck. He walked to the edge of the field and followed its plough line. His ears caught the sound of a windsock whacking; marking the end of runway. He came to the barbed wire fence that divided the field from the railway line. Another memory flashed in his mind. He'd caught his trouser leg that night, scaling the barbed-wire fence. Looking now, he noticed a swathe of black leather pinned to one of the jagged barbs, fluttering in the breeze. He left it there, certain it would match the hole in his trousers. He looked up the tracks. The line was a straight run into the city. Now he remembered walking along the tracks in the dark. He recalled reaching a bridge, he wasn't sure, but he thought it was near a farm. He peered ahead. Yes, he could just make out the dark shape of the old stone trestle, arched over the line. He proceeded along the tracks and reached the bridge. Beyond it, the embankment steepened and the line passed under the main road. The feelings of dread and revulsion he felt as he trod along the sleepers that night came back to him; the eeriness of it all. He came off the track and reached the bus shelter at Corstorphine; another flicker of recognition as he recalled sitting in it. A bigger picture began to form in his mind. It was raining. He was exhausted. That must have been why he'd stopped and waited there. Now, he stood in the shelter and looked idly at the timetable behind the glass screen; his memory clearing slowly. The first bus into town was 5:50 a.m. Of course, he'd taken that first morning bus.

'Evening.' The voice startled him back to the present. A man walking a panting German Shepherd approached him; its tail wagging. 'Don't take any notice of her lad, she's just an old softie! Couldn't bite through a biscuit, that one.' He said with a grin. 'Come on, Bess, we're off for home now.' Bess gave George a friendly sniff and turned on her tail. Then in an instant he remembered. He'd run into this man walking his dog before. George called out to the man.

'Uh, excuse me, but do you happen to remember me? It's been a while now, it was early morning, I was at the bus stop? Do you remember? You asked me if I'd fallen.' The man turned and leaned on a walking stick; a look of recognition came across his face.

'Heavens, lad, it's *you*. My goodness, you must have took one heck of a tumble, I could see that much.' he said with a nod. 'You had one heck of a bump on your head. I asked if there was anything I could do to help, but you didn't answer. I thought maybe you could do with a cuppa. You didn't seem quite right to me, a wee bit confused I dare say. Anyway, you're alright, I see. That's good. Of course, I remember you!' George thanked the man for his concern that morning and he continued on with his dog. A few strides later, he turned back to face George.

'Say, I found a motorcycle helmet after you'd gone. Might it be yours? I found it sittin' there in the shelter.' *So that's where it ended up.*

'Yes! Yes, that's mine.' He said struggling to contain his excitement.

'Well if you come on back to my house, you can take it back,' the man offered, motioning ahead. George realised then; the old man could be a great help to him. He might be able verify his memory loss, help him prove there was a reason he hadn't gone to the police straight away. Back at the house the old man told him all he could remember; it wasn't a lot, but it was something. It was clear George was disoriented when the man had run into him at the bus stop.

'Like I say, lad, you didn't seem quite right to me.'

'Thank you so much. You've been so helpful, more than even realise.' George smiled. 'Well, if I can be of any more help, don't hesitate to drop in.' he said.

George made his way back to the bus shelter with his helmet tucked under his arm. He jumped on the next bus into the city and hopped off at Haymarket. He walked briskly back to his flat on Grove Street, his head filled with a renewed sense of hope and self-confidence. He studied his door momentarily from a safe distance before climbing the steps and letting himself in; scared to make a sound or turn on a light. He climbed into his bed and had the best night's sleep he'd had since the accident.

CHAPTER TWENTY-FOUR

He meant to wake early. He wanted to catch Lorraine as she came off the night-shift; to tell her about his adventure and about meeting the old man with the friendly dog. When he woke the clock read 11:00. It was too late. *Never mind*, he thought, *I'll catch her later.* Meeting the old man had given him hope and a new perspective about the events of that night. He began to remember things from before. How the bike hadn't wanted to start that day, about how he hadn't been able to find the new helmet he'd bought for Lomond. He'd settled on bringing the old, cracked one because he was already late to pick her up. Now he realised it had likely split, with Lomond's head taking the brunt of the impact. He could almost feel her pain. Why hadn't he listened to the little voice that warned him not to go. *Not tonight.* It had told him. He'd ignored it and now all this.

Just before noon he slipped out the flat and headed directly to the Meadows to look for Mint. He wasn't there. *Well, I Guess I might as well go now and get it over with,* he decided. It hadn't been the original plan, but his conscience was prompting him and this time he decided he would listen to it. He walked to the police station; a red-stone building that seemed to be glowing in the afternoon sun. It sat on the corner of St Leonard's Street and a narrow, cobbled street running towards Holyrood Park. He could see the steep face of the Salisbury Crags silhouetted in a gap at the end. For a fleeting moment he considered doing a runner into the park. He imagined himself climbing to the top of the cliff and jumping off. *There over and done with.* He looked up curiously. He could make out the shapes of two lithe stick-figures holding hands on the top. *That could be me and Lorraine* he mused. He climbed the well-worn, hewn-granite steps of the station and entered. He told the enquiry desk he'd like to report himself as a witness to an accident; a motorcycle accident. They saw him without hesitation. He was shown to a small room with a metal table and chairs painted glossy, battleship grey. He took a seat and almost immediately, two officers came in; a man of about thirty and a woman in her early twenties. They asked for his identification. When he told what accident he had information about, they retrieved a small tape recorder from a supply drawer and informed him that they would be recording the interview.

All-in-all, the process was much easier and painless than he expected it to be. The questions were straightforward. Time, date, location, details as they occurred. At the end, the male officer switched off the recorder and looked at George.

'You've done the right thing lad. We'll have to charge you for now though, for leaving the scene of an accident, for failing to report it. Depending on the circumstances we might have to charge you with reckless endangerment too, but in the end the formal charges will depend on whether the girl recovers. For now, you'll be released and you'll receive a summons to testify in court. As I said, you've done the right thing here.'

'What about the old man?' asked George.

'His address in Corstorphine is on record now and we'll be speaking with him soon.'

George asked what the maximum penalty might be in a case like this. The male officer was direct.

'If the girl recovers and is able to corroborate your account of the events that night, it'll make a big difference in the court's ruling. If she's sustained no permanent damage and there are no charges levelled by the parents, a heavy fine and community service will be the likely outcome.' He asked about his bike. They told him it was sitting in the police compound. The female officer said they'd examined it and the skid marks at the scene of the accident. They'd calculated the speed the bike was travelling as well as George's reaction time, information they were not at liberty to disclose just now. As a matter of formality, George would be required to identify the bike as his. Depending on a number of factors, he may or may not get it back eventually.

He had a bounce in his step as he walked out of the station. *Confession is good for the soul.* He'd heard this once and now it rang true. He made his way back to the Meadows and was delighted to see Mint. His friend was so pleased and relieved for him.

'Come on, let's celebrate! he said, placing his hand on George's shoulder and almost frog-marching him towards their favourite watering hole. On their way to the bar, Mint relayed the intelligence from his D.S. friend. It correlated with what the police had told him. They met up with some of Mint's street friends at the bar. George was soon caught up in some of their wild stories, the time passed too quickly and before he knew it, he'd missed meeting Lorraine before her night-shift. Mint treated him to see a war flick at the old theatre and afterwards they sat under the park lights and talked deep into the night.

He left Mint and staggered back to his flat along his old route.

No need to hide anymore, he was no longer a wanted man. He let himself in noisily and snapped on all the lights; just because he could. Falling into bed, he reminded himself he needed to stay awake so he could meet up with Lorraine after shift. He lay there staring at the ceiling, reflecting on an extraordinary day.

He was convinced that by re-living the accident and going to the police with his story, he had somehow negated the wrongs he'd done. It *re-booted* his self-confidence. He knew it took inner fortitude to confront his fears and demons. He learnt his lesson.

For the second time in his life that he could remember, he'd put someone else's needs before his own. He sacrificed himself because he *needed* to own-up to what he'd done. Now he could move forward with his life. He thought about Lorraine's advice, how facing your fear was only the first step. How shining a light on imperfections would allow him to see them clearly; how real change took time. Though he hadn't done it for the praise, he hoped it might garner some respect from outsiders. Perhaps, Lomond's parents might see him in a kinder light. Within minutes; he'd dozed off.

CHAPTER TWENTY-FIVE

Ian was transferred to the Royal Edinburgh Psychiatric Hospital. They were going to keep him under observation, *indefinitely*. It was a horrible place to visit, even more horrible to reside in. The wards were under heavy lock and key with nurses stationed at the entrance like prison guards. The rooms were divided into non-descript yellow cubicles, each with tiny matching barred windows; the whole place felt dingy and depressing. Paint peeled from the walls, sometimes removed and chewed upon by some of the patients. The smell of faeces, urine and vomit throughout made the stomach churn. Innes was certain being in here could only make a person feel worse; no matter their state of mind. It felt like the end of the road. While visiting her brother, she saw other young people whose lives had been lost to drugs. Many of them looked defeated and disconnected as they peered hopelessly from hollow, darkened eyes. Those that weren't heavily sedated were restrained in their rooms. Seeing them helped her make up her mind. She picked up the pay phone and punched in the number and answer machine clicked on.

'D.S Jordan, its Innes, I think I can help,' she said. 'I've remembered a few things.'

Innes accepted the invitation from Lomond's mother. She would attend her birthday gathering that Friday. Even though it seemed slightly inappropriate since the guest-of-honour may not be present as it were. She needed to let Tyrone know. Fridays were the day she cleaned the meditation room and he depended on her to do it. In truth, she was growing a little tired of being Tyrone's maidservant; dusting and sweeping, polishing his brass. She was beginning to feel used and un-appreciated, maybe it was time she found a real job; something nearer to home, one that actually paid her a decent wage. When she got home, a message had been left for her to contact the police. She did straight away and made an appointment to see D.S. Jordan. The, taking a deep breath she called Tyrone to break the news. Just as she suspected, he didn't hide his disappointment, said he was counting on her. A special delegation from Bhutan, in the Himalayas was coming. Innes apologised, feeling terrible, but she held her ground. This was something she needed to do. He was still talking when she hung up the phone.

A part of Tyrone wished he hadn't lied. There was no delegation coming from Bhutan—or anywhere else. The truth was, he looked forward to her weekly visits. Increasingly, she'd become a pleasant distraction from his other bleak dealings. It gave his ageing ego a charge. Though once a charming and handsome man, with his pick of young adoring women, he was now beginning to wither. His features had become overly angular and awash in grey. Sweet Innes seemed to be about the only person left in his life who idolized him, the only one who could nourish his flagging self-image. More than once he'd tested her level of devotion; by brushing his hand casually across her ample breasts, or down her back and across her taut young bottom. He'd even moved in for a kiss once and he nearly got one back. He wondered if she was still a virgin. He doubted it; and so, what if she were? More than once he'd confided, telling her special men like him had extra special *needs*. Age meant nothing, only dedication and purity of heart mattered.

'You're so important to me,' he'd flatter. But now she wasn't coming, now she was hanging up on him? There was something else. An envelope sat on top of a pile of unopened bills and notices on the mahogany desk, waiting to be opened. He knew from the postmark where it had come from; his mother's solicitors. He poured himself a triple measure of stiff malt whisky. Raising the hexagonal crystal glass to his lips he closed his eyes and downed half the fiery liquid. It felt fiery and treacle-soft as it slid down his throat and into his gut. He waited for it to take effect; for his courage to arrive. Finally, he picked it up and sliced open the top with his hand-carved ivory letter opener. *'Dear Mr. Monteith, it is with deepest concern that we write to you following our last communication of the 16th...* He skipped on. *'We await your instructions and anticipate that this matter can be settled post haste. Yours Sincerely...Senior Financial Adviser, Heathcliff & Son.'*

'Damn, damn, bloody *damn.'* he said before smashing his glass against the wall. So, there it was. Tyrone's world was collapsing around him. He knew it was only a matter of time before his other *indiscretions* would demand accountability. A wave of anxiety gripped his chest. Laying the letter aside he got up and headed for the upstairs bathroom. Careful to avoid his reflection in the mirror, he opened the medicine cabinet looking for his sedatives. He couldn't find them. 'You forgot to get a bloody re-fill you absolute twat!' he scolded himself. Closing the cabinet door, he stared mockingly at the haggard face looking back; a greying man with a quickly retreating hairline. Time had not been kind to him and he looked much older than his years. He pursed his lips in self-disgust. His dark past floated in and out of his consciousness, like a phantom haunting a dilapidated manor. He'd buried his demons but they were threatening to rise and consume him; his chest tightened again. Suddenly he saw another face in the mirror. Not his own, but the craggy, wizened face of the Hermit. Then, for a fleeting second, he was no longer standing before the mirror in his bathroom. He was staring into the gaping maw of a wild and primitive place, but just as quickly as it came the vision was gone. He felt the small amount of inner fortitude he had left begin to crumble. The sight of the Hermit plunged him into deeper gloom and desperation. His little meditation group had been mesmerised by the old man. That was not the effect he'd hoped for. They'd listened to him so intently, were sucked into his stories in a way they had never been drawn into his own.

'*Shit.*' He muttered to his reflection. 'I'm losing *everything*. My crazy fucking mother! *She's* to blame, that wretched old bag!' As far as he was concerned, it was *she* who wanted to sell the house out from under him. *She* who wanted to take away his home on India Street, to strip it of his beloved tapestries and everything he'd acquired through his years of clever scheming. If he didn't come up with a solution quick, he'd be left with nothing. He'd be living on the street, disgraced.

Tyrone had accepted many years before that as long as he coveted material possessions; the path to true spirituality would always elude him. Once he'd admitted this to himself, and that he hadn't the willpower to change it; he embraced using his *gifts* for material gain; for power and status, and to lure young women into his bed. Despite preaching there was genuine freedom in love; he could not seem to implement this in his own life. Inside he was a weak and deeply insecure man. He loathed the powers-that-be for making him this way; for cheating him of the lofty place he deserved. Moreover, he quietly loathed who he had become. He knew most people did not see the envy that drove him, he hid it so well. However, it was certain a few did. In all his past relationships, he'd always ended up controlling them both mentally and physically; convincing himself that he was *protecting and cherishing* them. He knew he was avaricious; out of control but he couldn't stop. He'd led a cold, lonely and detached life. A life fed by other people and material things. He used the belief he was created for a higher purpose to rationalize his behaviour. Despite how in-sincere, he convinced himself he was entitled to unlimited carnal pleasures. But now, with such pleasures growing fewer and further between, he was determined not to let any of them slip through his fingers.

The doorbell rang, interrupting his thoughts. He descended the staircase in his silk Japanese "happy" coat, a gift from a former student. He opened the door and Innes was stunned when she saw him; his robe hanging open, revealing his bare body. He reeked of stale whisky and his eyes were mere slits against the unrelenting rays of the sun. She almost turned and walked away, but the look of relief on his face stopped her; she couldn't bring herself to desert him. To her, he had always been the epitome of the spiritual *ideal*. She didn't want to see him like this. Like a once grand marble statue crumbling from his lofty pedestal.

There seemed nothing serene or sublime about him now. Tyrone ushered her inside with a deep and dramatic bow. She followed him into the lounge and by the large bay window. Almost immediately, she realised she'd made a mistake; he never needed her to clean for him. As he broke into ranting soliloquy of accusation, condemnation, and logorrhoea; she grew angry with herself for believing him; only a simple-minded sycophant would follow so blindly. He just needed someone to prop him up. She began to doubt if there was any truth to his stories whatsoever. His epic adventures in Bhutan, Nepal, and Tibet, and all the great spiritual teachers who'd "blessed" him and his work. Maybe they were all mere legends he'd created and came to believe for himself. They supported his delusion of self-grandeur.

'Do you know, before he sent me away to boarding school, I had a string of different nannies,' he said, topping-up his glass, 'attractive young things they were. I remember *him* doting on them all, fawning on them in front of my mother; the self-centred *bastard*. Our house, I won't dignify it by calling it a *home*, was like a ball of toxic gases always ready explode.' He looked up to the heavens. 'That first visit to school, the wrought-iron gates, the long driveway and pillared entrance. I was only seven years old. *We'll take you along to your dormitory now, say goodbye to your parents.* Footsteps along dark, cold corridors and never-ending staircases. I never stood a *fucking* chance! They ragged me about my name. '*Tyrone the twat, 'Tyrone the titty-baby*. My father, the sick son-of-a-bitch, he was nothing but ashamed of me. "Get off your bony arse and show some *guts,* for Christ's sake." He couldn't stand the sight of me; took out his belt whenever he felt his disappointment justified it. Sure, my mother tried to speak up; but he'd just slap her 'round a bit too. He was a *fucking bully.* "Let the worthless little twat speak for himself!" I was just a kid for Christ's sake!' The way his voice slurred was making her feel increasingly uncomfortable. Now it seemed she was witnessing him fall from grace; becoming a purveyor of darkness.

'Em, Tyrone, I'm only here to clean for you, I thought you have important guests arriving?' she told him.

'To bloody *hell* with that.' he said, rolling his eyes and curling his lip. 'That was just a ploy to get you here. You mean you really believed me?' He sniggered derisively. Innes wanted to leave. 'Nah, it was just me hoping to get in your...' he caught himself. 'It must be a shock to you huh?'

'Well then, if you won't be needing me, I think I'll just...' she said, eyeing the door.

'It was *Mother* who convinced me to marry her, you know, Beth. "Do it for your father," she said; what an absolute joke. It was doomed from the bloody start. She wasn't the person she seemed, first she has a secret child by another man behind my back and if that's not enough, the whore ran off and married her best friends' husband. That's what I get for marrying the cleaners bloody daughter. She got her comeuppance though, saddled with looking after his bloody brat in the end and...' he trailed off, 'My father died right after the wedding anyway, had a stroke shagging his accountant in the storage room. And guess what I did? I took every scabby photo of him I had, tore them into tiny little pieces and threw them into the bloody fireplace. "Burn you bastard burn,"

I screamed as I jumped up and down with glee. There isn't one image of that hapless bully left anywhere.' he laughed, his tone seemed delirious and Innes feel her heartbeat quicken, the usual excitement she felt in his presence had turned to abject fear.

'Anyway, I really think I'd better...'

'Hey, wait. Don't go yet. You wanna know my big secret, Innes? How I contact the dead?'
Despite her fear, she was curious to see if he would reveal his finest *trick*. She'd seen him impress new followers with it so many times. "Some of us are blessed with the gift." He'd boast. Tyrone gestured to the Ouija board sitting on a three-legged sandalwood table; apparently from India. 'Go ahead, pass me the board and a wine glass from the cabinet.' Innes did so and watched as Tyrone fumbled with the wooden board, clearing a place on a near-by table. She had never actually thought of the Ouija board as a legitimate way to contact the dead. She watched intently as he stood the glass in the centre.

'Go on, put your index finger on the edge, don't be scared'
Curious but guarded, she placed her finger on the glass and almost immediately she felt it begin to move. *Was this part of the trick or was he using some kind of dark magic?* Instantly, the image of Lomond popped into her head.

Poor Lomond lying in a coma, would she ever wake up?
The fact she had come to mind made her worry Lomond may be dying.

Lomond felt herself spiralling out of control. She was being sucked headlong into the indigo tunnel, against her will. A black fog rose and enveloped her. She was frightened, and had no idea what had just occurred, or why she'd lost control. Then she heard her name being called and a glint of crystal almost blinded her. She saw a man with a girl beside him. It was *Tyrone,* and *Innes.* The fog began to dissipate, revealing the silhouette of a young girl; a girl about her own age. The figure flew directly at Tyrone, swirling madly around him, as if poised to attack. A deep masculine drone was coming from it; '*stop, stop, stop*' it chanted. Lomond watched as the figure took deep heaving breaths; the chest area swelling out freakishly and swelling with a gale of black inky mist; it billowed forcefully towards Tyrone, enveloping him in a swirling cocoon. Then the young girl streaked around the room causing chaos before the entire space was engulfed by a raging black storm. Back in the physical realm, the glass on the Ouija board moved; shooting to the letter "F" then "I" with an abrupt and precise movement, taking Innes and Tyrone by surprise. Books dropped from the shelf with heavy *thuds,* a pile of papers burst into the air and a glass globe fell from its place; smashing to smithereens on the wooden floor. Innes pulled her hand away from the glass but is continued to move of its own volition, frenziedly spelling out, "F-I-N-D M-E" over and over again. "F-I-N-D M-E" each time faster and faster until it was a silver-white streak. Innes jumped up from the table, trembling. She had no idea what to say or do, she was frozen to the spot in terror.

'Shit! What the hell did we just do?' Tyrone said, ashen faced and making no attempt to disguise his horror. He reached out to touch Innes, his hand shaking. It was clear he wanted more. Innes saw his eyes were lustfully scanning her body and she knew if she stayed a moment longer, something would happen; something that shouldn't. She didn't trust him.

Moreover, she didn't trust herself either. Though she now knew his true nature, he still seemed to have some strange hold over her. She was both frightened and exhilarated. For a brief second, she even imagined herself being taken in his arms and carried to the sacred altar of his bed.

'Uh…I have to go now,' she said nervously. 'I… it's getting late and my parents will be worried.' she lied. Tyrone realised he could have her. He'd learned to smell and target her vulnerability. His body took the next step. His hands reached out and grabbed at her jumper, he felt her breasts, his eyes closed. He knew she was his now. This was the moment he'd been waiting for since she'd joined his group. Immediately, Innes backed away from his groping hands. She rushed out of the door.

Lomond was shocked by what she'd just witnessed, by the desperate spirit and the narrow escape for Innes. However, there was no time to ponder her friend's fate, as without warning, she felt herself being projected into another realm; a place of many different colour energies. Here, there were no spatial boundaries. The energies were morphing into human features. She saw Mrs. R., in what had been her corporeal body. She became aware of the hermit's physical features. She'd seen the *auras* human bodies emit, now she was witnessing human forms materialise from colour energies; energy into matter. In this surreal carnival, there seemed to be no thought process. A sense of interdependence kept the energies alive; each one aware of every movement, reaction and form of the other. Lomond felt herself expand and become a flaming ball of fire. Like a cannon ball in the maw of a muzzle, she was projected back down the tunnel and into the physical realm.

Effortlessly, she spiralled through the material walls of the hospital and into the HDU ward. There, she drove through the crown of her own bandaged head and reunited with her body. George caressed blond tresses free of the dressing and tubes stranded on the pillow. He lifted a wisp of hair from her damp white brow. Lomond felt his warm breath brush her eyelashes.

CHAPTER TWENTY-SIX

An iced birthday cake with sixteen candles sat on a medical cart at the foot of the bed. On the floor, a small cooler kept the chocolate-mint ice cream cold. Mac and Beth sat on one side of the bed. On the other side were Innes and Lomond's friends Maria and Tracy. Maria was from Gdansk in Northern Poland. Her long blond hair seemed to complement Tracy's dark locks. Tracy, or Theresa as she was called, had an Italian father and a mother from Glasgow. They were all waiting for Lorraine to arrive. Lomond was breathing on her own, her breaths were soft and even; unlaboured. There was anticipation in the air as they glimpsed, nervously to one another with covert sidelong glances. Every now and then, each of them thought they detected the trace of a smile on Lomond's lips, but no one drew attention to it. The cake lay unlit as they waited for the sleeping princess to awaken. The silence was broken by Lorraine's entrance.

Lorraine acknowledged Innes and in no time, everyone was introducing themselves; discussing how they knew each other. Lorraine complimented Innes' creative get-well cards. She was sorry she'd somehow missed seeing her during her few short visits. Maria spoke matter-of-fact.

'Innes hates hospitals, so she's in and out quick.' She was unaware Lorraine and Innes knew each other outside. Then it happened. There was no doubt about it. There was an audible gasp and Lomond opened her mouth. They cupped their hands over their mouths to stifle their excitement. Beth seized the moment and started them off,

'Come on everyone, let's sing *Happy Birthday* to the birthday girl!' By the end of the first chorus, everyone had joined in and the excitement was building. '*Happy birthday dear Lomond, happy birthday to you...*' They waited. Lomond didn't stir. They waited longer. The disappointment was palpable, it showed on their faces. No one wanted to cut the birthday cake yet, as if it would somehow jinx Lomond's miraculous awakening. Mac leaned towards Lorraine and whispered,

'*What about George, Lorraine? Did you manage to get hold of him?*'

'Yes...I did.' She answered.

'Well, is he coming?' Beth sounded both anxious and hopeful.

'Actually, he's here,' Lorraine said, a reserved smile appearing on her face. 'He's waiting down the hall. He wanted to be sure you really wanted him to come in.' Mac nodded as Beth rolled her eyes in resigning agreement.

'I'll go get him.' Lorraine said. A few moments later all heads turned as George walked in.
Tracy looked to Maria, her face twisted in question.

'He's the one with the bike.' Maria whispered.

'*Oh…*' George's expression struggled to hide his shame. He felt horribly naked; a part of him wanted to do a runner, another part wanted to be there for Lomond, whatever the consequences. He stood at the foot of the bed, unable to look at Lomond or her parents. He looked to Lorraine sheepishly. Mac came up beside him and placed his hand on his shoulder.

'Sit down, lad. We've all been waiting for you.' At last George plucked up the courage to gaze upon Lomond with her pale, familiar face resting on the pillow. As he stared at her memories came flooding back. All the times they'd been together, the times they'd leaned in close after riding out together on 'Power," both of them laughing, Lomond's youthful cheeks flushing from the sting of the wind and him leaning down to peck the tip of her wind-blown nose affectionately. They'd been a "rite of passage" for each other, careering together through the traffic of the adult world; flashing the "peace" sign to those who caught them in their fleeting act; and anyone who dared criticize them.

One particular thought brought a smile to George's solemn face. Lomond had spotted their school's headmistress in the car ahead of them. She took the opportunity to lean over and toss a rose onto the windscreen; a rose George had snatched from an unobservant street vendor. The headmistress recognised Lomond of course. She was so furious, she called her parents and told them of the "outrageous conduct of their daughter." This was when George was officially tagged as "trouble on wheels" by her parents.

George broke into a full grin as he recalled the day; he was only half surprised when the face on the pillow twitched a sly smile. He wished he could remember it out loud with her. But he didn't want to mention the bike. He leaned in close and whispered self-consciously,

'Remember all our fun times together, Lomond?' Everyone sat or stood frozen; they'd seen the tiny response. The eyes jump, the corners of the mouth drawing up. George took a breath and whispered again, 'Remember the wind flying by us and our talks of an adventure cross-country?' He looked at her face for response.

He wasn't getting through as everyone had hoped.

'Go on George. We've all sung 'Happy Birthday,' now it's your turn, sweet sixteen after all eh.' Lorraine urged.

'You wouldn't ask me to do that if you heard me sing.' he said shyly.

'Oh, go on,' Mac encouraged too, 'it doesn't matter how it sounds, it'll be fine.' George reminded himself of why he'd agreed to come. This wasn't about him or any other face in the room. It was about doing the right thing for Lomond. Clearing his throat, he broke into a soft, faint rendition of *Happy Birthday.* Everyone felt certain Lomond would still hear him regardless. He sang with his voice breaking up and giving way to throat-clearing at several points. As he sang the chorus for the third time, what started as a tiny grin, grew into a lingering smile. Lomond's eyes fluttered and opened slowly. Then, clearing her throat, she whispered hoarsely,

'You never could sing in tune, George,' before her eyes closed again. George brushed an errant tuft of hair from her forehead.

'Hey, Lomond…it's time to wake up. You plannin' to sleep your life away?' She spoke.

'What time is it?' Her eyes opened again, sensitive to the harsh glare of the overhead lights. She squinted confusingly around the room, taking in the unfamiliar surroundings; the gallery of staring faces.

'Hey, where the hell *am* I?' she croaked, a look of panic over-taking her face. Lorraine dashed off to share the news with the ward nurse. Beth was exclaiming between tears,

'I can't believe it, Mac. I just can't believe it!' Mac went to his wife, wrapping his arms around her, both their eyes glistening with tears. As they moved towards their waking daughter, George reckoned it was time to go. Mac stepped to Lomond's bedside and took her hand in his.

'Oh, my sweet lass, we thought we'd lost you.'

'What am I doing here?' she asked, taken aback by the bizarre scene.

'You were in an accident, a bloody bike accident,' chipped in Beth, unable to hide the sneer in her voice. 'But you're okay now.' she added softer. Lomond stared at everyone gathered in her room; Innes, Tracy, Maria and George...

'George?'

'I'm here, Hi…' George said coyishly from the doorway. Lomond smiled and caught site of the cake at the foot of her bed.

Is that…?'

'It's your birthday, we're all here to celebrate with you?' said her father. Mac stopped George as he saw to make a quiet exit. 'George, you can't go before the cake is cut!' he said and they exchanged a pleasant, knowing smile. Lorraine returned and was given the honour of cutting the cake; paper plates were loaded with squares of chocolate sponge. George was given the first piece and Maria spooned on chocolate-mint ice cream. As he held his plate nervously, George still felt the urge to set it down and get out of there. A moment later Dr. Robb popped her head in, clipboard in hand and he slipped out. A short time later, Maria, Innes and Tracy were thanking Mac and Beth for having them and filing out.

'Well, young lady,' the doctor said with a kind grin, 'you certainly had us all a bit worried!'
Lomond was still bewildered.

'How long have I been here?' she asked. With Beth and Mac looking on, the doctor explained to Lomond how she'd been in a motorcycle accident and she'd sustained a blow to the head. This had put her into a coma for the last four weeks; and now she was awake. As she shined a small flashlight into Lomond's eyes, she asked,

'What's the last thing you remember?'

'Well…' she realised quickly everything was a foggy blur. All she could remember were obviously dreams; fantastic dreams.

She couldn't put anything into words.

'That's alright, this is quite normal,' said Dr. Robb. 'It'll take time for your mind to catch up with your body. Try not to worry. We'll be working with you. There are special counsellors and therapists to help you fill in the gaps.' Turning to Mac and Beth, she informed them a therapeutic team lead would meet with them the following morning, to map-out the best recovery programme.

The next morning, an increasingly-alert Lomond was moved to the rehabilitation wing to begin the physical and psychological therapy until they were certain she had the strength to cope at home. Her parents would help her settle in.

'I still don't remember how I got here.' Beth took her hand and said,

'I should have known what you were planning that night. You were wearing that powder-blue jacket! I blame…'

'The blue jacket?' Lomond interrupted, asking to see it. When she saw the rips and blood stains, her memory found the night. She remembered waiting for George at the bottom of the hill, getting on the back, pulling on her helmet. One after another, like audio-visual dominoes, the memories filtered back into her mind. Her parents' warnings echoed in her head.

In the days that followed, there were lapses as Lomond would momentarily forget where she was, she couldn't grasp the idea she'd been in an accident, or that a month of time had passed. But gradually, bit-by-bit, the pieces were coming together. The therapists reminding her rehabilitation was a slow process, patience was the key. Her mind and body would eventually synchronise, they hoped she would make a full recovery. However, this was said with the knowledge that many patients never quite return to their former selves.

PART 2

CHAPTER ONE

Lomond was convinced everything would go back to normal once she was home. That in light of all she'd been through, her parents would give her more freedom. She was sorely mistaken. In fact, her movements were even more restricted than ever. Her mother laid down new rules. She was only permitted to spend time with her friends at certain times, at home and with at least one of her parents present. This didn't bother her at first, she didn't have the strength to go out for long anyway. But day-by-day, as she grew stronger; the same old minor irritations grew into full-blown aggravations. When they did start allowing her to venture out the house; they insisted she tell them exactly where she was going, for how long and who with. Worse still, she was expected to call home every bloody hour, on the hour and the ice-rink was entirely off-limits. Worried she might somehow be involved in another accident; sometimes they even resorted to following her, just to make sure she wasn't meeting up with George. Incidentally, despite them taking advantage of his help in the hospital; now they didn't want his bad influence anywhere close to their vulnerable daughter.

It all came to a head her very first day back at school. As this was to be her last year, Lomond had secretly decided she would be leaving at the end of the summer term. She had no intention of sitting Highers; a complete waste of time in her eyes. Lomond was in a cheery mood when she set off. She was looking forward to seeing Tracy, Maria and all her other friends; even *pain-in-the-ass* Trudie. When the Year head, Mrs. Scott popped her head in classroom during Reggie, she wasn't surprised.

'Welcome back, Lomond.' She smiled. 'Would you mind coming by my office during break? We need to go over your timetable.' Lomond was horrified and furious to be informed her parents had decided she would be repeating her last year of school. They thought, and the school agreed, she would benefit from the extra time to help her pass her exams. By the end of the school day, she was ready to explode. She stormed home and threw open the front door, following the sound of activity to the kitchen. Her mother was standing over the stove stirring a pot of lentil soup and Lomond stood seething behind her.

'Uh, you're home sharp' she said surprised. 'What's happened, now?' she added taking one look at Lomond's face.

'How dare you! How dare you go behind my back and decide my future, without even discussing things through with me?

Who are *you* to decide *my* life?'

'Now just you wait a minute, young lady. If you're talking about repeating your last year, it was the school who contacted us! They wanted to know what we, *as your parents, were planning to do about all* the time you've missed. I'd hardly call that going behind your back! We've just done what any responsible, concerned parents would.'

'But what about me and what I want? Don't I have my own god-damn brain, my own flipping opinion?' Beth was doing her best to remain calm. The last thing she wanted was a repeat of what happened before; She was unconvinced about the stability of Lomond's mind.

'We both just want what's best for you for god's sake. Why don't we wait till your father comes home? We can sit down together and discuss it then.' Lomond lost control.

'Don't even think you're going to hide behind dad! It's not gonna happen. I'm sick of you. You tell everyone I mean the world to you, but we know the bloody truth. I really don't mean a god-damn thing do I? You don't want a daughter. You want a speechless, brainless rag doll you can twist into position to suit you. Well, to hell with you!' Lomond thundered defiantly up the stairs and turned her music on full-blast.

By the time her father arrived home, she had it fully rehearsed.

'You can just bloody well forget it. I am *not* staying an extra year as that school, no matter what the hell either of you say!' She glowered. Her father was contrite.

'Why don't you just think it over angel. Think it through before you decide. Then, if you *really* don't want to go…I guess we can't force you.' It was clear Beth was livid. She had no intention of backing down. Knowing his wife's mind, Mac shot her a warning glance before she could contest. He knew that if they had any hope of Lomond agreeing to continue with her education, it needed to be on her terms, for her own reasons. Lomond glared hatefully at her mother before letting out a scream that reverberated through the kitchen. She turned her back on them both and left the room; cursing under her breath.

CHAPTER TWO

Recovery was a slow game. Lomond had to face the reality her body didn't work quite the way it used to; something as simple as stepping up onto a bus challenged her depth-perception. More than once she'd stumbled and almost fallen, catching herself at the last moment. During her ongoing physiotherapy sessions, she'd discovered the right side of her body had been more affected than the left. Her therapist tried to be encouraging; it just takes time for it to re-learn how to do the things it used to do. The scans revealed a small lesion on her brain, but the doctors were confident it would heal with time, that new synaptic pathways could be created relatively quickly. Having patience and persistence would be key. However, in no time at all, Lomond became agitated, bitter and lazy; it was a battle to get her to do her exercises. Although being warned she would tire easy and to keep at it; she used this as an excuse to avoid following the doctors' orders. Her mother nagged incessantly and the tension at home escalated.

'Have you done your exercises today? Lomond, the doctors know best. If you want to get better you need to do what you've been advised.'

'Yes! I've done them.' She'd lie. The way her mother tried to control her whole life made the resentment she felt towards her seem justified. 'Let me see you doing your side-step exercise then, I'd like to see if it's any better.' The farce would continue.

'Piss off! I'll do it when I'm bloody ready.' Lomond would hiss. Beth did her best to contain her frustration and fear, but she couldn't ignore the fact Lomond still couldn't do basic things without difficulty. She stumbled climbing the stairs, misjudged the distance to the pantry shelves; the simplest of tasks were causing her great anxiety. Mac trusted the doctors. They seemed to think Lomond was progressing just fine; that she'd regain full control in time. Healing didn't stick to a schedule.

'Leave me the hell alone!' Lomond shouted one morning from the bathroom where she had taken to retreating; her bedroom was beginning to feel more and more like a prison cell every day. 'I'll do them when I'm ready.'

'It's Lorraine on the phone for you.' her mother countered; her patience nearly evaporated.

'Well, why the hell didn't you just *say* that then?' Spat Lomond, throwing open the door and struggling down the stairs. She'd been wondering about Lorraine, if she'd get in touch. It had been weeks since she left the hospital and not a word. She was coming to the conclusion her interest was purely professional after all. Lorraine suggested they meet at The Old Town Book Shop in Victoria Street and Lomond agreed willingly. She didn't mention her plans to her parents, *Screw them!* She thought.

Lomond left discretely and took the bus into town, getting off at Greyfriar's Bobby and pausing for a moment, as she always did, to look at the statue of the famous Skye terrier. They'd learned about him in school, how Bobby had guarded his masters grave in Greyfriar's Kirkyard for fourteen years, until the wee dog died in 1872. The story had touched her heart. Suddenly, without warning, the sun's rays reflected off the water in the top tier of the fountain on which the statue sat; the glare blinding her vision. As she looked into the water, she was amazed to see the reflection of Bobby; the little dog alive and well; wagging his tail.

'Hello little friend.' She whispered, smiling. She was sure she heard a soft voice reply,

'Hello.' Then, in an instant, Bobby disappeared from view, leaving behind a sense of warmth and peace and she wondered if what she saw was a trick of her imagination. She walked, down into the Grassmarket and along Candlemaker Row; taking a brief detour to look at the vintage clothes in the window of Armstrong's. She crossed over to the foot of Victoria Street, stopping again at

Iconic Design; the iridescent colours fascinated her. She noticed the pitch of the sun as it shone in on the facets of a crystal hanging in the window. It transmitted a rainbow of colour and something struck a familiar chord within her. Like a feeling of Déjà vu, something triggered in the back of her mind. What was that? The sound of singing distracted her. A pleasant looking young man with an acoustic guitar was sitting cross-legged on the wall on the other side of the road. Carefully, she stepped down the curb and crossed over, moving towards him. For a while she stood listening.

'Sing it again,' she requested, 'please, if you don't mind.' The sun cut through the early spring leaves, causing dappled pockets of light to dance in sympathy to the rhythm of the music he played.

'Well, what you gonna give me then?' teased Mint, keen to keep her on the hook. He appreciated the way she'd stood listening so contentedly to his new song. The one he'd written with his buddy George in mind.

'Well, how 'bout I tell you my name?' said Lomond coyly, drawing herself up to her full 5 feet 3 inches and staring him straight in the eyes.

'Deal.' he grinned strumming the four-chord intro. As he picked up the melody line and began humming along; Lomond felt a warm swelling in her chest.

'In the dark hour of sleep, do you see who I am?' Somehow, the words seemed to echo an unfathomable feeling she'd been unable to shake off the past few weeks. It must have something to do with the coma she decided. Like the remnants of a dream, fragments kept repeating. It was as if she'd brought part of the deep trench of nothingness back to the physical world.

During one of her therapy sessions, frustrated, she'd demanded to see the medical records of her time in hospital. She was convinced they were hiding something from her. Maybe they'd reveal she'd been all-but ignored in the physical world while she floated aimlessly out in the black void; but deep down she knew that wasn't rational. As well as her friends and family, she knew she'd had the best care from her devoted nurse, Lorraine. Even so, the feeling of being abandoned persisted; festering inside her and making her feel resentful. *If they can do without me, I can do without them.* Everyday life became stupid and trivial to her.

What does it matter if I catch the bus or not, or if I miss a therapy appointment? Why not just get on the bus and ride till I can't ride any farther? Mint's lyrics filtered into her consciousness again.

'Dark days, dark nights, silent mind, silent thoughts…' A swirling cloud began to form on the horizon of her mind. There was something poised, hiding in the recesses of her memory, trying to surface. She could sense it. But she couldn't reach it. It remained in the shadows, as if hidden behind a dark curtain.

'*Remember, Lomond. Remember.*' A voice seemed to whisper from somewhere within. *Maybe the coma caused my awake and sleeping minds to split. Is that even a thing?* At times, when the sensation was at its *loudest,* she'd felt the need to lie down, to search her mind in the same way you would try to remember a fleeting dream. Twice, she'd been certain she was on the verge of bringing it to the surface, whatever it was, she could almost *see* it, like writing on paper. But then it vanished. Slipping through her mind's grasp like sand through the fingers. Now, Mint's lyrics made her think whatever she felt belonged to another realm of consciousness; an out-of-the-ordinary realm of experience. She wanted to hear him sing it again.

'So, what's your name then?' he asked as the final chord resonated through the air.

'It's Lomond.' She answered.

'No way! You're *Lomond*?' Her defences leapt to the fore; she was confused. People usually laughed or complimented her name. Before she could grasp the nettle, Mint went on. 'You're the girl who was in a coma, George's friend, right?' Lomond took a step backward and seeing her reaction, Mint added quickly, 'Hey, don't worry. I know George. He's a mate of mine.' He extended his hand. 'They call me 'Mint,' by the way. Don't tell me he never mentioned me?' Lomond felt the blood rush to her face. It dawned on her she'd barely felt the urge to see George since coming home. She had no idea why she was avoiding him. Not so long ago she'd have given almost anything to be on the back of his bike. Maybe it was the accident or the bloody state of her powder-blue jacket? She never blamed George for what happened to her, she knew it wasn't his fault. He'd never taken any risks that might have put them in danger and his bike was safe. Yet now, the mere hum of motorcycle in the distance would provoke every nerve in her body. Her throat would begin to close up and her eyes would search the approaching traffic in a panic.

'Mint?' she searched her mind to recall any mention of the name by George.

'Aye, strange name I know, that's what I get for having hippies as parents.' He noted Lomond's uneasiness and wondered if it was the mention of George that had upset her. He also wondered if Lomond knew about George and Lorraine, he quickly changed the subject. 'You've been out of hospital a wee while now, I hear? I bet that's been a bit of an adjustment.'

'Like a chicken coop, if you really wanna know.' she reacted, a resigned grin spreading across her face.

'That's a bummer, it sounds pretty rough,' he responded, showing true concern. 'It must be strange coming back into this unpredictable world.' His words carried a deeper meaning for her than he realised. Lomond was impressed, he seemed different; someone intelligent who knew how to listen. All her other friends seemed to think being in a coma was somehow *cool*; a chance to visit some exotic wonderland. No one really considered what it might have been like for her.

She wanted to tell him how her rehabilitation was long, dull and depressing. How it was difficult for her to accept how badly her coordination was affected, and even harder to admit she needed help. Home-life was a constant battle; her parents' concern was *stifling her.* She was starting to fear the accident had changed something deep inside her. There was a constant nagging feeling she had forgotten something really important.

'So, you wrote that song?' she asked instead. 'Is it for George?'

'Yup, words and music. You think it'll be a chart topper?' Lomond smiled at his little quip.

'The lyrics, I… they really speak to me. It's like they describe my life since the accident. It's funny; people seem to think being in a coma is something exotic and mysterious. As if being flat on your back for weeks, separated from reality is somehow exciting. Well, I promise you, it's not! It's a bloody deep dark hole and you still feel in it when you wake up.' Lomond gave him a sidelong look; he was still listening; a look of genuine compassion on his face. She glanced at her watch. 'Shit!' She'd agreed to meet Lorraine at 2:30 and she was late. 'I need to go. I'll be back later though. I want the words to that song Mint!' she shouted over her shoulder. Mint strummed a few chords and started humming the tune again as he watched Lomond cross the road. He thought for a moment she was turning to wave, but realised she'd lost her footing and was heading for a fall. Luckily, a quick-thinking passer-by caught her arm and saved her grace. Mint wondered if George knew the problems she was still having.

CHAPTER THREE

Lomond was delighted to spot Lorraine browsing the shelves as she entered The Old Town Book Shop. She looked so different out of her nurse's uniform; like a regular person. The two embraced.

'You know, it's funny,' Lomond said, the meeting with Mint still on her mind. 'I think the accident has changed me. I mean really *changed* me. It's almost like a bit of my mind is missing, if that makes any sense?' Lorraine was ready to offer a professional opinion when Lomond added, 'Anyway, I owe you a debt of thanks for looking after me in hospital. I understand it was your idea to bring George in?' Lorraine felt a sense of dread at the just the mention of his name. Tactfully, she shifted the topic of conversation to Tyrone and his meditation session.

'You know, one time I was there, when you were still in a coma, I had a vision of you. How strange is that?'

'Did you?' said asked in surprise. At the same time a ghostlike memory of Lorraine flashed through her mind.

'This is going to sound just as crazy as it was for me seeing it, but while I was meditating, you came to me in a flaming ball.' As soon as the words were out, Lomond felt a jolt to her senses and a bright light flashed between her eyes. In her mind, Lorraine held the vision of Lomond as she'd appeared in the flame. For a few moments, it was as if the two of them stepped outside real time, as if they were transported to another place and time; another realm. Then the sounds of the real world, the outside traffic and people's voices came in again. They looked at each other in a daze, unsure how to respond. In that instant, Lomond felt Lorraine was someone she could confide in about everything. In a quiet corner of the shop, Lomond opened up, telling her all about her hatred for her parents and her longing to escape their control. About her plans to leave home and travel to other places as soon as she'd left school and how she planned to ask George to help her make her great escape. When she noticed Lorraine's face cloud over and her eyes become distant, she changed the subject.

'You know, I was thinking I might try *dowsing* to help me decide what to do.' she said. 'Have you ever heard of that?' Lorraine shook her head even though she had. She was sure she'd heard something about it being connected to witchcraft. 'Well, my Great-Aunt Martha showed me how to do it when I was little.' Lomond continued. 'She's dead now, but I still remember how.' Lorraine was unsure about encouraging Lomond along this path, she wondered if she'd had such thoughts before the accident. 'See, you start by holding a thread with a needle at the end of it. You keep your hand very still and ask yourself a question, to find the direction of your *'yes'* response. Over and over you repeat it until the needle moves in one way or another. It could be left to right, back and forth, in a circle, whatever. Well, this shows you the direction the thing will move if the answer is yes. Then, when you have it, you do the same thing to find your *'no'* response, which will be different. Everyone has to discover the responses that work for them.' Lorraine listened, not sure what to make of Lomond's plans. Had the coma really *changed* her as she suspected? 'My Aunt told me our brains take in everything we see, hear, and experience. It files it all away in little compartments and by dowsing; we can access the information and use it to find answers.'

Lorraine wasn't convinced there was any validity in what Lomond was suggesting, although she was relieved the conversation had steered away from the delicate subject of *George.* She suggested they go and check out the "new-arrivals" at the front of the shop and Lomond happily agreed, she felt somewhat honoured the older and wiser woman wanted to hang out with her.

'Hey, maybe I should dowse about *George.*' She stated half-jokingly. 'You know, he loves me, he loves me not, he loves me, he loves me not.' Lorraine's face flushed scarlet and Lomond wondered if she had a boyfriend of her own, maybe she was envious. As they made their way down the aisle, a book caught both their eyes. Lorraine was first to pick it up.

'*The Principles of Light and Colour*' she read aloud. 'You know, I've been interested in learning about healing with colour for a while now. Innes told me about it.' she half-lied. The memory of the way she'd used the orange at Lomond's bedside was still fresh in her memory.

'How did you meet my old neighbour anyway?' Lomond asked curious. Lorraine explained their first encounter, how Innes had pointed out the relationship between colours and chakras and their use in meditation. As she spoke, Lomond felt another jolt to her senses; her brain seeming to light up inexplicably with deep excitement as Lorraine talked; as if something was trying to make itself known. She kept it to herself. Lorraine paid for the book.

'Hey, let's hop it.' Lomond suggested. 'Shall we go check out Iconic Design? I had a peek in the window on the way, I love that shop.' Lorraine smiled and nodded in agreement.

The colour from the window could be seen glowing from across the way. The two young women stood street-side; fascinated by the visual spectacle in front of them. The afternoon sun was hitting the facets of a dangling cut crystal, sending spectres of colour shooting out in all directions. A small and wiry old man with a straggly grey beard looked up as the doorbell jingled. He grunted an indifferent greeting and continued to polish a green gem nestled in a purple swathe of velvet resting in the palm of his hand. The girls hovered, taking in the ambiance of the little shop, waiting until he'd finished. Every now and then he held the stone up between his thumb and index finger, to an incoming beam of light. He fanned the fingers of his other hand behind to assess the sheen. After a few minutes, Lomond made a move towards the door in resignation. Only then did the man clear his throat and mutter,

'Something I can do for you young ladies, or are you just browsing?'

'Well actually, I was interested in a crystal; a crystal to use for dowsing.' Lomond announced unashamedly. The old man gazed over the top of his spectacles with a knowing look.

'I see. Then it's a pendant crystal you'd be looking for.' He said, taking in the appearance of Lomond and Lorraine for the first time. 'Here, let me show you what I've got. Now, I'm no expert on dowsing, mind you.' He added, his facial expression suggesting otherwise. He led them to a glass case set apart from the others and one crystal immediately caught Lomond's attention.

Unlike the others shaped like cones, ovals and crescents; this one was an orb cupped in a silver wrap. The man noticed where her eyes rested and smiled.

'Aye, she's a wee beauty, now isn't she?' he winked. 'Course, you've gone and picked the most expensive one in the case. Cost you three pounds that one.' Lomond sighed. That was way more money than she had. She told him she'd have to wait, but she'd be back.

'I wouldn't wait too long, lass. A unique gem like that won't be here long.'

Lorraine and Lomond walked up the hill on Victoria Street, passing Nicky Tam's pub and turning right onto George IV Bridge. They decided on a coffee at a little café just further up towards Chambers Street. Suddenly Lorraine remembered Innes had been asking after Lomond. She also told her about the meditation group, and Tyrone; the group leader. Perhaps she'd like to go along? There was a good deal more she thought she ought to tell Lomond too, but she kept quiet about that; a serious talk with George was in order first.

'Here, I was thinking. There's a craft fair on this Sunday at the Assembly Rooms. Maybe we could meet up there, you, me and maybe Innes?'

'Sounds fab!' Lomond said, her mind instantly thinking of dowsing crystals and shards of colour.

'It's a date then!' Lorraine said, hugging Lomond good-bye. On the bus ride home, Lomond thought again about the strange look that came across Lorraine's face when she'd mentioned George. She wondered what it was all about. Was there something she wasn't sharing? Did something happen at the hospital she didn't know about?

CHAPTER FOUR

Having heard nothing from Tyrone since the Ouija Board incident, Innes decided to check in on him. It wasn't something she *wanted* to do, but something told her to do so nonetheless. With her guard raised, she resigned to make a quick appearance then announce she had somewhere else to be. When she approached the house on India Street, she was surprised to see a large *FOR SALE* sign outside. No-one answered when she rang the bell. She pressed her face to the little prismatic panes framing the door, but there were no signs of life inside. *What? Did he move out? Did he go off on one of his famous trips to the East?* Feeling puzzled and a little dejected, she headed home. Although a part of her reasoned it was unsurprising behaviour from Tyrone, and probably for the best if he were gone. Another part was filled with uncertainty and all kinds of wild scenarios played out in her imagination.

Back in her room, she tried to work on her holiday project for school but no ideas would come. Her mind was still distracted by the situation with Tyrone and her anxiety about the pending line-up at the police station began to rise. Although it seemed a good decision at the time; the more she thought about having to testify about what she'd seen that night, the more it worried her. She was starting to regret coming forward at all. Her mother's annoyingly tentative knock on her bedroom door brought her back to the present. *Why does she not just speak out? Everything is so goddamn proper and polite in this family.* She got up and pulled open the door aggressively. Her mother's eyes went straight to the array of books and art supplies lying on the desk.

'Oh, there was a bit on the news,' she said. 'I think it had to do with that man you mentioned, that one who runs the meditation group.' There was a smug look on her face. 'It was a piece about the rise in the Edinburgh property market and they showed a house on India Street, and part of its interior. There was a room full of tapestries and Asian do-das, just like you described in that 'meditation room.' They said they were taking offers over a hundred thousand pounds. A hundred thousand! I remember when houses in that neighbourhood went for no more than fifty; isn't that amazing?' Innes couldn't find the words or will to respond. 'Do you think it could be the same place?' her mother asked pointedly.

'How should *I* know? I didn't see the TV, *you* did.'

'I just thought…'

'Mother, we both know you don't *think*, so…'

'Oh, I see you're getting on with your holiday project?' her mother said, not wanting to set off an argument. '

'Yes, Mother, I *am*. But now, I need a break.' She side-stepped her mother and headed downstairs, leaving her standing in the doorway.

'Don't forget, you said you'd stay in with Ian tonight.' her mother called after her. 'Your father and I have tickets for the theatre!'

'I don't need reminding, I'm not a child.' Innes shot back as she reached the front door. Since being discharged from the hospital, her brother was her main priority, but now all this business with Tyrone was distracting her. *Would he really just up and disappear without a word?* She recalled their last disturbing encounter. She wondered if it was the tumbler of whisky that brought out his dark side, or maybe that was the real Tyrone. His long and emotional confession about his childhood replayed over in her mind. *What was he trying to tell me? What was he trying to justify?* Remembering also how she'd been *tempted* that day filled her with guilt and self-loathing. She needed to speak to someone about it. If there was anyone, she could talk to about it, she felt she could trust *Lorraine,* although these days she seemed to have enough troubles of her own.

Her breath formed a cloud in the crisp biting air. It was one of those cold snaps Scotland often gets in the springtime, although the sun was glowing in the sky, the cold wind showed no mercy. Innes buried her chin inside her long scarf and made her way up Lothian Road. After checking out what new films would be showing at the ABC, she made her way towards The Old Book Shop. She liked the selection of books to be found there.

Walking along Bread Street, she stopped outside the Art College. She gazed lovingly at the multi-coloured arched windows, rich with Gothic stained glass. Then she continued down the West Port and into the Grassmarket. She'd been waiting for, *The Principles and Colour,* by Edwin De Babbit, but it was nowhere to be found in the paranormal section. She approached the woman behind the counter and asked about it; perhaps they had copies through the back.

'Oh, I'm so sorry deary, the last copy was *just* purchased, but we'll be getting a new order in next week. I could keep one aside for you, if you like?' the woman said helpfully.

'No thanks, I'll just see if another store has a copy.' she told the woman, struggling to hide her disappointment. She'd set her mind on getting it today. *How could someone else be interested in it?* She turned and walked dejectedly out of the shop. Just as she was just reaching the bottom of Victoria Street, she heard someone calling her name.

'Hey Innes!' It was Lorraine. The two waved enthusiastically from either side of the street. 'I've got something I want to show you!' Lorraine shouted. After a quick embrace, she fumbled around inside her bag and pulled out the book. For an instant, Innes felt betrayed it was Lorraine who'd taken the last copy. But when she reconsidered, it pleased her to know they shared the same interest, and she could always borrow it. Like Lomond, Innes now looked up to Lorraine. Despite it being she who introduced Lorraine to the metaphysical world, Lorraine was older, more mature, she had ambition. She seemed to know what she wanted in life and how to get it. Innes was desperate to discover her vocation, but she couldn't decide what it should be; artist, nurse, teacher, librarian? It was so hard to know which path to take. Lorraine noticed the look of worry behind Innes' glasses.

'Are you ok?' she asked. Is there something on your mind?'

'To tell you the truth, between my parents, my brother and school, I don't know if I'm coming or going.' She told Lorraine about all that happened with her brother and the court case, and her worry that Ian was still caught up in the drug scene. As stressful as this all seemed, Lorraine sensed there was something else.

'Innes, is that all that's bothering you? I mean, you don't have to tell me, but....' Here was her chance. Innes was desperate to speak to someone about what happened with Tyrone; especially about him coming on to her, touching her and about her lack of resistance. Although, nothing happened, she was still finding it difficult to admit it to herself. Instead, she told Lorraine about the house being up for sale and there being no sign of Tyrone anywhere.

"What do you worry might have happened?' Lorraine was a little concerned over Innes' state of mind. 'I wonder if it has anything to do with the hermit who visited.' She added, thinking of the profound effect the man had on George. Innes shrugged; she was still feeling desperate and reluctant to share the whole truth. Lorraine also had things on her mind she wanted to discuss, but now wasn't the time.

'Here, I gotta get back home,' Innes changed the subject, 'but if you haven't made dinner plans, I'm making curry. I promised my *mother* I'd keep an eye on Ian while they went to some stupid show. You're welcome to join me?'

'That would be great,' Lorraine smiled, 'I *love* curry.'

As Lorraine helped her prep the chicken, she remembered George might be stopping by at her place, although it wasn't a given, she hoped he wasn't hanging around waiting for her. As the curry simmered, her thoughts turned back to Lomond. She remembered the nights she'd spent sitting by her bed, holding her hand. She was certain there'd been some kind of special connection; something supernatural. She was certain she'd felt an inexplicable, palpable energy pass between them. She thought again of seeing Lomond's face emerging from the orange blaze of light in Tyrone's meditation room. She felt pulled to tell Innes about this strange occurrence and about how things were with George, but she resisted. It frustrated her that their *relationship,* if indeed you could call it that, was getting in the way of her friendship with Lomond too; it had to be dealt with. In the meantime, it was wearing heavily on her conscience. Part of her wished and hoped it might just take care of itself. There was no denying the *honeymoon phase* was over. True, things were still good, but more and more often were incidents where George would lash out at her for no reason. She was finding his insecurities harder and harder to take. The lump in her throat was becoming a permanent lodger.

Innes watched as Lorraine drained her coffee cup and ran her tongue over her lips. *Now's as good a time as any* she thought.

'So, are you still on with George?' she asked, feeling somewhat awkward about the whole situation since Lomond had woken up. Lorraine's conscience seized her at the mention of his name and she looked longingly into Innes' eyes. She wished there wasn't this cloud of secrecy over their relationship. Since Lomond's recovery, it had grown much worse. Now she felt caught between two sides of an abyss. On one hand she was the nurse who'd willed Lomond to regain consciousness; she'd breathed the orange colour energy to help it happen. But she was also the *other woman*, the one who'd fallen for someone else's boyfriend. She was ashamed to admit a part of her had even hoped Lomond would remain unconscious. If only she had the courage to say what was on her mind.

'We're just friends really,' she lied.

Just then, a glassy-eyed Ian shuffled into the kitchen with a cassette tape in hand. Unaware her brother had managed to sneak a couple of mates into the house and up to his bedroom to get blazed, Innes turned to him and said chirpily,

'Hey, stay close. Curry's almost done.'

'Cool, I'm absolutely famished.' he mumbled, avoiding eye contact. 'Here, I got this tape, very cool sounds. How about after dinner we…?' He looked up and caught his first glimpse of the young woman sitting with his sister. '*Shit.*' he breathed. The two looked at each other like deer caught in headlights, Lorraine wracking her brains as to why he looked so familiar.

'Uh, do you two know each other?' Innes asked, unaware of the drama that was unfolding. Lorraine's memory replayed the moment she'd been confronted, held her at knife-point as she walked across the Meadows that night. She remembered pleading with him to consider his sister, something she never knew to be true, until now. With her emotions surging, she made her excuses and quickly skirted around Ian, heading straight out the door.

'I tell you what, sis' he said with a cocky, self-satisfied grin. 'I'm so hungry I could eat a scabby horse. Just shout me when what you got cooking in your cauldron is ready, then we can check out the music.' Innes stood staring at the door, shaken and confused as her brother stood glassy-eyed and grinning at her like a lunatic.

CHAPTER FIVE

George wasn't there when she got home. He must have decided to spend the night at his own flat after all.

'Hey Lorraine!' Helen screamed over gushing tap-water and blaring music, 'I'm in the tub.' *When are you not,* she fought back the urge to shout back. Instead, she retreated into her room and lit her sandalwood-scented candles. She needed so badly to find peace of mind but there was no hope of that. Ever since Lomond had regained consciousness, Lorraine felt her emotional connection with George swinging like a pendulum. She moved between feeling enthralled and elated to feeling as though she were drowning in a sea of doubt. One-minute trusting him to do the right thing, the next convinced he'd leave her at the drop of a hat for Lomond. As she sat in the flickering candlelight, an image came into her mind. She saw Lomond and George riding on Power together. Lomond with her arms wrapped around him; her golden-brown hair flying behind her. She worried George missed the younger girl's lust for life, the excitement; that he was growing bored of her. Already it seemed their sex-life had become a bit like a routine; he was always in too much of a rush for morning coffee. Her head told her to stop being so naive and insecure but, in her heart, she sensed something was wrong; as if the writing was somehow forming on the wall.

She felt ashamed about her true intentions for meeting Lomond earlier that day. She'd hoped some of her vivacity would rub off on her, that she would be able to suss out what made her so special. She'd also thought that by confronting her fears, they might prove to be unjustified and would vanish. On the contrary, though merely a girl, she realised Lomond was a formidable competitor. A tear rolled down her cheek and panic began to grip her chest. Had she surrendered her body just as freely as other girls she judged so harshly in the past? The worst of it was, she knew she wouldn't be able to resist questioning George the next time she saw him. Even though she knew it would make him feel cornered and that he'd react. His fuse seemed to be shortening each and every time she confronted him over their situation. Helen burst into the room.

'I've simply *got* to tell you the news, Lorraine. I'm going on holiday with Hector! We're going to Benidorm, we're off next Monday. Can you believe it?' *Of course, I can believe it. This is what you do!* Fighting back the urge to project her own misery onto her friend she tried to appear happy for Helen. She wished it were she and George going away on some romantic adventure; that their relationship had even matured to this stage. How far from the truth this was. She doubted it would ever reach there; that would mean all the complications had been worked out. Helen noticed her grim expression.

'Hey, cheer up. You'll have the flat all to yourself. Just you and George, think of that!' she said with a naughty, grin. Then Lorraine burst into tears and before she knew it, she had venting all her pent-up anxiety about George; a veritable tidal-wave of twisted emotion came flooding out. To Lorraine's surprise, Helen listened intently and offered her worthwhile advice.

'Listen, I know you didn't ask, *but* I think you should tell Lomond what's going on, fess up. It's the secrecy that's doing you in, girl! I mean, that way you can let Lomond know how you feel about George and find out if she even *wants* to be with him. For my money, I doubt she even does. At least this way you can find out for certain and clear your conscience.'

'That's the trouble,' Lorraine said, looking pitifully at Helen. 'I mean, *I* actually want to tell Lomond, I've told him it's the fair thing to do, but he won't have it. He said he wants to do it himself, in his own time. The longer this lying and deceit goes on, the worse I feel.'

'Well, I guess I can understand his point too.' Helen said,

bobbing her head in measured agreement. 'If I were Lomond, I think I'd rather hear it from George than you. No offense, but the relationship- if there even is one still- is between the two of them.

'He gets angry if I even mention her name.' Lorraine said sadly. 'I get the feeling he doesn't want to commit until he can work out who he'd rather be with!' Wanting to make her friend feel better and annoyed that George was making her feel so unhappy, Helen was tempted to point out that Lomond was just a daft young girl, not a mature, sophisticated woman like Lorraine. Instead she said,

'Sounds a bit like a guilty conscience to me. I think if it was *me*, I'd put my foot down. Enough *is* enough. Say to him, either he tells Lomond what's been going on, or you're finished. Simple. You know, 'shit or get off the pot!' Lorraine couldn't help but giggle at this, she felt her mood brighten. She rather fancied the idea of laying it on the line to George once and for all.

Helen might be bold and brassy, over-the-top most of the time; but at least she was direct. She got to the heart of matters and Lorraine really liked that about her. Suddenly, she remembered why she'd wanted to share a flat with Helen in the first place.

'Thanks so much. That's really helped me Helen. And

you're dead right, enough is enough!'

Feeling some resolve over how she'd proceed with George; her thoughts now turned to the incident in the park. She'd almost forgotten the disturbing revelation at Innes' house. What were the chances it was Innes' brother who'd accosted her? She didn't know quite what to do about it, or if in fact, she should do anything at all. Innes and her brother were going through a hard-enough time, the last thing she wanted to do was make things worse. She pondered over events that had brought her to this point in her life, about how things were shifting. This whole situation with Lomond and George had changed something in her. The one thing she'd always found rewarding was tending to the needs of others, patients, friends and family, colleagues. Now it seemed this sense of satisfaction was disappearing, gone from her job and her personal life. It was as if she was losing sight of herself.

George was waiting for her the next evening she came home after her shift. She was genuinely happy yet somewhat surprised to find him there.

'You've come back to me.' she said, regretting the words as soon as they passed her lips.

'What's that supposed to mean?' George seemed tense.

'Oh, nothing… I just missed you, that's all.'

'Sorry, hen. I know I'm a bit crabbit, but it's just the waiting. I wish it was all over and done with.'

'The court case?'

'Of course, what else?' She wondered if he had anything else on his mind.

'Have you spoken with Lomond?' she asked, bracing herself for his reaction. George stiffened.

'You need to keep your nose *out* of that, Lorraine. I've told you already, I'll tell her when *I* think the time is right.'

'Look, I'm not trying to meddle George, but you need to understand this isn't easy for me either. We're involved with each other and I feel like I'm living a lie. I was with her yesterday and could barely look her in the eye.'

'Well, if you *feel* like a liar, then that's your problem. You shouldn't be going to meet her then.' His tone was cold. A tear rolled down her face.

'What about you, then? Doesn't this bother you, going behind her back this way? I mean, this is a girl you supposedly had, or *have*, feelings for.'

'Look, I *don't* want to keep going over this again. I'm getting a bit sick of you pestering me all the time to be honest. It's driving me fucking nuts. I've told you I'll deal with it. I've got bigger more important things to worry about just now. Please just leave it at that!' George felt a pang of guilt as he saw the look of pain on Lorraine's face. He touched her cheek and she leaned into him. 'I know it's a hard time for both of us.' he said, his tone softer. Lorraine considered her words.

'George, I'm sorry, really, I am. I know you're worried about going to court and you don't want to rock the boat, but this can't go on. It's just not right.' The weight of her words hung in the air between them for a few moments. Deep down, George hated that he was avoiding the issue, the fact he couldn't just get it over with confused and frustrated him.

'Okay, I hear you,' he said, I'll try fix it.' Lorraine sighed and held him close.

'Let's just let it go for now.' She resigned. 'We can sleep on it; tomorrow's a new day.' Finally, she felt a glimmer of hope about their relationship.

The serenity was short lived though. After spending the night together and him promising to spend the day with her; first thing in the morning, George was straight on the phone making plans to hang out with Mint.

'We're going to see a movie, come along with us if you fancy.' George offered, sensing her irritation.

'Its fine, I've got other stuff to do anyway.' She lied, angry about being made to feel like an afterthought, yet again. She liked Mint well enough, but George was making her feel used. 'You just go enjoy yourself with your friend, don't mind me.'

George showed up at her flat that night with left-over's from Brattisanis Chip Shop. It was clear she wasn't as pleased to see him as usual, despite the peace offering.

'Hey, what's the problem now?' George demanded; crossing his arms on his chest.

'Do you even have feelings for me anymore, or not?' Lorraine blurted out, the tears following quickly.

'For Christ's sake, Lorraine! What is going on with all this? You're like a nagging wife already. It's really pissing me off.'

'George, something has changed, you must feel it too.' The look of pain on Lorraine's face was the only thing that stopped him walking straight out the door.

'Look, of course I have feelings for you, but I think we both need space. Lately you're always up my arse, demanding to know what I'm doing, where I'm going, why I'm not doing this or that. I don't get why the hell you're acting this way!'

'It's Lomond!' Lorraine shot back; beyond exasperated by the way things were left. 'I've tried to tell you. It's all about her not knowing about us and you not seeming to *want* to tell her. I can't deal with the guilt. You don't want me to tell her and as long as you keep us from her, it doesn't feel right. I've told you time and time again about how I feel but you're just ignoring me. Well, I'm sorry George, but until you tell Lomond about us, I can't be with you anymore. I can't keep living this lie!' The tears were now streaming down her face.

'Lorraine, this is all on you. I've got enough to deal with without all this Lomond shit! I do *not* need the fecking aggravation.' As she sat in the armchair, sobbing as she looked out the window, he moved towards her.

'Okay, Lorraine. I still can't understand why you're so obsessed with Lomond, but I promise I'll tell her, and soon. And when it's done, I'll let you know.' Now Lorraine doubted whether he ever actually would. To her it was feeling more and more as if he was stringing her along.

CHAPTER SIX

When his mother wrote to say she planned to sell the house on India Street, he ignored her at first. To hell with what she wants. The letters from her solicitors received much the same disdain; he threw them in the trash unopened. Only when the *final demand* arrived by special delivery did Tyrone reluctantly, and with the aid of a considerable jolt of whisky, open it. He would be evicted by force from the property, if he did not leave voluntarily within three months. His only hope, he decided, was to pay his mother a visit in St. Andrews. As he left the house and walked to Waverly Station, he was mentally preparing himself. It would take some doing to charm and persuade her to change her mind. Once on the train, he plonked himself down by the window and as it chugged out of the station and headed west, the brick, concrete and stone gave way to fields of golden corn swaying in the soft breeze; he began to relax.

At St Andrews, he jumped in a taxi to his mother's from Leuchars Junction. How was he going to dissuade her? Threaten her with exposing family secrets if she balked? Maybe even something more severe if she failed to see reason?

'No, Tyrone, I will not move back to the city. I'm eighty-three years old and it would be too much strain for me. I have good friends here and if anything should happen to me, I'll be looked after.' She told him flatly, it was clear she was not going to budge. In compensation, she was prepared to buy him something smaller, a quaint cottage; a modern flat if he fancied. Neither interested or appeased Tyrone. He wanted couldn't leave India Street he told her; as always, he refused to consider the needs of anyone other than himself. He announced he would need to stay with her whilst the house was in the process of attracting a buyer. In actuality, he was intent on formulating a plan to keep the house; he'd find a way to change her mind somehow.

His mother, Mavis, lived in a small, traditional house in the seaside town of St. Andrews. It was so old, Tyrone had to stoop to get through the doorways. Storing a few of his irreplaceable possessions in the tiny guest bedroom just in case, he was forced to sleep on an uncomfortable daybed in the living room. As if it wasn't degrading enough being forced out of his home, salvaging his priceless collectables in cheap cardboard cartons like common junk was just about more than he could take. Although he knew living with his mother was only temporary, being around her brought back memories from his childhood he wanted to forget.

Mavis became quickly exasperated by her son's ceaseless complaints. However, her friends seemed to be intrigued by Tyrone.

'What a respectful man your son is, Mavis.' Morag commented after Tyrone offered to walk her four dogs, 'He's such a proper gentleman. Tiny' simply *adores* him, don't you, Tiny?' Mavis grew increasingly suspicious as more neighbours approached her singing his praises.

'What a lovely man you've raised, Mavis.' another commented.

'Such a fascinating individual, you must be so proud!' Her best friend Ethel gushed. 'Can he play bridge? We should have him up on bridge night.' Becoming known for his long, meditative strolls about the neighbourhood, Tyrone would always stop and charm the old ladies. His arsenal of compliments seemed unlimited. On one particular day with a distinct chill in the air, he headed to Law Mill, at Lade Braes. There, he sat on an old wooden bench watching the sweep of the water and the ducks as they glided effortlessly downstream. While contemplating his dilemma, he regarded the way the daffodils bent in the breeze on the river bank, then after a while he set off, raising his collar against the rustle of the wind; he knew what he had to do. The only question remaining was how?

The house on India Street had never actually belonged to Tyrone;
he'd merely stayed on after his mother re-married after the death of
his father. Her new husband Stewart, owned his own house and
they had been happy enough there in St. Andrews, until his
untimely death just over a year ago. Over time, Tyrone had grown
confident in the claim he thought he'd staked. When his mother
passed on, he assumed the house on India Street
would finally be his; obtained by occupation and by default.
However, he hadn't reckoned on Stewart McNaughton. Before his
death, the greedy, controlling interloper had brainwashed his
mother into looking at selling India Street to use the money for a
world cruise; and God knows whatever else. Tyrone was enraged
to think about all his father's hard-earned money being spent so
frivolously on his stepfather's pleasures. He was nothing more than
a scoundrel. The irony was Stewart and Tyrone were much alike.
Both considered themselves to be *entitled* men; deserving better
than others. Both projected the idea they were in special
communion with their respective "powers-that-be". Stewart was
a fastidious pillar of the church. He'd moved to St Andrews in his
retirement, eager to secure himself a position of religious

importance in the congregation. Every Sabbath he would shuffle up and down the aisle quietly in his suede shoes, handing the collection purse decorously to the head of each pew before returning it bulging with cold coinage and folded notes. He was convinced his place in heaven was pretty much secured through his religious servitude. His great moment in death, much to the disgust of Tyrone, was to surrender his worldly goods to the Kirk; the Church of Scotland. He had no intention of Tyrone getting a penny of his money; he hated Tyrone. He thought of him a pompous no good parasite. He'd made humble, yet scant provision for Mavis. She would hold the lease on his house for the duration of her lifetime, but her tenure was conditional on payment of a monthly rent to the Church.

Before she had met Stewart, his mother had even suggested they convert the basement of the India Street house into a self-contained flat for her with its own entrance and a back door opening into the garden. This would leave the rest of the house to Tyrone and his "interests." At the time, he had been dead set against this idea. He'd complained it would be far too much work, too much dust and after all, the basement was his wine cellar; he had nowhere else cool enough to store his much-prized collection. Maybe on reflection, he should have agreed to the renovation. A basement conversion would have added value to the house, and it would have prised some money from his mother's bank account. Now she wanted to sell the house, so she could continue to live in St. Andrews. It made him sick with rage. She was *old*, she had enough money. What did she need more for? It wasn't as if she was going on a world cruise, now that sanctimonious old husband of hers was dead. No, rather she was just robbing him of his rightful home. Well, he wasn't going to stand for it. He was adamant. He was going to persuade her to let him stay or, she could move back to Edinburgh and have one of the rooms on the first floor, or they could renovate the basement like they talked about before.

'No, Tyrone. I am telling you; I will not move!' There was finality in her tone. 'I want to live out my life *here* in peace and quietude and that's what I'm going to do. It would be better for you to have somewhere of your own to live. My mind is made up Tyrone, I need to release some money and I'm going to sell, no matter what you say; I don't need money worries at my age.'

When he told her outright, she was only thinking of herself; that she should consider *him* for once, she'd replied candidly and firmly.

'Tyrone, from the time you were a child in knee-breeches you've had an air of self-importance about you. What is it about living on India Street that matters so much to you? Why can't you let it go? Is it so you can say you live in a big house, to impress people with what you have? I think that's what it is. It's time you looked at your own motives, rather than questioning mine or Stewart's, god rest his soul.'

'I'll go away again then, and travel.' he replied with a hint of childish defiance.

'Well, Tyrone, I'm quite sure you'll do what is best for *you*. Time away might be just what you need; give you some perspective. In the meantime, I'll instruct my lawyers to put enough money aside from the sale to help you get re-established. That's as good as you are going to get. Maybe you should think about finding yourself a proper job.'

'A *job.* ' he huffed under his breath. He knew exactly what he needed to do now.

Tyrone focused his energy on planning and scheming. Who could help him re-establish himself as a spiritual leader; one deserving of all the compensations he believed were afforded to his lofty status? Who could he take into his confidence with such a delicate matter? As he watched the meandering of the river from the bench again, he considered a visit to see the Hermit might be in order. But what would he say? Particularly to someone who placed no importance on material assets. What light could the Hermit, who lived off the land and off seemingly thin air, shed on his predicament? There had to be another way. He rose to his feet, he had a train to catch. He'd return to the house in Edinburgh, take a quick inventory of all the furnishings and items he could sell quickly at auction, if the worst came to the worst. But before that, he'd make a stop at the estate agents.

'Good afternoon, Tyrone.' said the sultry voice behind the desk, seemingly unphased by his unannounced visit. At around forty and somewhat striking, Vanessa's flowing and lustrous red hair was swept back in a French roll and her large breasts poised invitingly like ripened fruit. She didn't seem to mind the extra notice Tyrone gave her ample bosom. His eyes were now fixed on her as if she were the only woman in the world.

'Please, sit down and make yourself comfortable.' she said, her eyes locked on his. 'Can I have my girl get you tea or coffee, a soft drink?'

'Coffee, thanks,' he responded with a saccharine smile, 'milk, no sugar.' She nodded absently to her young assistant, who immediately got up and left the room. Tyrone was glad to have a moment alone with her. As the agent in charge of the house sale, she was a key player in his big plans without even realising it. His cover story was to inform her he'd be looking to purchase a tenement flat in Morningside; for once India Street was sold. But his plan was far more specific than that. Business concluded, he took a deep breath and focused his gaze on her.

'How do you fancy a little trip to St Andrews this weekend Vanessa? You drive I take it? You see, my mother lives there as you know, and she would be delighted if you'd come by for Sunday lunch, after service?'

'Why, that's most kind of you Tyrone and yes I have a lovely Silver Mercedes Convertible.' she smiled, but not too overtly. 'I'd be delighted.' Vanessa was quite accustomed to receiving attention from men; she received lunch and dinner invites almost daily. However, Tyrone represented a very special kind of man to her; a man of genteel refinement, an "evolved" individual. Reminding her to keep an eye out for a property that he could buy, one suitable to his stature in the community; he smiled and said he looked forward to seeing her Sunday. Rising to his feet, just as his coffee arrived, he took Vanessa's hand and kissed it chivalrously before saying,

'Pick me up at the house about ten then? Adios.'

On India Street, Tyrone was met with abject silence. The house seemed huge after living in his mother's poky home; particularly with none of his beautiful personal possessions providing the ambiance. He wandered about the rooms, reflecting on the past, the secrets it held. His heart ached to think his time there was limited, unless he could force his mother's hand. The thought of someone else living within its walls gave him palpitations, filled him with anger and defiance and fear. The old bookcase in the sitting room…the oriental rug in the formal dining room…the antique mirror hanging above the mantle in the study; they all might bring a few bob. No, no, no. He'd leave them right where they were. He had not finished with his mother yet. He would find a way to stay for good, one way or another.

CHAPTER SEVEN

Lomond was bored to tears. As she sat surveying the variety of artwork pinned to the wall, in pastels, watercolours, pen and ink, she couldn't get why other people failed to see what she saw; the coloured energy was floating about everywhere. She didn't understand why they insisted the subject be drawn *realistically;* she was good at capturing the *essence*; the colours that radiated. Mrs. MacFinnie, was beyond exasperation with Lomond and her refusal to follow the O Level curriculum outlined so clearly. Despite warning after warning, every piece of work was *'a surreal barrage of colour'* or *'an assault on the senses'* as she called them; unlike anything she'd seen. Although deep down, Mrs MacFinnie couldn't deny Lomond had natural talent. She saw it in the effortless almost unconscious way she applied water or oils to paper and the energy radiating from her paintings; but she had to learn to follow the rules

'I can't make it the way you want it!' Lomond told her, frustration bubbling over.

'Look, drawing is not about getting it the way *I* want it. It's about *discipli*ne first, and then it's about *freedom.'*

'How is telling me what to paint and how to paint it

freedom?'

'I'm talking about the process we need to follow to reach *freedom of expression*,' Mrs. MacFinnie explained. 'Freedom starts with being able to master how things *actually* appear, their form. Then you can present your *own* vision of them, how they appear to *you*.' Mrs. MacFinnie's thoughtful explanation was lost on Lomond. Her mind was already fantasizing about her own vision of freedom; and it looked like George. Despite his showing up at the hospital on her birthday, George had yet to call Lomond. Safe to say, she'd made no effort to contact him either, but she'd expected him to be the one to make the first move at least. She didn't want him thinking she was chasing him.

Furthermore, she still hadn't decided how she felt about him after everything that had happened. She never knew; he may have moved on and found someone else. There was also still the issue with her parents. Although they'd softened about George, almost appreciating his help bringing Lomond out of the coma; their hatred towards his motorbike had not changed at all and they couldn't forgive him for nearly taking their daughter's life.

Dawdling through the park on her way home from school, Lomond received another harsh reminder of the effects of her coma. She misjudged the size of a pothole and found herself lying flat on her face in the grass. Adding to her embarrassment, a young teenage boy practicing football rushed over to help her to her feet.

'I'm alright, honest, I am.' Lomond said, brushing dirt off her skirt and blouse and hurrying off. A short distance away and out of breath, she came to a stop at the main road. Whilst standing waiting to cross, images began flashing through her mind: the bend in the road and the glare of headlights, the sound of grinding brakes, squealing tyres, glass shattering and the grating of metal-on-metal. Then she remembered a strange sensation of being airborne before the searing pain as she collided with asphalt, then *nothing.* She stood transfixed on the curb; the traffic flowing past her. In her confusion, every car became the car that hit them and every driver a reminder that any moment things can turn *fatal.* Suddenly, colour began to flow all around her and she allowed its invigorating energy to take over. With it came the thought this energy could transport her to imaginary places she somehow knew-existed. *There's got to be more. This can't be all there is to life.* Freedom was about having the tranquillity needed to plunge into the unknown. No thoughts, no distracting pictures in the mind. It was about freeing yourself from life's expectations, about mastering how to break away from society's norms, without any re-percussions. She realised there was only one way for her to achieve this; and that was to leave home. Only then would she be able to take charge and lead a life of her own choosing. *I can't just leave home like that,* she reasoned and a plan began to materialize, *I'll need a job, money, a place to live.* That was it, she decided she'd stick it out at school until the end of the term, play it cool with her parents and after that it was *Bye-Bye!* See *yaanon!*

With a renewed sense of excitement, she secretly checked the *Evening News* and the *Scotsman* for jobs. She quite fancied hotel work, thinking this could provide her with an income and post-escape accommodation, she could do that. To her dismay, most ads included the dreaded caveat: "experienced individuals need only apply" or "college student welcome" and she was neither. There was one that caught her eye but it was a way out in Dalwhinnie, out in the sticks. It had a train station and a distillery but little else; only truck drivers stopped there. She didn't really fancy that.

The day of the Craft Fair came and something told her she needed to attend, no matter what. Surprisingly, her mother had agreed to let her go, provided her father drove her there and picked her up afterwards. Although desperate to go, Lomond was adamant not to suffer this level of control. Whilst her mother was at Easter church service and her father was out with Shuna, she slipped out and jumped on a bus to town. As she approached the Assembly Rooms on George Street, she saw the broad granite steps leading to the portico entrance were peppered with people. Immediately, she spotted Lorraine leaning against one of the pillars at the top, Innes stood next to her, looking somewhat gaunt and sickly she thought. Lomond held back for a moment, taking the opportunity to study Lorraine, unnoticed. Out of her uniform, she looked prettier than you might imagine. Although it was clear she never dressed to draw attention; her flair for style was evident. The lovely woollen, teal scarf wrapped loosely around her neck stood out against her auburn hair and cobalt-blue jacket. Innes appeared more subdued in her muted mauve, home-knitted scarf. Lomond's became aware of a soft blue glow bouncing off Lorraine's shoulders; she was drawn to the colour. The energy she felt from it made her want to express her inner thoughts.

'Hey Lomond!' Lorraine called noticing her and she climbed the steps towards them grinning broadly.

'You guys been waiting long?' she asked breathlessly.

'Just a wee bit,' Innes said. 'Come on, we better get a move on, the line is getting deep already.' The three paid their entrance fee, which they discovered also entitled them to a 'free cup of coffee and a *mystery gift*. Apparently, the number printed on the back of their tickets corresponding to a number posted at one of the stalls inside. *Who'll find their number first?* Lomond wondered, thinking of it as a game.

Inside, the grand ballroom was an absolute feast for the senses. They were mesmerized by the huge circuit of stalls with so many lovely things to look at, there was a real buzz in the air. The range and variety of products was stupefying. There were stalls selling dozens of types of incense sticks and the most beautiful candles; in all colours, shapes and sizes. Others offered hand- knitted jumpers, silk scarves, plush soft toys, homemade jams and chutneys. The many oils with the potential to energize the whole body, mind and soul filled the air with a cocktail of scent. As they wondered around taking it all in, they kept their eyes peeled for their lucky numbers. Innes was the first to spot hers.

'Twenty-five!' she screeched. The stall belonged to an older woman who looked to be in her seventies. She was offering cures for arthritis with devices such as ionized bracelets and shoe insoles. Devices she said incorporated special magnets or copper.

Both metals relieved pain. They combated the progression of chronic musculoskeletal disorders including rheumatoid arthritis she promised them.

'You'll all be my age one day, dearies,' she chuckled, trying to win them over. Much to her disappointment, Innes *mystery gift* was a pair of shoe inserts. Lomond was on top form, a combination of the company and being able to revel in the energies floating all around. Her humour was infectious, to the extent both Innes and Lorraine momentarily forgot their personal problems. Lomond pointed out the stall with rows and rows of hanging gemstones. They all quickened their pace towards it, only to slow again when they noticed the frosty-faced old man sitting on a folding chair behind the make-shift counter. He was doodling in a notebook and seemed to be the only stall-holder not actively luring people. As Lomond and Innes '*oohed*' and '*aahed*' over his wares, Lorraine realised her ticket number matched. She waved it front of his eyes, breaking his artistic concentration. The other girls were secretly envious; especially Lomond.

'Choose your birthstone from one of these boxes.' he said flatly, pointing to dozens of compartments brimming with gems. Lorraine's birthstone was Garnet, for January and she chose the fiery orange Mandarin version. 'It's considered a great gift to symbolize friendship and trust.' he muttered while wrapping it in red tissue paper. Lorraine thanked him. 'Perhaps you'd like to see your birthstones as well?' he said turning the box towards Lorraine and Innes. 'They're just a few pennies each, and that's old pennies.' He went off on a tangent. 'I tell you, it's pounds, shillings and pence all the way to ma grave for me. I'll not be doing anything different come decimal day. They've just withdrawn the ten-shilling note you ken. It's a pure disgrace, confusing the hell out of us old folks like that.' Lomond recalled how they'd been practicing for 'the big change over' at school. None of them understood why there needed to be a new currency anyway; why mend something that's worked fine for so long already? As he was ranting on, Lomond noticed something in his face that disturbed her. She didn't know what it was, but immediately lost interest and turned away, beckoning the girls to follow her.

'There's something in his face I don't like it at all.' Lomond declared once they were out of earshot. Lorraine gave her a disapproving look. He'd given her a free garnet; she wished Lomond was a little less critical sometimes.

Innes gasped and gripped Lorraine's arm.

'Look! It's *Tyrone, o*ver there, with that pretty red-head.' she was half whispering and inside, half relieved to see him with someone closer to his own age. It was quite a sight to behold. There he was arm-in arm with an attractive and powerful looking woman who seemed way out of his league. To add to the hilarity, he was wearing a Hindi Sherwani, making him look totally out of place. For Lomond, who was seeing Tyrone for the first time in the flesh, that she could remember, she saw nothing but an actor; a man whose whole demeanour was a performance. The redhead seemed enchanted as she laughed affectionately and batted her eyelids. Lomond was not impressed at all. Even at her young age, she saw straight through his superficial veneer, sensing a spoiled man who didn't like himself really. Suddenly, she was overcome by the feeling she'd been in his presence before. She couldn't say when or where, but she'd encountered this energy. Next his dull colours and darkness seemed to consume her and for a moment she wasn't there in the room. Everything became chaos. She saw swirling black energy and flashes of light from a crystal glass, a deafening rumble with it. She put her hands to her head. Individual letters sprang to mind, they were jumbled up and no matter how hard she tried she could not work out what they spelled. She felt a presence in all this array of moving energy and she heard a soft pleading voice in her ear,

'The bookcase, the bookcase…' Lomond jolted as a hand rested on her shoulder. She was relieved to see Innes standing beside her.

'Are you ok Lomond, you look as if you were in a trance, like you seen a ghost?' Taking deep breaths to steady herself; Lomond nodded her head and smiled.

'It's ok,' she whispered 'but maybe I *have* just seen a ghost.'

With the crowd suddenly thickening, Tyrone disappeared, propelling the redhead forward with the palm of his hand on the small of her back; controlling her movements like she was a child. Lomond drew in close to Innes.

'What do you see in him?' she asked, unable to hide her disdain. Innes was embarrassed by the thrust and unwitting implication of Lomond's question; she couldn't believe her 'attraction' was that obvious, she side-stepped.

'Do you know, the first time Lorraine met him, she didn't like him either, did you, Lorraine?'

'Well I must admit, he wasn't at all what I was expecting,' she admitted, but I guess I got used to him and well, I liked the meditation group, so…'

'You know, he's selling his house.' said Innes.

'Is he?' replied Lomond.

'Yep, I saw the FOR-SALE sign at the door and my mum saw something about the property market on the news, they were showcasing a house on India Street, I'm sure it was Tyrone's; if it is, he's asking for over a hundred thousand pounds for it.'

'Good afternoon, ladies,' His drawl took them by surprise. 'How are you all doing this fine day?' He asked without sincerity, singling out Lomond with a long stare. All three of them nodded and forced a smile. 'We've been to visit my mother in her country house haven't we dear?' he stated, dragging his eyes away from Lomond and nuzzling into neck of the red-headed woman.

'We sure have Ty.' She cooed proudly.

'Vanessa here works at Elite Property Services in the New Town,' he gloated. 'You know, it's just *amazing* the way the price of property is rising in that area' His tone condescending.

'Ty stands to make a pretty penny.' Vanessa added with a wink.

'I'm selling the house, well sort of selling it,' he stuttered. 'My mother, you know, she's moved to a lovely house in St Andrews.' Tyrone looked directly at Innes. 'Good thing I'm around to make sure we get the best price; that we're not taken for a ride!'

Tyrone recalled how pleasant his mother had been to Vanessa. It was clear she saw her as a prospective daughter-in-law. Someone who could change him and in doing so, bring his mother peace to live her life. He knew if he played his cards right for now, soon there'd be no more quibbling about *who* gets *how much* from the sale. There was only him now, his sister had died lied long ago. He needed that house, was desperate for it to help him maintain his self-indulgent lifestyle. He'd also considered the possibility of moving in with Vanessa, as his wife. Maybe he could live off the money his mother would give him from the sale of India Street. It would be a fresh start to live the life he felt he *deserved*. The fact Vanessa seemed to love the house on India Street as much a him meant she was his best ally regardless if the house sold or not. Vanessa also had plans. She saw herself living in Tyrone's large Georgian house, saw herself entertaining her friends and family there; the address would give her *Kudos*.

'Vanessa was saying prices haven't peaked yet.' Tyrone announcing as if were of general interest; or by way of stroking her ego.

'If you can hang on to it, it'll be worth a good deal more by this time next year.' Vanessa added.

'Well, if *anyone* can persuade Mother to hold off selling, it could only be you, mother *adores* you!'

'Oh, and I just adore her, *too*' she said fawningly. As they turned to leave, he touched Lomond's hand and an electric shock coursed through her.

'Has nobody told you it's rude to stare?' Tyrone said in a low deep voice.

'Sorry,' stammered Lomond, 'I just thought I saw…well I mean, well I am not sure what I mean, really.' She hung her head.

'What are you talking about, saw something like what?' he demanded. Lomond's eyes looked distant as she spoke.

'Well, it was like moving energy, a black mist and, the voice of a young girl; saying words I couldn't make out.' She thought she saw a flash of fear in his eyes.

'What's your name girl?' he asked glaring at her.

'Lomond.' She answered, bristling.

'Lomond? What kind of name is that? A strange name for an strange girl eh?' he sneered before turning to Vanessa with a wry smile 'Come on, it's lunchtime, I'm absolutely famished.' With that, the pair turned on their heels and headed away, with no further regard to the girls.

'*Oooh*…who do you suppose is buying?' Lomond quipped sarcastically. The girls couldn't help but snigger at her insight.

'Think they're headed for the George Hotel?' she said, half of her desperate to follow them. The well-known, opulent hotel was exactly the kind of place he would take a lady to try and impress her; or grant them the privilege of impressing him. It was then Lomond noticed Innes, she looked altogether disturbed by the whole scenario.

'What was all that about Lomond?' she asked. 'A girl's voice, what did you…?' Before Lomond could answer, she felt a hand rest gently on her shoulder and turning, she came face-to-face with a smiling, silver-haired old man dressed in rather shabby cloths.

'I believe it was you I gave a message to a while back?' he said through crooked teeth.

'Uh, I think you've mistaken for someone else,' she said politely. 'I've never seen you before…have I?'

'Oh, most certainly you have,' he said, grinning broadly, 'in the old house with the cellar? You are the one who is to discover me.' Lomond was confused, something was bothering her. She dropped her gaze to consider.

'Could you…' when she looked up, he was gone. She glanced around, scanning the crowd but there was no sign of silver-haired man.

'Hey Lorraine, did you see where that man went who was just talking to me?'

'Uh? An old man…?'

'Yeah,' she interrupted. 'the old man in shabby clothes, he had silver-hair?'

'Sorry, I don't know what you're… maybe it's time we got moving.'

Lorraine answered, beginning to worry Lomond was suffering some after-effect of the accident. As they headed to the next row of stalls, the words the man had spoken kept echoing in Lomond's ears. She was certain he was there; his appearance wasn't just her imagination; or was it? That morning she'd awoken with a powerful feeling that big change was coming.

Now she wondered if it had something to do with him.

There was so much to take in as they flitted from stand to stand: so many commercial and handmade products, demonstrations of all kinds, modest offerings of modern and ancient. Lomond revelled in the oil-scents as she passed by Aroma therapists. She wondered whether to invest her money on a tarot reading, but the reader, a dumpy-looking woman in ancient hippie garb, sent her a bad vibe.

There were books everywhere, far more than in The Old Bookshop even. Innes was drawn towards a beautiful luminous display of fine silk scarves, their soft sheen like a healing balm to her soul. They seemed to whisper to her. *We can help you, choose the colour that suits you and it will soothe you and care for you.* Innes moved along the row of colours and found herself most drawn to a rich pink. She touched it, afraid to ask what it cost. Lorraine offered to buy it for her, as a gift. The vendor with honey-coloured skin smiled and told her pink was the colour of the young.

    'It'll draw the love and support you need in your life.' she promised.

Lomond caught up and her attention was pulled to a multicoloured display of pyramid-shaped bottles on another table at the stall. They were elegant, tapering from a narrower square at the neck to a wider base and capped with rounded gold tops fitted snug into the shoulder. It was the colours of the contents that spoke loudest to Lomond. Each bottle contained a duo of complementary coloured water; separated by a fine layer of what could only be oil. There was red with gold, yellow above purple, green with violet, blue over yellow; even transparent colours. She counted forty-nine altogether, virtually every permutation you could think of. Her fascination deepened when she picked one up and tilted it. The colours didn't blend; they remained separate, moving in a heavy, almost sensual way. She picked up the indigo and purple and held it up against the light. The deep colours shone, luminescent, almost translucent and her captivation was mounting. Gazing upon it, she felt something pulling her to another realm. Then she saw herself lying in her coma and feelings of an altered state of consciousness fleeted in her mind. Immediately, she knew she had to have it. The crystal pendant was no longer an issue. Her eye was drawn to a written notice stuck to the next stall; *Radiant Colour Readings, By Sorcha, Free to Ticket Holders 15, 45, 75, and 100.* Excited, she pulled her ticket from her pocket and double-checked.

'I have number seventy-five!' she said to a small vibrant woman of perhaps forty. There was an openness and trust in her face.

'Does that mean I get a free reading?' Lomond gushed. 'Indeed, it does,' the woman smiled. 'Would you like to have one just now?'

'Oh yes, yes, I would!' she said enthusiastically, despite being nervous about what to expect. The woman extended her hand.

'My name is Sorcha, it means *radiant* in Gaelic, hence

Radiant Colour Readings,' she laughed. 'Please come in and take a seat.'

'I'm Lomond.' She took the woman's small and delicate hand. 'Is that a Highland accent?' she asked loving the soft Scottish lilt in Sorcha's voice.

'Aye, indeed, it is, lass. I'm from Nairn.'

'Nairn, I'm not sure where that is.'?'

'It's on the coast, on the Moray Firth, not too far from Inverness and once described as the Brighton of Scotland.' Lomond felt at ease.

They sat facing each other, next to rows of pyramid bottles.

'Now, what I'd like you to do, Lomond, is to pick four different bottles in the order you are attracted to them; most to least. Can you do that for me?' Lomond nodded. 'Now, set them out in a row here on the table from left to right. Take as much time as you need.' Lomond placed the Magenta-pink -on the table followed by pink-blue, red-violet, yellow-green. 'Now, pick four more bottles you are *not* attracted to, and put them in a row behind the others.' Again, she laid them out in a row, orange-orange, violet-indigo, orange-blue and gold-indigo.

As Lorraine and Innes watched curiously from outside the booth, the woman began to interpret Lomond's colour choices, conveying their meaning in an easy-to-follow explanation. As the reading went on, Lomond found herself more and more transfixed by how accurately Sorcha identified how she was feeling and the events in her life that weighed heavily on her shoulders, simply by her colour choices. *How could Sorcha know so much about my life, everything I'm going through, just from the colours I've chosen?* The woman continued by suggesting she was going to change direction, that she was making plans to find a job and leave school.

'It's going to happen soon,' she added pointing to the last bottle, the yellow-green. 'There is a quest you have to follow, the gold-indigo is there waiting for you to find and develop a psychic, spiritual path, this is a *journey* you will undertake, facing the dark and entering the Light. However, it's not just about what's going to happen today or tomorrow,' she explained, 'the patterns you choose to make and the conditions you create for yourself will shape your lifestyle. You've set your heart on finding a job haven't you?' Lomond explained how much she felt she needed to get away from her parents. How she was looking for something in the hotel business. 'I can tell you this,' the woman said, observing the colours she'd chosen, 'there is a strong connection to the colour magenta…and tea parties and a search for someone. A search that is long overdue, I believe.' Lomond frowned, somehow parts of what she was saying rang true, but she couldn't think why or how? 'I feel a choking sensation around my throat Lomond, do you feel this at times? Lomond thought for a moment.

'Yes, sometimes I do, but it's not like I'm the one choking, I feel a pressure, like someone is showing me they are.'

'Calm your mind Lomond, sit quietly and try to see or hear who this sensation belongs to, what they are trying to tell you.' Lomond closed her eyes and Sorcha continued, 'There are loose ends in your life that would benefit from being tidied up. You have been through many difficult emotional events, including a near death experience.' Lomond nodded in agreement. 'Well, now it's time to un-scramble all the loose ends. You are very intuitive, and you know you are. I believe during your near-death experience, you observed many different energies, you developed your intuition and spiritual awareness. However, since you decided to return to the realm of the living, you've avoided this inner spiritual knowledge.' Lomond could barely breathe. 'It's time to remember Lomond, to heal and become the person you were meant to be, your true self. Soon you will begin the real journey, one that will connect you with the 'I' consciousness you were born with. Ok,

now sit for a moment. Take a deep breath, feel your body relax.'
Lomond obeyed willingly, everything became still and Sorcha's
tone grew softer. 'Now, what do you see?' she asked and Lomond
felt her body becoming light. She no longer felt the chair beneath
her, could hear no external noise. She saw a rainbow of flowing
energy, orange, yellow and magenta and she could almost make
out a form within; a woman surrounded in flowing pink robes. A
soft voice came from the figure.

'Welcome Lomond, you have found me. Now you know
what you must do to reach me. Keep this feeling with you always;
use it to come to me. I still have much to teach you.' Slowly, she
became aware of Sorcha's voice again, aware of the heaviness of
her own body. Fully back into the moment, she beamed at Sorcha.

'Thank you, so much, that was amazing.' Lomond said in all
sincerity.

'I can see you took a great deal from that Lomond. You
know you have the answers, you just need to find the ways to
access them. Can I ask, do you see the colours around people
Lomond?'

'Well, sort of I guess, yes I do…'

'Let me explain a little about what you're seeing. Colours
surround every living thing, but most people can't see them. They

are called the *aura*. It's also known as the electro-magnetic field. *Your* aura is so expansive Lomond, emanating such strong vibrating colours, it tells me you are a truly gifted intuitive.' Although still with many questions on her mind, the reading was complete and Sorcha handed Lomond her card. They exchanged smiles and she took Lomond's hand.

'Let me know how things turn out dear, won't you?' the woman said kindly. As she left the booth, Lomond realised the colours in the bottles had made her feel strangely *alive*. She wanted to know more about it and she wanted to know how Sorcha did her readings, she definitely planned to see her again.

The women moved out into the rising hustle and bustle and for the third time that day, Lomond saw the blue colour radiating from Lorraine. Unable to contain herself she turned to her and said;

'Lorraine, you know I see the colour blue all round you today; like it's your *aura* or something. I saw it twice earlier and now I see it again. I don't know what this means, but Sorcha said the blue in my second bottle represents the healing I got from someone. It must be you, Lorraine. You're the nurse who helped heal me.' Lorraine took Lomond's hand and led her aside. Holding it tightly she closed her eyes and imagined again, the orange energy that connected their consciousness' while Lomond lay motionless in the hospital bed. Now, they both experienced the orange energy fill their bodies and flow between them, as if there were no separation. Momentarily, they were transported beyond the ordinary dimension, suspended in a pool of warm flowing energy that was simultaneously inside and outside of them.

'Is that what you did for me in hospital?' whispered Lomond, as if it were something deeply intimate. 'I know you did; you don't even need to answer. You helped *heal* me and in a way that was way beyond being my nurse.' She gave Lorraine a deep, warm embrace. 'You are a very special person Lorraine. Thank you so much.' As they made their way to the exit where they hugged and kissed goodbye, Lomond's mind was overflowing with all that had occurred that afternoon.

Later that night as she lay in bed reliving that *magical* moment with Lorraine and thinking about the reading, she began to wonder *where* she'd been while in a coma. Did her consciousness somehow find another way to function, in a different dimension? Might that explain everything, all the strange thoughts and feelings? There was something about the magenta colour; the mention of the tea parties and of finding someone. As she drifted off to sleep, she saw the image of the old man again and a strange indigo-coloured tunnel.

CHAPTER EIGHT

The sun shone brightly through the pale-yellow curtains of her bedroom; casting coruscate gold upon her face. It woke her from sleep like a warm kiss, and then a moment later her mother's shrill voice from outside the door shattered her harmony.

'Lomond! I am telling you, you will *not* be leaving school, it's out of the question. All your cousins have gone to university and got their degrees and you will too. Once you have it, then you can travel, or do whatever you want to do, but you need to get it first. You need it to land a decent job; you can't live off your looks you know.' As she ranted on, Lomond's mind wandered off, dreaming of her journey to freedom. 'Lomond? Lomond! Are you listening to me?' Lomond stayed silent. 'Ah well, what can I expect? You were always going to be *different* from the family.' Lomond jerked back to the present.

'What?' She jumped out of bed and threw the door open. Her mother was already halfway down the stairs. 'What's that supposed to mean?'

'It's nothing, never mind.'

'Oh, no, what the hell did you say? That I'm *bound to be different*?' she yelled after her, but Beth was now down in the kitchen. Lomond's mind kicked into overdrive. What was she talking about? Her mother was the type who chose her words carefully. *Does she know something? Was she referring to the accident, -or something else?* Lomond retreated back into her room, slamming the door. Frustrated about not knowing, she threw herself on her bed and thought about her mother; how they had never been able to relate to each other. It seemed they were complete opposites in most things; particularly regarding her father. *That's just how mother-daughter relationships are, isn't it?*

Although she had issues with her father, most of them were because he was always siding with Beth over her, but she loved him regardless. Why did she not feel this way about her mother too? She hated the way she controlled Mac, the way she put him down, labelling him as dim-witted and incapable of making decisions. Sometimes, it seemed to Lomond her father had just given up; resigned himself to be her doormat. He often said that agreeing with Beth was simply easier; anything for a peace. However, she could see how much doing so had limited him. Lomond was different, in her mind, peace at any price is no peace at all. There was no denying she'd felt 'different' from her mother for as long as she could remember, she felt like an outsider in her own family. But, what did her mother meant about her 'always going to be different?' Did she mean different from her? That they had nothing in common? She had a gut feeling it wasn't that at all, but it was pointless to try and talk to her about it. Just then, Lomond felt something tug on her senses, she heard voices in her mind, a conversation taking place somewhere else:

'This falls on you, you know. This never would have happened if you...'

'Me? What did I...'

'Well, didn't get that defiant attitude from me!'

'Now, Beth . . .'

*'Don't you dare, now Beth **me** McIlroy Mitchieson! You've always let her have her own way, constantly undermining my authority. If I'd known you were such a spineless...'*

'Shhh...she might hear you for god's sake!'

'Oh, we can't have that can we? God forbid she finds out the truth...'

'What the hell *was* that?' Lomond said aloud, her heart pounding in her chest. 'That was my parents voices, what am I hearing? What *truth* was Beth talking about?' Convinced more than ever there was something to Beth's offhanded quip; she was determined to find out what she meant. Wracking her brains, she decided that if any information, clues would be anywhere, it would be in her father's desk. That's where he kept anything of importance, anything private. She considered when might be a good time to snoop. On Tuesday her mother would be serving tea at the Women's Guild in St. Cuthbert's Church and her father would be hard at work; that would be the day.

When Tuesday arrived, Lomond pretended to be under-the-weather, 'Lady problems' she told her mother so she could stay home from school without suspicion. No sooner had they left the house, an unexpected anxiety and paranoia set in, *What if one of them comes back unexpectedly and catches me going through their private papers? What would they say . . . and think . . . and do?* More importantly, she was petrified at what would she find in the desk? Shuna, her faithful Golden Lab, followed her around as she checked every room in the house, just to make sure. She even checked the back door was locked and her mother wasn't just out in the garden pruning her prized yellow rose bushes.

Although satisfied she was alone, she could not shake the feeling of being watched. She put it down to the dog who never took her eyes of her. Okay now it was time. She hurried to the walnut desk by the window in the lounge and turned the little brass key in the lock. Inside, everything looked so neat and tidy: her mother's handy work, no doubt. Making a mental note of where everything was placed, she began to flip through the row of manila folders, meticulously checking the label on each. A half-dozen files in, just after *Cambridge Insurance*, she came to one labelled '*Certificates.*'

She slipped out the file and opened it, the first document was her parents' marriage certificate. She smiled as she scanned the page, noticing her father's name in the first column; 'McIlroy Stuart Mitchieson', then in the second, 'Maude Millar.' Lomond stared at the name in confusion, she read it again.

'This can't be right.' She whispered. *He was married before? Why keep it secret*? There was nothing on the back. She laid it down and stared out the window, trying to imagine her father being married to someone other than Beth. She told herself she wasn't really bothered; some people marry more than once; the past is past and all that. Catching sight of another handwritten certificate, she took it out. The handwriting on this one was difficult to read. As she mulled the document over, she could just make out the name 'Elizabeth Violet En...' the rest of the surname was blurred' but further read nee Riley, all of which were written in the column next to her father's, and the date of their marriage. The date, it must be wrong, it was three years after Lomond was even born, they told her they married before she was born. A thought terrified and excited her. Maybe Beth wasn't her real mum, maybe it was Maude? Surely not, Beth must have had an affair with her father, while he was married to Maude she reasoned; that would explain it. Then when he found out Beth was pregnant; he did the right thing; he divorced Maude and married Beth and they became a proper family. That must be it. He was trying to make things right for her, for his daughter. Though dreading to delve any deeper, she couldn't stop herself looking for more. The bold black print jumped out, 'Death Certificate.' She scanned the page and gasped when she saw the name, 'Maude Mitchieson.' According to this, they didn't get divorced and Maude died earlier the same year her parents married. What must have happened? Lomond began fanaticizing there must have been a beautiful romance between her parents. It must have been for them to have kept their love secret, so as not to hurt Maude. Cause of death… the words 'gas inhalation.'

'What the f…' The dog began to bark and she early jumped out of her skin. She heard the sound of the post dropping onto the tiles at the front door. Lomond glanced up at the brass carriage clock on the mantelpiece, she didn't have long. She was torn between closing the desk and searching for the truth.

'What the hell, I need some answers here.' She said out loud. 'Who is my real mum, bloody Beth or Maude, and why the hell did she die of gas inhalation?'

It occurred to her she'd never seen her birth certificate before, there'd never been any cause to but now she needed to. She began searching frantically, it must be here, unless they've hidden it. Was this some kind of full-blown conspiracy, or perhaps something more sinister? She leafed through the files looking for the heading, then she found it. Inhaling deeply, she acknowledged the name on the top: Lomond Lee Mitchieson. Her eyes moved quickly to the signatures at the bottom. Father: McIlroy Mitchieson; Mother: Maude Mitchieson. *What the hell*? Beth was not her mother. When, if ever, were they planning to tell her? What were they waiting for? What other lies were they telling her? How could her father give Beth such power over someone who was not even her child? How dare she think she could control her and steal her freedom. Never in her young life had Lomond felt such rage, such a sense of betrayal. She rested her head in her hands, she couldn't concentrate. Suddenly she was *nobody*, part of *nothing*. Her whole identity was destroyed. She wanted to know about Maude. Who was she? What did she look like? What kind of person was she? Most importantly, why did she want to die like that?

As her mind became a swirling ball of confusion, it dawned on her she'd never seen photographs from her early childhood, pictures of her as a baby; not a single one. There'd been some story about all their things being ruined when the old basement flooded. She considered, she didn't look much like her father, she must take after her mother, Maude. *Were there photographs of me as a baby, in my mother's arms?* She felt upset and betrayed. She told herself that no matter the outcome, she would force them to tell her the truth. She'd confront them about their lies, she had a right to know. She glanced again at the clock on the mantle. She needed to get out of this prison, away from these strangers and find some time to think. Her head was aching. She wished there was something to numb the pain. Maybe she should pour herself a drink, a *strong* one. Something she'd heard her father say often enough. Is this why he drinks, to help him cope with the secrets he had to live with? His Whiskey was always coupled with a *John Player's Navy Cut*. She hated the smell, but if cigarettes and alcohol did the trick for her father, maybe it would help her too. *Things are gonna change around here for damn sure.* No longer would she put up with their self-serving, sanctimonious *shit* she told herself. No more would she just 'go along' with things because 'they were her parents.' Whether they helped or not, she'd find out who she really was and reinvent herself. She would become someone no one could deceive or hurt again. Quivering, she returned everything as it had been and slammed the walnut desk shut, turning the tiny gold skeleton key. Suddenly, the sun penetrated the large sash and case window and shone in her eyes. Although unable to see, the warming rays cocooned her whole being, triggering a memory in her of a different way existing. Again, she tried to grasp it, to bring it into her conscious mind, but it wouldn't rise to the surface. Despite being unable to find the source, she appreciated the feelings of happiness and peace it gave her. She headed towards the hall.

'Shuna, let's go!' she cried, snapping the lead to her collar. The dog, in all her excitement bumped into the hall table causing the vase of flowers to teeter before falling to the floor. It smashed on impact sending water, glass and her mother's newly picked roses everywhere. Lomond stared at it for a moment before saying. 'Well done Shuna, just for rewards, she can clean it up.'
She grabbed her handbag, jerked open the front door and stepped

over the post, slamming it behind her.

She ran down the hill with the dog, not stopping until she reached the main road; she needed to get away from 'her parent's' house. Just the thought of them made her feel sick. Crossing over the road, she carried on walking. She wanted to cry, but she couldn't. She wanted to scream and shout, but no sound would come. Emotionally exhausted, she slumped down on the park bench and let the dog off the lead, staring straight ahead as she bounded around on the grass.

'Ughhhh!' she screamed towards the sky. *Who the hell am I? I've spent the past sixteen years living nothing but a lie.* More questions flooded her already-inundated mind: What could justify her parents' deceit? Why had her real mother, Maude, never been mentioned? Why did they need to hide her death? No matter their reasons, it had to stop *now*. As she reflected on her "so-called" life, a bigger picture began to emerge, and it all had to do with Beth. Beth and her fecking *church* and her fecking *friends* and their fecking impossible *standards*! It was *Beth* who brought misery to the family with this façade of always having to lead a "good and decent life"; what a load of bollocks. Forget having a mind of your own, we must keep up with the neighbours, with everyone else. We must get the decent job, the fancy car, the big house to fill with expensive pointless things the neighbours would approve of. Everything about the woman and her ideas were so fake. She thought to be a *good* and decent person, you have 2.4 *good* and decent children, feed into a *good* pension fund, invest in a *good* insurance policy, set-up a *good* funeral plan, and pick out a *good* (and nothing-less-than pretentious) tombstone. Then, pass all this shit down to your kids so they can perpetuate the whole "good and decent" pretence into infinity. The woman had no clue and she was a hypocrite, she came from a normal family; her mum was only a cleaner. The only reason she had a half decent job in the solicitors office was because she'd manipulated her way there.

A thought crossed her mind bringing her musings came to an abrupt halt. *Silly maybe, but…could Beth have had something to do with Maude's death?* Considering her mother's passive aggressive personality, maybe it wasn't so far-fetched, maybe they were both involved. Lomond returned to the moment and the greenery of the park came into focus. Her eyes took notice of the colours radiating and flowing around everything. Like thousands of vibrant rainbows merging together, extending their rays over every living thing. She blinked and took a long and deeply revitalising breath; it was all so beautiful. The vibrant energy patterns danced over the grass, around the trees, all around the flowers and the people strolling by. Everything was imbricated by this dazzling spectrum of energy. Seeing the colours triggered a familiarity in her, she felt a strong unity with them, but yet something felt missing. She vowed she would find out what it was. Other, darker thoughts found their way into her mind.

As if sensing her mood, Shuna, ran over, sat down beside the bench and cuddled into her. She closed her eyes, shutting off the spectrum of colour. It wasn't beauty she craved, it was a reckoning, and for that she needed a plan. Leading Shuna, she made her way to the nearest phone box and punched in Tracy's number. On the second ring she picked up. 'Tracy, I'm so glad your home,' Lomond said urgently. 'I need to talk to you. Can I come around?'

'Is something wrong Lomond? What's happened?'

'*Wrong* doesn't even begin to cut it,' she replied. 'I'll tell all when I see you, okay?'

'Okay sure, just come over.'

After checking the coast was still clear, she dropped the dog home and headed to the bus stop, jumping on the cross-town just arriving. As the bus meandered along, she gazed out at all the houses they passed; wondering what kind of secrets *they* all held. Sure, she imagined some of them must be truly loving households, with families sitting around the kitchen table chatting, laughing and sharing their unconditional love for one another. Or maybe that was all just a myth. A fantasy. Although her father showed her some affection, real love was never displayed in their house. The closest it came was at Christmas when, after a couple of strong drinks, he'd give her an awkward hug and wish her a Merry Christmas. She couldn't even count on one hand the number of times Beth had embraced her, or her or indeed her dad. Their 'home' was a cold and sterile environment where love was a contagious disease to be avoided, for fear it would spread and infect. Realising Tracy's stop was just ahead, she descended the stairs too quickly, losing her footing and nearly colliding with the conductress at the bottom, she was still so angry she didn't care. Five minutes later she reached Tracy's first floor flat in Montgomery Street.

The oldest of three, and only seventeen, Tracy was level-headed, down-to-earth, intelligent and fun. Unlike Lomond, she had almost limitless freedom. She was allowed to go anywhere; skating, clubbing, whatever, and she had a steady boyfriend, who her mum liked. Lomond had always envied her and wished Yvonne was her mother too. Often when visiting, she gave in to this fantasy. Tracy flung the door open, just as Lomond was about to push the bell.

'Christ sake, girl, you look *awful*!' she blurted. 'What an earth has happened?'

'I need a drink, a strong one.' Lomond responded.

'Come on in.' Tracy said, leading her through to the sitting room. Although she knew Lomond's parents would never approve, she could see how much her friend needed calmed down, and she would need it as Dutch courage to talk about what had happened. She poured a large *Bacardi & Coke* from the refreshments cart. Lomond took a sip and pulled a face before flopping down on the over-stuffed armchair. Then she told Tracy everything she'd found out. 'Do you know, I always felt something wasn't quite right if I'm honest. Don't take this the wrong way but you are *nothing* like her, and she never seems to want you to be happy like most mothers do, that's just not right.'

Lomond was surprised but comforted by the way Tracy had taken it all so nonchalantly.

'I don't know who I am anymore Tracy.' Lomond's voice

cracked.

'Listen, you are still Lomond, no matter what.'

'I don't understand, aren't our parents supposed to shape who we become? The fact I've been *lied* to and influenced by *her?*' Tracy lit a Consulate and passed it to Lomond. With the drink kicking in, Lomond reached out her hand. 'What the hell, might as well have one!' she said, emboldened. She took a long drag and instantly began coughing hard, her face turning red. 'Damn, how long's it take to get the hang of these bloody things?' she asked before taking another uncomfortable hit. Tracy laughed,

'No idea I don't smoke either!' The two of them fell into hysterics, rolling around on the floor. It didn't matter to Lomond that she felt nauseous to her stomach. It was worth it. 'I have an idea,' Tracy said. 'Something that will take your mind off all your family *dramas*! Let me get dressed, we're going out!' Lomond nodded her intrigue and approval.

Up in her classy and spacious room, they both got ready. Tracy helped Lomond with her make-up before styling her hair and giving her something daring and sexy to wear; a bright yellow scoop-neck dress that was sure to draw attention. Lomond loved the way she looked in the mirror. She promised herself to make the transformation permanent.

'Beth would have an absolute *shit-fit* if she saw me now, but to hell with her!' she laughed.

Thinking of what 'Beth would say' made her relish it all the more. A short time later Ramona arrived home from work, she greeted them warmly and told them they looked "very lovely' *before* suggesting they wear their vests as it was getting cold out.

'Don't be *silly*, Mother!' said Tracy playfully. 'Don't you know we're *young* and *tough*. We don't feel the cold like you *old* folks!' Her mother chuckled.

'Is Lomond spending the night with us?' she asked looking at them both. They nodded.

'If that's okay?' asked Lomond.

'Of course!' Friends needed no formal invites to the Avella household; it was so welcoming, so open and simplistic. Lomond was also relieved because it gave her an excuse not to go home. She would call 'her mother' and *tell her* she was staying at Tracy's and *tell her* were the operative words.

That night, they both went into town did a round of some trendy pubs. With false dates of birth pre- rehearsed, they headed first to the Chameleon in Abercromby Place. As soon as they entered the downstairs bar, a young man came over and offered to buy Lomond a drink.

'We'd both like a Blue Lagoon cocktail please.' said Tracy. The young man raised his eyebrows, but ordered them none the less. The Chameleon was *utter sophistication* with its subdued lighting, plush booth-style seating areas and quality décor. The latest tunes and flashes of light emanated from a discrete DJ platform, alternating red, yellow, green and blue. In front of the DJ box was a compact timber dance area; the rest of the floor was decked out in plush carpet. The clientele looked equally snappy, as if they were cut from the same cloth; guys in sports jackets and flannels or three-piece suits and the ultimate accessories, matching tie and top pocket handkerchief; the girls in velvet dungarees and platform shoes to tight fitting jumpers and short skirts.

As the music and drink filtered through her system; Lomond began to feel bold. She acted out an interpretation of how her mother might view their little night out. With her hands on hips she began to imitate her.

'Well, well, well Lomond, we never taught you to dress like that, just look at you, like a little tramp for all and sundry to see, and drinking as well, what a disgrace, whatever will become of you?' Lomond did a twirl and took a bow to peals of laughter from Tracy. The young man who bought them the drinks was still lingering; ranting on about how tired he was from working all hours of the day in a local law firm. After half an hour or so of listening to him, Lomond rolled her eyes and indicating to Tracy they should leave; he was worse than her mother. When he *finally* decided to go to the toilet, they quickly downed their drinks and bolted. Outside, they walked west along Abercromby Place, heading for the *infamous* Bandwagon Pub, in Frederick Street. They were met at the top of stone steps by a tall, heavy set man wearing a long buttoned up black coat.

'What's your date of birth' he almost snarled. Staring directly into his eyes and wearing an infectious smile, Lomond recited her date of birth convincingly. He looked her up and down, barely satisfied, but he waved them past. Navigating the short flight of steps down and into the Bandwagon, Lomond let out a sigh of relief, she had managed to bluff her way into this pub, and there was no stopping her now. The Bandwagon was different from the Chameleon; less sophistication but with more live music. It generated a more edgy and vibrant atmosphere. There was no real dress code here; it was Rock and Roll and Blues territory. The downstairs bar was a thriving place of noise and energy, while upstairs, it was more chilled, more laid back. Lomond and Tracy pushed their way to the bar where Tracy ordered them a Bacardi and Coke.

'Let's head down to the stage,' Lomond nudged, 'I want to see the band.' A large sign above the stage read, *Shorty Rogers and the Wranglers.*

The boom of the music reverberated through Lomond, like nothing she had ever experience before; she couldn't help but dance. This live music was a million times better than the radio. A man nudged her arm and shouted in her ear.

'Brilliant hey! That's Shorty, the one singing, he's just brilliant!' Accompanied by his two guitarists and drummer, Shorty belted out 'you ain't nothing but a hound dog', the girls sung and swayed along in their element. She got unapologetically drunk that night, enjoying herself more than she ever remembered. The numbing effects of the Bacardi and Coke let her forget all about her problems. She surrendered to the night, joining in a ruse with Tracy in which pretended to be airhostesses for Caledonian Airways and allowing the young men to chat them up. Them both dissolving into peals of laughter that they were so easily believed and for a moment, life felt tolerable again.

CHAPTER NINE

The constant shrill ringing of the telephone woke from her drunken slumber. *Christ, who the hell's that*? She really didn't want to leave the warmth of the bed, but Tracy was still sleeping it off and she suspected Ramona must have already gone off to work. Staggering along the hallway she reached the phone and lifted the receiver.

'Tracy's house.' She croaked, her head feeling thick and woolly.

'Why haven't you checked in with us, young lady?' her mother barked. 'We've been worried sick!' *Shit* thought Lomond, she had forgotten to call them.

'I've been busy.' She blurted...

'Busy? Doing *what*?' demanded Beth. 'Something so important you couldn't even let your parents know if you're dead or alive?'

'Just *doing.*' said Lomond vaguely; half-tempted to ask why the hell she thought she had the right to expect *anything* from her after lying to her all her life.

'*Just doing* is *not* an answer, Lomond. Just doing *what?*' pushed Beth. 'Your father and I have been absolutely frantic!' Another lie, thought Lomond. Maybe her father was worried, she thought, but her *mother*, if that's what you could call her, would be more concerned she was tarnishing the illustrious Mitchieson family name. As Beth ranted on about the importance of knowing her whereabouts, Lomond pulled the receiver from her ear and mouthed,

'U*h-huh, uh-huh, uh-huh…y*es, of *course* you're right, *Mother.* You're always bloody *right*!'

"*Don't you dare* take that tone with me, my girl!' Lomond had to bite her tongue to keep from launching into an all-out verbal assault.

'Your father and I will be expecting you home in time for tea, do you hear me? 5.30pm sharp and not a minute later, in fact, you can come a bit earlier to help set the table. Do you hear me?'

'Yeah, tea, *Mother*!' she said through gritted teeth before hanging up the receiver. 'Up yours, *Mother,* 'she said, 'you'll see me when I'm bloody well ready.' With the hangover beginning to take hold, Lomond jumped back into Tracy's bed and under the covers, the events of the night before began screaming into focus. *Damn, what a night!* She'd kissed a boy who called himself Dave, who'd immediately declared his undying love for her. She'd danced on a tabletop to cheers and applause and cat-calls to "*Show us your chebs!*" She'd made people laugh all night with her witty come-backs. Feeling as she did now, she wondered if it was all worth it. At least it had made her feel happy for a while, she reasoned, taken her mind off things. Thoughts of what she'd discovered the day flooded back into her mind. She felt heaviness in her chest; was struggling to breathe properly. She wondered how much drink she'd need to consume to erase it all from her mind. It was too late to leave it be now.

'Wow, what a night!' Tracy groaned between yawns and stretches. 'You were an absolute *blast* last night, Lomond; we gotta do that again soon.'

'Aye, we *gotta*.' agreed Lomond, still uncertain how she really felt about it all.

When she arrived, begrudgingly, at 'her parents' house', as she now thought of it, it came of no surprise Beth had intentionally left the table for her to set, just so she could blame Lomond for delaying teatime no doubt. Fussing about in the kitchen, Beth made no acknowledgment of Lomond's presence. As if sensing the mood, Shuna wagged her tail a few times before returning to her bed and keeping her eyes fixed on them both. Lomond kept quiet; she couldn't even stand to look at Beth for fear of what might come out of her own mouth.

'So, what's the problem *now*, Lomond?' Beth finally asked; her tone dismissive.

'Nothing.' Replied Lomond, too sharply.

'Of *course,* there is,' Beth countered, finally turning to face her, 'I always know when something's wrong with you, young lady. You can't hide your feelings from me, Miss emotional.' Lomond took a deep breath and had to hold back from saying '*you don't know a fecking thing about me*'

'I need my birth certificate.' She stated instead. Beth stopped dead in her tracks and Lomond saw her jaw tighten before she spun away so hide the panic on her face.

'And just why would you be needing *that*?' Beth said, feigning nonchalance.

'What's the problem like? Don't I have a right to see it?' Lomond shot back.

'You'll have to talk to your father about this; when he comes home.' Beth muttered.
Lomond was watching her reaction closely.

'Why do I have to talk to *him* about it? Isn't it in right there in the desk with all the other important papers?'

'I told you,' Beth said, nervously shifting her weight from one foot to the other, 'you'll have to wait until your father gets home. He's in charge of all the family papers!' Lomond's heart was pounding so hard it echoed in her ears and a searing heat rose in her head. She clenched her hands into fists.

'Well, if *you* won't get my god-damn birth certificate, *mother* then I'll get it myself!' she screamed, storming out of the kitchen and rushing head-long towards the desk in the living room. Beth lost control. She slammed her fist down on the kitchen counter, her face contorted as she yelled,

'That's your father's bloody desk, young lady! You'll damn-well respect his wishes or you'll suffer the consequences!' Lomond stormed back into the kitchen.

'Look you're frightening Shuna, see, she's cowering in her bed, because of you! And what are you talking about, *consequences*? We both know it's *your* bloody desk *too*. What the hell are you hiding? What don't you want me to see?'

'Just set the bloody table, Lomond!' Beth shrieked. 'You're not going to ruin another meal with your childish *drama*!'

'You know, it works both ways *Mother*. You think you know when something's wrong with me, when there's something I'm not telling you? Well, I always know when *you're* hiding something too. When you're *lying*! It's written all over your face.
So, what the hell are you hiding from *me*…or don't you have the

guts to say it?'

'I don't know what the hell you're talking about Lomond.' Beth lied, forcing herself to calm down. 'Why should we, I mean, *I*, be hiding anything? I'm just a mother trying to deal with an impertinent, vulgar-mouth daughter, and trying to prepare dinner!' Lomond took a step closer.

'Why should a bloody piece of paper cause such so much…anger?' she said, storming back towards living room. Lomond knew Beth was on the verge of completely losing it and that's precisely what she wanted. She needed a confrontation, a reckoning; even if it all turned ugly. Just then the front door banged shut in a familiar way. 'Let's just deal with this here and now shall we?' Lomond yelled, loud enough for her father to hear. Mac looked crestfallen when he walked into the room and saw the looks on both their faces.

'Well,' he said, 'nice to see you, Lomond.' *Not for long* she thought, knowing Beth was about to explode; she intended stoking the flames. 'So, is there something you two want to tell me?' Mac asked, his tone conveying he was uncertain he wanted to hear it. Beth shot her husband a desperate look.

'Uh, Dad, I need your help getting something.' Lomond said.

'Anything,' he said, hoping to diffuse whatever contention had rattled the two.

'I'd like to have my birth certificate please but Mum said I need to ask you for it? I think it's time I start taking responsibility for my own life and that includes having any papers that pertain to me.' Lomond held her breath and studied his face. For a few moments all was silent as he looked back and forth between them. 'My birth certificate, dad, I'd like to have it.' She repeated in case he'd missed it the first time. Mac and Beth exchanged a series of tense looks before Beth finally nodded a look of resigned defeat. Her father spoke first.

'Lomond dear, listen, there's a few things we were planning to tell you, when you were old enough to deal with them. We would have told you before, but with the accident and everything…' her father said, looking away. Lomond's eyes bored into Beth; she wanted to hear the words come from her, to hear her admit her duplicity. 'I think it would be best if you sat down.' Mac said. As the two of them took a seat, Beth turned and stared out the window in silence. 'Darlin', the truth is, I was married once before I met Beth. Her name was Maude and she; it was her, well…she is your biological mother Lomond.' The word *biological* rang dissonantly in her ears; Maude had given birth to her but she had never got the chance to be her *mother*. 'You see, Beth was Maude's best friend and when she…well, you see, she died and Beth agreed to marry me so I wouldn't have to raise you on my own.' Looking at the grave look on her father's face brought Lomond no satisfaction whatsoever, none of the smugness she'd expected to feel. Suddenly, as if Beth had been waiting for this moment all her life, she turned to face them both.

'And all for *Maude's* bloody child, what about my own? I gave up everything! My *friends*, a good *career,* my whole *world*! And all for what? A *spoilt,* ungrateful *brat* who thinks only of herself.' As Lomond listened, she couldn't help think about what a total crock of bullshit Beth was spewing out. This was all *their* shit, *their* lies, she reasoned. Surely Beth didn't expect her to believe she married her father purely to take up Maude's mothering duties? It sounds like she stole her best friend's husband!

'If you had to sacrifice *so* much, then why do it?' Lomond asked calmly.

'Because I felt sorry for your father, that's why.' Beth retorted. 'I couldn't see him having to bring a small child up on his own.'

'Oh, so, it was an *arrangement*, like a *charity* case!' Lomond stated, certain there was still more to this story and adamant she would find out. 'So, what exactly did you mean about having your own child, what child? Why haven't you had children of your own together? Is it because you have a loveless marriage?' she asked blankly. Mac shot his wife a glaring look and Beth lowered her head.

'Oh, we wanted to, believe me' she said with contempt, 'but we decided against it when we realised how needy you were, constantly clinging to me and so jealous of any other children.' Lomond felt like she wanted to scream, laugh, and cry; all at the same time. Did they *really* think her so naive?

'*Bollocks*! So, all this was just for my benefit then? What a right load of shite!' she shot back. 'I want to see my birth certificate right now. Oh, and I want to see photos of my real mother as well. There *are* photographs of her, aren't there? Don't tell me they were all ruined in the 'great flood' too?' Her father's unsettled expression said it all. The hatred in her voice surprised her as she continued. 'Look, if you two don't stop this bloody *charade* and give me the truth, I'll get it by whatever means I have to!'

'Angel…' her father began, attempting to console her.

'Lomond, don't you dare threaten *us*, you…' screamed Beth defiantly, making a move towards her before stopping herself. It was then Lomond realised she'd pushed the issue as far as she could for now. A dark silence permeated as Beth stormed out the room and back to the kitchen to finish preparing tea. Seeing the look of anguish on her father's face, Lomond wondered about the wrath he might suffer in the aftermath of this revelation. Beth was probably planning her retaliation already.

Although she hated Beth for the part, she's played in it all, she found it impossible to hate her father; in some ways it seemed he was a victim in all this too. He was just a man trying to make the best of a bad situation. The clatter of dishes from the kitchen and the look of defeat on Mac's face only confirmed her suspicions; there was more to this than any of them were telling her. She watched as her father sat on his chair, lowering his head into trembling hands. Nodding, she left the room and stomped up to her bedroom. Still shaking with rage, she stuffed a few things into a bag before hurrying down the stairs and out the front door, slamming it behind her.

CHAPTER TEN

Lomond stayed at Tracy's house the weeks following the confrontation, when one day her father phoned.

'Hey lass, Beth was taken to hospital last night with a dreadful cough.' he said sombrely.

'Oh, really?' said Lomond, trying to feign concern. She'd wished Beth dead so many times it wasn't easy.

'The doctors think it may be heart congestion,' he said, his words taking on an audible quiver. Lomond raised her eyebrows and felt a moment of vindication; *divine retribution*. Then she felt guilty, realising how her father must feel, this was clearly his way of asking her for help. Still, maybe, just maybe, she thought; Beth's heartless lies had finally caught up with her.

Her father went on to tell her the hospital, ward and room number. 'I know things are very difficult between us right now, but I would really appreciate it if you could see your way clear to visit her,' he said, sounding more forlorn than Lomond ever thought he could. Sighing, she decided that she would make an appearance; but purely for her father's sake. She didn't give a shit about *her*, but why add to her father's pain.

'I'll drop by this evening dad okay? Try not to worry, I'm

sure she'll be ok.'

A few hours later, she was almost disappointed to see that Beth seemed fine, apart from a deep, rattling cough. She felt entirely hypocritical as she sat by Beth's bedside; the conversation between them was false and clipped. Just as she was about to make an excuse to leave, her father arrived with a big bouquet of flowers. Laying his hand gently on Lomond's shoulder; he leaned over and gave Beth a kiss on the forehead. Lomond took this as her cue to slip out. All things considered; she found his show of affection towards Beth rather disturbing.

Over the coming days, things took an unexpected turn. An Echocardiogram revealed Beth was suffering from an 'underlying congenital heart defect' and she was fighting a bout of conjunctive heart failure. When her called to father tell her; all she could think about was how grateful she was not to be related to the woman. Since they had discovered her condition was far more critical than first suspected, Beth would be in hospital for a few weeks at the least; Lomond decided she would surprise her father and move back home to help him. He was at work when she arrived, but the dog was ecstatic to see her.

After several weeks away; the house looked different, it occurred to her how very few times she'd been alone there. She wondered what other secrets lay hidden in the emptiness of the house; what other schemes had been hatched within these very walls. Did she really want to know?

For the first couple weeks, Lomond never left the house at all. She saw nothing of her friends, Lorraine, Maria, or Tracy; and George barely crossed her mind at all. She was entirely happy with her faithful friend Shuna; she enjoyed having her all to herself, her father even let her sleep on Lomond's bed; something her mother would never allow. She felt as if the dog was the only person who *really* understood her, they had such a bond. Shuna would stare at Lomond, as if hearing every word, before cuddling right up to her. She felt nothing but unconditional love. Who needed people she thought? George called once; he left a message saying he thought it was time they "talked". However, to Lomond, with all that she had discovered about her past, their relationship seemed insignificant now. She considered confiding in Lorraine, but she wasn't ready. Instead, she distracted herself with cooking, cleaning and making sure her father felt cared for. After a couple of weeks, he began commenting she was 'looking a bit paley waley' and she 'should be getting out to see her friends' and after some persuasion, Lomond finally agreed and picked up the phone and after a few nights out with Maria, Innes and Tracy, Lomond felt more like her old self. She revelled in the attention she received from young men in the clubs and bars they visited, but there was one boy in particular catching her eye. The more time she spent with Mint, the more she felt an attraction; she liked everything about him: his music, his attitude, his laid-back Bohemian lifestyle. His creative nature stirred something in her; he didn't just *talk* freedom, he lived it. She began fantasising about them hitting the road together. Maybe they would hitch-hike or sneak on a train. She could sing along to his lovely music and together they could busk their way around the world. For the first time in as long as she could remember; Lomond felt an unexpected balance in her life. All that was about to change.

Somewhat intoxicated, Lomond arrived home after catching the last bus back from another night out. The house was silent and she figured her father must have gone to bed already. Shuna bounded up, wagging her tail frantically and circling her legs in excitement. Closing the front door behind her she noticed that the hall lamp was still on, casting a dim yellow light on what looked like a collection of photographs spread across the dining room table. Lomond approached and picked one up. It was a photograph of a young woman; a young, homely looking woman, smiling broadly with a baby in her arms; she felt as if she'd seen this woman somewhere before. Lomond noticed it was the same woman in all the photos, and looking closer, a much younger version of her father was standing beside her. Lomond realised it must be Maude, her real mother, and the baby, it must be *her*; she felt a sinking feeling in her stomach. A rustling sound coming from the lounge distracted her. She peeked in to see her father sitting in his usual chair by the fire, the last embers glowing in the darkness, an empty whiskey bottle sat on the side table. Shuna followed her into the room and plonked herself down on the green rug by the coal fire.

'You saw photos then?' he asked solemnly.

'Yes, I did, Dad' she said, inching closer, understanding how hard it must have been for him to bring out the photos; Beth would have surely raised holy hell if she found out.

'Thank you.' She said. 'Is she my real mum?' Her father tried to speak, but his words were slurred; he stammered, his tongue thick with the whisky. Whatever he was trying to say, it had all the emotion of a confession.

'I, I can't live with it any longer, angel,' he said, holding his empty glass to his lips. 'It's a lie, it's all a lie!'

'Look dad, I know Beth's not my…' Mac pulled himself up to a sitting position, holding the arms of the chair to steady himself. Lomond had never seen her father in this state before; it made her sad. She moved to the chair beside him and sat down.

'No, you don't understand, lass. Aye, it's true, she's *not* your mother, but neither was Maude.' Lomond felt a burning in her chest and a searing heat rose in her throat, taking her breath away.

'What? If Maude's not my real mother then…?'

'Wait,' her father said, the tears now streaming down the creases of his haggard face. He turned and looked directly into her eyes. 'You are *my* daughter Lomond, but not with Maude or Beth. I was young and carefree, and a little wild to say the leas and I fell head over heels for this young woman, Margaret. Our relationship was over by the time I moved back to Edinburgh, but I didn't know that Margaret was pregnant. I met Maude, we married and then Margaret contacted me and told me about the baby. She told me she couldn't look after you; her parents refused to allow it, and she had no way of caring for you herself. So, after much discussion, Maude agreed to adopt you and take you as her own, officially. So that's what we did. I'm so sorry, I know I should have told you all this earlier but…well, Beth wouldn't have it. Jumping to her feet, Lomond wanted to speak, to yell, to release her anger and shock into the world, but the words were stuck in her throat.

Lomond felt as if she were tumbling over the edge: 'There's one more thing you should know sweetie. They knew each other, Maude and Beth; they were best friends for years. Beth's mother used to clean Maude's family home and Beth would accompany her there during school holidays. Beth ended up marrying Maude's brother, a bad yin by all accounts. Lomond, Maude was not a well woman, mentally-speaking, a very good woman, but she had major problems; depressed all the time and…in the end,' he bowed his head, 'she took her own life. You were only three years old at the time.' Lomond sat in a daze, struggling to process all she was hearing. *That' why she recognised her.* 'I had a full-time job; I couldn't do it on my own, no way. It seemed like the most logical solution. Beth had divorced by then, so I married her. She'd been to hell and back already by then, living in a violent marriage and…' He took a deep breath, 'On top of that her own daughter disappeared; she was only seven for Christ's sake. So you see, I thought the whole thing would be good for you both. Like you would gain a new mum and Beth, well, I thought it would fill the void. I'm so sorry it's not worked out how I had imagined.'

'Oh my god, I feel sick.' Lomond spluttered feeling more alone and terrified than ever. It was as though bolts of lightning were penetrating the deepest recesses of her brain, the circuits of her mind sizzling. Her father's words became a jumble of sounds coming from voice light-years away. She staggered to her feel and towards the door. *Wait. If Maude wasn't my real mother, who and where is my real mother, does that mean she is still alive? Do I have brothers and sisters, aunts and uncles I've never even met?* 'Oh, my god!' she cried, running from the room as if she were running for her life. Stumbling up the stairs and into her room, she broke into hysterical sobbing. The darkness of her past had finally found her. She jumped into her bed and pulled the covers tight around her head. She felt like a dark and dirty secret. Something neither Mac nor Beth ever wanted to utter again.

CHAPTER ELEVEN

Lomond remained in bed until early afternoon when she heard her father leave the house. When she went downstairs, the first thing she noticed was that all the photos were gone from the table, returned to their usual hiding place no doubt. Seeing her, the dog slunk out of her bed and stood leaning into her legs. She crouched down and wrapped her arms around her; Shuna was always there ready to offer love and comfort when needed. Despite choosing to share the pictures, and the truth, with his daughter the night before, now she realised there had been none of her real mum, only Maude. Lomond wondered what had made her father decide to come clean, she suspected it was something to do with Beth's surgery, planned for later that day. Due to her weakened condition, the doctors had only given her a 50-50 chance of pulling through, but they had no choice but to operate as she needed the heart-valve replacement. Perhaps Mac wanted to tell her the truth in case Beth didn't pull through, however, Lomond instinctively knew she would live, she just knew; she was a tough old boot. Already, she felt changed by her father's revelation, as if it had stolen her innocence. Daddy's little girl was now gone, a bitter, confused and mistrusting person left behind; a girl who envied others and lacked any sense of belonging. Also, with the end of the school year drawing closer, it would soon be time to leave for good. Lomond was damn sure she would be going somewhere no-one knew her.

She shuffled to the kitchen and made herself a coffee. With cup in hand, and Shuna trailing behind she then headed through to the lounge and stood staring at the walnut desk. There was only one objective in her mind now, she had to find out her real mum's full name. This, she hoped, would help her discover her own identity. She switched on the radio and her favourite song of the moment blasted out, she sang along,

'Me and you and a dog named Boo, travelling and living off the land, me and you and a dog name Boo, how I love being a free man.' If only she could take Shuna with her and leave this place. Uplifted by the thought of finding freedom, she threw caution to the wind, set her cup down and began rifling through the desk. A file named 'Beth Riley' jumped out at her. 'Riley, so that was her maiden name.' she mumbled, setting it aside for later. For now, she was on a mission to find something, anything about her real mum; Margaret. It wouldn't take her long. Flicking through a folder of old post, she came across a wrinkled and tattered letter, the address at the top read; *Margaret Ferguson, 12 Rowlands Terrace, Perth,*

Scotland. She scanned the content quickly, a sentence halfway down stood out. *I can't afford to look after our baby, you will need to take responsibility, come and get her as soon as you can…* with her heart racing, Lomond copied the contact information onto a note pad and returned everything as it was before closing and locking the desk. This was all she needed.

It was a harsh slap in the face for her to learn Beth would be returning home soon. She'd enjoyed taking on the role of woman of the house and looking after father. A few days later, Beth was carted in *via* wheelchair by her obedient husband. No sooner was she in the door, she immediately slipped back into her role as a tyrannical control freak; it was as if nothing had changed. In an attempt to soften her attitude towards the woman, Lomond tried to remind herself what her father had told her about Beth's daughter going missing. However, there simply no way of breaking through Beth's hard exterior. It all came to a head a few days later when Beth tried to stop Lomond going out with her friends. She used her wheelchair as a barrier, preventing her from leaving the house. All the while, spewing a harsh, verbal tirade about how Lomond had no right to go out without her permission. This pushed Lomond over the edge. She shoved Beth aside, storming straight by her and out the front door; unaware that Beth had gashed her leg on the wooden vegetable box lying on the floor.

When Mac arrived home a short time later, Beth lamented through angry tears,

'She viciously attacked me Mac, she tried to slam me into the wall, just look at my leg, I could have bled to death!' Although he didn't for one minute believe her melodramatic version of events, he was deeply disturbed that things were getting physical. When Lomond returned later, she stormed past them both and retreated into the bathroom, slamming the door. She sat on the side of the tub trying to catch her breath, her mind struggling to cope with the barrage of thoughts and emotions swimming around in her head: the unbearable situation with Beth, the trauma of the accident, her relationship with George, the unspoken *thing* she couldn't quite put her finger on between George and Lorraine and the unexpected feelings she was developing for Mint. She wanted nothing more than to flee, to run from her life and not look back, the only thing stopping her was the thought of leaving Shuna behind.

Suddenly she felt she was being watched. *That can't be*, she reasoned, scanning the space around her. *It's must be my nerves, my imagination, or maybe I'm finally losing my mind!* Then, as her eyes fixed on the wall opposite, a swirling, transparent mist settled on the small yellow bench across from her. As she stared into it, it began to change, a shape forming within. The mist transformed into the figure of a person, a man with flowing ivory-robes billowing outwards from his form. *Oh my god, I am losing it.* Flashes of gold appeared around him, mixing with the pure whiteness, almost blinding her with its radiance; never before had she seen such colours. They were more luminous and brilliant than anything she thought possible. Now fully manifested, the figure stood watching her silently. She closed her eyes and counted to five and when she opened them again, he was still there, just looking at her. Despite how impossible the situation seemed, something felt familiar; it was if she had seen this before. This eased her mind and as she began to relax, the figure became more substantial. She was transfixed on the moving energy and array of colours. A sound penetrated the silence in the room, like the buzz of static electricity. As she strained to hear; her ears began to hurt. Just as the pain reached a feverish peak, there was a burst of blinding white light. She realised she had left her physical existence and had become immersed within the same energy as the figure. Although there was no external sound, she could hear him speaking to her telepathically.

'You are *different*, Lomond. Do not be afraid to *be*, that is your gift. Remember I am with you. One day soon, this will all make sense, one day soon *you will discover me*.' Unable to verbalise her thoughts, all Lomond could do was watch as the figure receded into a churning ball of white and golden energy, before instantaneously collapsing into a tiny pinpoint of light. Then it disappeared completely, leaving not even a trace.

For several moments Lomond sat, unable to process what she had seen. Had it really happened? Surely not. However, she couldn't ignore that in meeting this strange figure, she'd experienced a sense of wholeness she'd never felt before. For the first time she felt complete, loved, cherished even. Imprinting the experience into her memory, she vowed to herself she would never forget this feeling. In times of darkness she would call upon it, this "spirit of the bathroom," What a place for a supernatural being to come visit her, she thought, a bloody *bathroom*. A loud banging on the door jolted her back to reality.

'Open this damn door immediately young lady!' Beth screamed.

'Leave me the hell alone, you demented old witch!' she fired back.

'Out, just get out here right now Lomond! Your father wants to have a word with you about your violent behaviour.' Enraged, Lomond flung the door open, just missing Beth in the process. She glared at her before heading straight into her bedroom. There, she began stuffing clothes into her rucksack; intentionally leaving behind all her childhood toys and treasures. When she came out, Beth was still sitting in the hallway, her arms crossed like a queen on a royal throne. Without a word, she went straight down the stairs and past her father. The tears were beginning to run down her cheeks as she gave the dog a hug before walking out the front door, leaving it wide open behind her. Mac hung his head in regret as he watched his daughter flee. Beth screamed from the top of the stairs,

'That's right, run away. Run off to your degenerate friends. You'll be back with your tail between your legs when you need money, or when they all find out the bloody *truth* about you, you'll see!' Figuring George was probably working; Lomond headed straight for the Meadows, hoping Mint would be in his usual spot. He saw her striding towards him from a distance, her hair flying behind her and rucksack on her back; he suspected trouble. He waved and when she drew closer, it was clear from the look on her face she was going through some kind of crisis. He wouldn't get into that unless she gave him an opening.

CHAPTER TWELVE

It was no surprise George's boss wanted to keep him on. Despite his disappearing acts and 'problems' with the authorities, he loved getting his hands greasy, tinkering with engines and best of all, he knew the *sound*, the perfect thrum any experienced biker wanted out of an engine. Bikers came from miles around, specifically because George had the hands and ears for a motorcycle. Once the guys at the garage found out it was Lomond who'd been on the back of the bike when he took the spill, they used every opportunity to rib him about it. He decided there was no way he was going to feed the rumour mill by telling them about Lorraine as well. In the weeks following the accident and Lomond's recovery, he immersed himself in work and ignored the off-handed comments.

Later that day, George met Mint at Brattisanis at the bottom of Morrison Street,

'Saw your Lomond today.' Mint said right off, 'She had a rucksack stuffed full to the top. Said she had a big blow-up with her parents and was lookin' for a way to get out of Edinburgh; wants her *freedom*, she said.' Mint watched George's eyes glass-over, a look somewhere between relief and concern, but he never responded. 'Does she know about Lorraine?' he asked, wondering if that might be part of the reason Lomond was so desperate to get away.

'Hell, *no*…at least not from me!' George said, clearly irked and making the point perfectly clear. 'God damn it! What the hell is it with everyone? Can't a man keep his business to himself?' he fired.

'Whoa, easy man.' Mint said. George stood up quickly, as if the space between them had suddenly become too small. 'Didn't say it was any of my business, only that she wants the lyrics to the song I wrote for you, said she'd be back. Just thought she might start asking awkward questions, so I wanted to know how things stand with her . . . and with Lorraine. Don't wanna be stickin' my big boot in it, do I?' George gave another sigh, less vociferously this time before sitting back down.

'Yeah, I'm gonna tell her. I just haven't fixed when yet. Thing is, I wanted to get my bike back first, so I could take her for a spin. You know, show her things haven't changed that way. See what I mean?'

'Yeah bro, I'm right with ya, playin' it cool eh,' Mint said, picking up a sugar packet and dumping the contents into his mouth before offering one to George, he waved it off. 'I dunno, man. She doesn't seem the type to like surprises to me. Maybe you just need to be up-front with her. Like, tell her now so she's not makin' plans for the future with you, you know? I mean, especially if you're gonna be with Lorraine. Feel where I'm comin' from?' George sighed; his face gloomy.

'Yeah, man, Lorraine's on at me too to get it over with. Says she can't take the secret any longer. She's been seein' Lomond and feels she's deceiving her. How the hell do you tell a girl you've moved on? That you want to be friends, but nothing more?'

'No easy way for that man, unless she's ready to move on, too. Till you talk to her, how are you gonna know? Maybe it's a big deal over nothing. Has she even been in touch with you since she got out of the hospital?'

'No, not really man.'

'Well then, there you go.' The waitress brought their steak and chips over and they began tucking in. George chewed things over in his mind, thinking about taking Lomond on a nice bike ride and where things might land with Lorraine, with or without Lomond in the picture. He and Mint said little else as they worked their way through their meals. George stared out of the window as he ate, imaging his future could be seen in the passing clouds. It was clear Mint thought he was playing with fire; leading two women on the way he was. George went back to his own place on Grove Street, the best place when he needed space and peace to think. However, he couldn't relax, he realised he'd done enough thinking already; that it was time for action. He headed down to the phone box on the corner and dialled Lomond's number. After a few rings, it answered, it was her father. Lomond wasn't at home; she was staying with her friend. He gave George another number. He lifted the receiver to dial but doubt appeared and stopped him. He'd phone her another time he told himself with cold feet.

Lomond sat alone at the kitchen table in Tracy's, a newspaper spread out in front of her. An advert for a cleaner/waitress at a hotel in Roslin caught her eye. *No experience necessary; room and board included.* Realising Sorcha, the colour seer she met at the fair, lived out that way too, she picked up the phone and dialled the number on her business card. Sorcha told her it was a nice establishment, in fact, she ate there often. Then, she offered her kindly to come visit and they could check it out together.

'Come by anytime, I'd love to see you again.' she said.

Lomond called the hotel and spoke with the manager, a man called

Robert, he seemed really keen and offered her an interview later that day if it suited. An hour later, a smartly clad Lomond hopped on the bus to Roslin from St. Andrew's Square, ready to change her future.

The bus trundled slowly down the narrow main street and where Lomond noticed a small flower shop, a chemist and a post office among a cluster of local businesses; beyond that, quaint single-story cottages ran along either side of the road. Looking down the side streets, she saw slivers of what looked like council houses and newer builds. Alighting opposite the post office, Lomond navigated her way along, feeling nervous as she walked.

The sign was large and colourful, *The Roslin Hotel*. She entered through the large wooden door, tripping clumsily over the threshold; she was thankful no one saw her. The place looked deserted. She pinged the little bell on the reception desk and waited. Echoing banging sounds and a trail of lime-dust footprints leading off down the hall suggested the place was undergoing some kind of renovation. She pinged the bell again and few moments later, a woman emerged from the back, out-of-breath and wiping her hands on her pinney.

'Hey there, lass,' she said, smoothing an errant lock of hair from her face. 'How can I help you?'

'I'm here for a job interview.' Lomond replied grinning. The woman looked at her blankly. 'Looks like you're pretty busy around here,' she added nervously.

'Aye, that we are, lass, it's all go. It must have been Robert you spoke to no doubt. He never tells me anything,' she said half in jest. 'If you just wait here, I'll go and fetch him for you okay? Can I give him yer name, hen?'

'It's Lomond,' she answered smiling politely. 'Lomond Mitchieson.'

'In fact, on second thoughts hen, just follow me tae the lounge.' The woman requested,
'It's about the only place no caked in dust the now!' Lomond followed her, careful not to stumble over any of the tools strewn about the floor. 'Can I get you a cuppa?' she offered.

'Uh, thanks. Yes please, if it's no bother.'

'No bother at all hen. Take a wee seat. My name's Andrena, by the way, but folks call me *Dreanie*.' Turning, she took a few steps and shouted at the top of her lungs, 'Robert! Robert! There's a wee lass here 'bout the job.' A moment later, a ghost-like figure appeared in the doorway and Dreanie roared.
'What the hell now, Robert. Why yer covered in stour. Look at you

man, what a mess.' Lomond tried her best not to laugh but a snigger escaped her lips; neither of them seemed to bother. 'This is Lomond,' Dreanie said, shaking her head at him. Robert wiped his hand briskly on his trousers before extending it.

'Eh, hi, pleased to meet you Lomond. Sorry I'm a bit dusty, but with . . . well, you understand.' Lomond nodded. 'We're putting in a new bathroom in at the front of the hotel and giving everything a general face-lift. So, you can imagine, there's dust everywhere.' he said, attempting to brush the grey patches off his trousers. Dreanie cut in,

'Did ye get scones like I asked ye?' she asked.

'Oh damn,' he answered, rolling his eyes. Sorry no scones, I forgot to buy them.

'For goodness sake. Well you'll need to send Jock, or Jimmie, or yer misses to get some then. We've got a funeral at two o'clock and I've nae time to bake them fresh!' Robert nodded and pulled an exasperated face at Lomond before changing the subject.

'You know Roslin is turning into quite the tourist *destination* these days. "*Toney*", some might say. There's so many out-of-towners visiting, wanting to see The Chapel. We need to be on top of our game and keep up our reputation as the best hotel with the best accommodation and very best staff.' he winked proudly.

'Of course, I can understand that.' Lomond answered, doing her best to sound like an adult.

'So, what kind of work experience do you have young lady?' Lomond was worried about how she was going to answer this.

'Well, truthfully, I have *none,* yet really. I've only just left school you see, but I *really really* need this job and if you'll consider me for it, I promise to work extra hard and I'm a very fast learner.' Robert liked the look of Lomond, something in her face and the way she spoke told him she would be a good worker, someone to be trusted. He also liked that she had a bit of grit about her. The truth was, except for Dreanie, who'd ran the kitchen for over ten years, staff rarely stayed long at all, a season or two at the most. Robert put it down to the hotel being too far away from the excitement of the city for most people. Robert described the duties the job entailed, which would essentially make her an *all-rounder.* Lomond nodded enthusiastically as he spoke, despite none of them sounding particularly exciting. Then, he offered her the job, there on the spot. Lomond was delighted.

'Oh yes please, that's fabulous!' she gushed, 'I can't thank you enough, although, there is one other thing.'

'What's that then?' Robert said.

'Well, I really need somewhere to live too. The advert said

the job came with a room and board, is that sill on offer?'

'Yes, that should be fine. We can sort all that out.' He answered. So, it was agreed, Lomond would be taken on as a combination of cleaner come waitress, come kitchen hand, come whatever else needs done. They shook on it. Robert led her to her room, a small-but-cosy cubbyhole, located in the original part of the hotel, the part that had escaped previous renovations and remodelling. All the rooms had timbered, vaulted ceilings, and a small window looking out over a quaint courtyard. Lomond was surprised to notice an old Royal Mail stagecoach sitting outside hers. The entire plot was rich with geraniums making it a veritable field of blazing colour. 'I'd be more than happy for you to start tomorrow, if it suits you? I would really appreciate the help to be honest.' Robert said imploringly. Lomond looked around the room; it was nowhere near ready to move in. She opened her mouth to speak but Robert got in there first. 'Emm, yeah, it'll take a day or two to get the room ready for you; we hadn't expected such a quick response to our ad to be honest.

Will it be possible for you to take the bus from town maybe? Or, if you know anyone more local you could stay with, maybe that would be easier for you?' It was obvious to Lomond they really needed her and this made her feel so happy.

'That's totally fine, I can ask someone I know who lives near the village, see if she can put me up for a day or two; if not, I will use the bus no problem.'

'Oh, that would be *wonderful* then!' Robert said, clearly relieved to finally have the help he needed. Lomond followed him back down the main staircase and to the lounge where Dreanie had laid out their tea.

'I really appreciate you giving me this chance to prove myself, Robert. I promise, no matter what, I'll be here tomorrow, come rain or shine.'

Lomond set off to the address on Sorcha's card. In her excitement she forgot to ask for directions, an old lady waiting at a bus stop set her on her way. She was relieved to spot Sorcha's sign, *Good Health-For-All*. She could see two Irish Setters inside a conservatory, pounding their tails and barking in chorus unison. Sorcha appeared behind the double glass doors and welcomed her in.

'Don't mind these mutts!' she said, a smile spreading across her porcelain face, 'they can't get enough attention, this pair. Down you two, *down*! Come on through.' She led the way to a living area at the rear of the house. Lomond took a deep breath, savouring the aroma of smouldering peat coming from a lovely black wood burning stove. Lomond noticed the room was strewn with the same lovely silk scarves they'd seen at the fair. The settee was decked out with Indian throws. Sorcha invited Lomond to sit at an old-world looking wooden table with her where dozens of her coloured bottles were set out in neat, organized rows. The two Irish Setters had stayed firmly by Lomond's her side, she seemed to be their new best friend. 'They're a good judge of character, those two,' Sorcha winked. She pointed to one of them, 'That's Aurora, named after the Aurora Borealis,' she laughed. 'and the bigger one, he's my boy Borealis; or Boris as I call him for short.' Lomond was intrigued to see Aurora wore a purple Bandana and Borealis a yellow one.

'I love their Bandanas; I'll have to get one for my dog.' said Lomond as she stroked them. 'Such beautiful dogs Sorcha, how did you get them? Have you had them since they were puppies?

'Well actually, I really don't know, they came to me in a magical way. When my marriage was failing, I went home to Nairn for a holiday, and as I was sitting on the beautiful golden beach, I had a sudden image of a red dog running across the sand, and then there was two of them. It seemed they were *willing* me to find them. It was such a strange experience but after that the vision just stuck with me, that night, the next day, the one after that. The thought of having a dog uplifted my spirits, I felt drawn to having one. The vision only grew stronger as the days passed too. A week later, on my journey back home to Edinburgh, I felt drawn to drive to Grantown on Spey; something I've never done before. Well, I parked in the main square and walked across to the bakers on the far side. Then I sat inside a coffee shop for a drink and the first thing I noticed was a small hand-written advert pinned on the wall, "FOR SALE – Two Irish Setter Dogs" it read.'

'Wow!' Lomond grinned.

'I know crazy eh! Well, without a thought, I rushed out to the phone box over the road, without even touching my tea. The gruff voice on the other end told me he still had them, but if I wanted to see them, I'd better hurry up. It was only when I put the phone down, I realised I never even asked if they were red, but I told myself, if these dogs were for me, then they would be.'

Sorcha laughed and carried on. 'Well, I followed his directions and ended up at a run-down farm some way out of town. The guy seemed really dodgy and the dogs were tied up in an old run-down barn, they looked so sad. There was no way I would be leaving them at his mercy. Also, they were red. I ended up going back to the bank in the town and taking out the money. I'll never forget the look on the dogs' faces; it was as if they knew I was saving them.'

'That is such an amazing story,' Lomond said clasping her hands together.

'It was the last straw in my marriage too, it was a husband replaced by two red-heads!' Both the girls laughed. 'So, what about you Lomond, what's been happening since last we met?'

'Well, I got the job!' Lomond said excitedly. 'I've just had the interview already, thanks for offering to show me where it was.'

'Good for you, that's magic news and no problem at all.'

'There is one small problem.' Lomond said, looking thoughtful.

'Oh?'

'You see, well the room that comes with the job won't be ready for a day or two he said, I was wondering if maybe I could stay here till it's ready. I mean, only if you have the room and don't mind the intrusion. If not, it's okay; I will just get the bus.

'Have you spoken to your parents?' Sorcha asked, her tone somewhat serious. Lomond paused, she hated to lie and felt she'd be no better than her scheming parents if she did. She told Sorcha the unfiltered truth; the whole drama as it played out in her house.

'I know I seem young to be out on my own, but I have to be, its constant chaos at home. I need to take control of my own life as soon as possible. This job is my first step towards independence.' Lomond looked sad for a moment, 'The only thing I'll miss is my dog Shuna.' She said.

'Hummm, let me just say this, Lomond. Life is too short to hold a grudge against the people we love. Far be it for me to suggest you ignore your own instincts, but just be sure you won't be left with regrets. You really should let them know where you are, so they know you're safe at least; then you are welcome to stay as long as they need to.' Lomond doubted they were really bothered, but she agreed anyway. 'Come and look at this view,' Sorcha said, leading her out onto the terrace. It was quite breath-taking. The land beneath dipped steeply through scrub and copse before reaching a large pasture sloping dramatically to the valley below. 'That's the North Esk down there. I take the dogs for a run along it every day. There's an ancient Roman viaduct crossing the valley and a disused railway track that takes you pretty much all the way to Roslin.' Sorcha spoke as if she were taking it all in for the first time. Aurora and Borealis stood beside them also surveying the landscape. 'The locals talk about an old Hermit that comes here sometimes. They say he lives in a cave deep in the forest, surrounded by the ragged cliffs and the smell of wild garlic. Nobody knows where he goes, only that he's there sometimes and then he vanishes. It's reputed to have been used by William Wallace after the battle of Rosslyn around 1303. I've walked with the dogs down to the area numerous times and I tell you, Aurora is really sensitive to the energies there. She'll stop running all of a sudden and stare directly at something invisible. Baring her teeth and barking as if she's ready to attack whatever it is, she's seeing. It is pretty scary; I can't see anything at all. It's also pretty dark down there because of the thick green canopy over the glen, and you have to watch you don't trip over all the gnarly tree roots in the ground; aye, there something really magical and super spooky in the glen.'

'It certainly is a beautiful place. So, a Hermit you say, that's interesting,' Lomond's quizzical eyes roamed the changing landscape.

'The truth is, Lomond, I may not be here much longer. It all belongs to my husband; the land has been in his family for generations, but I plan to enjoy it while it lasts!' Lomond gazed fondly at Sorcha. Her soft proportions draped in colourful, loose attire all served to make her even more attractive, she radiated such warmth and generosity. *Why would any man divorce her, surely men must adore her!* she told herself. 'I'm too much my own woman for my husband's tastes,' Sorcha said, as if reading her thoughts. 'He's the *protecting* type.' Lomond nodded, even though she didn't really understand what that meant. 'Oh, by the way,' Sorcha said, remembering some big news. 'That man I noticed you talking to at the fair, the one with the glamour girl on his arm?'

'Yes…?' Lomond said, full of curiosity. Sorcha picked up a newspaper.

'He lives in India Street, right?' Lomond nodded as she places the paper in front of her. 'Well I think his house made the news. The police are re-opening some un-solved crime they think took place there, twenty years ago!' Lomond took the paper and began to read. A montage of thoughts and images flashed through her mind: a crime, visions of Tyrone's house, him and something she could just not quite grasp. A part of her felt she already knew something about it, she just couldn't seem to bring it to her consciousness.

CHAPTER THIRTEEN

A full day of cleaning and running around the hotel exhausted Lomond more than she ever anticipated, her feet hurt and her body ached in places she didn't know could; she wondered if would be able to keep up this pace all the time. Although her room was ready as promised, she decided to spend a few more days with Sorcha. Her world presented a whole new fascination for Lomond and the days spent with her were the most interesting and rewarding she'd ever had. Sorcha taught her much more about the world of colours. She explained the system she used to interpret them as a language, as well as introducing her to other forms of healing such as aromatherapy. Through all this, Lomond became convinced this was her true path in life.

The more she learned, the more she felt inexplicably drawn to colours and the energies they emitted; she experienced great surges of joy in their presence. This was the freedom she'd longed to live. It wasn't about getting away from those masquerading as her parents, or about having her own money to spend as she wanted. It was about following her heart and being self-empowered. It was about finding something that touched her, or even *called* to her in a

way that nothing had before. The bond she felt with Sorcha grew
stronger each day, she was like a long-lost cousin or an aunt.
Sorcha seemed so and it was so good to have someone who
understood what made her tick, someone she could trust.

'Lomond, hen, where's Robert?' Dreanie shouted from the
kitchen doorway with her hands on her wide hips. Lomond had fast
come to discover this was her way. 'I'm runnin' outta rolls here! He
was supposed to pick them up for me, that man is useless!' Roberts
wife, Lavender, sashayed into the kitchen with her beloved black,
wire-haired miniature poodle tucked under arm.

'More to the point, I'd like to know what's he's up to right
now, I can never find him when I need him!'

'Is it not a bit hot for wearin' that awfy great big coat?'
laughed Dreanie. 'The fur collar about covers your whole heed
woman, and you're not supposed to have that damn dog in here
mind, you ken the rules.' It seemed as if Lavender was a constant
nag to her husband, incessantly on at him.

"Robert, mind and collect the laundry, and make sure it's
been ironed properly this time, and remember to speak to the
postman about our mail left out on the doorstep letting it get all
wet!" Although she felt a little sorry for the man, she had to admit,
he was pretty forgetful and easily distracted. He never stayed with

one job long enough to finish it and he was a master of procrastination. Lomond imagined she would turn into a nag too if she was his wife. His latest project was the so-called "multi-function hall" which now boasted an elaborate and somewhat misplaced cherub and angel motif. He believed this was the *best wedding theme* possible by far; despite Lavenders objections that he would rather re-decorate the room with 'fat dwarfs' than deal with the clogged-up drains. As far as Lomond could ascertain, the hotel had been in a constant state of disarray ever since Robert and his family took it over seven years before, rather than bringing order, they brought an air of controlled chaos to the place. Robert barged through the swinging doors blanketed in grey powder from head-to-toe.

'Unbelievable, woman, bloody *unbelievable*! Why did you send me to the attic? Couldn't you have managed the schedule for clean linen more sensibly? I've fell through the bloody ceiling! Now there's stour and plaster all over the damn bedroom I just spent the last week renovating, and we've guests arriving in less than an hour. What the hell do we do now?'

'Oh my god Robert, you are absolutely useless!' Lavender said in her faux-aristocratic voice, shaking her head in disgust. 'Daddy was right, you're positively incompetent.'

'Incompetent? I'll give you bloody *incompetent*, miss too-good-to-get-out-of -bed-before-noon! For once in your oh-so privileged existence, why don't you make *yourself* useful? All you can do is stand around and bitch. Call the bloody linen suppliers or get in that lovely new, custom-made BMW which, might I remind you, I paid for, and go buy some new bloody sheets. Or are you too exhausted from dragging that pitiful excuse for a dog around and feeding your face with bon-bons? Really, woman...*do* something...anything!' Lavender threw him a look of exasperation before stomping up the stairs. Robert shook his head, 'Lomond darlin', you come with me, won't you? Christ sake, what a mess. What an absolute *mess*!'

'Maybe ye should call the plasterer!' laughed Dreanie. 'Old Jimmy will be sitting down in the bar, he may be totally pished mind, but that never stopped him patchin' up holes before!'

Lomond followed Robert into the bar. It went silent as they entered as countless pairs of blood-shot glassy eyes turned to stare at them. He looked so comical with his grey matted hair and stour-covered clothes. As if to announce his presence and authority, he walked over to the wall-mounted fan and without thinking, pulled the cord. A shower of thick black dust spewed all over him, adding a layer of sticky soot to the grey and white patches on his face and clothes. Everyone in the bar broke into peals of laughter.

'You of all people oughta know to *never* to use that fan.' said old Jock as he supped his pint.

'Why is everything *my* responsibility? The damn thing should be kept clean and working. Lomond, lass, can you get to cleaning that tomorrow please.' He muttered before directing her to grab the Hoover and follow him back upstairs. Catching sight of old Jimmy nodding-off in his usual chair in the corner, he yelled, 'Hey, Jimmy! Wake up, mate. Fancy making a few bob?'

'Do I *look* fit enough to make a few bob?' Jimmy said, partially rousing from his stupor before easing his head back down and dozing off again. Robert grabbed him by the elbow,

'Come on, up mate. We have an emergency and it needs your expertise. There's a pint or two in it for you if you're quick enough about it too.' Old Jimmy staggered to his feet and steadied his wobbly legs,

'A free pint? Shite, that'll be a first!'

'Lomond! Lomond!' Dreanie's voice hollered from the kitchen.

'I guess you better see go what she wants,' he sighed, annoyed by the interruption. 'But come up stairs when she's finished will you?' Lomond put the Hoover down and made her way into the kitchen.

'Quick, hen, take this food to table ten afore it gets cold, would you? What's that raj done now?' she asked. 'Sounds like a right ruckus.'

'Oh, he yanked the cord of the fan and it threw dust all over the place, including all over him! Not one customer could keep a straight face, they were hysterical!' Dreanie chortled as Lomond picked up the plates and headed for the dining room. On her way back, she ran into the tall and ever-haughty Lavender.

Lomond glanced at her blond coiffure hair with its excessive volume of large curls. No doubt she thought they complimented her facial features, but it really made her look rather gaunt and tragic. She was still wearing the heavy black suede coat and carrying the dog like a clutch purse. Her hand, with it's highly manicured, pillar-box red nails looked like it might suffocate the life out of it. Just then, two patrons entered the building, glancing around anxiously as the state of the place.

'Excuse me, but we're here to check in I think.' One of them said to Lomond. Just as she was about to step behind the reception, Lavender sauntered up behind her.

'*I'll* check them in if you don't mind. You just get back to your duties in the kitchen please.' She glared at Lomond before flashing a fake smile to the guests.

'Your names?' she ordered rather than asking. Lomond shook her head. So much for the "Scottish welcome" Robert had banged on about so much. "Always treat them as if they were your long-lost relatives and you are delighted to see them,' he'd instructed; it was clear Lavender didn't get that memo. Just as Lomond reached the kitchen, Lavender shouted out to her, 'Lomond. *Where* has the check-in register gone?'

'I don't know, Robert had it last.' She answered, struggling to hide her growing irritation.

'Then go and *find* him then,' she hissed impatiently, 'and bring it back here where it belongs! It's so hard to get good help these days.' She mumbled for the benefit of the guests. Lomond bounded up the side-stairs two-at-a-time. She found Robert trying to clean up the rubble in the bedroom. He was none-the-wiser about where the sign-in book was, so Lomond raced around all the common areas, eventually finding it in the dining room.

'You'll be in room number ten, top of the stairs and turn left,' Lavender instructed the couple.

'That's the room where the ceiling fell in,' Lomond whispered to her.

'Yes. Room *ten*,' she repeated, choosing to ignore her. 'If you'll just follow me. Robert? Robert are you up there?' she hollered from the bottom of the stairs, as if calling for the hired help.

'Lavender, ten isn't ready yet remember?' Lomond repeated.

'Rubbish, of course, it's ready!' she said dismissively. 'I *ordered* it to be made ready hours ago…Robert!' She yelled more shrilly this time. Robert appeared, still covered in dust and soot and a new layer of something green. The guests glanced at each other, looking increasingly concerned. 'Perhaps we should look for somewhere else if you're not…'

'Please, Mr. and Mrs. . . .?' Robert said reassuringly, through dust-caked lips.

'Uh, Cecil and Cynthia Beardsley.' they answered hesitantly.

'Well, Mr. and Mrs. Beardsley, if you just follow me, I'll put you in room nine. I'm quite sure you'll find it to your liking.' The three exchanged smiles before leaving his wife and Lomond standing at the bottom of the stairs. Lavender bristled away; a dismissive nod left in her wake.

CHAPTER FOURTEEN

It was 10pm by the time the kitchen closed its hatch for the day. Dreanie suggested they go to the lounge for a drink and although Lomond was beyond exhausted, she welcomed the opportunity. Dreanie's sense of humour had brought laughter and lightness to what was otherwise a pretty rough shift. As they propped themselves up on bar stools, Lomond with her Coke and Dreanie sipping on neat scotch, the cook began to tell her a story.

'Do you know, my dad died sixteen years ago and for those years since, his soul has been held prisoner.'

'How can someone be held prisoner after they've died?' Lomond asked confused.

'Well you see, his old witch of a wife, who never really cared about him anyway, has kept his ashes on the mantelpiece for all those years, like some kind of trophy.'

'That's terrible.' Lomond said.

'Aye it is lass,' Her voice was cracking with emotion, 'and now I've heard *she's* finally died, and I thought I would be getting him back, but *her* daughter's gonna mix them together and scatter them in the bloody back garden! Well, over my dead body. I've told her he belongs with me; I'm the one who really cared about him. I warned her, I told her if she doesn't set him free his spirit is going to come back and haunt her. And I told her,

I'm going to report her to the police, because it's just no right.' Being so cheery so far, it was a surprise for Lomond to see her overcome by emotion, she was unsure what to say. Then, without a word, Dreanie got down from the stool and headed for the ladies. Lomond sat contemplating for some moments, she thought about her own father and how she might feel if it were here in the same situation. She could easily see Beth doing something similar. Then seemingly random words and ideas filtered into her mind: being a prisoner, the police, ghosts, haunting…?

A face slowly manifested in her mind. It was Tyrone in his India Street house. A silver-haired old man was with him. Shadowy thoughts and words on the tip of her tongue…*Shit! What can't I remember? What are these buried images trying to reach the surface?* Her eyelids began to droop, a small slit remaining. Through it, she could see the outline of a potted plant on the bar, so luminous it was almost *golden.* As she stared, it seemed to expand outwards until she no longer saw the plant, just a lambent, opaque mist obscuring and dominating everything within her line of vision. Then the mist rose up and engulfed her.

She became part of its very essence, could no longer feel her own body. Feeling both frightened and exhilarated, it was as though her physical body no longer existed, only her mind remained. Rather than feeling lost or abandoned, she felt *free*. Totally unburdened, *liberated*. As the solid features of the room began to melt away, she strained to identify a sound, a sound that that reminded her of times when her father had driven beneath massive electricity pylons; like the static crackle of high-intensity power lines. All connection to time and space vanished, and as the mist began to clear, a figure came into view. A ghostly apparition that appeared to hover, suspended in thin air. She began to hear soft lamenting sounds. Words to a hymn she recognised, being sung by a young child. The figure turned to face her and she saw a child-like face forming from the spiralling wafts of grey mist. It glared at her, its sunken, dark eyes boring a hole in her mind. Then, as if by telepathy, it spoke to her,

'Look at *him* Lomond, it was him.' Lomond homed in again on the two men, Tyrone and the silver-haired old man. She homed in on *him*, and with what felt like no effort at all, she could hear their conversation.

'I am neither your judge nor jury.' the silver-haired old man said.

'Then *help* me.' Tyrone begged. 'Free me from these bonds, please! You have the power.'

'I'm afraid I cannot,' said the Hermit, 'You must learn to see beyond that which is in front of your nose. All around us, here in this very room, energy is moving. Energy that belongs to those you have done great injustices to. They are here waiting Tyrone, and divine retribution is coming your way, soon. This is the path you have chosen and now you must walk it.' The voices receded into the background and Lomond could hear a faint beckoning. She focused her senses and found herself standing beside an older, plump woman, a woman whose face she somehow knew. Then, as if through sound and a sixth sense, the woman spoke to her.

'Lomond, you found your way back.' As she conveyed the thought, her pink dress bellowed, becoming almost at one with the surrounding mist.

'Mrs. *R?*' Lomond asked, unsure where the words came from and whether she had actually uttered them. 'This is quite *strange*, I mean, meeting you here after all these years.' Both confusion and clarity occupied her mind.

'Oh, but my dearie, it hasn't been that long at all.' The

figure responded, an etheric smile parting her lips. 'It was just a few weeks ago we stood in this very place together.' With this, memories of being with Mrs. R. again flooded from the depths of her mind. Not memories from her childhood, but scenes from the recent past.

'Oh, my god!' Lomond exclaimed, half in fear of what she knew to be true.

'Yes, lass, you're remembering now, I knew you would.

'So you know, about my accident?' Lomond breathed.

'Indeed, I do,' Mrs. R. responded, 'I know all there is to know about you Lomond.' Suddenly, Lomond felt a great connection with this spirit being; an inconceivable *oneness*. 'Though I have passed on, I exist in the nothingness, of the energetic vibrations of infinite consciousness, you have found the passageway, like tuning a radio to the right station, you have freed your mind from your physical body, and now you have the ability to tune into this energetic higher consciousness whenever you choose.'

'Wake up, lass. It's time to wake up!' Lomond jumped, ripped from the space between two realities. Dreanie was gently shaking her, she felt sick to her stomach. It was if she'd jumped back into her skin from a distant place.

'Are you okay, dearie?' Dreanie asked, seeing the far-away look in her eyes. 'You must've been deep in never-never land' she added. Lomond rubbed her face and pulled an errant lock of hair back into place. She attempted to rise from the stool but sat back down quickly; her legs too wobbly to hold her. For a moment, she couldn't remember where she was, she was entirely disorientated but the face of Mrs. R. lingered in her mind.

'I, I guess I must have dozed off,' she muttered, feeling somewhat embarrassed.

'Come on lass, off ta bed with you.' Coaxed Dreanie.

That night, Lomond dreamt of Tyrone and the old man with the silver hair. She revisited the house on India Street. Had she imagined the young girl she had seen and who had pleaded for her to find her or was it real? Was she in fact asking her to do just that? If this was the case, what did it mean and more importantly what should she do about it? With these thoughts swimming around her mind, she eventually fell into a deep sleep. As the sun rose above the horizon in the morning, it shone through the curtains, causing her eyes to flutter open. Immediately, Mrs. R. came vividly to mind and with this vision; the pieces of the puzzle began falling into place.

CHAPTER FIFTEEN

'Innes, I'm so glad you agreed to meet. There's something I need to tell you, but you *must* promise not to tell anyone ok?'

'Of course, what is it?'

'Well, it's going to sound pretty bizarre, but it's important…it's about Tyrone.' Innes was silent in anticipation. 'When I was in the coma, I had all these strange experiences and they're all coming back to me now. I'm getting flashbacks, as if I'm somehow reliving them. One of these is the time you visited Tyrone and something happened. He came on to you and you were both playing the Ouija board?' Lomond paused to survey her friend's face for a reaction. Innes hung her head and a tear rolled down her cheek.

'Oh my God, how do you know about that?

'That's what I'm trying to tell you, I was there Innes. Somehow, I managed to be there, even though my body was lying in the hospital bed, in a coma. I can only describe it as like being in some other realm, like a ghost, yet somehow I was still alive.' The tears were now streaming down Innes' face.

'Are you alright?' Lomond asked concerned, 'He really has done a number on you hasn't he? Have you spoken to anyone about it?' Innes shook her head.

'I just learn to live with my feelings, that's all I can do. I'm angry at him, but even angrier with myself. I don't know why, but a part of me was actually attracted to him and maybe I led him on. I really can't explain how, but it was as if he had some kind of hold over me. Even though he repulsed me and I saw him for his true ugly self, for some reason I was drawn to him.'

'Maybe you were drawn to him because of his surroundings, his lifestyle, his fancy home, because of his so-called knowledge and power he had over others?' Offered Lomond.

'I don't even know why.'

'I think you do Innes; you must do. You went to his house knowing full well what he was like, but you chose to push it to the back of your mind. There was something you needed from him wasn't there? Something you knew only he could give you. I think that deep down inside you why you went there.' For some moments, Innes was deep in thought.

'If I really think about it, if I strip it all back and really look at my own actions, not his, I think I saw him as a way out, a way of escaping life with my parents, and my brother. A part of me thought Tyrone might love and take care of me. I imagined myself living in that big beautiful house of his.'

'There you go, there's your answer then. Attraction comes in many forms and I understand how, at that time, Tyrone was filling a huge gap you felt in your life. You know, if Tyrone worked an ordinary job and lived in a simple flat; I guarantee you would not feel the same way about him, and I mean *him*. I can see it was down to all the trappings, everything he was offering you at a time when you were vulnerable. He fooled you into thinking he was a stepping stone to your freedom Innes, but he isn't. It's more like out of the frying pan and into the fire with him.' sighed Lomond. Innes began to laugh.

'Hell no! I guess I just never really thought it through properly, I let my imagination take over.'

'That's not all,' Lomond said, 'The main reason I wanted to see you was to talk about a ghost.' Innes inhaled sharply.

'What about ghosts?' she asked.

'Well, when I was watching you both using the Ouija board, things began to go crazy. Books were falling off the shelves and I saw a whirlwind of swirling black energy. The figure of a young girl appeared from it; she was begging me to find her.' Innes began to tremble, the hairs on her arms stood up and she clasped her head between her hands.

'Oh my God, that's what the board was spelling out Lomond,

'Find me', I remember now. So, it was real? It was a real ghost coming forward with the message?'

'Exactly!' answered Lomond.

'What are you suggesting Lomond? What do you want me to do? I can't see ghosts, and I wouldn't want to either.'

'You clean for Tyrone, don't you?'

'Yes, well I did, until all that happened.'

'Do you still have a key to his house?'

'Well, yes, I've still got that. He gave it me so I could clean up after the removal, if it happens, after the men have taken out all the furniture. Apparently, his mum made him do an inventory of everything, so none of it really belongs to him. His mother owns all his prize paintings, his statues and probably the whole contents of the house. I think it must be worth a fortune.'

'I don't know about that, but I need to get in there. I need to see the place and attempt to contact this young girl. After all, she asked me for my help and I can't ignore her, I have to help her.

'You can't be serious Lomond; you are going to try and contact a ghost? It all sounds a bit woowoo, and bloody dangerous.'

'It's serious stuff.' echoed Lomond. Innes thought about trying to contact the ghost for a moment, but felt it was a bad idea.

Not only would they be breaking and entering, it sounded like shear madness. Despite this, she felt utterly relieved to have confided in Lomond about her awful experience with Tyrone, it was if a weight had been lifted. Lomond had not judged, questioned, or been angry with her. On the contrary, she felt their conversation had forced her to see the part she played in it all. Thanks to Lomond's insights, waves of happiness washed over her and finally she felt free. She decided she would help Lomond no matter what.

'I have a key to his house Lomond, let's go find our ghost.' They agreed to meet at seven o'clock the following night at Tyrone's house in the new town.

Innes' hand shook as she fumbled about trying to insert the brass key in the lock. Lomond was outwardly calm but inside, her nerves were jangled. She had never summoned a ghost before and she had no idea how to. As well as feeling anxious about sneaking into the house unawares, the thought of seeing the ghost filled her with fear. The girl that appeared during the Ouija board experience was full of pain and rage. Unleashing such an angry spirit might bring her a whole load of trouble. However, the words "Find Me" kept resounding in her mind, she knew she had to do it; they had to find the girl. Once inside, they shut the heavy front door as quietly as possible and entered the magnificent lounge. Dusk was falling and the street lamps shone orange beams of light into the room, illuminating their way and offering a moment of comfort. They knew it was not safe to turn any lights on, the large un-curtained bay windows offered no privacy whatsoever. No doubt the neighbours would be keeping their eyes on the property. There was also the possibility that Tyrone could arrive home and catch them at any moment. The musky smell made Lomond feel as if she might sneeze. The furniture and trappings were still positioned exactly as they remembered and it was as if Tyrone's malevolent presence was still there, lurking in every corner of the old Georgian house. White linen sheets were haphazardly thrown over some of the furniture and Innes shook her head as she pointed to the layer of dust covering Tyrone's precious collection of ornaments. His favorite chair remained uncovered; an empty crystal glass sat on the small table beside it. As they cast their eyes around the room, Lomond pointed out all the spider webs, they were everywhere, shimmering in the corners of the high walls, on the glass side lights, hanging from the chandelier and in all the nooks and crevices on the large bay windows. Innes was surprised about how different the house felt. The desolate, haunted macabre dwelling filled her with fear.

'I swear I think I'm gonna pee my pants if we hear or see anything.' She whispered. Lomond suggested they sit cross legged on the floor and rather than demanding the ghost appear, they should just be silent and see if anything happened. After sitting for what seemed like an eternity, the silence was broken by a soft whooshing noise and a soft pale mist appeared in front of them. As they both stared wide eyed, the mist disappeared leaving behind the figure of a young girl. Just as before, Lomond could hear her pleading in her mind,

'*Find me, find me, find me.*' She was sure she could make out other figures in the mist too, hanging in the air beside the young girl. 'Find me.' mouthed the apparition as she faded out of sight and Lomond's vision of the room returned to normal.

'Did you hear that?' asked Lomond with a shudder.

'No, I didn't hear anything, but I swear I saw a young girl, did she say something to you?'

'Yes, again. She's asking me to find her, over and over again. How do you think she died?'

'How the hell would I know that? You're the one who seem to be able to communicate with her.' said Innes, flashing Lomond a fake smile. 'It could have been the plague or something. You know, all those years ago when tons of people died?' Innes said as an afterthought. 'Why don't we light a candle, it's getting really dark?'

'The plague?' laughed Lomond. 'I don't think so. This ghost is not that old. I think she might have been murdered.' She looked at Innes who was grabbing a candle from the mantle-piece. Lomond sensed something was terribly wrong in this house, she felt a heaviness, a feeling of doom spreading from her feet right up to her neck. The feeling grew more intense as it gripped her throat, she couldn't breathe, a deep husky cough escaped from her quivering lips.

'Christ Lomond, please. I nearly jumped out of my skin! Shall we start in the attic?'

'I'm sorry, yeah good idea, isn't the attic the place where most people hide dead bodies, or is it the cellar?'

'God's sake, listen to you! "where most people hide dead bodies" You'd think we were bloody detectives. "Dead bodies" are not everyday conversation Lomond. Perhaps all this is just our imaginations playing tricks on us, what do you think? Either that or we are both crazy.' Innes let out a hysterical laugh,

'I think this young girl is pleading with us to find her body.' stated Lomond.

'Did she say Tyrone had killed her?' asked Innes.

'No, all she said was "find me." God you talk about me? Now you're suggesting Tyrone killed her?' Lomond sniggered, but something deep inside her felt uneasy. With the candle lit, the two girls ventured out into the magnificent hallway.

Lomond led the way, clutching the candle in her right hand as they climbed the three flights of stairs to the attic. The wooden steps creaked under their weight and the highly polished, brass stair rods shimmered and reflected strange shapes from the light of the candle's flame. Outside, it was growing darker and the house felt increasingly damp and cold; they were both shivering. The Flame flickered from the movement of Lomond's hand shaking hand causing shadows to dance across the large oil paintings - portraits of Tyrone's ancestors.

'How grimacing and foreboding do they look? I've never liked them. There's a look of madness about them don't you think? I always feel as if they are watching me, even now.' said Innes.

'Aye, for sure.' muttered Lomond, reluctant to look at the portraits and keen not to prolong their time in this house. Although this was all her idea, panic was beginning to set in. Her heart raced and she felt lightheaded. They stopped at the top floor to catch their breath. Holding onto the black metal balustrade, they peered down the long flight of stairs they had just climbed. Lomond signaled to the heavy wooden doors with brass handles flanking the long corridor.

'We'll check them one at a time,' she said 'starting with that one over there, follow me Innes.' She led the way, turning left and walking towards the gable end of the house. Gingerly, Innes turned the handle of the carved walnut door and it creaked as it slowly swung open.

Lomond gasped in amazement; what a beautiful room. A sumptuous looking king-size four poster bed was centered on the back wall with heavy velvet powder blue drapes hanging from the top of each side. They were edged with maroon tassels and a maroon tie back secured to large brass claw like hooks at either side of the matching headboard. A lavish maroon silk bedspread was thrown back, revealing matching pillows and pale blue sheets. It all gave off a rich and opulent look. It was accentuated further by tall brass lamps with ornate clear glass shades on the oak bedside cabinets and Persian rugs were scattered over the highly polished wooden floor. Innes shivered at the soft creaking from the floor boards as Lomond walked over to the window and peeked out; all was quiet in the street below.

'We need to find the attic,' Lomond said quietly, 'Maybe we're looking for another small stair, it might be behind a door or something. We'll need to open them all to check. Have you seen the attic before?'

'No, Tyrone forbid me from ever coming up to the third floor, he said it was his private quarters.' They moved from door to door, opening them to check. Finally, they opened one that led to a narrow staircase.

'Yes, here we go.' said Lomond, pointing to the door at the top of the stair. Just as she placed her foot on the first step, the shrill sound of the phone ringing downstairs broke the silence.

'For Christ's sake!' said Lomond. Innes was doubled over.

'Lomond, I can't breathe. I'm so scared.'

'Come on, keep going.'

'I don't think I can, it's not right Lomond.'

'Remember our plan. We need to help the girl; we just need to.' cried Lomond.

'No, it's not that, it's the bloody phone, the fact it's ringing is not right; it's been disconnected for over a week! Tyrone said he didn't need it anymore since he's moved in with that Vanessa.' The two girls stared at each other.

'That can't be right.' said Lomond. 'Let's go and check it.'
Hanging on to each other, they crept back down the stairs, the light
from their candle illuminating their way. The old-fashioned black
phone sat on the hall table. Gingerly, Lomond picked up the
receiver and held it to her ear.

'There's no dial tone, nothing, it's dead.' said Lomond. A
second later, another bell rang, reverberating all around them. The
girls clutched each other in terror.

'What in the name of God is that?' said Lomond.

'Oh, I recognise that sound. It's the old servant bells on the
wall in the kitchen. Every room in the house has a pull cord that
rings to the kitchen, to let staff know someone wanted attention.
It's a pulley system. Tyrone had a habit of ringing them for this and
that, water for his Whiskey, sometimes even just for a bloody chat.'
said Innes. The shrill ringing from the kitchen triggered goose
bumps over their skin and the flame from the candle dipped
momentarily as they stared at each other, their eyes wide with fear.
Lomond shielded the candle's flame with the palm of her hand,
petrified it would blow out and leave them in inky black darkness.
They peered back down the hallway to the front door, terrified they
would see Tyrone or even the ghost standing there. They tip toed to
the kitchen and Lomond placed the candle on the large oak table.

The brass bells on the wall above the fridge shone in the candlelight.

'Look, the one still moving slightly, that must be the one that was ringing.' Lomond read the label above it out loud.

'Cellar.'

'God no, not the cellar; I can't stand that dark and dingy place. It's full of nooks and crannies and shelves with wine and god knows what else on them, and it stinks awful. I do not want to go down there at all Lomond.'

'Well, be that as it may, but someone or something is directing us there, so we have to go. Where's the door?' Asked Lomond

'Oh man, it's over there.' said Innes, pointing reluctantly to the wooden door just next to the large red Aga. 'Tyrone forbade us to *ever* go down there, unless we were with him. I think he was worried someone might steal some of his beloved wine or something. I watched him once when we came back up and saw where he hid the key.' Innes bent down and ran her fingers along the skirting board, stopping when she came to a very small hole in the wall. She pulled out the key to the cellar door. It opened slowly and the pair stared into darkness. Lomond picked up the candle from the table and they descended the stone steps. Innes was right about the smell; Lomond felt nauseous. It took some moments for her eyes to adjust to the darkness as the candle's flame danced around the stone walls. She could see rows and rows of neatly placed wine bottles in a wooden wine rack. She smiled.

'Think we should open one and have a party eh Innes?' Innes shook her head vehemently as Lomond pulled out a bottle and wiped away the dust from the label. She had no idea what a good wine was. She shrugged and slid it back into its cubby hole

'What did you say Innes?'

'I never said anything, I just heard you speak.' said Lomond.

'I never said a…'

'Look!' said Lomond 'over there, there's the mist again, its clearing.' Both girls stood frozen to the spot in the dimly lit cellar and watched on as the pale mist receded to reveal the figure of the young girl. She looked about seven, a petite figure with long ringlets of golden hair falling around her neck like soft golden leaves bobbing on ripples of water. The way her energy moved ever so slightly gave her an ethereal look. She looked beautiful and angelic.

'Can you both hear me?' She said in silent honey tones and both girls nodded in amazement. Innes sucked in her breath momentarily and her bottom lip quivered. The flame from the candle flickered wildly and tendrils of golden light streamed forth from the girl. 'There but for the *Grace* of God Go I, as I take you back in time Lomond, back to events that occurred in both of our childhoods. I will show them to you like a movie and you will watch as the truth unfolds.'

They stood in silence and a picture began to form in Lomond's mind. She saw a young girl playing with a toddler on a pink rug. Past the child, a homely, kind faced woman sat in a green armchair by the coal fire, knitting a small pink cardigan. Then a tall slim woman with coarse brown hair came into focus. She was pacing up and down and Lomond could see there was bruises on her arms and face. She seemed to be shouting but Lomond couldn't hear the words, her face was full of anguish. The girl playing with the small child seemed happy; she paid no attention to the tall, slim woman. The lady in the chair placed her knitting on the wooden side table next to her and stood up. She pointed to the green floral print sofa and gently pushed the other woman towards it who nodded before laying down. Then the homely woman picked up the small child and kissed her forehead before taking the older girl by the hand and leading them out the room. As the picture dimmed, Lomond felt herself blink, the awareness of her physical body returning.

She marvelled at how completely disconnected she had been from it. A deep sense of relaxation washed over her, and now in her mind's eye, she saw the clear image of two large concrete lions on either side of steps, a brass number six and a brass letterbox on a shiny black door. The kindly woman pressed the brass doorbell and shortly after it opened. The kindly woman entered with the small child and older girl, then blackness descended.

Lomond heard a soft voice speaking to her.

'Remember the day you came to the lounge and the books were flying off the bookcase, well that was me, I did that with my energy. I concentrated my mind on moving the books and hey presto, they moved. Because I had so much practice already it was easy.' The apparition continued with a mischievous smile. 'Back then, you were between the living and dying consciousnesses. That day you were drawn to the Ouija Board's vibrational energy frequency, but also because your friend thought about you as well. She tuned into your frequency, just like tuning into a radio and you heard, Lomond, you heard it. You picked up on the telepathic connection and became locked into that frequency and *zoom,* here you came.'

'I wondered how that happened.' said Lomond silently.

'Are you really a ghost?' thought Lomond.

'Yes,' the young girl laughed. 'Yes, I am a ghost. I need you to do something for me Lomond. Will you take a message back to someone, someone who I have been unable to reach? I can't reach her because for years she has been bitter and lost, her heart is physically broken. There has been no healing, no peace or reprieve from her dark thoughts. The darkness has engulfed her, but she needs to know that…' A loud bang caused the girls to jump and the apparition disappeared in an instant.

'What the hell was that? Let's get out of here.' said Lomond, grabbing the candle. 'Come on Innes.'

'Oh my God, the kitchen light is on,' said Innes as they ascended the stairs, 'I pray to god it's not Tyrone.' The two girls stumbled into the kitchen where they came face to face with Tyrone.

'My God, what are you doing here Innes?' His face was aghast, then the surprise switched to anger in an instant. 'How dare you enter my house without my permission and go snooping around. How dare you!' He made a grab for Innes.

'Run!' screamed Lomond 'Run.' Tyrone was holding on tight to Innes' arm.

'I can't.' she cried.

'Give me back my keys you little bitch, give me them to me now, or I'll shake the living daylights out of you. So, you want to go down to the cellar, do you? Well that's easy arranged.' he growled as he dragged a screaming Innes towards the cellar steps. 'As for you,' he turned, addressing Lomond, 'You are my worst nightmare. You're the one who's polluted Innes, tarnished her very soul you have, evil is what you are. I will deal with you, oh yes, you can bank on that. I will be *your* worst nightmare whether asleep or awake. I will seek you out and there will be no peace or happiness for you, that is a promise.' The look of hatred on his face was so intense. Lomond knew she would have to act fast; she would have to catch him off guard. She threw the candle at Tyrone's head, at the same time moving to grab Innes from his grip. Just then, a grey mist enveloped Tyrone and he waved his hands frantically in the air, letting go of Innes.

'Run Innes, now, run!' cried Lomond as both girls made a beeline front door' Lomond grabbed the handle frantically and flung the door wide. They ran out from the house and down the street. Lomond glanced over her shoulder expecting to see Tyrone coming after them. However, just as he appeared in the hallway, the door slammed shut in his face with a loud thud, keeping him inside. 'Oh my god…let's get out of here!' cried Lomond into the wind.

The girls flopped down onto Innes bed, their breathing gradually slowing and their nerves steadying.

'What the hell was all that all about?' said Lomond. 'I am so confused. I can't believe we never got the last part of the message and I've no idea how to connect back with her, without going back into that house.'

'No chance.' Innes responded. Lomond continued, unphased.

'Thinking back to the images I saw in my mind when we were in the cellar, I think the tall slim woman might have been Beth and the kind looking one Maude, there was something about them that I recognised. Then, there was a baby and a young girl. Remember Innes, the ghost began by saying, "by the grace of God go I", do you think Grace could be her name?' Innes shrugged. 'Anyway, if it *was* Beth and Maude I saw, then why and what could the ghost of a girl have to do with them?

Could you imagine me telling Beth all about Tyrone, breaking into his house, she would have a hairy canary!' replied Lomond with a giggle.

'I don't know what you were doing, what you saw or what you said, I think I was asleep' added Innes sounding confused. 'Do you think Tyrone had something to do with whatever happened to this 'Grace' and that's why she's stuck in his house? Maybe you should go to the police.' said Innes.

'Well actually, when I was staying at Sorcha's, she showed me a newspaper article about the police re-opening an unsolved crime in India Street, so maybe they are already investigating Tyrone.' said Lomond. 'Anyway, what do we actually know? Little to nothing really. It's like that TV program, *Dixon of Dock Green*, the one my *so-called mother* has to watch every week.' Lomond sniggered. 'So, we stroll into the police station and just say "Hi Mr. Policeman, we just want to tell you we broke into a house, and we talked with a ghost of a dead girl and I threw a candle at the owner and we legged it." What do you think will happen? We will get bloody charged and thrown into prison, or the loony bin.' laughed Lomond.

'Well police or no police, there is something very sinister going on in that house and Tyrone is at the bottom of it, I'm sure of that.' added Innes.

'Aye, but mind he threatened me Innes, and I have to admit, his threats scare me, they scare me a lot.'

CHAPTER SIXTEEN

Lomond agreed to meet George on Saturday evening, but as the time neared, she began to question her own motives. She wasn't sure how she felt about him anymore, nagging doubts filled her mind but she couldn't bring herself to just drop him; not yet anyway. She tried to convince herself that enough time had passed and seeing him would bring closure to the ordeal they'd been through. She wasn't sure if the butterflies in her stomach were due to apprehension or anticipation, but she had a strong feeling that he might somehow hold the key to her future.

She dolled herself up, her light brown hair swept up with ringlets falling neatly behind her shell-like ears, framing her heart-shaped face perfectly. The crooked, coy smile in the mirror reflected the satisfaction she felt with her creation. George had gone to some trouble, too. He didn't mention to Lorraine where he was going, nor did he wear any of the shirts she'd bought for him. Instead, he put on freshly laundered jeans and a black T-shirt with a bike-rally logo. He'd also shaved, slicked back his hair and sprayed on some *Brut*. Lomond sat perched on the low wall beneath the four Rowan trees around the corner from the hotel, waiting patiently for George to come. She'd decided to avoid sharing her personal life with the hotel staff; there was already enough gossip traded about there. Her heart felt light and she felt optimistic for the first time in a while. She looked up at the branches bursting with leaves and the candelabra shapes of their promised blooms and she thought about that icy night in February that had side-tracked her life; it seemed like a lifetime ago, so much had happened since then. Still, she couldn't help but conjure visions of herself and George on the promised journey to "freedom," cruising the wide-open spaces far beyond Edinburgh. The sound of "Power" preceded the striking sight of George as he came around the corner, bang on time. Although it wasn't "Power" he was riding. It was another Honda in for repair he'd taken for a "test run," a liberty he may have to answer for when he returned. The new pink helmet he'd forgotten to bring for Lomond that night was strapped to the back of the bike. With a small nod of recognition, he brought the green and chrome bike to a stand-still before releasing the helmet and passing it to Lomond.

'A loaner.' he told her by way of explanation. Lomond stood for a moment, taking in the scene, George and the bike, the helmet. She waited for the fear to grip her, to stop her getting on; it never came. She shrugged before buckling the helmet strap beneath her chin and climbing on the back behind him. Her arms found his waist with familiar ease. Then he released the throttle and away they roared in a blur. Despite the accident, she was not afraid. She relished the familiar sting in her cheeks from the cool wind and nuzzled into George's leather jacket. *This is the life!* She told herself. *It really doesn't get any better than this.* Beneath her, the bike leaned to the right like a huge green feline shifting its weight; flexing its impressive muscles. They rode up past Milton Bridge Junior School, pausing a moment for oncoming traffic before George aimed the bike straight across the road. Following the windy tree-lined country road, they wove on towards the main road leading to the town of Biggar. Lomond knew this road well and she knew that for a biker, it was a *Nirvana*. Dozens of well-cambered curves where one can lean in tight and intimate with the bike. As they drew up the hill and into a swelling bend, George dropped down a gear and accelerated to get a sharp burst of speed before they came out onto the straight.

Above them, the Pentland Hills rolled out, green slopes studded with sheep and white lambs oblivious to the rushing world around them. Below, on their left, patches of wood and wildflower fields stretched out far and away to the foot of Lammermuir Hills.

This will have to end sometime, but don't let it end now Lomond petitioned the powers that be. George pulled into the car park adjacent to the Flotterstone Inn and came to a smooth stop. He dismounted and offered his hand to Lomond. Playfully, she threw her legs over the seat and landed plumb in his arms.

'I'm as happy as Larry!' she beamed, realising how silly she sounded, but not caring. George smiled but inside he was wrestling for the right words. He planned to come clean about Lorraine, he'd promised her he would, but now that it came down to it, something stopped him. *I can't just tell her now, it wouldn't be fair*, he told himself. Instead he stood looking at her, taking all of her in, remembering her fire and spirit; the qualities that had drawn him to her in the beginning. He'd wanted someone to share the thrill, the kick of adrenaline he felt when straddling "Power" and there she was. He was certain she felt just the same way when they were strapped as one to his exhilarating machine; or he knew she used to at least. Lorraine was afraid of speed and danger; she'd made it clear from the beginning she would *not* be joining him on his two-wheel adventures. Bikes were not for her she told him, risking your life just for the sake of it opposed her sensibilities.

'Fancy a lager?' George said.

'You know it!' Lomond answered, her lips parched from

the whip of the wind. George ordered two Shandies and brought them outside to sit at one of the picnic benches in the beer garden. They sat facing each other, the long shadows of the approaching evening light playing artfully on the edge of Lomond's face. He searched his mind for the right opening, but all he could think of was how much he liked her sense of adventure; something he missed with Lorraine. Lomond interrupted his jumbled thoughts.

'George, I'm sure you know I've been to hell and back since the accident. I had a huge bust-up with my parents, found out a bunch of *awful* stuff about my childhood. Now I hate them, really *hate* them for all their lies. I've moved out on my own. My dad's called me a few times, I feel sorry for him and I love him no matter what, I love and miss Shuna too but I despise Beth, I want her out of my life for good. I just can't deal with her anymore. Nothing will ever be the same at home again, that's a given; especially now all their bullshit lies have come out.' Lomond noticed a look of disapproval on George's face; like he found her attitude spoilt.

'You should really think yourself lucky you *have* parents, people that care about you.' he scolded, as if she were a child.

'Well, yes, you're right—at least I do have *parents,* if you really want to *call* them that, but you have no idea the hell they've put me through. The mess they've made of my life, and theirs.' She raised her glass to her lips and realised she should expect no sympathy from George. It was clear he didn't understand all she'd gone and was *still* going through. Lomond was thankful she hadn't told him more. If he knew her questionable parentage, he might throw it back in her face she thought. George straightened his back and smirked,

'Are we not being a wee bit *dramatic,* Lomond?'

'A wee bit *dramatic*?' she fired back, losing patience now. 'I've no mother for god sake, no *real bloody mother,*' she said, forgetting he didn't have one either 'Beth isn't even my mum, I don't even know my real mum. How much worse can it get!' she ranted unapologetically. 'I've been majorly betrayed and lied to my whole life, surely you can understand that!' she said, bursting into tears. 'What's worse then? I'd rather have no parents at all rather than having so called parents who lie to you your whole fucking life?' George was taken aback. He hadn't expected this; particularly after the way her parents had acted in the hospital. He searched for the right words to say. He knew too well what it was like not to have parents. 'Honestly George, what the hell am I supposed to do, what would you do?' she cried.

'Well, what do you *want* to do, Lomond?' he asked, a part of him regretting he wasn't able to be a more understanding, a little more tolerant at least.

'What I *want* to do is find my mother, my *real* mother. I know her name, I dragged it out of my dad, Margaret Ferguson, and she's from Perth. I don't think I'll ever feel right about any of this awful mess until I find her, *if* she's still alive. I need to know how the hell I ended up abandoned. Don't you ever want to find your mother? I don't even know your last name George' He shrugged,

'Why would I, never knew her, the surname on my birth certificate is Giles, Do you have an address?'

'No, well, *yes*, I have an address but it's an old one from years ago. I'm sure she's probably moved on by now.'

'Still worth a check.' George pointed out. Then he paused before adding pensively, 'You know, something about that rings a bell Lomond. I think my uncle lived in Perth or somewhere near there a long time ago. I never met him, or any of my relatives as far as that goes. They dumped me in a children's home until I was fostered out.'

'That's crap for you. Maybe it is worth checking though like you say.' Lomond said. 'I'm gonna ask the barman if they have a phone book for Perth, you never know!' with that she sprung up from the bench with new found enthusiasm and headed into the pub, coming back out a few moments later with a thick directory in her hand. After a quick thumb through the pages to F, there she found three Margaret Fergusons and a fair number of M. Fergusons; one of them was listed at the very address she had.

'Wow, Lomond. That is crazy! It was so easy. Are you going to call her? I think you should.'

'Yeah, well, what will I say exactly? I mean…'

'Don't over-think it. Just tell her you think you might be her long-lost daughter. I'm sure she'll fill in the rest.' Lomond bottomed her beer; her head was spinning with excitement. It was all so mind-blowing.

'Have you got some change? I've only got a few shillings. I don't want to start talking to her to be cut off because I run out of money.' George handed her some loose change from his pocket, as they walked back into the pub.

'Good luck girl.' he said as she headed for the pay phone on the wall beside the bar. Smiling nervously, she picked up the receiver and stared at the number she'd written on the piece of paper, Perth 26224. Then after taking a deep breath, she placed her finger in the hole and started dialling. A woman's voice answered on the fourth ring and Lomond dropped a couple of extra shillings into the pay slot.

'Hello, Ferguson residence?' The voice was soft but clear.

'Hello, um, well sorry to bother you, this might sound a bit strange. You see my name is Lomond, I'm sixteen and well, I think you might be my mother.' Lomond could barely believe the words coming from her own mouth.

'*Wow*,' George whispered, shaking his head in disbelief. He watched on as she talked for a while, he could hear her responding to the voice on the other end, then there was a pause before Lomond gave out the number of the pay phone before saying goodbye and hanging up. For a while, she stood with her eyes closed, holding receiver in her trembling fingers before fumbling it back onto its cradle. 'Well?' George asked, unable to contain his curiosity.

'She said she'd have to call me right back, there's a few things she needed to take care of. Oh my God George, it's her. She sounded pretty shocked to hear from me.'

'Well I'm sure Lomond, you just called her up out the blue and told her you're her daughter, she's bound to be in shock.' Before Lomond could respond, the phone rang and she grabbed the receiver. The barman gave her a quizzical look.

'Yes, yes, tomorrow,' she said nodding whilst looking at George pleadingly. 'Yes, I'll be there tomorrow.' George stared at her, wondering what was going on. 'Any chance you could give me a ride to Perth tomorrow, please? I really don't want to go by myself!' she pleaded. The idea of a long bike ride with Lomond behind him, and the wind in their faces as they sped up the road was too much to resist.

'Okay, sure. I think I can get a loaner so I should be able to take you, I'll have to get back early mind.' Lomond squealed before flinging her arms around George's neck.

'You're an absolute sweetheart, thank you so much!' she said. *I can't keep putting off telling her about Lorraine*, he thought to himself. *I'll tell her how I still feel about Lomond. Tomorrow after the trip to Perth, I've got to do it.*

CHAPTER SEVENTEEN

D.S. Jordan was finally making head-way in the attempted break-in at the hospital pharmacy. There'd been three eye-witnesses, including Lorraine, who were able to identify the young man seen in corridors in the early hours of February 18th. It was Ian, Innes' brother; a young man with a troubled past. When they brought him in for questioning, D.S. Jordan connected the two events. Ian was scared. He'd *really* screwed this time and he knew it. It had been a chance situation, he explained, a crime of convenience. He'd recognized the pharmacist; he'd seen him at a flat on Old Dalkeith Road a couple of times, a flat where kids went to get a fix. Ian was just one of many drug users who knew this flat and one day while coming out of school; he'd spotted the man. He'd seen him cross the street and turn into the hospital employee entrance. A streak of curiosity made him follow, it was a golden opportunity he told the detective. So he'd followed the man into the hospital and along the ground floor corridor until he disappeared into a room. It was then Ian noticed the pharmacy door was open. He couldn't contain his excitement; all those drugs right there, within reach. Then later, when his body needed stuff; he'd talked himself into going back to the hospital. Ian gripped the arms of the chair as he explained all this to detective, realising what a ludicrous defence he was presenting for himself.

'I mean, it was just all there for the taking!' The detective was surprisingly sympathetic to Ian's situation; she'd known dozens of unfortunate young men just like him. She offered him a deal: give up the names of the two men who'd attacked him outside his parents' house, cooperate with their arrest, and the attempted break-in charges would be dropped. She would recommend he get treatment in a rehab centre, provided his parents assumed full responsibility. She could make no guarantees, but she would suggest to the magistrate they start him off in Spittal Street; a minimum-security facility. So, with the signing of a formal document, Ian was taken into protective custody, leaving Innes off the hook for any future identity parades.

The following morning the two thugs were behind bars. It turned out they were enforcers working for the hospital pharmacist who'd been dealing prescription drugs on the streets. Innes went to visit her brother.

'You know, sis, I don't know where things went off the rails, but I've had plenty of time to think about it, and it seems like so many young people these days are angry and scared. All we see is violence everywhere and war, war, war! It's like we're being programmed to become pissed off, to *hate,* to be *paranoid.* All adults can do is talk *at* us and tell us everything we're doing wrong. They don't seem to care what we're all about. Mum and Dad are perfect examples. How did Mum not even miss all the pills I took from the cabinet? Do you get what I'm saying?' Innes lowered her eyes and nodded. There was surely enough guilt and blame to go around. She knew their situation was far from unique.

'They're always bloody bitchin, 'do *this*, don't do *that. I* mean, what the hell! How can I act in a certain way, to please *them*, when I don't know who the blazes I am as a person?' Ian looked imploringly into his sister's eyes. 'You know, sis, I have no idea who the hell our parents really are, what they're about. Except for the god-damn money they never seem to have enough of. Do you know them?' Innes shook her head. 'What the hell is that all about? Parents and their children living some weird, pointless existence like god-damn mindless robots. Well, I don't *wanna* be a god-damned mindless *robot*!' Ian said, hanging his head and sobbing uncontrollably into his hands. Innes moved closer and wrapped her arms around her brother. Sure, he was unwell, but what he'd said made sense. She felt the same sadness and desperation about her parents, her life. They were both victims of the same mind-numbing hypocrisy, the same senseless head-games that sent people over the edge. As she held her brother tightly, she suddenly had a vision of herself in the future. She could see herself helping others like her brother; other lost and mixed up young people. She decided she would see if Lorraine knew anything about how to become an addiction counsellor. Maybe she could somehow incorporate her love for art too, as a form of therapy.

Back at Lorraine's flat, George began feeling guilty about the time he'd spent time with Lomond behind her back. As he waited for her to come home from her shift, he paced nervously back and forth in front of the bay window. Then glancing out onto the street below, he saw an unexpected sight, Mac and Lorraine were on the corner talking to each other.

'What the *hell*?' he said out loud, 'What the hell does Lorraine have to talk to him about now Lomond's out of hospital?' *They must be plotting something,* his suspicious nature told him; that was what people did. Maybe, he wanted her opinion on a health matter he tried to reason, she is a nurse after all. Or maybe it's something to do with Lomond's progress. Or maybe he'd figured out George and Lorraine were having an affair and he was trying to protect his daughter by 'having a word.' Whatever the reason; George wasn't happy about it and when she walked in the door, her smile was met with harsh accusations. 'So, you're meeting Lomond's dad behind my back aye? What the hell Lorraine?' Dumbfounded, she tried to explain,

'I was only…'

'Don't even try to bull-shit me Lorraine. I have eyes you know!' he spat.

'George, if I were going to do something behind your back, do you really think I'd do it right out front of my flat for you to see? 'George shot out the palm of his hand, dismissing her words and stormed out of the door. The night he'd told her about his past came into her mind and she realised she was up against a wall with this. He had major trust issues and it was clear her love and affection hadn't brought about any real change in him. He was still his own worst enemy, he couldn't help but sabotage himself. *Oh, God, what have I gotten myself into?* She asked herself as she stared out the window. She watched him run cross the street beneath the garish yellow lights and disappear onto Marchmont Road. Little did she know that as he strode away, his mind was on Lomond and their road trip scheduled for the next day.

At least now I won't have to tell Lorraine about it. Save myself that nightmare headache! He told himself. After all, *she* was in the wrong, talking with Mac behind his back, the very man who could have had him locked-up. So *what*, he told himself, soon he'd be out on the wide-open road, in the beauty of the countryside with a girl to match. He deserved that much at least.

Even when he'd cooled down later on, he couldn't bring himself to go back and apologise to Lorraine. So, what if she *hadn't* schemed with Mac, she *always* had a way of pissing him off anyway. Even if he *had* over-reacted and falsely accused her, he couldn't face it. As his mind switched to Lomond, his list of problems seemed to mount up, weighing heavily on his already troubled mind. His driver's license might well be revoked and he didn't even want to think about the whopping fine he'd likely have to pay. What about his bike? The last time he'd seen Power, it was clear it needed a whole lot of work before it would run right again. They might even fire him at the garage if the court case went badly. Then there was Lomond, and the accident. He'd almost forgotten that. She would have to make a complete recovery if he wasn't to be charged with a criminal act. *Christ, I didn't even ask how she was doing since the accident!* And now he'd received two formal notices from the courts as well, one to his home address and the other, hand-delivered to his work, what an embarrassment. The hearing was set for May 4th and he was required by law, to report to the Court of Session in the High Street by 9:15 a.m. He was entitled to free legal counsel if his finances warranted it but given that he was earning a reasonable income, he wouldn't get it. This was going to ruin him. His only release was Mint, but even he was becoming none-too sympathetic.

'Man, you're crazy. If I had a woman like Lorraine, shit, I'd crawl on my hands and knees if she wanted me to. Lomond seems like a sweet kid, but that's what she is, brother, a kid!'

'You just don't get it, man. I can't go back. The damage is done mate, I've screwed up big time.'

'What's so *final* about it all?' Mint asked, 'People screw up every day. Just apologise and make a decision man. You're playing with fire and someone is going to get seriously burned!' Mint struggled to figure George out and the lack of understanding was becoming more mutual. Why would *he* beg forgiveness from a woman like Lorraine? George asked himself. Did that mean he felt something for her? That he secretly *fancied* her? Is that what this is all about? Was he the kind of guy that *liked* having his every thought and decision catalogued the way Lorraine did? Every emotion discussed and analysed until he had no private thoughts left at all? Maybe he enjoyed having to account for every single coming and going? Well, this was not what George wanted, not by a long shot. He needed trust and unconditional *acceptance. No strings.* Most importantly, he needed his freedom. He needed to be able to go where his heart led and the wind carried him. Between the two girls, it was clear Lomond fitted the bill better, not Lorraine. He wondered what he had even seen in her in the first place?

CHAPTER EIGHTEEN

Lomond was delighted to receive nearly five pounds in tips, compliments of the generous American guests staying at the hotel. Although Sunday lunch was a tough shift, it was worth it. She couldn't wait to put the money in her secret "travel fund box," an old tea tin she fancied for its elaborate Asian design. As soon as she reached fifty pounds, she decided the time would be ripe. Then she'd be off on an adventure to *who-knows-where*. In the kitchen, Dreanie was barely visible through clouds of steam rising from the pots grouped strategically on the stove.

'Called the police, I did, about ma Da's ashes,' she said between orders. 'I could hear the policewoman tryin' to hide a snigger, told me it isnae a police matter, but one for a lawyer. Well, ma lawyer already wrote a letter to that shite bag of a daughter, so guess I'll just need to wait and see now.' Lomond expressed a look of sympathy, but Dreanie didn't look up; she just kept stirring the pots.

'Your life seems like such a drama.' said Lomond shaking her head. As she stood waiting for Dreanie to come back with a clever quip, something began to materialize in the puffs of steam behind her; it looked like the face of an old man. Not so long ago, Lomond would have found it hard to believe what she was seeing, however, after her recent experiences; anything seemed possible. The face spoke to her,

'That's ma daughter for ye,' it said, 'she loves a bit o' drama. Can ye tell her I'm glad ma ashes got her thinkin' o' me again. I ken I done her and her brother and sister wrong, but I do love them all dearly. Tell her that would ye, hen?' Lomond could still hear Dreanie's voice rambling on in the background as the figure spoke, then a hand grabbed her arm making her jump.

'What the hell's the matter with you, hen? You was starin' like you was in some kinda trance!' Dreanie looked concerned.

'You're not going to believe this Dreanie, but your father was just there talking to me, he was standing right there behind you.' Dreanie's eyes went wide and she spun around surveying the empty space behind her. 'He wanted me to give you a message. He said he was glad all this business with his ashes got you thinking about him again and that he was sorry for everything. He said to tell you he loves you. I feel kinda *weird* saying but…'

'Well, that is a strange one isn't it,' she interrupted with a curious grin, 'I'm not sure what to say for a change. I dinnae not believe you. Aye, the ashes have made me think of him more again. Say's loves me huh? Well…' The *ping* of the oven timer interrupted her. 'Anyway, we best get a move on dear; here's still loads to get done.' Lomond could think of little else but meeting her real mother later that day; she struggled to keep from telling someone. *Do I look like her? Will she like me? Will my coming back into her life bring back bad memories of how she lost me?* Her thoughts turned to poor Maude, then to Mac and Beth and the 'callous' thing they'd done. One thing Lomond felt for certain, she would love this woman, her blood mother, no matter what.

George arrived on his borrowed wheels at the agreed time. He sat outside the hotel with his heavy black biker boots planted firmly on the ground and the engine whirring; he drew more than one pair of curious eyes. Seeing him there, oozing confidence made Lomond feel safe; that was just what she needed at that moment. He handed her the pink helmet again and for a split second, the colour triggered a memory of her last encounter with Mrs. R. on the other side. She swung a leg over and wrapped her arms around George's waist and with them both settled, he popped the throttle and they set off with a roar; zooming along the road out of Roslin and onto the main Penicuik Road. He took a side road cross-country that led them to the foot of Pentland Hills and soon enough, they were flying along the straight; all their plans and destinations vanishing momentarily with the wind. They headed over the Forth Road Bridge, the immense suspension bridge over the over the Firth of Forth always impressed Lomond. She looked down through the slits at the rippling blue-grey of the water flowing far below and she felt exhilarated. Up, and to her right, her eyes were drawn to an old train chugging it's way north over the famous red iron rail bridge. She closed her eyes and her heart raced as she reminded herself that within the hour she would be meeting her real mother, finally.

They'd arranged to meet Jock, Margaret's man, at a garage in Perth. When Lomond removed her helmet, he let out a gasp,

'Christ lass, Margaret, your mum is in for some shock!' He exclaimed, 'You two could be sisters.' They followed behind Jock and in less than ten minutes, they pulled up in front of a mid-terrace council house. He beckoned them to follow him inside. Lomond felt sick and her legs were trembling as she crossed over the threshold, this was the moment she'd been waiting for. Then, there in the lounge stood her mother. The two of them stood speechless for some moments, surveying their striking similarities. They had the same petite build, the same hair colour, although her mother's was flecked with grey. Then, they embraced each other warmly.

'This is my friend, George,' Lomond managed to say, the nerves evident in her voice. George nodded in acknowledgement. 'It's very nice to meet you too, George,' Margaret said, looking him up and down and shaking his hand. She gestured for them to sit on the sofa together. Sensing the delicacy of the situation, Jock invited George out to the garage, to see an old bike he was working on; George readily accepted. Once alone, although clearly nervous, Margaret wasted no time explaining to Lomond what had led to their separation.

'I was young and carefree when I met your father and he was a good man. We saw each other for a while, until he left Perth and went back to Edinburgh. Soon after, I found out I was pregnant, but I was only fifteen Lomond. My mother *insisted* I leave Perth until the baby was born and I was sent to a home for unwed mothers in Edinburgh. It was awful, all the young girls had to scrub and clean for their keep, right up until the day I went into labour. I had no money and we were forbidden to contact *anyone*. My mum threatened she would have Mac arrested for underage sex and thrown into prison if I even tried to make contact; I couldn't have that. Your dad was nice person and the two of us created you, our baby, together.' Lomond watched as the tears streamed down her face, thinking she might be too upset to finish the story, but she carried on. 'Well, when I finally came home to Perth with you, my parents decided I was an embarrassment to them. They hid your existence from our neighbours, from our friends and family. Then my mother forced me to give you up, to sign away all my rights to you, my own flesh and blood. That was when I called your father and he told me he'd had met a woman called Maude and they were in a serious relationship; I was broken hearted about it all. I told him all about you and how they were forcing me to have you adopted. Of course, he agreed to take you and I made a promise never to contact you, that I wouldn't bother him and Maude ever again. He said he didn't want to drag up the past and he felt it was for the best. As the years went on, I convinced myself you were better off with him and Maude, that you would have a much better life with them. Lomond was silent trying to absorb all that Margaret was telling her. She tried to picture herself in her mother's shoes and she felt sorry for the ordeal she had suffered. 'Later on I met Jock, we never married but we have two kids, Shaun and Denise, your brother and sister. I've told them all about you, they'll be back soon.' Margaret wiped her face with her apron and the two women smiled at each other. 'Well, enough of all that for now,' she said, standing up, 'I need to check on the dinner. I won't be a few minutes. Make yourself at home sweetie.' She said.

'Please,' Lomond called after her, 'let me help you.'

'Ah, it's no bother but if you want to, just come on through to my wee kitchen.' she invited.

As Lomond scanned the faces in photographs hanging on the kitchen walls; a slim, dark haired boy of around fifteen sauntered in. His face looked friendly.

'Hey, you must be Lomond, my big sister eh?' He threw his arms around her in a bear hug and Lomond noticed he smelled of engine grease. 'I'm Shaun. Mum told about me all about it, another sister, how cool is that?' he said, grinning ear-to-ear, 'Is that your bike out there?'

'Uh, no, that belongs to my friend, George. He's out in the back yard with your dad I think.'

'Nice…' he said. A few moments later, George and Jock entered the kitchen. 'Hey, mate, I hear that's your bike out front?'

'It's a loaner, actually, mine's is in the shop.' George lied, not wanting to tell them it was still with the police.

'*Sweeeet*! I absolutely *love* bikes!' said Shaun with an enthusiasm George recognised. 'I've been round 'em all my life, doing cross country and speedway and all that, and now I'm a trainee mechanic at a garage down the road.'

'Good choice!' said George, 'That's what I do too'

'Maybe sometime we could…' A sullen looking girl with fire-red hair and a round face burst into the room. She flung her bag on the kitchen floor and gazed critically at Lomond.

'So, you're 'her' then are you…the new 'sister'?' Lomond was taken aback by her abruptness, was unsure what to say.

'Hey, yeah…hi, I'm Lomond, it's nice to meet you.' she answered holding out her hand. The girl ignored it.

'Aye, well I've had a *shit* day so…' she narrowed her eyes. '*Boys*, what do you make of them? Shit-for-brain bampots right?' Lomond opened her mouth to speak but before she could answer, the girl spoke again, 'I'm Denise, by the way.' There was a smirk of her face and Lomond smiled back, however, she felt suddenly awkward, like an intruder. They all sat at the table and enjoyed a lovely meal together; it was clear Denise dominated the family dynamic. Jock said very little, he seemed used to the women-folk directing the conversation. Lomond wondered what it would have been like if she was brought up by her mother, as opposed to Mac and Beth, she tried to envisage herself as a member of the family at this table. She felt she would have preferred the seemingly casual and carefree parenting style of Margaret. It suited her much more than the starched collar, stern, 'children should be seen and not heard' lifestyle Beth had created.

It was starting to get dark when they said their good-byes. Despite Lomond and Margaret promising to talk again soon, she left feeling a bit let-down. It wasn't really what she'd expected for her first visit, although she was unsure what she had expected in the first place. All she knew was that even though she just spent several lovely hours with her actual blood relatives, they felt like total strangers to her. Her mum and siblings shared all their life experiences with each other, they had memories as a family unit, she was not part of any of them and it made her feel sad. She wondered if she would even fit in with them at all. A part of her also felt a little betrayed. She thought about the pictures of her maternal grandmother adorning the walls in the hallway. She questioned why her mother would have all these pictures up if she had been so hurt and distraught about being forced to give up her baby. In her opinion, her grandmother had a lot to answer for.

Thinking about this filled Lomond with anger, although she realised she would need to consider the consequences of her having this attitude. She desperately wanted to be part of the family and she longed to have a loving mother in her life. Venting her anger towards an old woman would likely see her being pushed out of the family all over again; it was evident they all had a good relationship with the woman. The fact Shaun and Denise had only just found out about Lomond made them ignorant to their Grandmothers wrong doings in Lomond's eyes. Regardless, she needed *someone* to vent off to about it. She had to find some way of confronting her grandmother for banishing her from the family. Thinking ahead, she began to plot. She would find a way of persuading Margaret to take her to meet her grandmother; the woman who had played God with both their lives and decided both of their fates.

As they sped back down the road to Edinburgh, the story of Margaret, her life and her children played over and over in Lomond's mind. The first twinkling of the night stars were visible as they stopped at the The Flotterstone Inn. The car park was full of cars and bikes; it was a popular place for people to come for a pint and a stroll around the reservoir. Other used it as a base to set off on treks up into the hills. Carrying their head-gear under their arms, they went inside and sat at a cozy table-for-two.

Lomond found she was unable to stop looking at George; it was as if she was seeing him for the first time. She couldn't work out what had changed but something felt different.

'What did you think of my mother?' she asked curiously.

'I'm not really sure,' he answered, trying to choose his words carefully. He tried to back-pedal when he saw the troubled look in her eyes. 'I mean, I'm probably not the best judge of stuff, but, well, it's just there seems to be something. I can't quite put my finger on it, but something seems a bit off…'

'What makes you say that?' Lomond asked taken aback. She looked him in the eye, 'Why would you say that? I mean, I thought she was amazing! I was just sitting here thinking how lucky I am to have such a young-looking and kind mother.' Lomond searched for hope in George's expression but it only reflected suspicion, she felt herself bristle. 'Clearly, she never *wanted* to give me up and…what about my brother then, is he bold wee rogue or what? Not sure *what* to make of my sister, though, I mean, she seems a bit dark, but I don't wanna jump to conclusions. Maybe she's just pissed off about having an older sister now, you know, not being the eldest in the family anymore. Still, didn't seem to stop her from taking charge, did it? I know they're only my half brother and sister, but I think I'm gonna like being their big sister.' George shrugged, he felt a bit dark himself, but he couldn't understand why. Although he was happy for her, something about Lomond's 'new family' made him feel uneasy and sad about his own life. He forced a smile and suggested they take a stroll before heading back.

At the edge of the reservoir, they looked out at the family of ducks rippling the water in the twilight and at the two men sitting in a small fishing boat with their rods in the water; floating as if in no hurry to go anywhere. Lomond noticed a cluster of old pine trees on a small island in the middle; they were bent forward like old men against the capricious habits of the wind. She hoped George would explain his mood, but he seemed unable to find the words.

'It's almost dark,' he said, 'I think it's time we start back.' Suddenly, it felt they'd said all there was to say. Something had shifted between them and it was clear they both felt it. Without waiting or warning, he turned on his heels and starting trudging down the hill, leaving Lomond trailing behind. She didn't know what she was feeling anymore. A part of her was angry, but there was also something else, a strange and unwelcome distance that wasn't there before. They rode home in silence and as he dropped her off, he muttered a simple,

'See ya round.' before zooming away into the distance.

Instead of going back to her lodgings, Lomond strolled absently down the single-track road towards the chapel; wild random thoughts ducked in and out of her head. It was a mild night but she barely noticed. She pushed open the rickety gate and entered the graveyard, sitting down on a wooden bench and staring up at the stars. A string of seemingly disconnected emotions bubbled up through her body and mind. She contemplated her 'good fortune' at finding her blood mother. *What could be better than that?* She reasoned. Then, Mrs. R.'s face came into her mind; as if she had just awoken from a long sleep and noticed her. Suddenly, she wanted to know who she was, *how* she'd seen her and most of all *why?* Why did she seem to drop in and out of her life like she did? In that very moment, she felt a strong connection with Mrs. R. and an even stronger desire to find out the answers to her questions.

CHAPTER NINETEEN

Lomond knew that sooner or later; she'd have to tell Mac about meeting her real mum. Whilst she couldn't care less what they thought about it, a part of her wanted to gloat. To brag to Beth about what a *fantastic* woman her mum was, nothing like her. There was also the matter of the ghost Grace swimming around in her head, if that was even her name. She was desperate to know what the unfinished message was and who was it for?

Bright and early the next morning, she was polishing the brass around the fireplace in the lounge bar. It was a traditional granite hearth with a gas-fire upgrade and soot would often dislodge and fall from the chimney breast. As she was sweeping the soot into a metal dustpan, a strange breeze suddenly rushed over her; it was too icy to be a draft. She felt a presence behind her and all the hairs on her arms stood on end. She turned quickly to see who had entered the room but there was no-one there. For a split second, she considered running from the building and out into the safety of the daylight, but just then, Dreanie and one of the regulars 'Old-Man-Brian' wandered in. She exhaled in relief although she still felt on edge, had Brian been spying on her maybe? With no one manning the bar, he went behind and helped himself to a pint, pulling out two coins and slapping them down on the counter.

'I should get a discount seein' I'm havin' to tap ma own lager!' he said, sounding half serious. No, there must be something else at play here, Lomond concluded. What she'd felt was a different vibe entirely. 'What's the matter wi' you, lass? You're as white as a sheet.' Brian said

'Aye, you're looking a wee bit peaky there,' added Dreanie, 'You see another ghost or something?'

'Well, I didn't *see* one exactly, but…' She was unsure about how much to say, 'I swear I just felt something.'

'Ah, that'll be ma old Da again.' said Dreanie, waving a dismissive hand.

'It'll no be your Da,' Brian said, 'He didnae bother to see you much in life, so why would he start now after death?' Brian roared. 'It'll be Ranald, the resident ghost,' he informed them in a matter-of-fact tone, 'gassed hiself he did, you've seen him afore Dreanie.' Lomond couldn't work out if this bit of banter was just playful yarn-spinning, regardless; she found it strange they thought it a laughing matter. She wanted to know more about this poor fellow who'd felt desperate enough to take his own life; maybe it would help her understand what happened to poor Maude. 'Ranald was the innkeeper here back in the nineteen forties, after the war you ken,' Brian stated before taking a gulp of his pint and wiping his mouth with the back of his wrinkled hand. 'Well, he was a bit of a miserly ol' boot. He'd been doon the mines when he was younger until he inherited this place from his aunt when she passed away; she had nae bairns of her own you see? So, he became the innkeeper and he stooped workin' doon the mines but he turned into a bit o' a loan shark. He kept a wee book under the counter wi the names o' the folk who owed him beer money. It was the tax inspector that finished him off. Since he'd been a miner, he thought he could get off without paying any tax. Well, when they set to askin' him for over two hundred pounds, he went into despair and hung hiself. It was a bit o' a shame and loads o' folk felt bad aboot it, aboot no paying their debts.' What a somber, tragic tale thought Lomond. She was confused as to why both Brian and Dreanie seemed so blasé about it and they were not the least bit ruffled by the fact Lomond felt the presence of a dead man in the room.

'So why is he still around?' Lomond asked, partly playing along but genuinely interested to know. 'I mean, is he unhappy?' She asked with a shiver.

'He's looking for retribution if you ask me.' answered Brian, clearly trying to scare Lomond with his dark and foreboding prevarication. Jimmy entered the lounge too.

'Tell 'er 'bout the chapel, Brian, that's the best part.' He said with a wink.

'Do ya want tae hear it?' Brian offered, a dark timbre to his voice. 'I have ti warn you though, it's no for the faint o' heart lass.' he added in the most ominous tone he could muster. Lomond nodded in curious fear. Brain emptied his glass and poured himself another. 'Well you see, a while back, ma pal worked as a kind o' Janitor for the chapel, keeping an eye on it and showing folk about if they showed an interest in it you ken? Mind you, it wasnae like it is the day, wi the shop full o' trinkets and guide-books and all that nonsense; it was just Roslyn Chapel back then. Well, he told me a tale he heard when he was a wee boy, a man told him about the private, family crypts under the chapel. This man said that one night, when the new moon was shining high in the heavens; he broke into the chapel and got into the crypts. He says he saw the corpses in them and all the deed bodies were laid out in their finery, as if they'd just deed the day before. He says there wasnae even any decaying he could see.

They looked as if they were just there sleeping, waitin' for some prince ti come and wake them up or something.' He took a quick slug of his pint before carrying on with his gruesome tale. 'Well, this local bloke was shrieking aboot it for years, haunted for life by what he'd seen. He ended going *mad* in the end, I heard. After that, the family ordered the crypts be sealed up with huge boulders to stop anyone else getting inside again, and that's how they are to this day.' Lomond noticed Jimmy's lips curl into a side-long grin and she wondered if there was even a lick of truth in any of it. It was obvious it was some kind of a highly-polished, local urban legend. How strange that she heard a story about the chapel so soon after her visiting it herself though. She promised herself she'd take a proper look inside soon; she was keen to explore it for herself.

As she sat in her wee room overlooking the courtyard that night, she thought about the bizarre appearance of Dreanie's father and the fate of the old innkeeper Ranald. She also wondered what had driven Maude into such despair. What terrible thing could have happened that forced her to abandon her child, her husband, her family and friends forever? The last thing Mrs. R. had said to her during their last encounter came into her mind, she'd pleaded with her to come back and visit. Why would she ask this? Why and about what would she want to converse with a ghost over?

How does a person *intentionally* cross over into the spirit realm anyway? She realised she had so many questions only Mrs. R could answer.

The next day, Robert asked if Lomond would work late on Saturday in exchange for Monday morning off. Lomond swithered, half hoping George would call her, however, when she discovered there was a buffet booked for an American Crusaders convention, she decided to accept. This would boost her travel fund over the target. Minutes before the group was due to arrive, Dreanie was still in the kitchen baking scones and there was flour everywhere, including all over her face giving her a ghostly look.

    'Well, hen, we finally got ma Da's ashes back, praise the Lord!' she said excitedly. 'The Police rescued them and brought 'em round to the house last night and now he's sittin' as you please on ma mantelpiece. I'm gonna take 'em down to the cemetery and spread 'em over my Ma's grave later the day.' Dreanie looked plaintively at Lomond. 'Say, do you have plans after your shift? You fancy comin' along?' Pleased to be included in such a momentous event, Lomond agreed willingly. She also liked the idea of a spin on the bike though so she called the garage to ask George if he wanted to take her out when she got back from the cemetery.

'Not tonight, Lomond, how about tomorrow afternoon?' she could hear a reluctance in his voice. 'Would that do?' She felt he was hesitant to see her at all; his usual cock-sureness was gone. In truth, he was sick of himself, not Lomond.

What the hell is wrong with me? Why can't I just come out and tell Lomond about Lorraine?
He'd come to accept he had feelings for them both, albeit in different ways, but he felt like a coward, a worthless lout who used women. Was he really attracted to Lorraine just because she'd given her body over to him so readily? He stood in the bathroom of his loft apartment, his reflection staring back at him with self-loathing. The same hatred he used to feel when he was in foster care was beginning to dominate his thoughts and emotions again; the abused was becoming the abuser. The dark side he never wanted to share with anyone was bubbling to the surface, he had to take control. With his mind numb, he peeled back the left sleeve of his shirt and surveyed his arm before reaching for a single-edge razor blade. He held it firmly between his forefinger and thumb and slowly scored the flesh on the inside of his arm. He watched as it sliced neatly and droplets of blood rose through the slit of the

wound like red tears. He stared at the wound sullenly, in a kind of self-satisfied trance. Then, within seconds his racing heart slowed to an even and controlled rhythm, sedation and satisfaction descended; he was back in control now. He didn't want to see anyone, not even Lorraine, *especially* not Lorraine he told himself. It was better that way. He thought about Mint, his conscience tried to persuade him he should at least confide with his friend about the turmoil going on in his troubled mind. Then with a fresh sense of calculated calm, he walked to his bedside table and picked up the letter, **"Official: For the attention of the Addressee Only."** He ripped it open and read, he'd been formally charged with reckless driving. He must surrender his driver's license within twenty-four hours. If he pled guilty, he must pay a fifty-pound fine, or he could go to court and defend his actions; the latter could result in more severe charges and penalties. He realised there was only one way he could get that kind of money quick enough, and that was to sell his beloved bike. He'd have to sacrifice *Power.* He slammed his fist into the glass-protected poster from last year's Bristol Bike Bash. What other option did he have? He could go crawling to Lorraine for help. *No fucking way.* Mint came to mind again…

A couple of miles away, Lorraine sat in her flat waiting. *Why hasn't*

George called? She wondered if he might actually be planning to see Lomond that afternoon, to finally tell her about their relationship, but she doubted he had the nerve.

'I bet he can't even work up the courage to call me.' She muttered. In pit of her stomach, she knew his silence meant things were not going to end well. She went to the window and stared out at the wet street below. The greenery glistened after a quick downpour and large puddles were dotted all over the street. A dark thought crept into her mind: *Maybe he's already made his decision and they're somewhere together.* The desperation was too much; it was worth the risk to find out. She trembled as she rang the number and was gratefully surprised when Lomond answered immediately.

'Hey, it's Lorraine, are you alone?' she asked.

'Uh, yeah…how come? Is something up?' There was a note of suspicion in her voice. Lorraine panicked.

'Em, are you free later? Do you fancy getting together?'

'Yeah, sure,' Lomond responded, 'I was planning to head over to the Meadows later. There's a street fair on, I thought it might be fun to check out some of the stalls, maybe go on a ride or two; you wanna join me?'

Lomond took the bus into town after work and the two girls met outside the entry gate to the fair as agreed. They greeted each other warmly and walked arm-in-arm checking out the rows of amusements before deciding to take a spin on the "Big Wheel." It was from the top of the ride Lomond spotted George and Mint below. She called down to them and eventually George realised where the sound was coming from. When he looked up and saw them together, he prayed silently the earth would open up and swallow him whole.

'Oh shit! No bloody way man.' he exclaimed; panic stricken. Mint nudged him.

'Uh, oh…now the shit is about to hit the fan!'

'For Christ's sake, Mint, don't let on!' George hissed, 'Whatever you do, please don't let on!'

'I really don't think it's me you have to worry about, mate,' Mint said as he watched the girls pointing at them and talking to each other.

'Have you met Mint already?' Lomond asked,

'Yes, I met him through George.' Lorraine answered. As soon as the words were out, she felt the blood rushing from her hands to her face. Then she watched in horror as the confusion on Lomond's face morphed into a look of disbelief and then betrayal.

'You and George?' Lomond sneered as an image of the two of them together flashed through her mind. She felt an overwhelming surge of anger. By the time the wheel came to rest at the bottom, Lomond was ready for a confrontation, but Mint was alone. 'Where the hell is George?' she shouted, rushing towards him. 'Where is that cheating piece of shit?' Mint took hold of her arms,

'Come on now Lomond, try and keep cool. I get you're pissed, let's take a walk.' As he frog-marched Lomond away, Lorraine was left alone and broken. As she stood there crying, she heard the unmistakable roar of a bike engine receding into the distance and it was all the confirmation she needed; George was guilty as sin and doing a runner as usual.

'Yeah cry bitch, cry your bloody heart out you back stabber.' Lomond yelled back over her shoulder, 'To think you actually pretended to care for me, to be my nurse, and my friend, what an absolute fucking joke!'

'That's quite the temper, you have.' laughed Mint, attempting to make light of the situation.

'I could claw his god-damn eyes out, and hers, and I wouldn't even regret it. I can't believe it. What a two-timing cheat, he's dating both of us?' Mint nodded.

'I know it's a hard pill to swallow Lomond, but…'

'I swear if I get my hands on him…and she better just stay away from me I tell you!'

Although he didn't want to diss his friend he felt compelled to offer some words of support.

'Look, it's always gonna hurt to find out someone you trust isn't who they say they are but know this. There's someone out there who'd treat you with more respect, someone who'd care enough about you not to cheat on you.' Lomond was taken aback for a moment. It struck her that Mint had so much about him; way more than George had portrayed. He was thoughtful, logical, charismatic and a real *individual.* Suddenly, she felt an overwhelming urge to somehow include him in her plans; whatever they might be now.

'Well, anyway. I really hope things work out for you; the way you want them you know?' He rubbed her arm tentatively before setting off on his own up the tarmac path. As she watched him move into the distance, something warned her to not let him go.

'Hey, wait a minute,' she yelled, hurrying after him,

forgetting for the moment the horrible mess her personal life had become. She caught up with him and the two of them walked casually towards the Royal Infirmary. On the way, Lomond was tempted to vent her anger further, to say a few more choice things about George and Lorraine; however, for some reason it seemed pointless, *childish* even. *There's someone out there who'd treat you with more respect, someone who'd care enough about you not to cheat on you.* His words calmed her.

By the time they reached the hospital, Lorraine had caught up with them.

'Lomond, I know this won't make it any easier,' she said, 'but I want you to know, I had no idea he was still seeing you. I mean, I had my suspicions, but I didn't know…or maybe I just didn't want to face it.' Lorraine looked crestfallen but Lomond just shrugged.

'I should have known there was something going on between you,' she resigned. 'I could see it in his face every time I mentioned your name, and I had a feeling; as if I already knew. I can't explain it, but it was as if I'd *seen* you both together, even though I can't have.'

'I hate to say it Lomond, but frankly, I think he's more

trouble than he's worth. I tried to be his friend, to help him, but he doesn't have the confidence or self-control to maintain an adult relationship. He can't seem to let go of his past.'

'You would say that, now wouldn't you? 'Lomond snapped, 'Well, no matter what you say, I'll always love him and I'll never turn my back on him. You see, that's the difference between our relationship and yours. What you had was just fickle, meaningless; it was going nowhere.' Lorraine looked devastated, 'George will *always* love me Lorraine, always!' she added, stamping her foot and walking away. At that moment, Lorraine felt like she would never get over the sense of guilt and the feeling of being totally used.

CHAPTER TWENTY

The more time Lomond spent with Mint, the more she knew he *was special* and she wanted him in her life. Instead of trying to fit him around her plans, as had always been the way with George, she found herself wondering how she might fit into his. He'd mentioned going to Inverness, maybe she could get him to invite her along.

George on the other hand, was at breaking point. He knew he'd managed to alienate everyone who had cared for him and he felt totally alone in the world again. He'd screwed-up plenty of times before, but this time he was hurtling towards rock-bottom and it felt like there was nothing her could do to stop it. If only he had treated people better. It saddened him to think Mint would never speak with him again. His friend had made it clear how much he disapproved of his behaviour towards Lomond and Lorraine, and rightfully so. Why had he not listened? Why had he been so reckless with their feelings? He needed to get away, as far away from the drama as he could. He thought about the time Lorraine dragged him along to the meditation class. Although at first, he'd been uncomfortable and stressed, it hadn't been all that bad in the end. In fact, his conversation with the hermit had most definitely changed his life for the better. It gave him the courage to report the accident to the police, which had ultimately resolved his problem there. Was Lorraine's safe and predictable lifestyle better in the end? Even with all the smelly candles and hocus pocus stuff she was into; he was starting to think so. His thoughts turned to the Hermit, despite being a stranger to him, George had believed in his wisdom. He felt a sudden urge to see him again, maybe he could help. With that in mind, he headed to Tyrone's house, praying he might know the old man's whereabouts, it felt like his last hope. Surely the Hermit would know how to steer him in the right direction, he would be able to give him advice about how to get out of the mess he was in, help him build bridges with his friends. He felt a glimmer of hope.

He parked his motor bike in the bay opposite Tyrone's house. Crossing the road, he paused for a moment and admired the impressive ornamental lions sitting at the top of the steps before bounding up them two at a time and ringing the bell. A few moments later the door was opened by a tall buxom woman with red coiffured hair. She looked him up and down.

'Um…hi…um, I'm George.' he stuttered.

'What are you looking for? We have no jobs here, if that is what you are going to ask.'

'Oh no, it's nothing to do with that, I…I…emm…'

'For goodness sake, spit it out then, I've not got all day.' She replied.

'Shut the bloody door woman, would you? You're letting all the heat out.' A voice hollered from somewhere inside. The lady shook her head in disdain and Tyrone appeared behind her. He looked both surprised and suspicious to see George on his doorstep.

'Ah, hi Tyrone, sorry to intrude. Is there any chance I could take a moment of your time, if you don't mind? I really need some advice.'

'You shouldn't have really turned up here unannounced you know; you need to make an appointment to see me actually.' George looked apologetic and turned to leave.

'Right, well if it's advice you're looking for then I'm most likely your man,' he stated with an air of grace. He stepping aside, forcing Vanessa to move at the same time. 'Come in then, I guess I can spare five minutes.' As George entered the hallway, he remembered the last time he'd been in the house but his thoughts were promptly interrupted.

'Where's your manners young man? Take your bloody shoes off!' the red-haired woman exclaimed. Obediently, he removed his shoes and followed them into the lounge.

'So, you want my advice, do you?' said Tyrone as he sat on his special chair. 'What is it? You want to know your future, or is it affairs of the heart you want answers on?' Although he wasn't keen on Tyrone and he felt uncomfortable sharing his private life with anyone, George started to confide in him about his affair with Lorraine and his obsession with Lomond. However, the more he spoke, the more he felt the guy was not to be trusted.

'Look Tyrone, I'm sorry to bother you with all this pal, and I appreciate you hearing me out, but I was hoping you might be able to put me in touch with the Hermit guy. He really helped me last time I met him, here at your meditation group. I don't suppose you've got a number or an address for him, have you?' Tyrone glared at him blankly for some moments before he finally spoke.

'The Hermit eh?' he said with the hint of a sneer.

'Aye pal, him. I really feel I need to talk to him, that he can help me sort things out you know?' Tyrone felt a rage swelling within him, rising to the surface. It took all his energy to contain it. *Why did they all want the Hermit over him? What the hell did he have that made people want to follow him, how as he the all seer?* That bloody Lorraine as well, he knew she was trouble from the first time he'd laid eyes on her, he saw right through her; the same bitch who turned his sweet Innes against him. And as for Lomond, the wild, dangerous one he'd met at the fair, the one who knew too much and could see into the souls of others, she was the one who'd forced Innes to betray him by breaking into his home; he still had every intention of making them both pay for that. He couldn't believe George was here asking for help to make things right with those heathens; but through 'the wisdom' of the Hermit; what a cheek. As the rage continued bubbling inside him; he knew it was time to seek his revenge.

George had landed in his lap and he was going to make the most of this opportunity, but he would need to think quickly.

'Sorry, the Hermit doesn't have a fixed address, or a phone number; but I think *I* might be able to help you George. Won't you stay for a drink?'

'Ah, no thanks, I better not, I've got the bike, I'm in enough trouble already with the law.' George laughed nervously.

'Oh, one won't harm,' Tyrone coaxed as he poured them both a stiff whisky. George took a gulp and it felt good, the burning liquid trickled down his throat and into his stomach; numbing his emotional pain.

'I tell you what George, I'll get my Ouija board out, and we'll get the answers you need from that.' George was unsure, he didn't really understand what that was, only that he'd heard they could be dangerous; he didn't see how it would give him any answers. However, he was so desperate, he didn't resist; the thought of facing a life alone seemed much worse. He followed Tyrone over to the large desk and looked with intrigue at the group of mini black statues sitting next to a gleaming paperknife. As he peered closer; he noticed they were grotesque, ugly looking gargoyle-like figurines. However, something drew him to pick one up; one with a single eye for a head. He turned it over and over in the palm of his hand, feeling as if it might reveal some secret information to him.

'Did you know your little friend Lomond broke into my house, George?' The question caught him off guard and he swung around to face Tyrone.

'Really?'

'Yes, really. You didn't know? I would have thought their 'little escapade' would have circulated half-way round Edinburgh by now.' George shook his head and returned his attention to the statue in his hands while Tyrone took a sip of his whisky. He had never found the answer as to why they broke into his house. Was it some childish prank or were they looking for something, and if so what? Innes knew his house inside out; she could have stolen anything at any time. It was all still a mystery and it tormented him daily. He'd wondered back and forth if it might have been the Ouija board they were after. He knew it had the power to conjure up friendly ghosts with messages of love and comfort, but sometimes it was more demonic beings that came forward to have their say and throw their tantrums; this was part and parcel of dabbling in it. To him, the Ouija board was his link to accessing other worlds, darker worlds; it was his pride and joy. Maybe Lomond knew that, and she wanted to steal it? However, if that was the case, why had he found them in the cellar? None of it made any sense and these questions had plagued him for weeks. He knew one thing though, if he didn't find a way to teach this 'wild one' a lesson, it wouldn't be long before she would be back to cause him trouble again in one way or another. Yes, he was going to show her just what happens when you go meddling in the occult. She would regret crossing the threshold of his home and rifling through his stuff and snooping around as if it were her right. Then, as he watched George playing with the statue, he had a flash of inspiration and in that moment, he knew just what he would do to get his retribution. Through George he would be able to punish them all, they were all connected after all. He sat back down in his favourite armchair and placed the Ouija board on the small round table in front of him. Then he placed a crystal tumbler in the centre.

'George come on over here and sit, please, and you can keep the statue you have in your hand. Think of it as a gift; I think it might be a lucky charm for you.' He smirked.

'Really? Wow…that's so kind of you, thanks. I'm not used to getting gifts, I don't know if I should accept it though, it looks expensive; I was just a bit drawn to it that's all.' said George, lowering his head.

'Not at all, I insist! You keep it George, truly, it would give me great pleasure if you take it.' Tyrone was grinning widely.

'Well, if you're sure…that's amazing, thanks.' He slid the figure into his trouser pocket and sat in the green armchair opposite Tyrone.

'Now, place the middle finger of your right hand on the glass George, just like I am.' instructed Tyrone. Suddenly George felt the energy in the room change, as if there was a build-up of electrical charge somewhere. The statue began to heat up in his pocket, it felt as if it was burning a hole in his leg, but he was powerless to move. He looked up to see Tyrone's reaction but he seemed oblivious. Then he watched as waves of swirling black energy surrounded the man. It seemed to be gathering momentum and he could hear a deep booming sound coming from its core. It began moving towards him and he was frozen in fear as he realised, he would soon be engulfed. As it merged with him, surprisingly, the fear subsided and he felt at one with it. Rather than it seeming alien, he understood it, he could feel his own energy being drawn from his body and mingling with the blackness; it was his friend, it had been all his life, it had helped him to survive through everything. In that moment he knew with certainty he would never again change to please others; he would stop trying to be the goody-two-shoes everyone else wanted him to be. He was his own man and they all just better accept it. What had all that lovey-dovey stuff done for him anyway? Absolutely nothing. He'd teetered on the dark side before and that was where he belonged, where he was most happy, at peace. Never again would he answer to anyone; he would be the master of his own destiny.

His finger nearly lost the glass as it shot across the board. It careered this way and that, as if searching for the right letter before coming to pause over the letter 'U'. Then it carried on, moving from place to place until it had spelled out the word,

'Unholy?' uttered George. He inhaled deeply and the glass continued; it wasn't done yet.
He watched fascinated as it shot to 'T', then 'R', then 'A'…

'Unholy Tragedy? What the hell does that mean?' he asked Tyrone confused. Before Tyrone could answer, a harrowing scream and the sound of smashing glass came from above. They looked up at the chandelier, it was swinging precariously from side to side, the crystal teardrops tinkling and chiming erratically. He felt a jolt as a crack of static energy exploded in a blinding flash, the powerful unseen force hit him, stunning him momentarily. As he recovered, he saw the swirling black mass moving towards him again, like a tornado imminent to hit the land. Unable to move a muscle, he watched helplessly as it penetrated the material of his pocket and concentrated its force on the statue. Then, as quickly as the chaos had unleashed itself, calm descended in the room and on George. Everything was just as it was before; as if nothing had taken place at all. It was at that point, Tyrone knew his revenge on Lorraine and her bloody troublesome friend was taken care of, he had just orchestrated a powerful energy exchange through the

Ouija board and their fates were sealed. Still trembling, George thanked Tyrone for his insights, whatever they were, and left with his new 'lucky charm' still warm in pocket. He could still taste the Whiskey on his lips as he sped along the city streets on his borrowed bike. As if on auto pilot, he headed out of town towards the Flotterstone Inn, he wanted another drink. He could have easily parked his bike and headed to a local, but something was pushing him to head out of the city. Maybe, he just needed to feel the wind in his face, he told himself, to breathe in the fresh country air? It might be just what he needed to blow away the dark cobwebs hanging over him.

Inside the Flotterstone, he ordered a wee dram of Whiskey and downed it, he ordered another…then another. After a while he started to feel mellow, carefree even; he almost forgot about the rising ocean of shit he was drowning in. Before he knew it, the bell was ringing for last orders. He signalled the barman for one more and downed it. He felt tired, but felt far less conflicted than he had a couple hours ago at least. Outside, the night air hit him hard, causing him to stagger. He shook his head to untangle the cobwebs, but to no avail, they were still as thick and wooly as they had been before he visited Tyrone.

'Tyrone!' he muttered. He couldn't make head nor tail or the man, and he still had no idea what had drawn him to his house that day. The voice of reason in his head told him not to get on the bike but his intoxicated state argued with him not to be so silly,

'Get on it and get home, you'll be fine, you're a good rider, the roads will be empty, why be stranded out here in the middle of nowhere?' A taxi was out the question anyway; he had no money left. He swung his leg over the bike and clicked the ignition key, revelling at the sweet rumble of the well-tuned engine. He smiled to himself, one thing was for sure; he could make any bike purr like a kitten or roar like a fucking mountain lion. Kicking away the stand he rolled the bike across the car park, the headlights illuminating the road ahead. Then he opened the throttle and set it free…

The evergreen trees stood to attention like soldiers along the sides of the road, the moonlight casting their shadows on the tarmac ahead of him. Suddenly, he felt a sharp pain in the side of his leg as the statue Tyrone had given him, dug deeply into his skin. He took his right hand off the handlebar, reached into his pocket to alter its position, but it wouldn't budge, it was caught in the folds of his trouser pocket. As he wrestled with it, the pain became worse and he began to question why the hell he had taken the stupid statue off Tyrone in the first place. Then, it was as if he couldn't hear, or see hear anything. He was floating higher and higher into the night sky, on the ride of his life. Almost the same as the night with Lomond, but without...he saw her face. *Damn, she's beautiful, there's no denying that.* He realised he loved her. *So, what was stopping me?* Moments from his troubled past flew by in a dream sequence. He revisited past events and forgotten places. He saw himself laughing along with Lomond, carefree as it was then, before everything. For the first time in his life, he really felt things; love and joy, pain and guilt, excitement, fear, everything swirled together in a melting pot of emotions. He felt true freedom. He saw Lorraine too, his memories with her passed through his mind fleetingly, he should have settled down with her; he knew that now.

CHAPTER TWENTY-ONE

Lomond was inconsolable. The last time she'd seen him, she wanted to scratch his eyes out. *Why couldn't I have been more understanding? It was my fault that he ran that day! Because of me he took the bike and rode off to drown his sorrows. What have I done?* Over and over the questions repeated in her mind. Tracy borrowed her mother's car so she could take Lomond to visit her family in Perth. They hoped Margaret would be able to provide the love and comfort only a mother can in times like this. As the three sat side-by-side on the sofa, Lomond told her mother all about George. About the difficult relationship they had, their accident and about Lorraine. How she had come into the picture as her nurse, her friend, then her love rival.

'His poor parents!' said her mother, 'They must be distraught.'

'He never had any,' Lomond wept, 'He spent all his life in foster care and children's homes.'

'How old was he?'

'Seventeen, his birthday was 27th April, he was a year older than me.' replied Lomond. 'He thought he might have family near here too, I'm sure he said a village called Luncarty I think.

Giles was their last name or something.' Lomond sniffled. Then she watched as her mother's face flushed and her neck turned beet red.

'*Giles*, you say? You're certain it was *Giles*?'

'Yes, I think so, why? What difference does it make now?' She felt a strange feeling in the pit of her stomach. 'Does that name mean something to you? Do you know them mum?' Rising from the sofa, Margaret began pacing the floor.

'Oh my god!' she cried finally before collapsing into the armchair, 'What am I going to do?'

'What is it?!'

'I…I'm so so sorry Lomond, oh my goodness. I should have told you before…'

'Told me what?' Lomond demanded.

'Well, I, I had another child Lomond, a son who my mother forced me to leave in a children's home. My birth surname was *Giles*. My mother remarried a violent drunk; he insisted on adopting me and me taking his name. His name was Ferguson.'

'What the hell…why did you…?' Lomond couldn't speak, she felt sick, this was too much. Her mother continued to sob. 'Oh my *God!*' Lomond gasped, jumping to her feet. 'This can't be real.' She began pacing the room clasping the back of her head.

'I was nearly fifteen, so, so young, when I had him and you were born a year later.'

'No…no, you can't justify any of this to me,' Lomond yelled, 'He was your son? He's my…Oh my…How could you?! What is wrong with you?' It was all too twisted for Lomond to wrap her mind around. Her head throbbed; her stomach wretched. She felt her brain spin out of control as her emotions reached snapping point. She screamed at Tracy to get her bag and car keys. Then she glared into her mother's eyes, eyes she could now see were just like George's.

'You disgust me. George was my half-brother and he; we never even knew it.' A look of panic spread over her mother's face,

'Oh, God, you two *didn't*…?' Lomond was horrified.

'No, mother, we *didn't*! No bloody thanks to you though!' Lomond was suddenly grateful for Lorraine coming into the picture. 'I've got to get out of here, away from you and all your lies.' cried Lomond. She flounced out of the house and headed for the car whilst Tracy bid Margaret an awkward goodbye. It was clear from the expression on her face she wondered if she would ever see her long-lost daughter again. The drive home was silent, they were both stunned by what had transpired and they both knew Lomond's life would never be the same again.

Lomond was sobbing uncontrollably when she burst through the door. The dog was so excited to see her she almost knocked her off her feet. She bent down and threw her arms around Shuna's neck, just as Beth appeared in the kitchen doorway; her face a mixture of concern and relief. Sitting on the sofa, Lomond blurted out everything that happened in the few months she had been living at the hotel. She told Beth about what had happened to George, about her meeting with Margaret and how the woman had held back the truth about having a son prior to her birth. She cried about the fact that now she would never be able to tell George he was her half-brother; it felt as if her life was dissolving into pieces right before her very eyes. Using the opportunity to let it all out, she also told Beth about Tyrone. How they had gone to his house unannounced and the encounter they had with the ghost there.

'By the Grace of god, I go she said. I think that was her name. She wanted to give me a message for someone, but I never got to hear it and I've no idea who that someone could be.' On hearing this, Mac, who had come into the lounge half way through Lomond's outpouring; stood up and poured himself a large Whiskey.

'Why did you think her name was Grace?' Beth asked,

'Have you been going through our desk again?' demanded

Mac, sounding uncharacteristically angry. 'That name should *never* be mentioned in this house, do you hear me? Why are you still trying to hurt your mother? I won't stand for it.' Lomond looked at him through her tears, confused about what she was hearing. 'All your life I've given you everything, let you away with everything, but that stops now. As if mentioning Grace is not enough, what did you think you were going to achieve by going off and meeting Margaret eh?

'It's okay Mac, leave this to me.' He tone was detached, emotionless. 'So a ghost wanted to give you a message you say?' Mac opened his mouth to interrupt. 'Be quiet Mac please, you only heard part of the conversation.' Unnerved by the familiar look on Beth's face, a look with the power to kill, Lomond began to stammer.

'I, um…well…sort of, but she never completed the message because Tyrone interrupted us.' She answered.
'Tyrone? How the bloody hell did you meet him? Well, this is really the final straw, now I've heard it all. After all your flouncing around, and tantrums, and daddy's little girl antics, now you're telling me you're seeing ghosts? You know nothing about life and *especially* nothing of death. Who do you think you are prancing in here looking for comfort and understanding, well you're not going

to get it here, let me assure you!' Beth had really let go. 'Mac, get her out of here. I don't care if she's seeing ghosts' or rifling through desks, just get her away from me.' Now she was shrieking, 'If I *ever* hear you mention the name Tyrone or Grace in this house again, I will personally wash your mouth out with soap and water; and that will be you getting off lightly, do you hear me?'

Mac never said a word as he drove Lomond back to the hotel and she in such a state of shock, she never even tried to speak to him either. When she trudged into the reception, she saw a message for her pinned on the board. *Margaret called, please get in touch as soon as you can.*' She turned the piece of paper over and over in her hand. A part of her wanted to speak to her mother but she was so confused about everything, she needed time.

The next day during her lunch break, she headed off to the pay phone in the village and called Margaret.

'Perth 26224?' the soft voice said.

'It's Lomond, what do you want?' said Lomond, consciously deciding not to call her mother.

'Oh Lomond, I am so sorry. I…'

'Look, I'm on my lunch break and don't have a lot of change

to feed the phone, please spit it out.'

'I want to know where George's body has been taken Lomond, I would like to pay for his funeral.' Hearing the words filled her with fresh pain. 'Do you know where he is Lomond?'

'I have no idea, why don't you do some telephoning around and find out for yourself?' Lomond yelled down the receiver.

'I love you Lomond…' she heard her mother say as she slammed down the receiver.

CHAPTER TWENTY-TWO

The frost on the grass shimmered silver from the rays of the mid-morning sun as Tracy drove through the gates of Morton Hall Crematorium and crawled along the tree lined road to the car park. The chapel and crematorium buildings were set back from the road, just a short walk down from the car park; their location helping to maintain peaceful and dignified surroundings. Tracy thought she could detect a whiff of alcohol on Lomond's breath next to her, not that it mattered, she wouldn't blame her if she had taken a stiff drink beforehand. Just as they got out of the car, another two vehicles pulled into the car park. They recognised one of them as Mac's, but the other one was new to them. Mac and Beth had decided they would attend the funeral. Mac wanted to support his daughter; although secretly he looked forward to seeing Margaret again. Beth was also curious about the woman whose child she had raised. Maybe by meeting her, it would shine some light on the way Lomond behaved. It was only when the other car had drawn to a halt, Lomond realised it was Margaret. This should be good, she thought, her two 'mothers' together. As Mac and Beth walked towards the girls, Lomond gave a subtle nod to her father, directing his attention towards

Margaret. A look of stoic resolution came over his face and he tugged on Beth's sleeve for them to head over and greet her.

'Margaret?' queried Mac, as she climbed out the driver's seat.

'Yes,' came back the reply, 'Hi, it's been a long time Mac.' Her eyes looked red and puffy, as if she'd been crying.

'It certainly has,' nodded Mac. Beth nudged him in the ribs, 'Oh, I'm sorry. This is my wife Beth.'

'It's nice to finally meet you Beth.' Margaret replied, a note of mild interest in her voice. 'Likewise.' replied Beth her tone as crisp and dry as the morning air.

'Have you travelled far?' Mac asked, trying his best to keep up polite conversation.

'Muirton, in Perth.' She answered.

'Oh?' interjected Beth with an exaggerated pensive look on her face, 'I think I've come across that name at my work in the law firm. Isn't it a council estate?' Mac rolled his eyes and offered Margaret an apologetic smile.

'Yes, it is,' she stated, looking at them both with a tight-lipped smile. More cars pulled in and before his wife could do any more damage, Mac suggested they should all move away from the car park. Maria and Innes emerged from another vehicle, whilst another dropped off Lorraine and Mint. As everybody began to make their way towards the chapel, a fancy silver Mercedes crunched across the gravel and out stepped Tyrone and Vanessa.

'What the hell is that awful man doing here?' spat Lomond 'He hardly knew him for god's sake, is this your doing Innes?'

'Well, I did tell him about George's passing.' she said apologetically.

'You did what? Why would you do that?'

'I'm sorry. I just thought he should know; he would've found out anyway.'

'Honestly? Have you no clue about anything Innes?' Lomond retorted. Then, to her horror, Tyrone began to walk in their direction.

'Well, well, well, if it isn't "Little Miss Housebreaker" and her side kick,' he sneered, 'I'm sorry, I can't remember your name,' he added, looking Lomond up and down.

'It's bloody Lomond, you know my name.' she snapped back.

'Well, *Bloody Lomond*, retribution comes in all forms, just remember that,' he threatened, 'there's consequences' coming to you and believe me, I'll be there to watch you suffer and I'll dance with glee when they do.' He turned abruptly to walk away, a malicious grin on his face, it was then he spotted Beth staring at him with a look of pure hatred on her face; he stopped dead in his tracks. 'Well I never, if it isn't old torn face,' he said, addressing her directly, 'the devil incarnate herself!'

'Hey! That's my mother you're talking to, you'd better shut up right now!' fired Lomond

'Ha! Beth's *your* mother? That explains it all then.' He laughed wildly. Enraged, Mac made a lunge towards Tyrone but Beth was holding on tightly to the sleeve of his jacket.

'Leave it Mac!' she hissed, 'he's not worth it.'
Just then, the hearse carrying George drew up and stopped outside the doors to the crematorium. Lomond looked at the various arrangements of flowers, one read *'To my beloved son.'* Seeing the words made her feel physically sick. George would never have wanted that, she thought. What an insult to receive a wreath from a mother who gave him away and only acknowledged him after death. Then she noticed another smaller wreath, the words on the card barely visible. She moved closer and read aloud,

'Unholy Tragedy – T.' Immediately, she wondered if the 'T' might stand for Tyrone, she couldn't think of anyone else it might have come from, unless it was Tracy; she'd ask her later.

Out of the corner of her eye she saw Tyrone was staring at the coffin, with what looked like a sly smile on his face. She realised she hated this man with such a passion; she wished it was him in there...

Margaret walked over to the hearse with her head bowed and a large rimmed black hat hiding her face. Lomond then watched on incredulously as Tracy walked over and linked arms with her new mother; she felt totally betrayed. *How could she do this?* More than anyone, Tracy knew how much she had suffered since meeting up with Margaret. As the two of them turned their backs on the hearse and faced Lomond, Tracy let go of Margaret's arm and walked towards her.

'What the hell Tracy?' she said sadly, 'She doesn't even deserve to be here, never mind being cosied up with you!'

'Lomond, come on. This is George's funeral; remember that. It's not all about you. The woman is *both* of your mothers and she's here grieving for her son *and* her broken relationship with you: try and think of other people's feelings too if you can? So, she made mistakes when she a teenager, don't we all? We're all human Lomond. I'm sure when we're older, we'll look back on *our* lives and wish we'd done or not done this or that. Who are you to be judge and jury? If you chose to carry this anger against her inside you through your life; you will miss out on the opportunity to create so many new memories. Think about your half-brother and sister too, you have the chance to build real connections there. You can have the love of the family you've been yearning for. Don't blow it Lomond. At least go and speak with her, she truly cares about you and loves you know.' As angry and upset as she felt about Tracy lecturing her, she knew everything she said made sense, she couldn't argue any of it.

As she stood watching the rays of the sun beamed down onto George's meagre wooden coffin, she felt his presence; it was as if he were standing beside her. She could almost see his form with the same charming grin that had attracted her in the first place. She focused on the colours surrounding him and she sensed a soft breath of wind envelope her. Then, a swirling mass of pink mist appeared and began to take on another human form. She recognised it at once; it was Mrs. R.

    'Go and talk with her Lomond. Remember that what happened is gone, it is in the past. No-one is asking you to forgive your mother for her mistakes, just to avoid judging or condemning her. If you build a relationship without the chains of the past; you will give your heart the freedom it seeks.' Suddenly, Lomond became one with the swirling pink colour and she saw again the alternative realms of existence she'd visited before. The memory of being in the indigo tunnel and the sensation of being surrounded in the colour caressed her. Sketchy images of incredible other worldly experiences came flooding back; she felt overwhelmed and ecstatic all at once.

Throughout the service, the sun cut through the stained-glass windows, casting an array of elongated multi-coloured shapes over the wooden pews and the faces of the people sitting in them. It was as if their other, less righteous sides were illuminated; their darker, shadow selves who expected 'his life would come to this.' Halfway through the service, Lomond slipped out of her seat at the front. Her eyes sought out Margaret who she saw was sitting alone in a pew at the back. She made her way up the isle and came to stop, gesturing for her mother to move along so she could sit beside her. Then, she took her hand and the two of them sat mourning their loss together.

'I think you should have this.' Margaret said quietly, reaching into her bag. 'It was part of his belongings, I have no idea what it is, but he had it on him when it happened.' She handed her a small ugly looking figurine. Lomond turned it over and over in her hand, a quizzical look on her face.

When the service ended, the sparse crowd shuffled solemnly from the chapel, out into the daylight. There was no line of immediately family there for mourners to offer condolences or words of comfort to. All those attending were invited back to the Roslin Hotel for a small buffet and some refreshments. Lomond was horrified when she saw Tyrone open the back door of Vanessa's car, and gently push Innes inside. Running over, she began to scream,

'Get out of the car now Innes, get out, you're not going with them and they are not coming back to the hotel!' She grabbed at the handle and the door swung open with so much force, it caused her to lose balance and nearly fall. Tyrone moved in quickly, slamming the door shut again. Regaining her balance, Lomond ran at him, kicking him hard in the shin before opening the door again. Not wanting to fall out with Lomond, Innes
decided it was best to jump out of the car. With his face twisted in agony and still rubbing his shin, Tyrone turned to Lomond,

'You are going to regret this, really you will. Everything is falling into place, you'll see. That old bitch over there Beth, your so called mother and your dad, well he has blood on his hands, and you…you're just a little nobody; a bastard with no idea about anything. I promise you this much, I'll find you and mark my words, when I do…'

'Shut up you old twat and get the hell out of here!' screamed Lomond.

The mourners who witnessed this scene lowered their heads and promptly headed for their cars; no-one wanted to get involved.

Standing at the door of the hotel, Robert welcomed what was left of the mourners and ushered them through to the dining where Dreanie had prepared a buffet.

'Everything's laid out for you: sandwiches, sausage rolls, cakes. The tea and coffee's over there and if yous want something stronger, and a guess some o' ye will need it, the bar's just through that door there.' She said with a warm smile. Although reluctant to mingle at first, after a couple of rounds; compliments of Mac, the conversation started to flow. Lomond couldn't settle at all though. Even in the company of people she could normally talk to; her friends, Mint and even her parents; she found it difficult to make small talk. As she sat with Maria and Tracy, Lomond noticed Beth make a determined move toward Margaret and just as she had done before the service, Mac gave Lomond a despairing glance before trailing after her.

'Funerals are desperately sad affairs; don't you think Margaret?' Beth asked. 'They make you realise time is precious and you should spend as much time as possible with family.'

'They are that.' replied Margaret. 'Time and circumstances can be strange things, though can't they? Often out of our control.' Mac wondered if now might be the time to butt in, the last thing he wanted to see was a full-blown cat-fight.

'How's life in Perth Margaret, do you have any family?' he asked

'I've got a good man and two teenage kids, Shaun and Denise. Typical teenagers, all over the place and bolshie with it, but I let them enjoy themselves while they can. Life doesn't get any easier as we get older does it?' she replied. *Why did I go there? Family and kids; Beth will be straight onto that.* Mac thought to himself. He was right enough.

'Children need guidance, control and a strong hand if you ask me.' Beth stated, 'Take *my* Lomond. She's had a good education and she's been taught respect for her elders. Some of the things I hear her friends getting up to, my god. The way they dress and flaunt themselves; it's no wonder the trouble they get into.' Margaret didn't bite, but Beth wasn't finished.

'If I had a teenage son under my roof, it would be exactly the same; discipline, respect, sticking in at school and getting a good job.' Margaret looked at Mac. It was obvious she was not going to get any time alone with him to talk. She excused herself under the pretext of going to chat with some of George's work friends.

Not wanting to be in earshot of any "conversations" between her mothers, Lomond had slipped out and seeing Shuna in her father's car, she opened the boot, clipped on her lead and walked in the direction of the Chapel. When she reached the grounds, she sat on a bench with the dog at her feet. She loved the way the soft breeze made the leaves rustle in the trees and the sound of the bird song. She thought about the love she had for her dog too; they shared a silent understanding. As she stared at Shuna, it was as if all the other sounds around her began to fade. Then she could see Shuna's energy expand and contract in a wondrous spectrum of colours. Colours she believed the dog could see too. She knew they understood each other; they could communicate without the needs for words. It was mutually healing and made her feel complete. The sound of a woman's voice caught both their attention.

'It's a very sad time in the physical world Lomond. The ending of a life is always difficult to accept, but you must ask whose sadness it is. Is it *yours*, his mother's, his friends; or is it Georges' sadness that *he* has lost the time to spend here in this world? Lomond recognised the voice, it was Mrs. R.

'He's gone, Mrs. R, I'm so confused,' replied Lomond. 'Everything seems so full of darkness, there's no light or energy in anything. People are just going through the motions, and I can see right through them. Why are they all so false?' she cried. Suddenly, Shuna lunged forward in a frenzied state, nearly pulling her arm out of her socket. With her teeth bared, she barked and snarled into thin air. Lomond tried to soothe her, but the dog was having none of it. Then, Mrs. R blew a gust of pink air towards her and Shuna, Shuna began to calm down. To Lomond's amazement, the figure of a young girl emerged from the pink cloud; the same girl she'd seen at Tyrone's house.

'You're sad Lomond, I felt your pain, I sensed your cry for help and it helped me find you. I need to thank you.' said the young girl. 'Now finally, I'm at peace and I'm free. I'm fee to travel in the universal infinite consciousness, where there are no boundaries. Lomond, this is all thanks to you.'

'Thanks to me?'

'Yes, it's simple really, because you prayed to God and kept me in your thoughts, because you cared about me and sent me messages of love, my soul was released from its earth-bound existence.'

'But I never delivered your message; I didn't know what it was or who it was for.' replied Lomond. Then she watched as the young girl faded from view and the dog settled down at her feet again.

'Well that was a nice little interruption.' said Mrs. R. 'Anyway, as I was saying, you can see right through the exterior façade that people display, you can see the real person and the life they were born to live.'

'So why am I different from other people? Why me Mrs. R?'

'Think how lucky you are to have this gift Lomond. To be able to see the colours around Shuna, to *feel* the force of energy that transcends her physical body. You have the ability to experience the colour and energy surrounding all living things. Do you not agree this is a blessing?'

'So how can I see *you*, if you're dead?' she queried. 'Again Lomond, we who have passed on become energy without the physical form. We can use this energy to form characteristics of our former self or the self that is most recognizable to the person seeing us…' As Mrs. R.'s dulcet tones began to fade, Lomond became aware of the surrounding sounds of the rustling leaves and birdsong again, and then Mrs. R. was gone. She looked into Shuna's dark brown eyes and for a moment, she felt drawn into her very soul.

'You really do understand me Shuna, I know you do.' She laughed, wondering what Mac and Beth would say if she told them she could have conversations with the dog. The thought she might be able to communicate with other animals intrigued her greatly; it was something she wanted to know the answer to for sure. She gave the dog a knowing look and a hug before easing herself off the bench and heading back to the hotel.

The formalities were nearly over when she returned and people were making moves to go their separate ways. As she put Shuna back in the boot of her father's blue Austen A40, she turned to face Beth.

'Come back with us Lomond, you, me and your father can have a talk.' Beth said, it was more of an order than an invitation.

'There you go again!' Snapped Lomond 'Deciding and planning my life.'

'No, no it's not like that, but we need to talk!' she justified.

'Yes, but it is like that. My friends are here, my half-brother has just died and you still want to run my life. I have a job here, in this hotel and I live here. I'm my own person and I'll decide what I do next thank you.'

'You still have no consideration for your family whatsoever Lomond, just like that woman over there!' retorted Beth, sneering over in Margaret's direction, unaware she was in earshot

'By *that* woman I suspect you're referring to me?' Margaret said coldly walking over towards them, 'Let me tell you something Beth, my family is my business and it that has nothing to do with you.'

'Oh, that's very rich coming from you,' Beth snapped back. 'I've been left to bring up your brat of a daughter and haven't we just cremated another *unwanted* child of yours today?'

'Good god Mac, whatever did you see in this vile woman?' Margaret said, her tone pitiful, 'I mean, I know I'm not perfect by a long shot and who is? But she is absolutely awful!' Lomond had had enough.

'My mother's right, you Beth, are a vile woman and this just proves it!' With this, Mac gave a hard tug on Beth's coat sleeve.

'Right, enough is enough! Let's just leave it for now; I think we've been through enough for one day.' His words were directed more towards Beth than Lomond. Lorraine, who had walked over, cut in,

'We're thinking of going over to the Flotterstone Inn, George liked to go there. Do you want to come with us Lomond?'

'Lomond, you go with your friends. Beth and I will make our way home.' Said Mac before his wife could protest. Lomond nodded in agreement before turning to embrace Margaret.

'I'll be in touch soon then,' she said, 'Have a safe trip home.' Then, without even looking in Beth's direction, she turned and followed Lorraine over to where the rest of her friends were waiting. Lomond glanced back at all three adults going in their separate ways and she decided she would never be like them, any of them. She would continue to be honest, to speak the truth.

'Ok, let's go then,' she said, 'leave the bloody *Grown-ups* to sort themselves out!

CHAPTER TWENTY-THREE

The car park was practically empty when they arrived. The Inn had only just opened for the evening and the diners hadn't started arriving yet. Inside, they pushed two table's together and ordered drinks before spending some time sharing stories and memories of George. After another round or two, the conversation broadened and they started to talk about their own lives.

'I see what you mean about your parents Lomond,' offered Mint, 'Especially your mum, she seems like she could toast bread with her breath.'

'I take it you are referring to *Beth*? You don't know the half of it; just ask any one of my friends,' Lomond gestures to Tracy, Maria and Innes, 'they know exactly what she's like. Every bloody day it's "do this, do that, work harder, get qualified, get a job, save money, on and on.'

'So the other one, the Margaret lady, she's your real mother right?' asked Mint.

'Jesus, what a right load of mistakes adults make eh? It seems your life has been full of drama because of all their antics. Can you imagine what they would do if it was us behaving like that?' said Tracy.

'I bet you wish Mrs. R was your mother eh?' blurted Innes, her comment bringing a look of confusion and intrigue to the others.

'Who the hell is Mrs. R?' asked Maria. Realising she'd disclosed something unknown by anyone else, Innes gave an apologetic look, however, when Lomond shrugged her shoulders; she took it as permission to continue. 'Lomond sees colours and lights and all that stuff; I don't really understand it but she knows things, and she communicated with this spirit lady called Mrs. R. she gives her advice.' They all looked at Lomond in disbelief, but eager to hear more.

'I know it makes me sound like a weirdo…but you see, when I was in the coma, I went somewhere else, I could see things as if I was actually there. It was like another world full of energy and colour, colours I didn't even know existed. I met another being there, a lady called Mrs. R; she was like my guide or something.

'Really?' exclaimed Maria in disbelief, 'Your guide to where…back down to earth? Come on, you don't expect us to believe that shite do you? It was probably all the drugs they were pumping into you.'

'Hey, don't be so quick to dismiss it,' Lorraine chimed in, 'No-one *really* knows how the mind works, like what's actually going on in there and what its capable of; it's all a bit of a mystery. Who's to say there's not things in us and out there that we can't see?'

'Did you ever *see* this Mrs. R?' asked Mint.

'Yes, well sort of, but when I see her, it's more like a sense I get, like everything around me disappears, and there's just her and I left; surrounded by this amazing magenta colour. I can feel that she's really caring and wise though; like a real homely person, but with a huge sense of freedom.'

'I've never told anybody this,' Mint said, 'but since by mother died, I feel like she comes to me sometimes, usually *just* as I am dropping off to sleep. I see this magenta mist descend in front of me and then it's as if I can sense her; I feel her presence and I can hear her voice; it's like I become part of her. I've never told anyone this before.'

'What was her name?' asked Lomond.

'Rose, Rose Robertson.' He answered. Lomond gasped and the group fell silent. Maria froze with a glass of wine touching her lips.

'Tell me about your mum Mint.' Lomond said, staring at him intently. Mint hung his head.

'Oh…she died years ago; I don't really want to go into the

details just now.'

'Oh, I'm sorry, that's so sad,' said Lomond. 'If you don't mind me asking, how come you're called Mint, like what's your real name? I've never even thought to ask before.'

'My real name is Malcom Robertson,' he shrugged, looking a little embarrassed, 'Mint was a nickname my parents gave me. When I started learning the guitar, I used to tell them I would make a mint from my music and they started calling me Mint, I guess the name just stuck.'

'Won't you please just tell me a little bit about her, just a little?' pleaded Lomond.

'Well, she was well into colours. You know, tie-dyed dresses and all that hippy stuff. She grew her own herbs, plants and vegetables and...' he looked a little reluctant to say, 'Well, she even talked to the animals; she loved them the most, they brought her great joy and happiness. She loved magenta as well, it was her favourite colour and she wore it every day. Some people even called her *The Magenta Lady*.' Lomond willed him to continue, her mouth hanging open in disbelief. 'You know, it nearly killed my father when she died. I couldn't cope with him moping around all the time, it was pulling me down. So, I decided to leave and well, here I am. I've never been to his new farm, it's up north, near

Kingussie. I bet my mother would have loved it there. I know he would love to see me but I've just not been able to go. I call him from time to time though.' He looked at Lomond, 'Maybe I should go and visit him, what do you think Lomond?'

'Em, well, I don't know really. I can't' think straight at the moment…I…' she was still trying to process all she had just heard.

'What about Mrs. R then, why don't you ask her for me?' he queried.

'I can't just *contact* her when I want, it seems she just pops in and out my life when she feels like it.' said Lomond.

'Okay, okay,' I think that's enough of this *other worldly stuff* don't you?' interrupted Tracy, trying to lighten the mood.

'Oh!' Innes jumped in. 'Did you hear the latest about *him*, that awful Tyrone? Well he's living back in India Street with that bimbo we saw hanging off his arm at the Assembly Rooms. Apparently, his mother very *conveniently* passed away and surprise surprise, he got everything he wanted. So now, him and Vanessa are all cozied up in that humongous house. I can just hear him now, "I live in India Street you know." Just goes to show you eh? Hey, remember that article you read in the newspaper Lomond, the one about the police re-opening an un-solved murder in the street? Do you know if there's any updates on that, like, are there are any links to Tyrone?'

'I have no idea Innes, but I'd put my money on it there is; I can just feel the guy's rotten to the core.'

'A part of me wants go back to try communicate with Grace again, if Grace is even her name, but I never want to come face to face with *him* again.' said Innes.

'I can assure you Innes,' smiled Lomond, 'there's no need for us to go back there and find the girl, no need whatsoever.' Innes raised her eyebrows and was about to question, but Lomond interrupted.

'Wait a minute, *oh my God,* what the hell?' she cried, 'The cellar, Maude and Beth in the room, the older girl with the small child and the ghost, Grace saying the words *find me…*' Lomond sucked in her breath, 'the black door with the number six…Tyrones!' Innes looked puzzled before her eyes went as wide as saucers.

'Christ Lomond, am I thinking what you're thinking?' she cried.

'When we broke into Tyrone's, I *thought* I recognised it because I must have visited it in my coma, but that wasn't it.

That feeling of déjà vu I had was *real;* it came from an actual real experience, I was there, I was the small child and the older girl…I think it was Grace, Beth's daughter' Lomond let out a long sigh.

'I don't have a clue about anything you're talking about Lomond, but correct me if I'm wrong, you broke into Tyrone's house? Are you both nuts? Why on earth would you do such a stupid thing? How come I never heard of this before?'

'Well…' Then, Innes gave them the whole story, exaggerating the details throughout for maximum impact.

CHAPTER TWENTY-FOUR

In that moment, Lomond knew she still had unfinished business with *ghost Grace* and Tyrone. She had no idea what it was all about, but she felt with certainty their paths would cross again.

All the adults in her life seemed to be a total mess living behind a mask of untruth. They were like robots; cloned into believing this was how life should be. They went to church and sinned all week believing that all they needed to do was ask God for forgiveness at Sunday service and everything would be alright. They were completely institutionalized; believing everything told to them by the minister, their lawyers and doctors to be gospel. They voted obediently for the next Prime Minister and Government because they believed their choices would make their lives better. Then, they had the audacity to complain when things did not live up to their expectations. It was all a joke! Lomond wondered if her peers even had minds of their own. Even the likes of Tyrone, who believed he was above it all, even he was a slave to the system. He claimed to have knowledge of the spirit world, but when it came down to it; he was driven by material wealth and obtaining a respectable "place" in society, just like the rest of them. The same crap was being passed down from one generation to another, until gradually, people were losing any sense of self.

The world and its inhabitants had become cogs in giant unfeeling, unthinking machine. Well not her.

Her eyes focused on the pine logs burning furiously in the fireplace. As she watched the flames, she could feel herself rising from them; looking down on herself and her friends. Most of them had their lives mapped out already, Maria was already talking about marrying her boyfriend, it wouldn't be long before she was just another housewife with a half decent postcode. Tracy would live her life as a hairdresser; her vivacious looks and personality helping cement her success. Innes would spend her life caring for others; thanks to the problems with her brother. She might get to Art College. Lorraine would now be the wounded nurse; confused and hurt by George but soldiering on with her mission to care for the world. Then there was Mint. She had to admit, the musician and confidante with hippy parents and taste for adventure was different; more of enigma. Suddenly without warning a burning log rolled out of the fire grate, landing on the black marble hearth. Billows of grey smoke began to fill the air. Lomond was the first on her feet. She grabbed the tongs at the side of the fire and picked up the burning log; the smoke stinging her eyes and making her cough. Then she threw the log back into the open grate; wiping her eyes to try to ease the irritation from the smoke. A figure appeared. She recognised it to be that of the Hermit.

'You *are* the one who is to discover me.' Without warning, she felt a chill run down her spine; as if the presence had engulfed her being. A nudge to her side made her jump.

'Wake up!' it was Mint, 'You were away somewhere else there for a bit.'

'Oh, was I?' she apologised.

"We're going now.' Said Tracy, 'I'll drop you back at the Hotel before I take Lorraine and Mint back into Edinburgh: Maria is going to drop Innes home.'

'Oh, okay…that's good,' said Lomond, 'Mint, what are you going to do?'

'Probably go home as well, what else?' he replied.

'No, I mean are you going to head up north to see your father?' she asked. He looked at her thoughtfully,

'Well, after our conversation, I am thinking I should go. I think I need to see him and his farm, it sounds like a step up from the hippy lifestyle we used to live.'

In that moment, Lomond knew with certainty Mint could offer her everything she needed, everything she wanted, a lifestyle with freedom at the core; she just had to convince him. That was her new objective, her only objective, to make him realise her was her destiny.